A DEADLY TRAP

Not knowing what waited for her on the other side, Ariane grabbed a handhold as she opened the door. There was no decompression, so she stepped to the threshold. The slate's alarm went off in her hand, vibrating as well as flashing red dots.

It felt surreal to look up at the status displayed above the door—calm green—then to look down at the slate and see blinking lights and the text WARNING! OXYGEN CONTENT INADEQUATE! TEMPERATURE DANGEROUSLY LOW! DO NOT EXPOSE SKIN!

At least the suits had been equipped with shrink-to-fit gloves, so she hastily saved the slate's data with a single action of her thumb. Still standing at the threshold, she reached around to flip the emergency disablement switch before stepping all the way into the gym.

The door closed behind her anyway.

She whirled, her breath starting to come faster. She'd toggled the mechanical disablement switch, yet the door had closed. She was beginning to feel persecuted, and those feelings became overwhelming as the lights dimmed and a text message formed on the back of the door:

HOW CAN YOU HANDLE THE GUILT, ARI? SOON YOU'LL HAVE NO TROUBLE SLEEPING. . . .

PEACEKEEPER

A Major Ariane Kedros Novel

Laura E. Reeve

A ROC BOOK

ROC
Published by New American Library, a division of
Penguin Group (USA) Inc., 375 Hudson Street,
New York, New York 10014, USA
Penguin Group (Canada), 90 Eglinton Avenue East, Suite 700, Toronto,
Ontario M4P 2Y3, Canada (a division of Pearson Penguin Canada Inc.)
Penguin Books Ltd., 80 Strand, London WC2R 0RL, England
Penguin Ireland, 25 St. Stephen's Green, Dublin 2,
Ireland (a division of Penguin Books Ltd.)
Penguin Group (Australia), 250 Camberwell Road, Camberwell, Victoria 3124,
Australia (a division of Pearson Australia Group Pty. Ltd.)
Penguin Books India Pvt. Ltd., 11 Community Centre, Panchsheel Park,
New Delhi - 110 017, India
Penguin Group (NZ), 67 Apollo Drive, Rosedale, North Shore 0632,
New Zealand (a division of Pearson New Zealand Ltd.)
Penguin Books (South Africa) (Pty.) Ltd., 24 Sturdee Avenue,
Rosebank, Johannesburg 2196, South Africa

Penguin Books Ltd., Registered Offices:
80 Strand, London WC2R 0RL, England

First published by Roc, an imprint of New American Library,
a division of Penguin Group (USA) Inc.

First Printing, December 2008
10 9 8 7 6 5 4 3 2 1

*To the U.S. Air Force and Army members
I've had the privilege to work with, and the
many other military personnel who heard the
call to duty and followed it without hesitation*

Acknowledgments

Most novels grow from many favors and much input. This one is no exception, and I apologize that I can acknowledge only some. First, my husband, Michael, deserves recognition for his encouragement and scientific advice, including his ability to simplify subjects ranging from quantum physics to cosmology. I am also indebted to my parents, Gerry and Norma, for their continuous support and for not noticing when I filched books from their library. I'm exceedingly grateful for the patient reviews and astute questions from my critique partner, Robin; my sister, Wendy; and my first reader, Summer. My agent, Jennifer Jackson, deserves all the accolades I can compose for her, after sticking with me through multiple manuscripts. Finally, thanks to Jessica Wade and the staff at Penguin Group, who brought this series into being.

CHAPTER 1

The name Pax Minoica might satisfy the damned latinized
League, but the Minoans don't care.

[Link to theories regarding modern Minoans encountered
in twenty-first century]

That's not the purpose of the name; the Senate's appeal-
ing to net-think nostalgia by hearkening back to pre-Terran
Earth. Two ancient accords, both successful, carried the
name of Pax Minoica. Alexander the Great brokered the
second, so the Senate gets the bonus of megahero
aura, helping them spin these treaties to citizens . . .

—Anonymous Sophist at Konstantinople Prime University,
2091.98.10.22 UT, indexed by *Democritus 9* under
Hypothetical Effect Imperative

The floodlights from *Aether's Touch* washed over
the vessel on the portside slip, enhancing its tor-
tuous lines and pulsing skin. It looked like an amoe-
bic parasite sucking life away from Athens Point
rather than a docked spacecraft using legitimately
leased resources.

"Matt? Get us a different slip. They're putting us
next to Minoans," Ariane said over internal comm to
the only other crew member on *Aether's Touch*. Her
fingers flew across her console and strengthened their

firewall, a precaution she took when docking at any habitat. She wasn't paranoid, only sensible.

"I'll talk to Command Post," Matt replied from the protected array compartment.

He sounded altogether too fresh and cheery, she thought sourly, because *he* had gotten rack time during N-space. The bright pumping into his bloodstream since they entered real-space had cleared his head. She, however, had to stay awake through N-space, and that meant clash, as most pilots called it. Clash kept her terrors at bay, her reflexes sharp, and her thoughts clear but jaggedly edged with irritability. Running her fingers through her loose, short curls, she felt them tremble against her hypersensitive scalp. The clash pushed uncomfortably behind her eyelids when she closed them, and the bright wasn't helping.

"That's all they can give us. All their class-C slips are taken." Matt no longer sounded cheerful.

"That's shit from the Great Bull itself. Who'd we piss off?" Ariane's question was rhetorical. Everyone followed the rules when Minoans were around, so she and Matt would suffer the most rigorous inspections possible from Athens Point Customs and Flight Records.

"We can't afford Minoan attention. Do you think they know what we're carrying?"

"Don't see how. I don't think this is personal; it's just bad luck." Ariane focused on the directional lights flashing at their slip.

"Bad luck all around. I already notified Nestor and told him to stand ready."

"Great—him and every lurker on this habitat," she said.

"The claims will be puncture-proof. Really."

She didn't answer. Among Matt's frustrating qualities were his unshakable confidence, good humor, and optimism. As a perennial pessimist, she doubted that he and Nestor could close the loopholes. By now, lurkers had seen their ship arrive and had their legal vultures ready to muscle in on the action. Once Nestor submitted their claims and the deadline expired, the carnage would start. Aether Exploration's claims would have to withstand everything from patent infringement threats to good old-fashioned claim jumping.

She oriented *Aether's Touch* and started Y-vector approach into the docking ring. Everything was right on track. She had time and was as curious as the next mundane, so she reviewed the video of the portside ship.

No mundane human, to her knowledge, had been on board a Minoan vessel. Net-think speculated that the outside skin was a partially organic composite, perhaps because of its mottled green-yellow color and the pulsing movement of conduits. Lights glowed through its hull, but didn't resolve into decks. Net-think also postulated that Minoan shielding allowed true windows in their N-space ships. Ariane couldn't guess where their referential engine was located or whether the ship was armed. She didn't dare direct her lights and cam-eyes toward the Minoan vessel again, as she didn't want to attract their attention.

She idly watched the approach video from the starboard cam-eye, happy to see the angular outline of a mundane ship. When she saw weapons pods, however, she magnified the video and frowned as the AFCAW logo slid by. Why would a military ship, in this case a lightweight cruiser, dock at Athens Point when it could use Karthage?

"Let's get through docking without a fuss. How's it look for flight records?" Matt's voice interrupted her deliberations about the cruiser.

Ariane chewed her lip.

"You're legal, right? Ari?" His voice became sharp. The logs on *Aether's Touch* would prove she'd stayed within real-space safety limits, but that wasn't the source of Matt's concern. She considered the cocktail of drugs inside her body. The street smooth she'd added to take the edge off the clash wasn't an approved supplement. On the other hand, regulations didn't *prohibit* smooth, and in this case Athens Point Flight Records got to decide whether she had used a safe dose.

"I'm not sure," she said reluctantly.

Matt swore.

"Look, I only added some smooth. Plenty of pilots use it, with no problems."

"But we're going to be hammered with every regulation possible," he said.

"How'd I know we'd be squeezed between Minoans and AFCAW?" Her voice rose and her stomach tightened. She should have made this run strictly by the book. *Too late now*.

There was ominous silence over internal comm.

"Matt?"

"AFCAW? Here?"

"Cruiser, lightly armed, docked to starboard."

"I'll be on deck for final connection." Matt cut off to lock down the array compartment. *Aether's Touch* was a second-wave prospector, and while she supported a crew of only two, she had the latest exploration-rated equipment. Sapphire-shielded crystal arrays held their precious cargo: information gathered through every possible remote sensor and telebot available on *Aether's Touch*. Physical samples were stored in the compartment aft of the vaults.

Ariane turned back to her console and concentrated on the approaching slip. The autopilot wasn't foolproof and any pilots worth their salary wouldn't let their ship attempt docking unattended.

Matt climbed to the control deck as station supply and recycling tubes were clamping on to the *Aether's Touch*. He was more protective of the ship than Ariane; she knew he watched the station crews critically through the cam-eye, ready to pounce on any safety deviations. Ariane's fingers danced over the smooth console surface. She turned over environmental controls to the habitat so they could run on station resources and power. Of course, Athens Point would bill Matt for every second of each service.

"Aligned and using station gravity. Switching over air supply." Ariane called out her checklist steps over intercom as was required by regulations, not that anyone needed to hear them. Matt knew when his air supply changed. She watched his reflection turn and sniff the air, his angular cheekbones, nose, and jaw showing a pleasing profile. He kept his blond hair short, cut in a military style that Ariane preferred. Not that she'd made her preferences known to him. . . .

She looked away. Matt was her employer, the civilian equivalent of her commander. Besides that, he was *crew*. The only way for a crew to work successfully was to keep the relationship professional. *I'll never make that mistake again.* Ariane clamped down on her thoughts, squashing the memories into darkness.

"Ah, fresh air." Matt sighed.

Ariane suppressed a smile. Only crèche-get could appreciate station air. Matt was a generational ship baby and carried the generational-line last name of Journey. Because of his upbringing, he considered any proven crew member to be family. Perhaps he was a bit too trusting, but this worked in her favor since she didn't have an authentic family or background.

She and Matt trusted each other, which was necessary because new space had its dangers. The generational ship that established the time buoy in the new solar system wasn't responsible for charting or resource discovery. That was the job of the second-wave prospectors, and Ariane liked being out in the lonely nether reaches for months on end.

"Let's see what's waiting." Matt leaned over her shoulder and activated the cam-eye feed from the dock.

Wearing colorful badges and crisp uniforms, three officials stood at the end of their ramp and looked as pompous as possible. They expected Customs and Flight Records, but not Station Ops.

"I've never seen all three officials on the ramp before, and certainly not in such clean gear." Matt widened the view to show the whole ramp, and they saw the reason Station Ops was present.

"What the . . . ?" she said.

"We're fucked," he said.

Several paces behind the three officials stood a tall figure with an elaborate horned headdress and robes that managed to look diaphanous while remaining androgynous. A *Minoan*. No one would have asked its purpose here; the Minoans rarely explained their business to mundanes. It stood, stopping traffic, in the center of the main ring corridor. A buzzing cloud of remotes, trying to record the rare occurrence of a Minoan on a commercial habitat, kept several meters away. Behind the billowing mass of remotes, well behind them, stood a few onlookers who were just at the edge of cam-eye view from the ship.

"Don't panic. There'll only be delays. They'll have to do a brain-wave pattern panel to detect and quantify the smooth." Ariane said this matter-of-factly, since the flight records official had all the appropriate equipment hanging from her left shoulder.

"As long as no one gets a whiff of our cargo," he said.

She nodded, her gut wincing. The waiting Minoan drew excessive attention to their arrival, more than Matt's messages or her delays with Flight Records required. The entire station was probably watching and loading video of the Minoan onto ComNet. They might as well have announced on the feeds that they'd made the most significant find of their lifetimes, which was far more important than her pilot license and rating.

After they opened the air lock, Ariane took a moment to digest the smells and the air quality, the unique signature of every station. Heavy equipment wasn't allowed on class-C docks; the mixture of perfumes, sweat, and spices overrode traces of ozone and lubricant. As stimulating as the scents were, the gray deck and panels of Athens Point were similar to those of other habitats.

She paused at the top of the ramp, disoriented. The panels near their slip should be covered with—ah, now they had been found and targeted. Advertisements aimed at Ariane and Matt, selected per their buying habits, opened and fought for space on the wall and even the ceiling. She knew better than to look up this soon on station, before she was used to habitat-g. For this very reason, the deck was off-limits to anything but operational and emergency announcements. The audio for the advertisements started yammering in her implanted ear bug; she pressed behind her ear and turned it off, since it would automatically activate for private and urgent messages. Turning the ear bug off, unfortunately, triggered higher volume from the nodes supporting the wall display. Every merchant she or Matt had ever used seemed to be trotting advertisements across the wall. After being isolated in new space for more than six months, she was unnerved by the discordant sights and sounds.

Ariane glanced past the officials. Hopeful advertisers were even peppering the Minoan. Its headdress extended its head organically and supported the requisite horns, jewels, and beads—apparently justifying the jewelry commercials. Hidden equipment obscured its head and face, and raised contours that sucked in light rather than reflected it. The "velvet-over-ice mask," coined by net-think, defeated man-made sensors and ensured that facial features or skin wasn't visible.

If Minoans had faces or skin. Net-think had more theories than she could count regarding the origin of the Minoans and who or what they were. Shortly after the Hellenic Alliance put mankind onto Earth's moon, the Minoans arrived. They offered the essential element for N-space travel to several other solar systems. At the time, they controlled the secret to making N-space time buoys, and a hundred years later, they still maintained that monopoly.

She looked away from the Minoan quickly, focusing on her scuffed boots. The officials waited. She jerked her head once to shake her loose curls and make them presentable. As she walked down the ramp, her boots made light, ringing taps, sounding deceptively delicate. Matt followed, his lanky stride making rude clunks. When she stopped, he put his hands on her shoulders and stood behind her, looking over her head. She felt tension in his hands through her coveralls.

"Athens Point welcomes the *Aether's Touch* into slip thirty-three. She's recorded as owned and crewed by Matt Journey, and piloted by Ariane Kedros." Station Ops used a clipped intonation.

"We'll start with the pilot, then move to the ship and cargo."

"We'll need proof of pilot identity." Flight Records handed Ariane the recorder. Proof of identity was unusual and she felt Matt's grip tighten on her shoulders.

"Great Bull–s—" Matt swallowed his expletive in deference to the listening Minoan. "What's going on here?"

"This is standard procedure, Mr. Journey," said Flight Records.

"No, it isn't, and I object to paying for retinal matching. The regs don't require—"

"It's okay, Matt. Let's pay, regulation or not," Ariane said. Antagonizing the docking inspectors wasn't going to speed things up.

She felt his hands relax and took this as acceptance. She held the recorder against her eye to take a reading and handed it back to Flight Records. Identity forgery in the autonomist worlds was almost impossible, because it required changing all primary and secondary documentation in crystal. Once written to crystal, always in crystal. The data couldn't be changed or erased, and both government and commercial security systems protected crystal vaults.

A false identity is impossible, unless your identity is created and paid for by *the government.* Her mind veered away from those thoughts. *I'm Ariane Kedros,* she told herself firmly.

"Any implants with artificial synapse interfaces?" asked Flight Records.

"No." Ariane shivered as the slim, humming detection wand waved over her head, neck, and back. Her implants were the common, innocuous kinds, used for communications, drug monitoring, or storage of personal information. CAW had outlawed synapse interfaces for piloting vehicles and denied air and space pilot licenses to anyone who still sported such an interface. Hospital vegetable bins were full of those who had jumped on the wet-ware craze a couple of decades ago. Early adopters didn't consider the viciousness of the anonymous hacker. Popularity of synapse interfaces waned in the face of the dangers. When they discovered that synapse-enhanced games could be used remotely for murder, the Senate stepped in and created legal constraints on synapse interfaces.

"Your allowed delta tranquilizer to cognitive dissonance enhancer ratio is . . ." The eyebrows of Flight Records went up as she read Ariane's profile on the slate. Frowning, she evaluated Ariane's small frame from head to foot. "Those are high."

"Medically evaluated each year," Ariane said.

Flight Records shrugged and held out the slate. "Unlock privacy control and approve dose-rate measurements, please."

Ariane thumbed the slate and gave her public password for voiceprint analysis. The slate downloaded readings from her implant and showed doses of d-tranny, clash, and bright, as well as radiation exposures. They would request the same from Matt, but purely as a health measure. For the N-space pilot, this was a compliance check.

Now was the time to admit she'd operated under smooth. At the least, she could bypass the brain-wave panel and Matt might quickly proceed into customs inspections. At the worst, they might fine her or revoke her license. Ariane drew a deep breath.

"I'm making a statement of personal status," she said.

"Don't, Ari." Matt's hands felt heavier.

"Hoping to get through this quickly, Mr. Journey?" A pleasant voice wafted toward them from the remotes in the corridor. Everyone turned to watch

Colonel Owen Edones glide through the swarm of remotes with his usual ease.

"What's *he* doing here?" Matt hissed in her ear while his fingers dug into her shoulders.

"I can formally vouch for Major Kedros and speed this up," Colonel Edones said. His black uniform with the light blue trim and insignia was pristinely pressed and tailored. He strode toward them. When he passed the Minoan, he nodded his head respectfully.

Strangely, the Minoan inclined its horns, backed away, and left them. Everyone standing at slip 33 watched as the Minoan departed for its strange ship. A few mouths dropped open. Remotes began to drift away, presumably to cover other areas of the habitat that were more interesting to their owners.

"What?" said Station Ops.

"Shall we bypass flight records inspection?" Colonel Edones asked. "I have business with Major Kedros and I can vouch for her, by signature."

Flight Records searched her slate, probably only now reading the notes appended to Ariane's pilot license that read "Member of AFCAW Reserve, rank Major, assigned to Directorate of Intelligence, rated to pilot light military air vehicles under seven metric tons and space vehicles OFSV-16, OFSV-19, Naga-20, Naga-21, Naga-24." She handed her slate to Colonel Edones, who applied his thumbprint.

Station Ops was peeved. "But our procedures—"

"Bypassed on my authority," Edones said, his tone quiet and implacable.

"We don't need your help, Edones." In contrast, Matt's voice sounded young and rough.

"Major, tell your boy to calm down. I'm carrying orders for you."

Ariane twisted away from Matt to face both of them. She understood Matt's antipathy for Edones, but she'd never figured out why Edones returned the hostility.

"You can refuse the orders, Ari. I'll sign the 932 that says you're necessary for your civilian job." Matt's face took on that familiar stubborn look. He had evidently read up on the regulations, but sadly, he didn't understand the true hold that AFCAW held over her.

"That'll never happen, will it, Major?" Edones had a small, grim smile on his face.

"I'll remind both of you that I make my own decisions," she said. "I'll decide after looking over the orders."

"Only under secure conditions. I suggest we talk, while Mr. Journey handles his inspections." Edones turned and walked toward his slip, apparently confident that she'd follow.

She felt a surge of resentment and wondered whether she could puncture his confident arrogance, just once. But if anything defined *Ariane Kedros*, it was her duties and assignments for the Directorate of Intelligence. She began to follow Edones, but Matt grabbed her arm and swung her around to face him.

"Ari, I can't go through this again. You understand?" His eyes were wide, his jaw muscles clenched and raised.

She knew what he meant. Matt had looked like that after he'd supported her head and kept her safe as she convulsed and vomited, purging her last celebration binge, her *reward* for getting through her last assignment alive.

"It won't happen again. I promise." Her voice was steady, but she swallowed hard as she remembered the rich taste of beer mixed with burning shots of liquor and the sweet smooth—all in quantities that could kill a bull. She was lying.

"Good. Don't take any assignment from Edones

until you talk with me." He squeezed her arm with friendly concern.

Deep down, she felt a tiny kernel of disappointment stir. She was sure Matt didn't believe her, but he wouldn't confront her. Why didn't he walk away and give her the contempt she deserved?

Matt watched Ari catch up with Edones. He shook his head. Whenever that smarmy colonel showed up, Ari would disappear on mysterious missions that Matt suspected were also dangerous.

He'd started to depend upon her. So much that he'd place his life in her hands—already had, for that matter. Just six days ago, he'd collapsed against the inside of the air lock in a punctured, barely operable suit. Ari pressurized the air lock and entered. After opening his helmet and checking his vitals, she'd proceeded to lecture him.

"We're almost at the end of the season and we can leave that bot. What we can't afford to lose is the ship, and I came mighty close; if we lost her, it'd be your own damn fault. Really, Matt, what's so valuable out there that you'd risk your life and ship?"

Standing there with her hands on her hips and that fierce expression on her face, Ari shamed him into silence. He reached into the webbed pouch on his suit, pulled out the bot's memory module, and held it up.

Her eyes widened.

"Is that a rhetorical question?" he asked.

She stared at him for a moment, and then started chuckling. That was what he liked about Ari—she knew that sometimes extreme measures were called for to get the job done. *That's probably why Edones keeps giving her assignments. The bruises and medical treatments she has when she comes back, the drinking she does—*

"Mr. Journey, I'm on a tight schedule!" The customs inspector still waited to examine the crystal storage and data systems.

Matt glanced down at the shorter man. When he looked up, he saw Ari and Edones turn onto the ring corridor and pass from his sight.

CHAPTER 2

The Terran Expansion League (TerraXL) and the Consortium of Autonomous Worlds (CAW), hereinafter referred to as the Parties, Conscious of the devastating power of temporal distortion weapons upon the fabric of the universe, and Convinced that the measures set forth in this Treaty will strengthen interstellar peace and security, have agreed upon the articles written in this Treaty. . . .

—*Preamble to Mobile Temporal Distortion (TD) Weapon Treaty, Signed Under Pax Minoica*, 2105.164.10.22 UT, indexed by *Heraclitus 17* under Conflict Imperative

"I see rank still has its privileges," Ariane said when she entered the mission commander's office on the cruiser. The compartment was large, by spaceship standards. A desk and two chairs were bolted to the deck. Behind the desk, the bulkhead displayed the seal of the Consortium of Autonomous Worlds next to the Consortium Armed Forces crest.

"Nice, isn't it? This connects to my cabin and is fitted with every device available through MilNet. But don't worry, this conversation can't be heard by normal nodes." Owen flashed her an innocent, boyish smile and winked one of his blue eyes. When he didn't close his face down into that bland politic expression, he could be handsome.

Ariane refused to be charmed. Owen was dangerous. He didn't have an innocent bone in his body
and he'd just admitted that he had control over what
MilNet documented. She regretted being on a first-
name basis with someone like him—what did that
say about her? *But I'm not anybody real, not anymore.*

She looked around. AFCAW crimson and gold
were liberally splashed about the cabin and furniture,
but something was missing. It took her a moment to
identify what, or specifically, whom.

"Where's Joyce?"

The hulking and pragmatic sergeant who followed
Owen from assignment to assignment wasn't present.
The saying "once you sell your soul to the black and
blue, you're forever theirs" wasn't hyperbole. She
suspected the Directorate always assigned Sergeant
Joyce and Colonel Owen Edones as a pair so they
could support, as well as observe, each other. After
all, loads of bullshit had rolled downhill onto these
two and they were the ones that had to clean up.
They were the only ones who handled certain secrets
that flowed from CAW to AFCAW to the Directorate,
secrets that no one wanted to know and everyone
hoped would die with these two men. *Secrets such as
my identity.* She knew how much work had gone into
her false records as well as those of others, and how
Owen and Joyce alone shouldered the burdens, responsibilities, and knowledge.

"He's TDY." Owen's voice didn't encourage any
questions and she didn't ask anything more, familiar
with the temporary duty orders that came from
Owen. She had no need to know what Joyce was
doing.

"When did the Directorate of Intelligence get its
own ships?" she asked.

"Thanks for noticing. Relax. There's no need to

stand on formalities after all this time." Owen opened cabinets in the side bulkhead, searching for something.

"I couldn't miss the Intelligence emblem on the air lock. Why would you be given command of a cruiser?" She remained standing and stared at the AFCAW crest behind the desk. Its clean midcentury design of the stylized Labrys Raptor had started with the Colonial Air Forces on Hellas Prime.

"The final treaty's been ratified and we're closing down Naga's temporal distortion mission. Can't your employer afford any feeds? Ah." Owen pulled out a bottle. He opened it, sloshing the dark liquid. "Want a drink?"

Yes, by Gaia and any gods of the Minoans. The amber highlights sparkled, and as he poured himself a glass, the sensuous smell filled the cabin. Her mouth watered as she regretfully measured her resolve, and whether she'd lose it with the drink. *Ari, other people don't think like that,* Matt told her. *Every drink isn't a struggle of control or a big decision. They either want it or they don't—if they don't, they decline it. Rationing and rationalizing your drinks isn't natural.* But for her, the idea of anyone not wanting a drink was unnatural.

"Shutting down the Naga systems puts you out of a job. No more secrets to protect," she said, trying to ignore the liquor.

That wasn't true. There would *always* be Ura-Guinn.

"Don't be naive, Major. We could always retrofit the Naga vehicle for kinetic weapons, but that's not our immediate concern. Someone has to ensure the TerranXL inspection teams depart with the same intelligence as when they arrived. They're still our enemy."

"You intelligence golems love all this intrigue and

secrecy, don't you?" She moved backward and sat down in the chair that opposed his desk to get farther away from the smell of the liquor.

"You're one of us now, so live with it. Your orders." He tossed her a military-issue slate. "Of all people, you should realize how important this particular treaty is. We've gotten to the crux of Pax Minoica. Fifteen years of dancing about the negotiation tables under Minoan oversight and we finally begin the drawdown of the weapons system that started it all. We're going to start destroying the warheads that damage nous-space-time, if we're to believe the Minoans. . . ." He let his words trail off, leaning back behind his desk. He took a deep swallow of his drink.

"No, *of all people*, I don't need to be lectured on the dangers of a temporal distortion wave." Her voice was harsh.

She thumbed the slate. It contained a copy of the treaty, which she paged through quickly. There were protocols to follow, inspections required by each side to verify numbers of warheads, schedules for destruction of warheads, blah, blah, and blah. She opened the orders next.

At least Owen kept her in-system. Karthage Point was a military habitat, under full AFCAW control and located near Hellas Daughter, the major moon of Hellas Prime. One of Karthage's missions was testing Naga systems, designed and built on Hellas Daughter. The first treaty under Pax Minoica had curtailed actual testing of temporal distortion waves. Now the test squadron, performing a dying mission, used simulations and tested guidance and targeting hardware without warhead packages. This last treaty finally dismantled the operational squadrons. Karthage also had one of these squadrons, with a complement of

TD warheads, qualifying it as an inspection site under the Mobile TD Weapon Treaty.

"This is different—putting me back into uniform. Why assign *me* as liaison to the Terran inspection teams?" She looked up to see Owen watching her. "Diplomacy isn't my forte and I'm not familiar with the Karthage facilities. You've got plenty of lackeys that can do this assignment better than I can."

"I have faith in your skills, Major. You can fit in anywhere you want, and be anyone you want."

Yet I can't feel comfortable anywhere, with anyone, she thought bitterly. She leaned back into the plush chair.

"I'm thinking of taking Matt's advice," she said. "Maybe it's time to resign my commission."

"Give up AFCAW protection? That would be foolish."

"You mean give up continuous observation and control." Her jaw jutted out in challenge, daring him to deny it. He didn't. She was watched because she was both an embarrassment and a liability to AFCAW. She tried to make up for it by doing her duty, by accepting these dangerous assignments from Owen, but when would her moral debt be paid?

"Before you hand in your commission, I'd suggest reading the next two packets."

Sighing quietly, she went back to the slate. The next packet required voiceprint access. She stated her name, rank, and service number, which were false like everything else. Was there ever a real Ariane? The packet opened and she read the first few sentences before she lost control, flinging the slate across the room.

"Are you *insane*?" The words hissed through her clenched teeth.

The slate hit the opposite wall, rebounded, and bounced over to rest on the floor near Owen's desk.

He calmly picked it up and handed it back. The slate, being military issue, took much more than her abuse to break.

She stared at the slate in his hand as if it were a cobra, ready to strike. "You're exposing me to my worst enemy. Isrid Parmet has dedicated himself to uncovering the 'war criminals' that destroyed Ura-Guinn."

"CAW has always maintained that everyone followed legal civilian orders. The government has taken responsibility and you are *not* a war criminal, Major. You operated under authentic and properly released orders. You did your duty." His tone sounded earnest and he continued to hold out the slate.

"Beating the patriotic drum won't work with me." Her tone was dry, but she took the slate back from him. It lit up at the touch of her thumbprint and reopened the classified report.

"Read the background. He's mellowed in the past fifteen years, with everyone talking about the possibility of finding survivors when ships reach Ura-Guinn."

"If he discovers who I am, I'll still end up a smear on the bulkhead." She skimmed the report on State Prince Isrid Sun Parmet, who was in charge of the TerranXL compliance inspection teams.

"The hide-in-plain-sight strategy can be effective."

"Sounds more like the dumb-ass-hiding-under-the-bed strategy." She looked up. "There's something else, isn't there?"

"Read the last report, which explains why I've chosen you for this assignment. I'm sorry, Ariane."

He hardly ever used her first name, and his tone made her apprehensive. She held her breath as she opened the last packet. It expanded to a set of twelve investigations of deaths, all within the last four months. She looked at the list, seeing a previous vice president of CAW, a previous AFCAW chief of staff, and a previous commander of AFCAW. Farther down, she saw *her previous* wing commander, squadron commander, crew comm officer . . .

"*Cipher*? Cipher's gone?" The name "Cara Paulos" smeared and blurred in her sight. She wiped her eyes with the back of her hand.

"Here, take this." Owen offered a tissue, which she used to wipe her eyes and nose and hide her face. She leaned back into the chair and took a few moments to compose herself.

Damn, Cipher was *crew*. Granted, she and Cipher hadn't always seen eye to eye. Not like Brandon. Ariane looked over the list again and breathed a small sigh of relief. Brandon wasn't on the list.

"The feeds said the vice president died naturally from heart disease, but all these other deaths? This can't be coincidence," she said.

"No, it isn't. CAW suppressed the unnatural causes of these deaths to keep the perpetrators unaware of our investigation. The common root cause was clever sabotage resulting in critical equipment failure. The exception is the catastrophe of Lieutenant Paulos's airline flight, which took eighty-five souls and left us hardly anything to analyze. We had a difficult time identifying bodies, much less finding a cause. That case is still open."

"Why didn't I hear about this?" She glared at Owen.

"Many of these people operated under false identities like yours, so you wouldn't recognize their names. And for the sake of security, I couldn't message you because the generational ship controlled all comm into G-145."

"You were supposed to protect us." Her teeth clenched as she fought the tears again. Poor Cipher. She'd been the nervous one, the dissenting one, al-

ways buried in her codes and comm. She hadn't deserved this.

"The signing of this final treaty seemed to be the
trigger. We were unprepared and our covert oversight doesn't lend itself to moving rapidly. I couldn't
find people fast enough, once we detected the
pattern."

Owen seemed sincerely moved, perhaps by the
loss of useful manpower or by failing an assignment.
She looked away. He hadn't *known* those people. He
hadn't *worked* with them. He'd never faced the moral
quandaries of operating the most powerful weapons
system known to mankind, or seen a comrade crum-
ble under that burden. Owen worked in a world with
clear boundaries and no regrets.

"Why just these names?" she asked softly. "More
people were, and still are, involved with TD weapons."

"True. There's weapons research and development
and maintenance and testing and storage—it took me
a while to figure out. That list is everyone who generated or processed the release order for Ura-Guinn,
with the exception of three people, including yourself."

"It's the Terran reprisal squads, isn't it? They're
out for revenge, like State Prince Parmet. He encouraged them, he's the one who should die—" Anger
rose from within her chest and heated her face.

"Without claiming responsibility on the feeds?"
Owen's voice was cold and slick as ice. "Think about
it. How could the Terrans know our classified release
process and our chain of command, *as it existed in the
past*—after I personally managed the vault and index
replacements? Where would they get the information?"

"You think an insider's involved?"

He nodded. "Someone combined classified information with AFCAW operational knowledge or expe-

rience. I want the *traitor* who helped these killers, more than I want them."

She shivered in the ensuing silence, realizing that she'd never before sensed hatred from Owen. Apparently, Owen did have a personal stake in this mission. *Now I do need a drink.*

She stepped silently to Owen's makeshift liquor cupboard, a repurposed personal hygiene cabinet. As she poured a glass of the liquor, she glanced at herself in the mirror on the back of the cabinet. Her face was thin from the last drop she'd run, her weight loss due to N-space. Her brown eyes sank into dark hollows and she looked brittle. From what she could see in the mirror, her crew overalls were worn and rumpled, hardly befitting an AFCAW officer. Under her right ear, the edge of her collar was unraveling into tufts of stiff orange fibers. Behind her, she saw Owen standing beside his desk in his perfectly appointed uniform, waiting for her answer.

She raised the glass with the golden liquor, deeply inhaling its aroma—she didn't know what it was, nor did she care—and met her own eyes over the brim. An exchange of honesty went through her like a shock. Who was she fooling? Could she pretend to be as composed as Owen, pressed and contained, while she was unraveling inside? She was in worse shape than her coveralls. Self-doubt seized her belly and she lowered the glass. *I can't do this mission.*

"Matt suggested I go for addiction reprogramming," she said conversationally, still facing the hygiene cabinet.

"What for? You don't drink or use on active duty. You're always in control." Owen's voice was confident. How did he know the extent of her control?

"I have the tendency to—to overdo things. Once in a while. When I relax."

"After the missions you've gone through, don't you think you deserve to have a drink or two?"

Of course she did. She also knew that Owen had an interest in keeping the status quo; he couldn't put her welfare ahead of his agenda. "I'm not talking about a couple of drinks," she began.

"That's no reason to undergo deep-psyche neural probes. AFCAW could hardly sanction the risk to your cover or to the information in your brain."

"Could you stop me?" she asked softly.

"Yes."

The finality in that one word was unmistakable. They both knew neural probes or hypnosis could crack the careful veneer of lies that protected her. Owen's caution only justified her random path through life. What was at the end of the path? Self-destruction, no doubt, and she didn't care.

She took a hefty swallow of liquor and let it melt down her throat and into her stomach. Her body relaxed. The alcohol stifled the sound of internal fraying. Her soul might be threadbare, but she could manage. *This is what I am.* She turned away from the cabinet and faced Owen.

"You said there are three of us left? Brandon, myself, and who else?" She tried to remember how release orders were processed fifteen years ago.

Owen answered as if the previous conversation had never happened. Perhaps it hadn't.

"The command post controller who processed the release order. He stayed on active duty and he's now Colonel Erik Icelos, facility commander at Karthage Point. With all the security required to keep the inspection teams safe as well as ignorant, Karthage should be a safe and controlled environment. Besides, you're forewarned now and you've proven your survival skills—you'll be there to protect him." He smiled.

"And Brandon?"

"Stubborn as ever. We advised him to move, but he won't budge from his current location. He's been uncooperative." Owen shrugged and annoyance flitted across his face.

Ariane smiled into her glass and took another sip of soothing comfort. She wasn't supposed to know where Brandon resided, but she had a vague idea.

Under her feet, she felt a faint but familiar trembling. She whirled and placed her hand flat against the back of the hygiene cabinet to feel the vibrations in the bulkheads. The sublight booster engine had started. The crew would soon fire orientation thrusters; the cruiser must have received clearance from Athens Point to disconnect.

"Damn it, Owen, I needed to talk this over with Matt."

"You've accepted your orders. Send him a message, but remember that your destination is classified."

"I haven't signed these orders yet. Matt—"

"He can surely get along without you for a couple of months. Besides, I'm not sure this sort of long-term employment is good for you. What if he learned the truth about you?"

"He never will." She shrugged at the implied, and worthless, threat. Owen wouldn't leak any hint of her past to Matt or anyone else. He'd spent most of his career obscuring "the mission" and would never sabotage his own handiwork.

"I could make things difficult for Matt and his little prospecting business. I could screw with his leases, question his permit."

This wasn't an idle threat. She kept her face impassive. Owen didn't need any more leverage over her, so why this extra pressure? She locked gazes with him, wondering why he always probed, always tried to get tidbits of personal information. Because what Colonel Owen Edones didn't understand, he couldn't control.

This was taking up precious time and Owen wasn't really offering a choice. She shrugged. Whatever honor she had left wouldn't permit her to walk away from the chance to find these killers, or to protect Brandon. As always, she'd follow orders. She gulped down her liquor, picked up the slate, and signed her acceptance.

"Matt and I are business associates, nothing more. I'll need time to prepare, sir. Do I have quarters?" She began her premission dissociation, changing her internal references. Owen was her commanding officer. She felt the change, almost like sliding into an invisible uniform. From Edones's face, he saw it also; he'd once remarked that she had a switch that flipped her into "military mode."

"Take hold. This is first warning for low-g maneuver," a deep drawling voice announced over the ship's nodes.

Colonel Edones smiled. "Better hurry, Major. Quartermaster's on deck two, port section sigma."

"Yes, sir." She saluted and left, but as she hurried toward supply for uniforms, quarters, toiletries, and other comforts, Ariane couldn't get Cipher's face out of her head.

Poor Cipher.

Ari had been six months away from pinning on captain's rank when Cipher was assigned to their crew, replacing a lieutenant who was transferred to Hellas Daughter. Naga was Cipher's first assignment out of sublieutenant preparation, and she received decent ratings in Naga technical training before coming to the Sixteenth Naga Strike Squadron. At first, Cipher was intimidated by her two other crew members, who had five, six, or in Brandon's case, even more years of experience, but she soon loosened up.

Ari remembered the day Cipher had come back from her first leave.

Ari pulled her head out of her locker and jumped. "Cipher! You're back. How was Pelagos?"

Cipher had entered the locker room silently. "It was okay." Cipher shrugged. "Pelagos isn't a prime planet, so I saw the sights within the first few days. They have good salons, though."

"I can see that." Cipher's hair was now bright orange. Personally, Ari didn't understand Cipher's urge to change her appearance on a moment's notice.

"Any news?"

"You've only been gone for five days. We're still holding steady after we took back New Damascus." Ari shook her curls and ran her fingers through her drying hair.

"No, I mean any rumor of Naga deployment."

"TD weapons are a threat that'll never be used, hopefully." Ari closed her locker and, as always, wryly grimaced at the tag that read K. ARGYRIS. Her family and friends called her Ari after her middle name, Ahrilan, and now her comrades did the same. Karen Argyris was a name she only saw on nametags and paperwork.

She turned to see Cipher, looking distressed and sullen, sitting on the bench, staring at the shampoo in her hands. Clearly, there was something else on her mind.

"Ari, I talked to Alex." Cipher's dark eyes settled on her, with *meaning* in them, as if she should understand that cryptic hint.

"Who? Alex Stavvos? You mean the squadron gossip, with the big mouth—always flapping."

Cipher didn't smile. "He said he saw you coming out of Brandon's room during early shift, after the STRAT-

EVAL party at the club. He said you looked. . . ." She didn't continue.

Uh-oh. Ari took a deep breath. *Is it too much to ask, Gaia, to let this slide by?* She looked around the locker room; luckily, the showers and lockers were deserted. She sat down, straddling the bench and facing Cipher. "We made a mistake."

"You're not going to deny it." Cipher turned and Ari looked down at the bench, not wanting to meet her eyes.

"No. Like I said—"

"What's going to happen now? You guys can't have a relationship and still be on crew together." Cipher's voice cracked.

"There's no *relationship*." Ari tried to keep her voice steady. She wasn't sure how she really felt about Brandon, but they'd made their decision already, for the good of the crew and their careers. Their relationship had been over almost before it began and they hoped the squadron commander would never hear of it. Depending upon how the squadron commander viewed their indiscretion, he could charge both of them with fraternization. At the very least, he'd break up the crew.

"So you guys had a one-night stand." Cipher looked shocked.

"That's a quaint way of putting it, but it's better than getting involved, isn't it?" Ari was confused. Since Brandon wrote both their evaluations, she expected Cipher to be relieved. "Otherwise everyone, including you, would suspect favoritism. We'd have to break up the crew."

"You shouldn't stay on crew after you slept together."

"Mistakes happen," Ari said calmly. *People get drunk and make mistakes—especially me.* "This is wartime and we make a good crew—just look at our ratings—and we shouldn't break up a good thing."

"But how can you work together?"

Ari wasn't sure how to answer this. She could work with Brandon because she could distance herself and take every conversation, every interaction at face value. Cipher worried about what people thought, what people felt, what lay hidden behind every decision, conscious or subconscious.

Instead, she said, "If you ask him, Brandon will talk to you about it. We'd like the whole thing forgotten, because we want to keep the crew intact. Do you want us to be broken up?"

Cipher shook her head, perhaps not willing to accept failings in her two senior crew members.

"We shouldn't have, well, gotten carried away. I admit that," Ari said. "But I hope you can forgive us, for the good of the mission."

"For the *mission*?" She turned and looked at Ari, outrage twisting her features.

What did Cipher want from her? Ari watched her stand and undress, her arms jerking and pulling at her clothes. The Naga crews weren't seeing action, but it was *wartime*, for Gaia's sake. Was Cipher hoping for a love story or a happy v-play ending? This wasn't virtual adaptive-fiction play, where the player could influence the story by tweaking parameters. Ari rubbed her temples. Nothing would be the same again. If she could take back her actions several nights ago, she would.

Cipher left a crumpled pile of civilian clothes on the bench in front of Ari. Without another word, she stomped off to the showers.

Ari shook her head. *Poor Cipher.*

CHAPTER 3

CAW's military arm (AFCAW) insists Ura-Guinn was targeted through civilian control, but they continue to classify the mission documentation and hide the perpetrators. The only conclusion can be that they're covering up a freelance military operation. Their militia has violated the Phaistos Protocols [see modern Minoans] and they must be tried as war criminals.

—TerranXL State Prince Isrid Sun Parmet, 2094.341.05.08 UT, indexed by *Heraclitus 12* under Conflict Imperative

The "window" in Isrid's study displayed one of his favorite views: afternoon clouds against the red horizon of Mars, viewed from the northeastern edge of Valles Marineris. He couldn't have a conventional window because of radiation, and this particular view wasn't possible from his location, the city of Roma Rossa.

The clouds building up against the Tharsis Montes volcanoes were a normal result of midnorthern summer and not due to the slight increase of atmospheric pressure. That mere increase in fifty millibars had been frightfully expensive, based upon diverting four comets over a century ago, and Mars still couldn't come close to sister Terra's atmosphere.

However, Mars wasn't going to receive terraforming funds any time soon, based upon the projected Terran Expansion League tax base. Millions of people forced to live in protected habitats on both planets would only support terraforming on, well, *Terra*, since Yellowstone's caldera had blown her friendly surface into an ice age. Yellowstone was a costly lesson in souls and biomass and ecosystems and species, as well as pride. Mankind learned that their footprints on Terra could never compare to the internal rages within the planet herself.

Inside his study, safe from climate vagaries and radiation, State Prince Isrid Sun Parmet relaxed after reading the Mobile Temporal Distortion Weapon Treaty for a third time. His back was straight, perpendicular to the seat of his stool. He aligned his feet square with his body and extended his arms on the low desk with his hands slightly curled into mirror images of each other. The lines of the lavish bamboo floor, shipped at great expense from a biome refuge on Terra, ran smoothly perpendicular to his desk. The window to his right balanced a large painting on the opposite wall, painted by a Martian artist and reflecting the muted colors in the study. Isrid breathed deeply and rhythmically while he practiced *somaural* exercises, methodically tensing and relaxing every voluntarily controlled muscle in his body using a master's sequence.

The treaty arrived with an attached comment. "SP Parmet, read carefully. Overlord Three expects strategic benefit. SP Hauser."

Isrid had hoped his exercises would give him insight into the strategic benefit that Overlord Three sought. He was distracted when transparent green-yellow froth crept across the study floor into the edge of his vision, carrying with it the faint scent of pine.

"You ignored the ban," he said aloud, rising to surface consciousness. The smell of pines receded, as did the colorful splash of his wife's aura on the floor. "I wasn't to be disturbed for four hours."

"Even for a drink?" said Sabina's soft voice from the doorway.

His second wife held a hot beverage, modeled after Terran tea, in her hand. Her small and taut body stood symmetrical inside the doorway, and no farther. Her short red hair cupped her head and neatly lay behind her delicate ears, while the smooth gray bodysuit showed every indelicate and muscular ripple on her body. Sabina was adept at *somaural* reading and projection, but Isrid didn't permit her in his study. He worried that her strong aura, perhaps a result of her willful personality, would taint his room.

He declined with an eyebrow. *I'm busy.*

"You've been here more than three hours. What are you studying?" Signing with almost imperceptible finger flicks and a shoulder shrug, she added, *You need a break.*

"I'm reading the treaty for dismantling CAW's Naga, versus our VTD-twenty drones and Falcon missiles." He stretched and relaxed his muscles. Of his two wives, Sabina was the one in whom he confided. This, however, was one reason he didn't risk having her accompany him to political events.

"Why torture yourself? You wouldn't have been allowed on the Terran team for negotiating this particular treaty, and for good reason." Sabina didn't know about his appointment yet.

"The overlord appointed me to organize and manage the treaty inspection teams."

Sabina projected disbelief and puzzlement, but Isrid didn't reply.

"It's a trap," she finally said.

"It's a test."

"Semantics." Her fingers flicked the Martian sign that translated to "a spoken word never has one meaning."

"The overlord and his staff need to know how far I'll go to support Pax Minoica."

Sabina nodded. She'd helped him craft a new public image, slowly softening his statements over the past five years. She understood the importance of publicly accepting Pax Minoica.

"You've convinced them that you've come to terms with losing Pryce and his family." A graceful curl of three fingers added the meaning "deceived" to her spoken word "convinced." A flip of the wrist added "brother" to "Pryce," which Sabina knew would cause him pain.

"Either that, or they think I've decided to wait. The overlord supports this as the logical course, considering the latest analysis on the glitch data." Isrid answered tonelessly and added no additional meanings to his words, because he was no longer sure how he felt.

"They place too much hope on the glitch data." Sabina's sneer made her feelings obvious; they were not ambivalent in regards to the Autonomists. Sabina felt she'd lost a child—since she and Isrid were going to have Pryce and his wife join their multimarriage so she could carry his child. The permit had been grueling to get and the chance was now lost. She had one son by Isrid, but she'd hoped for more.

"Even if their sun survived, the colony might not exist anymore," Sabina continued. "The temporal distortion wave would have caused coronal mass emissions and flares. If they survived *that*, then how long could civilization endure, shut off from supplies and information?"

Isrid nodded agreement. They'd had this discussion many times and he was empty, drained from years of pain and *wondering*. Was anyone alive in Ura-Guinn? Could they trust the glitch data?

It was so much simpler during the war. Both sides had TD weapons, although the Autonomists had followed the Phaistos Protocols to the letter with their manned, somewhat manual, Naga release vehicles and the Terrans had stretched the protocols to the limit with their standoff drones and missiles. Not interested in learning the physics behind temporal distortion, Isrid took the analysts' word for what it could do: A TD wave was capable of blowing up a sun.

They were terrible weapons; the Minoans were edgy about temporal distortion wave testing, and were always pestering for a moratorium. The analysts had all said that as long as neither side was losing the war and no one panicked, the TD weapons were good negotiating material.

But fifteen years ago, the Autonomists had detonated a TD weapon in the Ura-Guinn system and they weren't even losing, *damn them*. It was a surprise attack, later called preemptive by the Consortium negotiators.

The detonation didn't behave as predicted. No one had been brave—or stupid—enough to test a full-scale detonation, so unexpected results weren't surprising. Fifteen years ago, the temporal distortion wave at Ura-Guinn had destroyed the system buoy and generated a pulse through the entire time buoy network, called "the glitch." This pulse carried data that shocked both Terran and Autonomist scientific communities, while giving Isrid and others hope, however hollow. Contrary to scaled-down tests and simulations, Ura-Guinn's sun, specifically, its fusion engine, *might have survived*.

When it was discovered that ships transitioning out and in to real-space at the moment of the glitch were lost, it brought the consequences of war to every system in the League and the Consortium. The Minoans stepped in, asking TerraXL and CAW to meet at the negotiation table once more. Pax Minoica began, if rather unsteadily. The scientific communities analyzed the glitch data again. And again. They built the largest space antenna and scope ever attempted at Epsilon Eridani, but that didn't change the time they'd have to wait. With the buoy at Ura-Guinn destroyed, the information couldn't go any faster than the speed of light.

"The colony, if it exists, has gone through hell," Sabina was saying. "The autonomists should be punished as if they'd damaged a habitat."

"In four months, we'll have light-speed data. We'll be able to verify what's happened to the planetary bodies." Whenever he thought of that, he almost shivered with dread. He needed to know, but part of him didn't want to know.

"And *coincidentally*, the final TD weapon treaty gets ratified before we even know what's happened to Ura-Guinn," she said. "How could we have allowed that?"

"I wasn't in any position to delay negotiations."

He didn't add that his position was tenuous. She knew that. During the last decade, the political climate had changed and Isrid had been forced to change with it. The people and their leaders began to wholeheartedly back treaties that were originally only grudgingly supported because of the Minoans. Overlords began culling their staffs of rabble-rousers—those, like Isrid, who would not let the memories fade so easily. He had called for retribution, for revenge, but eventually found he was alone—unless the overlords or their staffs interpreted his speeches as an appeal for funds. Everyone still agreed that money was a problem.

"We'll know more after the light-speed data is analyzed," he added. "Then, in three years, the *Campaign
VII* will arrive and we'll have full access through the
new time buoy."

"Hmm, yes, an *emergency* generational ship. What
a contradiction. We helped finance the bulk of that
mission and when I say the Autonomists should pay,
why can't they reimburse us for those expenses?"

He didn't want to think about their financial situation. They had more years of debt-load than he, his
wives, or his children could live through. Other established Terran families were in the same position,
but this only made his position and salary more precious because of the competition.

"It doesn't work that way. I can't demand reim-
bursement from the CAW Senate directly." He
paused; Sabina had a point. "Since I'll be traveling
into CAW on weapon inspections, I could try to re-
finance with a Consortium bank, perhaps get better
rates and fees. I could find other investors to back
the Campaign ship."

"So you support this final treaty." Some of her
anger leaked into her aura; he could see it, so recently
close to meditation.

"I have to. Pax Minoica has become too strong to
withstand, at least politically, and we have to keep
the overlord's patronage."

Sabina nodded reluctantly. Her aura cleared back
to its original green shot with yellow. "How long
will the inspections take?"

"The actual inspection time is limited to one UT day.
I don't know how long the entire visit will take."

"Will you be taking Maria?"

Oh, how casually she asked that question! Isrid
watched her for a moment and felt for changes in
her aura. He didn't detect any. Once again, he had
no idea what she was feeling.

"Of course Maria will be on the inspection team," he said. "She's the best analyst with field experience that I have on my staff."

There was another pause as each waited for the other to betray an emotion. Both were masters of *somaural* projection, and both revealed nothing. Sabina spoke first.

"Make your decisions carefully. Our future with the overlord may depend upon this *test*." Her fingers flickered. *Remember that revenge is engraved upon your heart.*

Sabina turned smoothly and left. He knew she hoped to fan the embers of his anger, to keep it alive. Her aura faded, but the disturbance she had caused in his aura didn't. Her blunt attempts at manipulation were another reason she didn't accompany him at sensitive political occasions. Garnet, his first wife and the result of a contract between families, wasn't as proficient at *somaural* projection, but she made up for it with her compliant and tactful behavior. This compliance also resulted in banal sex—hence the need for another wife. At least Sabina could express herself sexually, although that could be a problem when Maria was involved.

Isrid cleared his mind of family annoyances and focused on the treaty. His pulse quickened when he considered *physically* visiting CAW military facilities. This was the first treaty under Pax Minoica that allowed on-site verification of TD warhead inventories.

A chime sounded and he opened a view screen on the far wall.

State Prince Hauser, personal aide to Overlord Three, wore a smooth tan suit that politely let communication through. The muted blue insignia on his upper left pectoral region proclaimed his position.

After exchanging greetings, SP Hauser said, "The first baseline inspection to verify numbers of systems and warheads will be initiated on 380.5 UT. You'll have to arrive at Karthage Point within a day of our initiation." *They don't expect us to move so fast.*

"SP, we've given up our best drone delivery systems. How can we justify this loss?" asked Isrid. *With no disrespect toward the overlords,* his head inclination and lowered eyes seemed to add. He might be overstepping his authority by questioning the terms of this treaty, but SP Hauser had a unique viewpoint because he'd been with the negotiating team.

"They have to destroy the Naga TD controller systems as well as eliminate the warheads. Since we have no manned deployment system, we've never been able to counteract the flexible Naga Force. Now Naga will have no fangs." SP Hauser waited, receptive to more questions.

"What if they refit the Naga vehicles with kinetic weapons?" Isrid asked.

"That'll be the least of our problems. We're in a new age, where we fight in the back alleys of industry and technology," Hauser said with a slight smile.

"You didn't obtain the names of those responsible for Ura-Guinn. Did you try to negotiate for them?" This subject was close to Isrid's heart and still made his anger burn. His operatives had learned that soon after the detonation, the military personnel who fired the weapon had managed to escape the system.

"Overlord Six asked for names during the early negotiations. CAW authorities said the records for that mission were destroyed at the end of the war." SP Hauser radiated annoyance. *They were lying. They're so easy to read.*

"My intelligence staff says there are still active reprisal squads."

"Isrid, we can't be associated with any of those teams, not now. It's of paramount importance that the overlords aren't sullied, in CAW's eyes, by *inde-*

pendent actions." Hauser's body language reinforced his words.

After SP Hauser signed off and Isrid downloaded Hauser's packet, he spent a moment dealing with his frustration. He practiced *somaural* breathing and built his wall to the world while he examined his feelings. If he didn't understand the roots of his anger, he'd never be able to control it.

The overlords had moved beyond Ura-Guinn, apparently willing to wait to see if the TD weapon had truly destroyed their colony. Hauser's packet outlined the alarming issues besetting the overlords, the issues that were of the highest priority for their staffs. The Terran Expansion League's planetary economies were in shambles. The League hadn't established new colonies for several decades, with the exception of those it had ripped away from Consortium worlds during the war. They also suffered the expense of rehabilitating Terra. The overlords now pinned their hopes on injections of technology to galvanize their industry and combat the deleterious effects from depending upon Minoan artifacts. "Never depend upon technology you don't understand and you can't replicate" was sound advice, but TerraXL couldn't afford such high principles while locked in economic struggle with the autonomous worlds.

Isrid examined SP Hauser's list of personnel, also provided in the packet. Isrid could choose six inspectors from his own staff for each of the two inspection teams. Hauser provided twelve names and at first glance, they were innocuous, but an autoshredding message attached to the list disturbed Isrid.

"Andre Covanni will be accompanying your team." The text from SP Hauser danced across his view port before dissolving.

Andre Covanni was the cover name for TerraXL's most effective intelligence operative. Andre was a shadowy legend during the war and he remained undercover to continue his work for TerraXL. Isrid suspected that Andre was the intelligence conduit to the reprisal squads, but he also knew Andre reported to Overlord Three. Had the overlords truly severed ties to those squads?

Isrid puzzled over the message. Was Andre watching Isrid to ensure that he put aside his own feelings and conduct the inspection properly? Or was Andre being provided so Isrid might command the reprisal squads, and thus subvert Pax Minoica?

Overlord Three was testing him; now Isrid had to figure out which answer the overlord wanted.

Walking out of the *Aether's Touch*, Matt bit back a yelp of surprise when he saw the departure list displayed near his slip. The AFCAW cruiser in the next slip, named the *Bright Crescent*, had disconnected. *Ari took the mission*. Otherwise, she'd have been waiting.

"Mr. Journey, are you paying attention?" The custom inspector's tone was severe.

I asked her to consult me first. He'd receive a call, of course, where Ari would apologize profusely. She'd say things like "this is something I have to do" and she'd knot her eyebrows into that responsible and earnest expression. Her dark eyes would be wide and worried about his reaction, hoping he'd forgive her. *Not this time, Ari.*

"Mr. Journey?"

"Yes?" Matt looked down at the inspector, whom he now privately called Mr. Customs.

Besides having no sense of humor, Mr. Customs had ridden him mercilessly throughout the inspection. Not that Matt expected a free ticket, but the inspector had to check every single seal on the ship, whether electrical, mechanical, optical, or recorded in solid state or crystal.

"Where would I have gotten illicit AI in the asteroids of G-145?" Matt asked when Mr. Customs insisted on checking every ruleset installed on *Aether's Touch* for piracy, whether it qualified as AI or not. He received no answer.

"Once I apply my seal, Mr. Journey, you have six hours to file your claims, or lose your rights of *pedis possessio*." The stout and stiff inspector made a grandiose gesture of applying his thumbprint to the slate before extending it toward Matt. "Your clock is ticking."

"Sure—I get stiffed with the short deadline. Everybody else gets two months to bid for leases," Matt grumbled good-naturedly, hoping to establish a rapport with the inspector. No one liked complicated CAW exploration law, in part because it was deeply rooted in old planetary mining law.

As Matt reached for the slate to apply his thumbprint, Mr. Customs whipped it away. He looked up from his empty hand to meet the inspector's eyes. Already too small for his face, they were squinted in anger.

"Who are *you* to question exploration and salvage laws? You're just crèche-get that passes through in your fancy ship. The people who lease your claims take the *real* risks, while you sit back and make royalties off the backs of others." Mr. Customs was standing as tall as he could and he only barely passed Matt's shoulder. His lips quivered, then split into a sneer.

Didn't this guy know anything about new space? Matt's anger and blood surged to his face. Mr. Customs took a step backward.

"You think my work is *safe*?" Matt held out his hand for the slate, leaning over the short inspector. "Next time, check your facts and see how many second-wave prospectors never come back from new space. Now hand me that slate before I make a scene."

Matt jerked his head toward the remotes fluttering on the edge of their privacy shields. The inspector's eyes darted toward their growing audience. He had no idea how close Matt had come to losing his life in new space.

They had less than ten days left in their prospecting season when Matt made his fateful decision. They'd already discovered the culture-shattering ruins on Priamos moon. If he'd stuck to the schedule, they would have continued to tediously assess large outer-system asteroids. Instead he abruptly decided to go in-system again, swinging by Priamos and its owner, Laomedon. Ari had raised her eyebrows when changing their course, but later, she admitted his instincts had paid off.

That's when they discovered the artifact floating in an empty chunk of space between the orbits of planet Sophia II and gas giant Laomedon. It had been too small and isolated to be caught in their original mapping process.

"It can't be natural, which means there was a *space-capable* civilization in this system." She stared at the readings that indicated a cylindrical object about forty meters by ten meters. "But what is it?"

"I don't know. The more important question: Why isn't it moving?"

"Everything *moves*, Matt. This thing might be stable because of Laomedon's orbit about the sun."

"No, it's fixed with respect to the sun."

"That's not possible." She checked the readings. "There's no sign of heat from station-keeping thrusters or antigrav."

"Everything moves in *real-space*."

"You're suggesting this thing has an active connection to N-space?"

"The only things that don't move in real-space, to our knowledge, are the Minoan buoys that are anchored in N-space. Too bad we don't know how they do that."

"Yeah, but we've got N-space travel *because* they do." She pointed toward another graph. "This thing isn't a buoy. It isn't emitting anything on the EM spectrum. There's no track and lock signals, nothing, and there's no known way to shut buoys down once they're initialized."

"They can be destroyed with TD weapons."

She looked away. "There's a healthy sun here. I don't think it was ever hit by a TD detonation."

"Ura-Guinn may still exist, right? So—"

"Why don't we launch our touchy-feely bot and get a closer look, huh?" The bot sent back some astounding close-up video once it was near the artifact.

"I've seen a lot of time buoys, even older ones, and that doesn't look like Minoan design or workmanship," Ari said.

"Amazing," was all Matt could say.

They weren't surprised when the bot had to fire chemical thrusters to resist the gravitational force from the artifact. Any simple N-space connection could generate a gravitational field; that was how the gravity generator worked on the *Aether's Touch*, as well as any other ship or habitat. It wasn't a strong field, but it affected the bot's navigation.

"Let's land it and see if we can scrape a sample or two," Matt said.

That's when everything had gone wrong.

"What do you mean it won't respond?" Matt demanded. "It's still feeding us data."

"Yes, but it isn't accepting commands. I can't get it to take a sample. Look at the video."

The bot walked around the cylindrical surface to the side toward the sun and oriented its solar panels for maximum exposure, yet it didn't need to charge its batteries. It didn't stop recording or transmitting, but it ignored all commands to move or take samples. Then they tried to make it return. No good. Finally, they tried abort commands. Nothing changed.

That's when he'd had the brilliant idea to go EVA to retrieve it, and keep the ship as far away from the artifact as possible. He was going untethered, keeping an open mike, with a thruster pack and several hours of air. His words when departing the air lock on *Aether's Touch* were "Don't worry, I'll have that bot back in no time at all."

When he got to the artifact, he was able to crawl on it because of the gravity field. His stomach felt strange, particularly when he crept about a midsection that had a diameter of only ten meters and a tiny circumference of approximately thirty meters. While his every action *should* cause an equal and opposite reaction, that was a real-space rule and it didn't apply to this artifact. It didn't roll or move, although it shuddered a tiny bit when he landed.

"What did you say? No time at all?" Ari's voice asked in his ear bug, twenty minutes and many creative curse words later.

"It's running away from me." Matt was sweating and puffing, making his environmental controls ramp up. The suit and pack weren't easy to maneuver, particularly when he needed quick, abrupt movement.

"Matt, hold on." She sounded worried. "I'm reading a signal. I think this thing suddenly switched on. The artifact's emitting—something."

"What?" He paused on the dark side of the artifact, staring at the bot that was less than a meter away,

taunting him. It seemed to have no problem using its wheels and multijointed feet to scamper around. *Maybe if I stay still, it'll come forward.* He crouched closer to the surface of the artifact.

"I think you ought to get off, Matt. I'm reading a faint, but repetitive, signal on a frequency in the microwave region."

That was when the bot shut off its lights, moved toward him, punctured his suit with one of its sampling arms, and retreated.

"What the *fuck*?" He backed away, seeing status lights inside the helmet blink red for a moment. Above his wrist joint was a tear about a centimeter long.

"What's happening? You're on the dark side and your helmet light sucks."

He backed away, clumsy in the EVA suit and unbalanced by the tank with thrusters. The suit was self-sealing and he heard the hiss of sealant expanding. The sealant fixed the leak, but it also stiffened and thickened the suit near a crucial joint, hindering his mobility even more. In the dim light from his helmet, he saw the bot advancing, both arms moving fast enough to blur.

"Matt?"

"It's attacking me—get away! What the—"

"I'm coming closer to give you better light."

"No! Ari, don't let the ship near, I don't want her systems compromised—hey! You piece of junk!"

He had rips in both arms and near the control panel on his chest. As he rolled backward and pushed off, the bot sliced an area near his left knee. His suit could take only so much abuse.

He pushed off hard enough to soar ten meters away, but when he tried to activate his thrusters, nothing happened. His status light indicated no connection. Without thrusters, he couldn't turn, but he

was happy to have his feet oriented toward the artifact. The bot's arms were reaching toward him. He
came down kicking and damaged one of its arms,
but received more punctures near his right knee and
left ankle.

Bright light erupted about him. Behind him, *Aether's Touch* had moved close enough to use floodlights. He grabbed the moving sample arm with his
left hand, feeling more sealant expand. How much
more could this suit take?

The bot's arm was stronger than he expected, jerking his torso left and right while his other hand
groped about, searching. He found the memory module and yanked. Luckily, it'd been designed for quick
disconnect. Pushing off with all the strength he could
muster in one arm and his stiffened legs, he rose
toward the ship.

He saw a status light on the bot's front panel blink
and go orange, but it still had power. It moved
around toward the sunny side of the artifact and he
lost sight of it. Tumbling slowly, head over heels, he
saw *Aether's Touch* come into view. The ship was so
close that he could see the seams in her skin. The
doors to her large bay were open and the interior
lights were on.

A rush of gratitude for Ari's quick thinking loosened his tense muscles. *Thank Gaia she never listens
to me.*

CHAPTER 4

A thought experiment I pose to my students: What if the Minoans didn't help mankind off Earth (Terra) or establish FTL (Nous-space, N-space) travel for us? We might never have migrated out of the Helios (Sol) system. To the contrary, we wouldn't have suffered spasms of planetwide economic and political destabilization, followed by warfare. At this point, some student will bring up the latest theory of alternate universes. . . .

—Marcus Alexander, Sophist at Konstantinople Prime University, 2042.261 UT, reindexed in 2093 by *Democritus 18* under Cause and Effect Imperative

"I don't see *you* dealing with punctured suits and insane bots!" Matt realized he was yelling and clamped his jaw shut.

Mr. Customs was leaning backward and squinting, refusing to give way to Matt's aggression by stepping backward. Matt took a moment to collect his emotions and backed out of the inspector's personal space.

"I apologize. I'm rather tired right now," Matt said stiffly. He didn't really want to make a scene that would titillate the lurkers. *Too late now*.

Mr. Customs looked at the watching remotes for a minute. His sneer had relaxed into a frown that looked ingrained and after a moment, he handed over the slate.

"I don't write the law, Mr. Journey." Customs

didn't make an apology, but at least he used a mild tone. "I'm required to personally inform you that you must provide proof of pursuit of discovery, plus justification of reasonable profit. That's in addition to proof of *pedis possessio* using manual or telebot methods."

The words came out in a rush and were probably meaningless to Mr. Customs, who turned quickly and shuffled his feet awkwardly as he walked away. From the gawky gait, he was newly assigned and a grav-hugger as well. Why would he have applied to work on a habitat in the first place?

Matt waited alone, except for clusters of remotes still cam-eyeing him. Where was his security? He fidgeted, about to put through another request, when the heads of two brawny security agents became visible over the curve of the deck.

"Mr. Journey?" One of the security team handed him a slate. Hired muscle was smart enough to ensure that they were paid with verified funds. Once they received their verification code, they relaxed into almost-smiles, which was possibly as friendly as they got.

"We can carry that, Mr. Journey," said one, extending a beefy arm.

Matt instinctively clutched the case to his body tightly. Then he realized that anyone watching through remotes would notice his overprotective reflex. No sense in giving hints to lurkers. Trying to look nonchalant, he handed the case over to security. Then he moved away from the docks as fast as he could with a safe lope, trying to get used to habitat gravity. When they entered the crowds on commerce levels, his security earned their pay, plus generous tips. Both men kept close to Matt so that their combined privacy shields kept the remotes at bay. They didn't let anyone physically bump into him and probe his implant firewalls.

They got to the burb-levels in record speed. After receiving admittance from Nestor's flat, Matt released the security team and entered.

"So, what was the deal with customs?" asked Nestor. No greeting after these six months, no how-are-you, but hey, this was Nestor.

"Only a dumb-ass grav-hugger with a chip on his shoulder."

"Yeah? It looked like your head was going to blow off during that fit you had."

"Did the node coverage already get indexed? Or did you set a remote on me?" Matt was still tense.

Nestor's tufts of blue hair bowed and waved to some fractal algorithm as he turned his lenses, which had one clear side, toward Matt. His propensity for using wearable interfaces, when most people used the myriad of available display surfaces, had earned Nestor the name of "Bug" at the generational orphanage. It was a name Matt knew he despised.

"I did what any lawyer or intellectual property broker would do. Particularly after foolishly broadcasting that you had such a good season." Nestor shrugged.

"I don't like being hounded by remotes."

"Who does? Anyway, where's that little pilot of yours? I always get a charge from her." Nestor made a rude gesture toward his groin. Matt rolled his eyes. If Ari were here Nestor would be all awkward worship and adolescent admiration.

"Ari went on some job for what's-his-face." Matt tried to keep the rancor out of his voice.

Nestor spent a moment observing him in silence, perhaps illegally collecting biometric data. "If you want a pilot who charges you, that's okay, but this one twists you up inside. You got to keep it professional."

Professional. Matt nodded vaguely. At one time,

he'd been objective about Ari. N-space pilots encountered unspeakable terrors during the drop, but those terrors usually didn't follow the pilots into real-space and haunt them in their sleep. The cognitive dissonance enhancer, nicknamed clash, was supposed to ensure that the pilot couldn't remember the terrors well enough to reexperience them in their sleep. After months of working together, however, Matt had determined that Ari's nightmares had nothing to do with N-space; they were fragments of her previous military missions. He always made sure he was in the small galley heating drinks when she staggered out for her shift, sometimes sweating and shaking. During this past exploration season, as Matt stared at her in that tiny galley, he knew he'd stepped over a thin and indefinable emotional line.

"Ari's a minor partner now." Matt tried to change the subject. He shook off the picture of how she'd looked, dwarfed in her large sleeping shirt with the faded symbol of a snake, with her hands clutching the hot drink. He'd gotten into the habit of stocking Hellas Kaffi, even though it was expensive, and sharing it with her during shift overlap. Generally, crèche-get didn't like strong flavors or spices, but there were two universal exceptions: coffee, even the generic kind, and reengineered cinnamon, when used *sparingly*. These flavors and smells seemed to appeal to the human psyche and instinct, regardless of environment and upbringing.

"So? Hire another pilot. Would she have a problem with reducing her seasons?" Nestor said.

"N-space pilots are hard to come by. Besides, whether I hire another pilot is *my* business."

"Hmm. I'm a minor partner now and I'm just giving you advice. Which perhaps you should heed, since you handled Customs so well." Nestor drawled his voice into sarcasm.

"He was new." Matt shrugged. He opened his data case and examined the crystal. Since crystal was extremely rugged, the specialized padding was a marketing ploy to make the crystal look better when inside the case. What needed sapphire-based protection were the connection sockets and sensitive equipment that made data into light before writing it onto crystal.

"He crawled all over the ship, even taking measurements in the array compartment to check for interference," added Matt. "I've never seen customs do that."

"Might be taking his job too seriously, but my money's on graft and greed every time. I think he was looking for something. He's on the take, you know," Nestor said.

"What?"

"Don't look so shocked. Many inspectors supplement their government income."

"Yeah—but shouldn't *I* be the one offering bribes? He never gave me a signal, not once." Matt was dismayed. "What's he paid for, and who's paying?"

"I'm not sure. When he came on-station, I checked up on him. The payments are small, so I'm guessing they're for information. When I discovered he'd been subverted so *quickly*, I widened my research to all of customs. They all get these small payments—from someone, for some sort of information."

Matt was relieved; it didn't sound as though *Aether's Touch* had been specifically targeted. This wasn't something he could ignore, but given the G-145 data, he had other priorities right now.

"Let's address that later. The clock's ticking." Matt winced at inadvertently parroting Mr. Custom's words. He thrust the open crystal case at Nestor. "Here's the source from the ship."

Nestor staggered as he carried the crystal over to

his "wall o' data." Nestor had decorated his small flat in a monochromatic style befitting any crèche-get, particularly a bachelor. Both the furniture and floors were plush and the same deep blue as his hair. The unwary visitor had to fumble for seating because the furniture showed only where edges contrasted against wall displays and shiny support ribs. The walls were currently awash with moving screens, but Nestor often changed the flat to an opulent all-encompassing blue.

The entertainment area allowed four people to be seated, but only if they wanted to be intimately acquainted. The "wall o' data" was programmed to look like glass and mirrored shelves of crystal art, but when long thin hatches slid aside, rows of protected sockets for temporary memory and crystal were exposed. If Nestor could afford to fill every socket with crystal, he'd almost have the equivalent of a vault.

Nestor rerouted data connections before installing the heavy crystal from the ship. He was one of those paranoid types who owned, rather than leased, his processors; he could physically segment his systems away from ComNet and still be functional.

"Let's see what we have." After puttering about, Nestor sat down beside Matt and turned off input over his right eye. On his wall, he displayed the indexes on Matt's data. The room was lit by displays on every flat surface, but Nestor outshone his screens with a shirt that had a rolling marquee of "hot young professional seeks limber arts type," followed by several sexually explicit scenes. The shirt threw flashes of light about, reflecting off the chrome and glass surfaces.

"Can you turn that shirt off?" asked Matt. "You're going to make me puke."

"Sure. You're not my type anyway." Nestor felt

around the front of his thin chest and the shirt became blessedly quiescent fabric.

They started defining the claims. The exaLOBs, the enormous amounts of large objects they had to release to public domain, weren't indexed, making it impossible for a casual browser to assimilate. This data would give researchers years of entertainment. Nestor, however, had the advantage of organization: precious indexes prepared by Matt. Nestor dove immediately toward the important indexes and whistled in appreciation.

"I thought this only happened in v-plays. You found evidence of *civilization* on this moon? Ruins of structures? I'll be damned by any-and-all-blessed-gods. Let's see if you've got proof of discovery." Nestor scanned for telebot data.

"The ruins weren't exposed on the surface, except at a tiny protrusion," Matt said.

"Physical exposure provisions are long gone," Nestor said brusquely. "After all, we're talking about space exploration and telepresence. Don't get me wrong, exposure would make the placer claim easier to define—what is this, a column outline? It sure doesn't look like architecture I've seen on Knossos."

Matt grinned. Nestor was going through the same sequence of assumptions that he and Ari had made. First assumption: *These ruins are Minoan.* Second assumption: *This is prespaceflight civilization.* Matt waited.

"I hope you didn't get excited about this," Nestor said. "Nobody gets rich off archaeological research, even when there's lease potential with the entertainment industry. And statute 1622.3 prevents mining of natural resources in areas of cultural importance."

"Wait." Matt cut Nestor's analysis short. He leaned forward and tapped out a sequence on the projected symbols on Nestor's console.

"Analysis of this protrusion indicated a composite made from sophisticated ceramics and directional polymers, much like the composite we use against cosmic radiation on the skins of our ships."

"Still, found technology is usually old technology," Nestor said. "They'll probably turn out to be old Minoan ruins."

"But it doesn't appear that any celestial body in G-145 supported Gaian-based life. Moreover, would the Minoans have abandoned an *inactive time buoy*?" Matt dropped the biggest bombshell of all.

Nestor took off his lenses and set them down. Tiny squiggles of light still ran down the left lens. He rubbed his eyes before saying, "I thought the only way to turn off a time buoy was to destroy it with a TD weapon."

"That's what the Minoans would have us believe. Of course, Ari and I are only making assumptions about this artifact—but everything points to a space-based civilization."

Matt told Nestor the entire story of the bot and the artifact.

"After I got into the bay's air lock, Ari chewed me out. Then she lectured me on the dangers of bringing the ship close to an uncontrolled artificial gravity source. I let her go on"—Matt shrugged—"because she saved my ass out there. *And* I got all the sensor data taken by the bot on approach to the artifact."

"Now I know why you submitted that problem report to DiastimBot Instrumentation. They started investigating, and they claim they haven't found a failure mode that produces the behavior you described."

"Keep on them," Matt said grimly. "If they can't come up with an explanation, I might take my business elsewhere. Maybe you can hint that my disposition could be sweetened with a partial refund or credit."

"They've asked whether you had it serviced by an unapproved facility or replaced any parts, perhaps with military surplus." Nestor's glance slid sideways questioningly.

Matt snorted. "Don't be ridiculous."

"That's what I told them." Nestor leaned back, looked thoughtful, and brought his fingertips together in a tent shape. "In a way, this may be good for us. The best and strongest way of proving *pedis possessio* is to leave markers, although that's not required these days."

"That bot's a hellishly expensive marker."

"Yes, but this is an unusual claim. We could learn a lot from this artifact and I bet we see all sorts of legal hijinks as everyone tries to get a piece of the action. Most of all, I'm worried about the Minoans." Nestor didn't have to add any more. The Minoans had a stranglehold over the creation of time buoys; would they permit mankind the means to end their economic control?

"It's too late. CAW had their blessing when the *Pilgrimage III* launched; there's no turning back now." Matt thought about the Minoan waiting for them when they docked. He wondered whether it was the result of random curiosity, or whether other G-145 prospectors had met the same observation.

"Without the Minoans, we'd still be shooting off satellites and hoping to colonize the Helios moon, for Gaia's sake—that's *if* we'd survived the Yellowstone extinction event."

"And we've repaid them with a century of lucrative trade. Besides, they're fanatical about following governmental controls. They won't be disrupting our exploration legal processes." Matt tried to convince himself, more than Nestor.

"Well, we've got future IP to protect. I've tuned and tested the girls; I'll let them loose on your first drafts." Nestor always worked the intellectual property issues within the claims first, considering IP to have more potential for making money. He put his lenses back on and made a show of cracking his knuckles.

Fortunately, they weren't treading on new legal ground. The mechanisms for laying down optical data in layers of crystal had come from the research and development on strange crystalline structures found on asteroids in the Konstantinople system by a relatively unknown prospector. What that prospector lacked in renown, he made up for in *wealth*.

Matt indulged in thoughts of financial independence, feeling a thrill of glee in his chest. Even at the small percentages given a second-wave prospector, this could be his mother lode. He could pay off the loans that loomed over decades and decades of his future; he might eventually own *Aether's Touch* outright. Ari and Nestor could end up with retirement nest eggs, getting their percentages from the complicated but time-honored system that CAW used to generate exploration and expansion.

Nestor displayed a representation of Matt's data, which looked like a round green blob with layers of wire shells. The wire shells represented Matt's initial claims and lease structure. This simple visual representation let them follow the progress of Nestor's agents, which were sophisticated but not as competent as full AI, of course.

"Go at it, girls," Nestor said.

A swarm of orange descended on the blob, probing and exploring the shells. Every once in a while, a small orange speck would separate and whiz by the screen, resolving into an avatar that looked like a female sprite with outlandishly large breasts. Nestor claimed he programmed his analysis agents for business purposes, but he did take liberties with their avatars.

A shaft of orange penetrated deep and swiftly into the data, causing both men to exclaim in surprise.

"Good work, Ari. Send results to a new viewport," Nestor said. A sprite flew close to the imaginary screen and winked.

"It's good to give them individual names, so you can make use of reward and competition patterns," Nestor said in an aside to Matt. "It supports their learning behaviors."

"Of course." Matt kept his voice as bland as Nestor's.

The sprite had a remarkable resemblance to Ari, although the real Ari certainly did not sport breasts of that size. Nestor couldn't take the hint that he wasn't Ari's type. What was her type? *Probably some stiff military dick like Owen Edones*, Matt thought sourly, although he was sure Ari had no amorous feelings for the man. Instead, he suspected she *owed* Edones something, and Edones twisted Ari's sense of obligation and duty for his own purposes.

The way Ari had left, without a message, really stung. This time Matt had *asked* her not to go. Didn't that mean anything to her?

"Here's the problem," said Nestor, unaware that Matt had taken a hiatus. "You mapped out the extent of the culturally significant ruins, but it may not be enough. We should make allowances for possible archaeological finds surfacing during mining or excavation outside that extent. Perhaps we should do the same for natural resource discovery. . . ."

While Nestor tested potential clauses, Matt shook off thoughts of Ari. He needed to concentrate on the future—*his* future.

"I want to divide up the placer claims for the

moon and the artifact. Make them smaller in scope and functionally interdependent," said Matt.

"That'll make your leases a bitch to administer."

"Smaller companies might be able to bid on the leases." Matt had a feeling this was the right thing to do, even if it necessitated more work for Nestor.

"On the other hand, you raise the overhead costs and the contractors have to adjust their bids, plus they'll have to share information. I strongly recommend you leave these as large, singular claims. It'll be a nightmare, mark my words."

Matt did mark his warning, but he also insisted that Nestor do the extra work. Aether Exploration, aka Matt, might suffer exponential administrative overload, but it gave him ways to leverage bidders against each other.

"It's almost time." The agents were fluttering anxiously about the time display and Nestor tapped them off. "We'll submit them and see how we fare."

Matt nodded and swallowed hard. His next few weeks would be spent reading bids. As long as his claims stood up legally and he "pursued discovery" within the next six months, he had "working interest" in the claim. He controlled who got leases to work the claims, and while some net-think mouths screamed nepotism, CAW exploratory law ensured that it was in Matt's best interest to lease his claims to the most efficient and effective companies. The government still got its percentage and, in a way, Matt ended up doing much of its job and being a front for the CAW Space Exploration, Exploitation, and Economics Control Board, or SEEECB.

When Nestor connected back to ComNet, Matt gasped as he saw the net-think activity that had already occurred regarding the return of *Aether's Touch*.

He watched Nestor submit the claims under Aether Exploration, Ltd.

"Don't worry." Nestor slapped Matt's back. "This'll be a real circus, so let me monitor our assets and IP."

Matt rubbed his temples. The environmental changes between the ship and the habitat had given him a pounding headache, and arguing with Edones and the inspector hadn't helped.

"There's something else I'd like you to do," Matt said.

"Standard fees apply."

Matt hesitated at this comment. Nestor might live in perpetual adolescence, but he was good at what he did and could demand high rates for his research. This job would be costly, but Matt needed it done. "I'd like you to personally do background checks on the inspectors for customs. Quietly and without subcontracting."

"You could hire my kid brother for that." Nestor fiddled with the settings on his view lenses.

"You don't have a kid brother."

At least not by grav-hugger standards. CAW classified both of them as generational orphans because they opted off their ships. Matt's biological father, with whom he had a passing familiarity, had opted off the same time as Matt but had settled only Gaia knew where. Nestor and Matt had met on Konstanti-nople Prime at the Generational Mission Orphanage of St. Darius, the wandering Ottoman saint that started the sect followed on generational ships. Nestor's opt-off point came at a younger age than Matt's did, their lives ruled by the almighty ship schedule so they couldn't control opt-off times. Contrary to Nestor's condescending attitude, *he* was the younger one, discounting time dilation and using absolute UT.

"If it's so easy, then you could work for half your standard rate," Matt added. "There's more. I'm looking for any unusual interest in G-145 prospectors, by either customs or *Minoans*."

"Still have to bill you standard fees." Nestor grinned. "It'll require, let's say, some *bending* of privacy laws. I'll also have to break Consortium bank security to figure out where the bribes are coming from."

"Okay, standard fees apply. I'll also pay for AI-accelerated time."

"Done, and have I got the AI for you! If you're willing to pay eighty percent acceleration, that is. I can't let it work for less."

Matt looked at Nestor doubtfully. "Is it legal?"

"I just told you we'll be breaking laws to track down the payments, and you're getting snarled up about the tools I use?"

"Fine. Use what you have to, just don't leave a trail to the company." Matt shrugged.

"Can I take this research wherever it might go?" Nestor raised his lenses but he wouldn't look at Matt directly, focusing on the wall behind him.

"Huh?"

"Suppose this requires digging into *somebody's* background?"

"You know everything about me, and—oh." Matt stopped. Nestor was referring to Ari. "You saw the background check on her. I did that before I hired her."

"Sure. Born thirty-five years ago on Nuovo Adriatico, entered military academy at twenty, parents are dead, et cetera, et cetera." Nestor waved his arms in vague motions. "All Gaia and good feelings, right? Conveniently there seemed to be no one who knew her way back when on Nuovo Adriatico."

"So? All the records were cross-checked and her references were solid. And she's been a damn fine pilot." Matt's stomach tensed with uneasiness. In a world where so many might be out of step, where any generational orphan might not be up to date on the latest music, v-plays, or recreational drinks and drugs, Ari always fit in well enough. Her records were correct in claiming she wasn't generational. She was comfortable in wide-open planetary environments where Matt crumpled and quailed. That behavior was so instinctual that one couldn't act around it.

"I'm saying there might be some dirt there and you'd better be prepared. What's an open, honest girl like her doing for someone like Edones? Ever think about that?"

Of course, he had. Matt didn't answer. Ari had experience beyond her known history, and every once in a while, she acted as if Colonel Owen Edones, who was superficially older and higher ranking, was her subordinate.

"I'm thinking she might be a *shadow*," Nestor said.

Matt burst out laughing. "You're running too many v-plays, you know that?"

Shadows were net-think myths: CAW agents with falsified records laid down in immutable memory by the government, usually so they could operate as assassins or do some other skullduggery. This made for good v-play, but changing immutable memory was impossible and rational citizens questioned the concept.

"Okay, okay." Nestor started chuckling too. "I just want to know whether I can follow this wherever it leads."

"Do what you need to do."

Matt had to have faith in his original background check of Ari. She rarely talked about herself or her history, but that wasn't necessarily suspicious. He tried to shove away memories of her nightmares and stifle all his doubts, particularly when he thought about Edones. For some reason, the assignments Edones gave Ari always led to binges. Her heavy drinking and recreational drugging, although legal, had been a point of contention between them. Matt had offered to pay for addiction reprogramming, but fear had flitted quickly over her face and she'd whispered, "Not allowed." He never brought it up again. After all, Ari had proven herself plenty of times aboard the *Aether's Touch*. She was *crew*.

He gathered up the case and packing materials for the crystal. For the next month, Aether Exploration had to allow bidders access to the exaLOBs of information they'd gathered during the prospecting season. Once companies applied with the SEEECB, they received access to the crystal sitting in Nestor's "wall o' data."

Matt picked up the empty case. Nestor was opening small transparent screens over his right eye. The images weren't sharp from Matt's viewpoint, but the tiny squares looked like porn v-plays. Granted, Nestor hadn't yet grabbed the v-play face shield, gloves, or other, ahem, attachments for the virtual experience.

"That's *so* juvenile—couldn't you at least wait for me to leave?" Matt headed for the exit.

Nestor looked at him, his uncovered left eye bright, blue, and unrepentant. "I checked with Carmen just before you arrived."

"Oh." Matt paused. "How's she doing?"

"Just as *experimental* as always. Said she'd like to see you." Nester snickered. "Well, what are you waiting for? It's been more than six months, hasn't it? So get going!"

Matt complied.

N-space pilots are hard to come by, Matt had said, and Nestor didn't know the half of it. Five years ago,

Matt thought he'd sunk to his lowest, both emotionally and financially.

A beer bottle sailed over his head, bounced off the bulkhead, but still managed to spray him. The fight broke out, directly in front of him. Grabbing both his newly served and nearly finished beers, he slid quickly down his chair to take cover under his table. Chairs and tables were bolted to the deck because this was just *that sort of place*.

Matt didn't usually patronize this bar, which catered to rough dockworkers and space crew and had a reputation for economical alcohol and drugs. But prior-military pilots on the down-and-out supposedly hung about this place, looking to find employment.

The *Aether's Touch* had been upgraded and now qualified as a second-wave prospector vessel, but Matt's debt load had grown to eighty years. He'd managed to get the Journey ship line to finance much of the necessary upgrades, considering he'd been born to that line and the *Journey IV* would soon be opening a new solar system. He still needed, however, an N-space pilot and he couldn't pay competitive wages. As added incentive, he tried throwing in company ownership and prospecting percentages, but he'd had no nibbles and he was getting desperate.

Anybody could get licenses for airborne vehicles, and private citizens could finance the training for operating in real-time space, working in orbital operations. Matt needed someone who could work both real-space and N-space, which was the kicker. Being qualified to pilot N-space was not for the mathematically challenged, since it required a capacity altogether different from aerodynamics and momentum-based physics. N-space didn't have the natural, and by now instinctive, forces like gravity or momentum or lift.

It was also physically demanding, because the pilot had to remain awake during nous-transit, the technical name for moving through N-space. During this time, they fought off subliminal terrors using drugs. The training was beyond the financial capacities of the average citizen, unless one received it through military duty.

The bar fight started with two men going at each other. Locked rigidly together, the men stumbled against Matt's table. Matt heard a high unintelligible yell and saw a small body fly through the air. He leaned forward and peered upward to get a better look. All three brawlers wore crew coveralls.

"Olaf, you'll be sorry, you—" The voice was that of a young woman, but the stream of profanity that followed could have burned the ears of any grizzled space veteran.

The woman, clinging to Olaf's back, moved her forearm up around his throat and executed a sharp movement that seemed expert and *military*, in Matt's opinion. Olaf let go and fell back insensate, pinning the woman partially under his body. The man he'd been going after staggered away, retching and hacking.

Matt crawled forward and pushed Olaf off the woman, who scrambled upright. She looked around and then ducked under the table with Matt, since the brawl started spreading through the bar like fungus across a growth pond. Matt saw she was small but older than an adolescent. How much older, he couldn't tell.

"Thanks," she said, extending her hand.

"It was nothing." Matt shook it, noticing uncommon strength in the slim fingers.

She had short dark hair that formed in loose curls wild about her face. Her brown eyes were bright but deep, set in a face that had the angular, hollow lines of an N-space pilot.

"You don't usually come here," she said matter-of-factly.

"No. I need to find a pilot for a second-wave prospector. It's a permanent job with ownership percentage, depending upon performance. Know anyone who's interested?"

The woman looked pointedly at the two beers he had beside him, so he hurriedly picked up the untouched beer and offered it to her. She took a long swig from it.

"Aren't you lucky?" She smiled and her face lit up, reminding Matt of angels from the paintings in the orphanage that depicted the trials of St. Darius.

She nodded at Olaf. The big man had started snoring, sprawled across the bar floor in front of them.

"That's my boss. I'm looking for new employment."

CHAPTER 5

Mankind learned to destroy life long before we understood its creation. Gaia sparks life on her planets, while
we struggle at terraforming. We researched the Minoan
time buoys and we couldn't understand the theory behind their constructive use, but our baser instincts uncovered the temporal distortion wave: a destructive
force that disrupts matter at quantum levels. When we
learned to rip apart the fabric of the universe, mankind's
true nature as the ultimate destroyer was revealed.

— *Rant: The Ultimate Destroyer and Why We Deserve
Gaia's Rage*, Lee Wan Padoulos, 2098.345.02.15 UT,
indexed by *Heraclitus 21* under Conflict Imperative

The air was warm and she smelled human sweat.
After twelve hours in the cramped Naga, she
should be immune to these scents. The edge of her
console dug into her side as she twisted in her seat.
An acrid taste spread across her tongue and her
stomach clenched, tightening into a ball. Her scalp
prickled as she glanced from Cipher's face to Brandon's face. They were sweating also, their faces shining in the sickly green instrument lights of the EM-
dampened Naga control center.

"Did you hear what I said? That probe is carrying
a TD warhead." Cipher's voice cracked. "The mission
brief was wrong. It's not an intelligence payload."

"You authenticated the wrapper. We authenticated

the orders. We executed as ordered." The muscle on Brandon's right cheek twitched.

"I broke the encryption on the payload packet. Time of detonation is—*soon*." Cipher's eyes were large, her short orange hair plastered to her head with sweat.

"We weren't authorized payload information," Brandon said.

It's too hot. Ari adjusted the environmental controls. Behind her, the discussion escalated in intensity, heating the small control center further.

"Ari has to get us out. Now!" Cipher was panicking.

"No. Orders are to verify final probe position." Brandon, as crew commander, tried to stick to their orders.

"No one knows what a TD wave—"

"Cipher, if that's an intel payload—"

"Ari, drop us out of normal space. It's starting."

She heard Cipher retch, then Brandon, both using their training to try to control their fluids. She felt bile rising in her own throat. The ship bucked and *stretched*. Console lights faded and recovered. Violent orange and red replaced sickly green. Multiple alarms went off.

"Ari—" Brandon gurgled.

Life, mission, security, operations. L-M-S-O. The hierarchy for handling emergencies. Save the lives of the crew, handle mission next, security issues, then simple operational problems. If the crew didn't live, the mission didn't get done.

Her console seemed farther away than it used to be. The center smelled of vomit. The twitching heartbeat signal from the time buoy was paralyzed. It fed the Penrose Fold referential engine and it *couldn't* stop, could it? That was physically impossible. She hit the controls feeding her previous calculations to the referential engine and prayed that they had an accurate lock from the time buoy. If not, they were lost forever.

They dropped out of real-space. Without drugs, without preparation, without references, she tried to pilot N-space, where normal senses could betray her and kill her—

Ariane woke with a gasp. Taking deep breaths, she stopped fighting her restraint webbing. Sweat covered her body. The air from the cruiser's vents felt cold and the skin on her arms and legs started stippling.

I'm Ariane Kedros. I'm a commercial pilot, with a reserve commission of major. The exercise of reinforcing her identity helped calm her. Lying in the dark of her cabin, she stopped trembling.

"Command: lights, slow." Ariane spoke carefully; the systems on the *Bright Crescent* weren't familiar with her voice.

As the cabin slowly brightened, she unfastened the safety webbing and let it wiggle to the sides of her bunk. She didn't remember getting into bed after finding her quarters. She sat up, relieved that the cruiser was maintaining light gravity. Her dream had been vivid, but at least it wasn't a waking terror that was indiscernible from real life.

She opened her locker and pawed through the mess she must have thrown together in the dark. When she found the d-tranny, she sighed. Delta tranquilizer was the space traveler's best friend. Everyone could take it because it didn't affect cognitive functions or reactions. It prevented the gradual and deleterious effects of N-space and, of course, wasn't supposed to be addictive.

Ariane pressed an ampoule against her implant and sighed after it drained and started dispersing the d-tranny. They said you couldn't tell when d-tranny entered your bloodstream, but "they" were wrong. *She* could feel it without displaying her doses from the implant.

She checked the shift schedule and tried to adjust her dosage of bright so she could adapt her sleeping patterns. Then she carefully laid out the rest of the ampoules, making sure she had enough d-tranny to get her through to her next requisition. During her active duty assignments, she rationed everything carefully. She snorted. *Sure, d-tranny isn't addictive.*

She put her ampoules into a folding packet she could keep on her person, inside her uniform. She remembered when Matt had suggested addiction reprogramming and shook her head. Exposing her secrets would be dangerous. Too many people wanted to rid themselves of the moral quandary that she represented. Would Matt be one of those? She also suspected the shadowy people in the Directorate that gave Colonel Edones his orders weren't above getting rid of her, should she become an embarrassment.

She was slipping back into her new persona, replacing "Owen" with "Colonel Edones" in her thoughts. She paused. She needed to send a message to Matt.

"I'm sorry, Matt, but this is something that I have to do. *Aether's Touch* will have a couple months' downtime and besides, this is an important mission. . . . "

Her voice trailed off. They were the same trite words, but for once, they were true. She wiped her message and started over, trying to be as earnest and forthright as she could, yet stay classified. She tried four times before she thought the message acceptable.

She sent it off, wishing she could speak to him directly. Matt was a bright boy, though. He'd trace the packet backward, calculate when and where it'd exited from MilNet, and determine she was in-system when she sent the message. However, in a system crowded with habitats, he wouldn't know that Karthage Point was her destination.

She went to the cruiser's galley and ordered a large meal. With her enhanced metabolism, she needed a hefty amount of calories to make up for the N-space drop. But her body craved more than food. She shouldn't have had that drink with Colonel Edones; her body was still pining for more alcohol, hoping for oblivion. She wolfed down her meal as she ignored the cravings and the sensation that her skin wanted to crawl off her body.

Back in her cabin, Ariane read the background information for the mission, making sure that all data stayed in the cruiser's storage vault. When finished, she replaced the sweaty sheets and got back into her bunk. As pilot of *Aether's Touch*, she was the one who lost both sleep and weight when they dropped out of normal space. Now she could catch up.

The klaxon and flashing take-hold alarms didn't wake her when the cruiser made its first deceleration adjustment for Karthage Point. Neither did the message alarm. She woke, groggy, to a crewman shaking her shoulder. He had to enter her cabin to wake her.

"The mission commander ordered you to the bridge," the crewman said. "Check your bright dosage, ma'am."

She thanked the young enlisted man and after he left, she opened her locker. As expected, a clean uniform awaited her, but she wrinkled her nose in distaste. When she was active duty, she'd never liked the intelligence arm of AFCAW. She never had to don the black and blue Directorate of Intelligence uniform for her previous missions under Owen's command. Now she was officially a golem. *So live with it, Major.*

"Take hold, take hold. This is second warning. Prepare for low-g maneuver." The male voice sounding through the cruiser indicated they were close to Karthage Point and preparing for an adjustment.

Ariane dressed quickly, grabbed her issued slate, and headed toward the bridge. The vector warning lights were flashing, fading from yellow into orange. The cruiser's crew were experienced because the adjustments had been precise and few.

"Major Kedros reporting to the bridge." She saluted the mission command chair, far removed from equipment consoles and occupied by Colonel Edones.

"Glad you could join us, Major." Edones's tone was biting. "Please take the comm monitor station."

"Yes, sir." Ariane cast a quick glance about as she went to the most useless position on the bridge, a station rarely manned on operational vessels. She and Edones were the only black and blue on the bridge; everyone else wore the green uniform of normal operations.

Grudgingly, she admitted that Edones knew what he was doing. Making her an intelligence officer isolated her from the operational crew members. No one glanced her way. No one was interested in a black and blue relegated to monitoring comm for some obscure purpose.

She slid her slate into the console as she listened to the bridge crew going through their checklists for approach to Karthage Point. She wished her military duties were as straightforward. At one time, she believed they were written in black and white with crisp edges. No longer.

"Take hold, take hold, take hold. This is third and last warning. Prepare for low-g maneuver." The pilot's intonation was singsong, almost bored. Everything was routine. Crew members on the cruiser had already stowed loose equipment and strapped themselves into their positions.

Ariane slapped her restraints on, feeling them

squirm and slide to keep her snugly in her seat. She frowned as her slate indicated an arriving personal message. Matt couldn't have found her so quickly, could he?

She had nothing better to do while the cruiser made its last adjustment. She opened the message.

It was from Edones: "Remember, Ari, that it's better to be the hunter than the hunted. Good luck."

Yes, I'll need it—and thanks for hanging me out as bait. Why had she agreed to take this mission? She remembered Cipher's anguished face from her dream. *That's why I'm here.* Cipher's military service had gone unmarked; the other victims were the same, murdered for doing their duty. None of them got a hero's funeral. She jabbed viciously at the slate, directing the note to be shredded.

The briefings and background packages regarding the assassinations were secured in the classified vault of the cruiser. She went through her slate, scrubbing everything that she'd be taking with her. She couldn't afford to be sloppy, not on this mission. Everything on the slate looked normal and supported her persona.

She never once looked toward Colonel Edones during approach and docking. Playing the good intelligence officer, she monitored comm patterns that were already being analyzed by AIs. Every once in a while, she reviewed an AI's sample, finding the expected operational chatter.

"Karthage boarding will occur at oh six thirty," announced Colonel Edones. He left the bridge without a backward glance.

Ariane checked her shift schedule. She'd board with Colonel Edones and afterward, she'd transfer to Karthage Point. Her orders were temporary; she was assigned to Karthage for thirty days. The deadline for completing all baseline inspections and verifying initial inventories was six months out. There was a chance she might not even see a Terran inspection team at Karthage, but right now she didn't have even half a plan regarding the hidden purpose behind her orders. She logged off her station and left the bridge.

No one likes devoting their life and career to a mission, only to have it pulled out from under them. The Mobile TD Weapon Treaty was doing just that to the Naga personnel on Karthage Point, which accounted for the sour expressions of Lieutenant Colonel Jacinthe Voyage and her two aides.

"Lieutenant Colonel Voyage is commander of the Thirty-second Strike Squadron, under the First Strategic Systems Wing." Colonel Erik Icelos, the commander of Karthage Point, was introducing personnel.

While Jacinthe Voyage seemed tense and sullen, Colonel Icelos was relaxed and friendly. As facility commander, he wasn't threatened by the loss of the Naga mission. Karthage Point was valuable to AFCAW and would always be operational. He wasn't worried about being transferred to another career field, being retrained, or worse: separated and abandoned. He also didn't show any underlying anxiety, if he knew he was targeted for assassination. Perhaps Edones hadn't yet told him about the murders. Icelos greeted Colonel Edones, and Ariane watched for familiarity between them, but saw none. Perhaps they'd never met each other in person.

Colonel Edones motioned to Ariane. "This is Major Kedros, who will be your inspection team liaison officer. She'll be your adviser for treaty compliance."

Ariane stepped forward and Icelos started slightly. He was a big man with broad shoulders. His blond hair was turning white and cut to tight fuzz about his head. Ariane didn't recognize him as the young command post controller from the Fourteenth Strategic Systems Wing, but he'd remembered her. In contrast to Ariane, he'd aged normally. He must have rejected the dangerous rejuv treatments offered by AFCAW. *Smart man.*

"Just a moment—got a priority message," said Edones, touching his implanted ear bug. He pulled out a slate and frowned at whatever was loading. "We've got problems, Colonel. Let's speak in your office."

The two colonels hurried away, leaving Ariane with the squadron commander and her aides. Jacinthe looked Ariane up and down, with a lift to her lip like a generational orphan facing a plate of dirt-grown vegetables.

"Got any Naga experience, Major?" asked Jacinthe.

"I became licensed to pilot Naga vehicles on a tour in maintenance, ma'am, in the Pelagos system. I also served on several STRAT-EVALS." Ariane's record could easily be checked, if Jacinthe was interested. For a moment, Ariane's jaw tightened as she thought of the lackluster career that Colonel Edones had designed for her.

"STRAT-EVAL scenarios aren't the same as putting in the years at ops, Major."

"Yes, ma'am." Ariane agreed, but the irony of the conversation almost made her laugh. Instead, she coughed. She'd read the records for Lieutenant Colonel Jacinthe Voyage, who'd left her generational ship after the destruction of Ura-Guinn. Jacinthe, who'd only seen peacetime operations, presumed to lecture Ariane on what it meant to be *operational*?

"Do you need a drink for that cough, Major?" Jacinthe's frigid gray eyes glittered.

Not the kind you're offering. Ariane shook her head.

"Fine. Then I'll show you the inspectable areas of the station."

Jacinthe Voyage had long legs and set a pace that made Ariane feel as if she was scurrying to keep up. She tried to lengthen her strides and remain dignified.

She glanced around at Karthage Point and decided it was a tight operation. The corridors, uncommonly clean and uncluttered, couldn't be compared to Athens Point because AFCAW didn't allow remotes on military habitats. MilNet nodes had to suffice and the only displays on the walls were for official use only. The station was trying to give her a newcomer orientation at the same time Jacinthe threw questions at her, often over a shoulder as they took a turn.

"You've worked for Colonel Icelos before," Jacinthe said.

"No, ma'am."

"Oh, I thought he recognized you."

Ariane made a mental note about Jacinthe's observational skills.

"You took the entry test for crew while stationed at Pelagos."

Once again, Ariane's jaw tightened. Apparently, Jacinthe *had* read her record.

"Yes."

"Didn't make the cut, huh?"

"No, ma'am."

Ariane was relieved when they reached the training bay. The treaty defined training facilities as inspectable areas because there were operational modules from the Naga weapons systems installed in the bay and there was room for possible warhead storage. Now Ariane could throw some barbs of her own.

"Colonel, since your training bay is so far from station entry, you'll have to blank all rosters, schedules, and daily orders from the walls between the two areas. You'll also have to suspend all crew training during the course of any inspection."

"That'll throw off our certification schedules. How much notification do we get?" Apparently, Jacinthe had paid less attention to the treaty protocols than

Ariane's records. Perhaps she was testing Ariane's knowledge?

"Each side is required to give two UT days' notification of inspection, and the notification must identify a specific facility. As the inspection team approaches, they must announce their intent to connect twenty UT hours away, then twenty minutes away. The facility to be inspected must allow inspectors to board within one hour of connection. By then, you must clear everything of intelligence value or anything that identifies personnel."

"I assume you can provide us with checklists, Major. We'll adjust them for Karthage and have command post drive the procedures." Jacinthe sighed. Her gaze went to the schedule board for the modules, showing which crews were inside for training or evaluation. She headed for an observation cab, motioning Ariane to follow.

Ariane glanced at the board also. The senior crew was under evaluation in the module they were entering. Since the senior crew designed all Karthage crew evaluations and training, a visiting senior crew from another squadron had to perform the evaluation. Three heads turned when Jacinthe and Ariane entered the cab, then focused back on their work. The cab, attached to the Naga module, had equipment that recorded everything that went on inside the module. On video, as well as through windows, Ariane saw the familiar interior of the Naga control center, although this was the Naga-26. The Naga-26 was the newest version of the weapons system and had been fielded after the war.

The evaluators were advancing the scenario clock to the authentication sequence. Ariane looked at the crew undergoing evaluation. This was the senior crew for the squadron, and the commander was only five years behind Ariane in rank and *apparent* age, but to her worn senses, they seemed much too young.

"Captain Dumas and Captain Atropes have spotless evals on their records, but Lieutenant Hawking has only been with them for two months." Jacinthe nodded at the third and youngest crew member, sitting at comm.

Inside the training module the comm panel warbled, signaling special execution orders. Ariane watched the crew smoothly begin their authentication using the classic triad. This crew had tempo; they were well trained and familiar with each other's reactions.

"Commander's order authenticated—approval given."

"Comm's order authenticated—approval given." The young lieutenant was quick, double-checking his encryption codes efficiently. Ariane was suddenly reminded of Cipher.

Then came the classic pause in the sequence as the crew waited patiently for pilot authentication to complete. The pilot had to ensure that the orders loaded into the navigation panel correctly, and more importantly, the pilot performed decryption and authentication on the target position. All three crew members had to agree that they'd received valid and authentic orders to execute a TD weapon.

Ariane's eyes automatically slid to the panel on the pilot's right, where the N-space "coordinates" should display as blobs and rotate through several dimensions. However, this was the Naga-26 and the NC display had been moved higher and to the *left* side of the pilot display. She watched the blobs brighten and deform as the pilot initiated transformations.

"Pilot's order authenticated and approval given," the pilot said after making the rotations and verifying the results.

The crew picked up their original rhythm.

"Enter comm prearm sequence."

"Entered."

"Enter pilot prearm sequence."

"Entered."

"Commander prearm sequence entered. Download targeting information to warhead."

"Target set downloaded."

"Enter—"

Jacinthe abruptly muted the speaker, causing the evaluators in the cab to key their ear bugs a bit higher.

"The NC display hasn't been on the right side of the pilot's station since the Naga-twenty-four," Jacinthe said.

Ariane knew her head hadn't moved; only her eyes had betrayed her and only with a flicker. Regardless, she'd been carried away with the checklist and she was going to have to wipe away her memories; otherwise they'd betray her again. She turned to face Jacinthe, forcing herself to stare unflinching into the cold gray eyes. She hated having to look up at the woman; Jacinthe was tall and willowy as a result of her generational origins.

"I'm pilot qualified on the older systems," Ariane said easily. True, maintenance officers had to shuttle around the Naga vehicles, even through N-space.

"Really?" Jacinthe drawled the word, dosing it with suspicion. "And as a *bus driver*, you learned ops execution checklists?"

At Jacinthe's insult, several heads turned to watch their conversation instead of the crew. Ariane changed the topic quickly.

"Colonel, the Terran inspectors will want to see inside these modules." Ariane couldn't afford being rankled by Jacinthe's ops snobbery, so she let it go.

"I have to let them inside?" asked Jacinthe.

"Yes, ma'am. Any area that's big enough to hold a TD warhead can be subject to inspection, as long as it's within the inspectable area. We expect them to push that to the limit for the chance of catching classified tidbits; getting intel for free, essentially."

Jacinthe's lips thinned as she pressed them together. She glanced at the crew inside the module one last time before striding out of the observation cab. Ariane followed. Outside, Jacinthe's aides were standing quietly aside, waiting.

"These modules are made from operational systems. Even the static displays are classified." Jacinthe stopped and turned, almost leaning over her.

"That's why I'm here: to assist you in controlling sensitive information." Ariane didn't step back.

"Sure, you're here to *help*." Jacinthe's lip curled and she lowered her voice so only Ariane could hear. "You're not what you seem, Major, and I don't like mysteries. I've still got a mission to meet and I'll keep crews operational until the last TD warhead is shipped out for destruction. Got that?"

"Yes, ma'am." Ariane kept her voice wooden. How had she gotten on this woman's bad side? The irony of being older and more experienced than Jacinthe made her want to grind her teeth again.

"Lieutenant Santorini will help you establish our treaty compliance procedures." Jacinthe's voice rose, loud enough for her two aides to look up from their conversation. She turned on her heel and stalked off, waving for an aide to scamper after her. The remaining lieutenant reluctantly walked toward Ariane.

Ariane's ear bug chimed. It was an urgent private message from Colonel Edones.

"The Terran overlords are already playing games with us." Edones's voice came through clearly, even through the chaotic encryption used in AFCAW facility nodes. "They moved faster than we expected, scheduling two inspections simultaneously. I have to get to Pelagos and prepare that squadron; they're not as far along as Karthage. You're on your own, Ari."

"Wait, Colonel—is Parmet traveling with any of the inspection teams?"

"He's leading the team coming here to Karthage. The itinerary and roster have arrived at command post. You'll do fine, Major." Edones cut the link from his side.

Ariane closed her eyes:

"Major Kedros?" Young Santorini wanted instructions.

A cold knot of fear formed somewhere between her stomach and her heart. She was going to face her worst enemy alone, hiding behind an identity that didn't even fool the Naga squadron commander. *Hung out as bait.*

Damn you, Owen.

CHAPTER 6

"Hear me and index my life" is the lament of the grain of sand on the beach. Citizens document all aspects of their lives, from plucking nose hairs in the morning to evening masturbation—in childish attempts for attention. Luckily, indexing requires meeting objective AI imperatives, yet tireless AIs can't keep up with the deluge of drivel that's written into crystal lattice. Democritus and Heraclitus have spawned more than forty models *each*, and I question the soaring costs we face each year for more vaults.

—*Minutes for Senatorial Subcommittee on Consortium Tax Structures*, Senator Stephanos IV, 2104.352.04.11 UT, indexed by *Democritus 7* under Metrics Imperative

Ariane watched Colonel Edones depart Karthage Point. He saluted Colonel Icelos briskly, acknowledging the facility commander's permission to depart the station, then walked into the air lock for his ship.

She was no longer angry; after all, Edones hadn't been looking over her shoulder on any of her plain-clothes operations. *Although Sergeant Joyce was on three of the missions . . . hmm.* Honestly, those missions really had required two operatives. Edones had faith in her and figured she could take care of herself. *You always come through when it's crunch time*, he'd said after one mission, after she protested that she was piss-poor at planning.

Ariane disagreed with his assessment that she was right for the intelligence field, but never voiced her opinion. Why was that? *Probably because he's the last remnant I have of my previous life, of the real Ari.*

When she first met him, *Lieutenant* Owen Edones had a generic face that was eminently suited for the intelligence field. His blue eyes were as bland as his expression, perhaps a result of the institutional lights and colors in this small room. Under other circumstances, Ari supposed, this was an interrogation room.

"There's risks associated with the rejuv procedures," said Edones. "Your genetic tests say you're an ideal candidate, but you're under no pressure to undergo any of the offered medical procedures or surgical alterations. You can take only the relocation and records-wipe, although your new identity will be more effective, more stable, with a change in appearance."

A chance for reinvention, a new life—and I'm having problems making a decision! Ari paced in front of the table, where the lieutenant had laid out the different slates, all waiting for her approval or refusal. She hadn't seen anyone since this had started, not even her squadron commander. It had been one black and blue after another, once their ship had managed to come out of N-space and dock at Thera Point. Brandon had lost control, enraged because the crew wasn't warned about the mission payload. Then the three of them were separated.

"What are Cipher and Brandon doing?" she asked.

"I can't tell you that, ma'am. That would be a violation of—"

"Yeah, yeah. Violation of personal privacy, classified material, need-to-know only. Did I cover the pertinent regulations?" She was rude to Edones not because she outranked him, but because she'd never liked intel types.

"Yes, ma'am, most of them. We're trying to perform identity changes and we're tampering with vault substitution and AI indexing. This would be highly illegal, under any other circumstances."

"Not to mention *impossible*." She stopped pacing and stared at Edones. "We're told that once recorded, everything stays in immutable crystal. Only AIs can alter indexes in rewritable memory, to allow true objectivity. Are you saying that AFCAW is destroying and replacing whole vaults for us? That AIs will be reindexing multiple vaults of new crystal?"

The expense made her giddy. Should she be grateful or frightened? *What will I owe AFCAW?*

"I won't go into the details." Edones placed his immaculately manicured hands on the table before him. They remained quietly folded together while he spoke. "Suffice to say, AFCAW will be going to great lengths to give you a different identity, with different records."

"To cover all the important asses?" She wrinkled her nose and frowned. "There's no way to obscure the loss of Ura-Guinn. Or the executive order to use the TD weapon."

"Those holding public office are prepared to take the consequences, since they've ended decades of warfare by bringing in the Minoans. You should be concerned with your own future."

She resumed her pacing, although she could barely hear her footsteps under the active muffling inside the room. She could only take four paces, then turn, take four paces . . . Now that she had a chance for early separation, she wasn't sure she wanted to leave AFCAW. Ever since her teens, she'd dreamed of the promises of space flight and getting her commission.

Her goal had always been to fly military spacecraft, as long as she could remember. Without the military, she'd be adrift.

"Can I stay active duty?" she asked.

"If you wish, but you won't be allowed to work Naga operations. There's also the Reserve, if you want to keep your commission. But we'll hash out the details of your new life later."

"How many of these new lives are you putting together?" She watched his lips tighten. *I don't have the need to know.* Quickly followed by the realization: *I'll never see Brandon again.* Her stomach knotted, though she hadn't eaten in hours. How long had she been here anyway?

"Won't there be some record, some connection, to our past? How will I find the others?" Her voice rose.

"Consider yourself lucky that your immediate family is gone and you're not having to jettison them. As for your fellow crew members, no one has expressed an interest in your future." Edones gestured at the slates that quietly waited for signatures. "Captain Argyris, you have decisions to make."

She picked up the nearest slate, the one offering rejuv.

"What does it matter, then?" she asked, a reckless edge in her voice.

"You should read the cautions," Edones said. "Our rejuv technology is still in its infancy. Your gene structure indicates a ninety-five percent chance of success, but there're possibilities of debilitating side effects."

Ari ran down the list of questions, answering in the negative until one made her pause: "Have you been diagnosed with any addictive personality disorders, or have you been treated for any chemical addictions?"

Only a couple of days before this mission, this mission that had changed everything, Cipher had confronted Ari and urged her to go in for an addiction diagnosis. *Just because I got carried away at a bar*. She hadn't lost control, but somehow Cipher had marked the amount of smooth and alcohol she'd taken that night. Ever since the episode with Brandon, Cipher seemed to think she had the authority to nag Ari about her behavior.

Well, Cipher, if you've got no interest in my future, then you've got no basis for criticism! Ari jabbed at the slate with her stylus, marking "no."

"Any problems?" asked Lieutenant Edones.

"Of course not," she answered brightly. She handed him the signed slate, reaching for another one.

"Hey!" Matt ducked as a remote went too far, trying to zoom over and pluck some of his hair. His privacy shield had been breached.

"Invoke emergency privacy shield, one-six-five-beta-psi-sigma-lambda-two," he quietly chanted for his implanted mike.

Nothing happened in the crowded bazaar. Kiosks blared, so he repeated the password. Remotes still buzzed over his head and crowded in on him like a thicket of insects, focusing their cam-eyes on him. Pedestrians, probably instrumented, edged into his personal space. Remotes ordering goods for their owners floated out of his way, but activated mikes and swiveled cam-eyes to follow his progress. He'd become a minor celebrity as net-think picked up a whiff of what he'd discovered in G-145. Now someone had cracked his emergency privacy shield code.

Matt resorted to using his *second backup emergency* shield; like any other Autonomist citizen, he kept several in reserve. A few remotes dropped to the deck, unable to get out of the shield radius in time.

He looked down at the chattering and whirring remotes, cut off from their owners and driving software, and invoked his disablement password. Thankfully, they went still. He wasn't sorry in the least; he had every right under CAW privacy laws to disable them.

To someone uninitiated to habitat life, this might have looked like magic. *No, all it takes is money, and I'm spending it like a drunken spaceman.* Matt paid a ComNet fee, via the use of an emergency privacy shield, to take away the meshed node network coverage that the remotes needed for navigation and guidance. Shields were merely ComNet algorithms that calculated an approximately two-meter sphere centered on his waist. The emergency shield had cut off all comm to those specific remotes, but hadn't disabled them. ComNet had charged him a much heftier fee for sending a disablement signal to every node inside the shield.

Unfortunately, shields were invoked by passwords that could be guessed or hacked because they didn't require voiceprint analysis. Net-think bemoaned the fact that users had to make up their own passwords and change them frequently, but not many citizens knew how to take technical advantage of this weakness. *Somebody knows, apparently.*

Bending down, he scooped up the disabled remotes. They were probably worthless for tracing their owners. Most standard modules in kits performed an autowipe if the remote experienced a privacy shutdown. He dumped them into the shopping bag attached to his belt.

Matt looked up. The remotes clustered at the edge of his newly established shield hid the upper bazaar levels from his sight. He had originally wanted to revel in his favorite noodle dish, made from one hundred percent hydroponically grown sources, in this case algae.

He wasn't hungry anymore, not after battling remotes all the way from the ship's berth. He'd only been going after comfort food that reminded him of growing up on the *Journey IV*. It also reminded him of Ari. He already missed dragging her out to eat at this shop, where he enjoyed watching her stoically choke down the noodles and make polite comments. Having her around seemed to fill the corners of his life.

Carmen, on the other hand, didn't fit into any part of his life, by her own pronouncement. *You have to play by* my *schedule*, she told him. Carmen worked in finance; in fact, she worked for the bank that held some relatively small loans on the crystal and referential engine in the *Aether's Touch*. Finance was one of those jobs that involved social climbing, so Carmen was a busy woman. She'd decided that Matt wasn't suitable for upper-circle social gatherings, where the elite of Athens Point engaged in verbal sparring and judgmental gossip. Thus, he hooked up with her only for rousing but infrequent sex—not that he didn't enjoy *that*—which might include some business on the side.

Matt retreated to the docks and his ship. He didn't want to contemplate the cost of his next privacy bill. Commercials pursued him, wrapping around corners and trying to catch his eye because he'd turned off their cacophony in his ear bug.

Once inside the *Aether's Touch*, he ignored the messages clamoring for his attention. On his own ship, he could have privacy, and privacy meant blessed silence. He didn't even feel like browsing his music library.

After he ate something from a ration pack in the

galley, he wondered if Nestor would be interested in dinner. He made the call, requesting face-to-face secure comm. A responder said that Nestor was busy, but would call back.

Well, there's nothing else to do but what I'm supposed to be doing. Matt reluctantly buckled down, combing through messages and evaluating bids. Some were from large enterprises, where the bid was proposing not so much a contract, but a threat of assimilation and absorption. Many of the small companies bidding might initially appear independent, but he expected most were fronts.

His queue chimed gently; Nestor had sent a message rather than calling back. Before he opened it, he noticed it had a delay trigger. It had been wandering ComNet since Matt went for lunch in the bazaar. He frowned. Usually this was the resort of somebody who needed the message payload off their own local storage. They'd send it to wander about as a vagrant, trying to find temporary residence here and there, avoiding housecleaning programs and security scans.

Matt called Nestor and got the autoresponder again. Regardless of Matt's opinion of Nestor's appeal to the opposite sex, Nestor did entertain women in his flat every so often. He'd be cranky if Matt disturbed him during such an interlude.

Nestor's message had no video or audio, and had only one line of text: "The demon on your back is better known than the demons hiding along your path." The message also carried a large encrypted payload, adding weight to the possibility that Nestor was trying to reduce local storage—but Matt happened to know that Nestor wasn't running out of room.

Matt tried his standard decryption and nothing happened. What game was Nestor playing? Matt recognized the quote from his time at the orphanage on

Konstantinople Prime. It referred to a verse that they had been required to memorize.

"The Chronicles of St. Darius, Chapter One, Verse Ten."

He guessed correctly that Nestor had keyed the decryption to his voiceprint plus a specific phrase. The packet opened, revealing three packages. The package labeled CUSTOMS immediately worried him. The second package was ominously labeled KEDROS. The third was unlabeled.

Perhaps he shouldn't have had Nestor hound the customs inspectors. Likewise, he wasn't sure he wanted to see the "Kedros" package—would it tell him what hold Edones had over Ariane? Instead, he picked the easy path and opened the third package. *Uh-oh.*

"Stop download!" he yelled.

Aether's Touch, or rather her information system, paused the download.

"This is a onetime transfer of unique images. Cancelation may damage images," said the system. The same message flashed on the view port on the wall.

Matt hesitated. By opening the package, he'd initiated several downloads from temporary storage scattered about ComNet. This package was huge! Some of the contents, currently suspended across two physical locations, were rulesets. He tried an urgent call to Nestor, which went unanswered again.

"Have I got the AI for you!" Nestor had said. At the time, Matt had only been vaguely suspicious because he'd said "AI" and not "agent," but Nestor frequently overrated his agents. He even named them, although only AI models with their unique model numbers had identities. There was a big difference between agents and AI models, or "AIs." AIs could *vote,* for Gaia's sake, provided they passed their identity and self-reflection tests. Once they passed their tests, they owned their rulesets and guarded them jealously. In a way, their ruleset was like a genome.

Developing AI required a license. They were hard to get; CAW only granted licenses to individuals, not organizations, and net-think claimed only ten people across the six prime worlds were licensed to work with AI. Nestor wasn't one of them.

If this was an AI, transferring it would require an expensive chunk of ComNet resources. Here they were at the beginning of the twenty-second century and extra bandwidth was still pricy. No matter how ComNet expanded, via satellite, zeppelin, optical line, wireless, meshed node network, the demand always grew to fit the bandwidth.

Matt shook his head. More importantly, he'd have to resort to using crystal. He'd just replaced the crystal on *Aether's Touch* by getting a loan—*thank you, Carmen*—against his future lease revenue. If he continued the download, the AI might take up partial residence in crystal. What a waste of money; but the only other option was to deny the download and, depending upon whether Nestor was wiping his track, damage the payload.

Cringing at the cost and hoping fervently that this AI didn't use illicit rulesets, Matt reinitiated the download. As he feared, this took enough bandwidth to cause his system displays on the ship to hang, pausing, waiting . . .

You'd better not be fucking with me, Nestor. With nothing better to do, Matt savagely grabbed his shopping bag and dumped out the disabled remotes he'd collected at the bazaar.

Five remotes hadn't made it out of the privacy shield in time. One looked entirely different from the others, which he hadn't noticed when he'd scooped them all into his bag. He'd built remotes himself from kits, and this one didn't have the standard little antigrav motor that could be unhooked from the other parts, the parts that people usually personalized with paint and fins.

Matt picked up the quiescent remote with the mottled gray-green skin. Its surface seemed oily, not mechanical. He sniffed. A faint organic odor rose from the remote. He'd never encountered a dead animal, but he could imagine that one would feel this way: limp, broken, and still warm. It *felt* the way Minoan technology *looked*.

With a shudder, he dropped it and looked around wildly, checking status displays. If this remote used Minoan technology, the ComNet disablement codes might not have deactivated it. The remote might be faking inactivity, yet still funneling data to its owner through some other mechanism.

"If I've been transferred to anyone else but Matthew Journey, then I've been stolen. This may indicate that Nestor Agamemnon Expedition, originally from the *Expedition VII*, is in distress." The downloaded AI's speech was patterned after Nestor's voice, but bland and emotionless.

That's more obvious than the Great Bull's balls. Matt bit back his response, since he didn't know how mature this AI might be. This was clearly a self-aware AI and it might still be in training, which meant that Matt's sarcasm could be detrimental. He noted on the view port the AI had the model name and number of "Nestor's Muse 3," which might indicate an obscenely complicated ruleset with Gaia-only-knew what sort of imperatives. Or the name might only be the result of Nestor's conceit.

"This is Matt Journey and you're aboard the *Aether's Touch*. Stay in quiescent mode until I give you a command."

The AI shut down without comment. Matt set his

security so that only he could activate the AI, and
only from within the ship. After putting the remotes
carefully back into his bag, he locked down the systems on the *Aether's Touch*.

He left the ship, followed again by a swarm of
remotes. After leaving the dock levels, he turned into
a circular commercial storage area. Since it was commercial, not public, its proceeds paid for a facility
privacy shield. No remotes allowed. His pesky fol-
lowers had to circle impotently, hoping to catch him
emerging from one of the numerous portals.

Matt glanced about the interior. He walked to an
empty spot on the circumference, finding an available
locker. Like everyone else inside the storage area, he
avoided showing curiosity about other people's business. He opted for the best security and slid his hand
under the privacy plate, feeling for the fingerholds.
He provided charge account numbers from his personal storage implant through the small electromag-
netic field about his body, adding a retinal identifier
and an additional access code for the locker.

With the seemingly inactive remotes safely locked
up and more than half the following remotes lost
circling the storage lockers, Matt felt a little better.
Now for Nestor.

Nobody answered at Nestor's flat. Sighing, Matt
paid to extend his privacy shield farther and asked
for entrance, providing a sentence for voiceprint and
a retinal scan. The flat allowed him to enter.

Suitable seduction music was playing softly and
the flat was set to low light, causing shadows to criss-
cross the floor.

"Raise lights," Matt said.

Nothing happened. Did he see a shadow shift?
Matt whirled. He didn't see any more movement,
but now he noticed the wall screens. If Nestor were
entertaining, he'd have erotic art displayed on the

walls. If he were meditating, he'd have a calming blue on the walls. Instead, Matt saw open and busy view ports. Nestor's system was shredding rewritable memory and executing emergency cleansing.

Matt crossed quietly to the bedroom and peered through the opening. His legs buckled.

Oh, Nestor. By Gaia and all her prophets.

Nestor hung from the ceiling in front of Matt. His wrists were tied behind his back, hoisted tightly up to his feet, causing his body to arch abnormally. A strange metallic scent came at Matt in waves from the darker-than-midnight-blue spots on the carpet. There were dripping sounds in the darkened room and enough light from the walls to see that Nestor's throat was cut. The wound gaped and bulged, dripping along his abdomen.

Matt crouched and vomited. His hands were on the carpet, his fingers splayed, and his right fingertips touched something warm and wet. He jerked his hand away and rolled back to sit on his heels. Tears squeezed from the corners of his eyes and rolled down to his neck.

"Emergency code," he croaked.

A beep from the flat's system indicated the embedded ComNet nodes were waiting for the one code that would always be recorded and transmitted, regardless of privacy shields. "Nine-one-one, emergency code nine-one-one."

"Stay down and keep your hands away from your body," said a cold voice behind him. The owner of the voice paused, perhaps waiting for data, and then authoritatively added, "Mr. Matthew Journey."

"Wait, I'm a friend, a business partner."

They stunned him anyway. As he went through the unpleasant jerking on his way to unconsciousness, Matt wondered why they'd bothered to let him into the flat.

CHAPTER 7

Why support Pax Minoica? Frankly, we need Minoan
time buoys for N-space travel and we *will* defer to their
wishes. I assume you're familiar with the video of Qesan
Douchet claiming responsibility for sabotaging a Minoan
ship—where he spouts vitriol yet doesn't notice the
shadow pass overhead. Crystal has preserved the pris-
tine surgical hits destroying his hardened bunkers, as
well as the finality of genetically targeted bioweapons
that we still don't understand. Minoan "justice" wiped
out Douchet's tribal gene sets, *forever*. Today, anyone
of Terran Franko-Arabian descent should have his or her
DNA analyzed before visiting. . . .

—*Interview with Hellas Prime's Senator Raulini*,
2091.138.15.00 UT, indexed by Heraclitus 11,
Democritus 9 under Conflict, Cause and Effect Imperatives

Per her authority under Pax Minoica, Ariane
stopped all Naga operations on Karthage Point.
She released personnel assigned to Naga maintenance, training, and mission operations from duty,
but restricted them to the barracks and public areas.

She required special support and services for the
treaty inspectors, but that wasn't the hard part. She
also needed inspector escorts with suitably high
clearances, which resulted in this pool of people she
faced in the amphitheater. Unit commanders tended

to stick junior officers with these duties, since they had appropriate clearance and access to intelligence material. She had no time to prepare training packages for these duties, and at her request, Karthage Point Command Post scheduled an all-hands briefing for everyone assigned special duties for the inspection.

Her heart sank as she looked over the rabble of young officers, with a few noncoms thrown in here and there. While the treaty was an interesting break in the daily grind at Karthage, no one in this amphitheater was happy to get saddled with extra duties.

"The intel golems are having a festival, with all these games and intrigue." The conversation carried to Ariane. She looked coldly at the offending young officers. They were ops, slouching in their seats with confident indifference.

As the volume from private conversations grew, Ariane glanced at Lieutenant Santorini standing to the side of the stage. He only gave her a smirk in return. She wondered whether she'd have to grab everyone's attention in some undignified and embarrassing manner.

"Ladies and gentlemen, the commander of Karthage Point." The voice was crisp and cutting, the sound of an experienced aide.

Conversation stopped and there was a whooshing sound as everyone stood at attention, Ariane included. She watched as Colonel Icelos made his way down the aisle, receiving sidelong glances as he strode along. There was a certain *feeling* in the room that made her think that Icelos had earned the respect of Karthage personnel. She'd worked in units that had various outstanding, average, and even loathsome commanders; she knew what the glances looked like when the troops wouldn't follow their commanders into the head, much less into a battle. Being liked by your troops was optional; having their respect and trust was necessary.

"Take your seats," Colonel Icelos said when he reached the stage.

The sound of three hundred people sitting filled the amphitheater.

"I shouldn't have to tell any of you how important Pax Minoica is to *all* the Autonomist worlds. So whether you come from a prime planet or not, you've been handpicked by your unit commanders to support this great peace initiative."

Ariane kept her eyes on Icelos as he spoke. She didn't believe the bit about being "handpicked," but he had the right mixture of ease and toughness and honesty—Gaia, even she wanted to work for the man! She had a flashing glimpse, a memory of a quiet, earnest blond lieutenant who slipped in and out of the Thera Point command post. This was a man worthy of protection and she reminded herself of her real mission: *Find the assassins before they find Icelos. Before they find me.* Interesting. Her unconscious mind already assumed more than one person was involved. She wrenched her attention back to the amphitheater.

"This particular treaty is the linchpin of Pax Minoica," Icelos was saying. "I expect everyone to give Major Kedros their full attention and support."

Her cue.

"Thank you, sir," Ariane said. He nodded and their eyes met for a moment. She tried to express her gratefulness in that glance. As he exited to stage left, she touched her slate and displayed an unclassified diagram of Karthage Point on the large surface behind her.

"The areas that can be inspected, per the treaty, are shown in red." MilNet nodes amplified her voice.

"In any of those areas, the Terran inspection teams must always be escorted by our two-person teams. All of you are assigned a shift and an inspection team, so check your schedules. Those of you who will be interfacing with the inspectors should read the treaty protocols. Remember that you must speak through interpreters, unless the inspectors indicate otherwise."

There were murmurs and snickers. Someone called out, "Can't they speak common Greek?"

"Only if they want to," said Ariane. "Many of the interpreters are TEBI, from their bureau of intelligence. If your inspector doesn't need to use an interpreter, you should be cautious, since that inspector doesn't *need* state oversight."

Her audience straightened visibly. They could no longer pass this off as a joke.

"Let's go through the players who we know, starting with State Prince Isrid Sun Parmet." Ariane had their full attention now. Video of the state prince played on the walls.

"During the war, Parmet rose to the position of state prince by running the League's military intelligence. After Pax Minoica began, he diverted his best people over to their new civilian intelligence agency and helped it grow into what we know today as TEBI."

Hands flew up and Ariane had to stop for questions. She generally answered the questions about Parmet's legendary exploits with "that's classified beyond our current need-to-know" (true) or "I wouldn't know" (not true).

"What about the rumors that Parmet sanctioned torture for interrogation of prisoners of war?" asked a maintenance officer, his eyes wide.

Ariane paused as the chord of fear ran through her. She knew all about the League's methods employed during the war, as well as the dispensation granted to commanders of both sides under the initial treaties of Pax Minoica. Both sides proclaimed victory in the long struggle and as long as one doesn't *lose* a war, there are no war crime trials . . . *thank Gaia and any gods of the Minoans.*

"Actions committed under valid orders, on both sides, cannot be questioned. The records have been sealed," Ariane said.

Her audience noted her pause and more questions followed in a surge of babble.

"Why demand reprisals for Ura-Guinn, when he's committed war crimes himself?"

"He's behind the reprisal squads, isn't he? They bombed the—"

"The Terran overlords have always protected him—"

"—sign this treaty anyway? We should keep Naga as an intersystem offensive vehicle. Fucking morons—"

"—could fit Naga with conventional weapons and—"

"*Quiet.*" Her voice cut through the jabber. She froze the displays and collected the reins of control. The room calmed.

"We've all sworn an oath to uphold the Consortium of Autonomous Worlds," she said sternly. "That means supporting this treaty to the best of our abilities, regardless of our personal feelings. On the other hand, we must continue to protect Consortium interests. You can bet the Terran inspection teams are out for any intelligence, military or industrial. We know that because we have dossiers on the team members and they're rarely who they claim to be."

Having grasped their attention again firmly, she displayed video of a man and woman.

"Two people listed ostensibly as translators are top TEBI agents. Nathaniel Wolf Kim and Maria Guillotte have served Parmet for years, and our intelligence considers them the most dangerous of the team. They often work with an agent code-named 'Andre Covanni,' whom we've never identified. We suspect he may also be on this team since Karthage Point is one of our *most sensitive facilities*."

There was silence as she paused and displayed checklists.

"Before the inspectors arrive, everything of operational intelligence must be hidden, including rosters, schedules, requisition lists—*everything*. All station displays will be suppressed and only your slates can access your schedules. Use privacy mode on your slates during the entire inspection period. All slates are programmed for autowipe and if you lose one, report the loss immediately to Command Post. Remember, proper control is still required for TD weapons, so make sure you're glued to those inspector teams when inside storage and maintenance zones."

Pausing for breath, Ariane looked at the faces in the audience. Most were earnestly following the lecture. She hoped the inspection went quickly and smoothly. For her, this inspection was primarily a way to distract Terran intelligence from the *truth*: Icelos's identity, her identity, and her true past. If the Terrans were behind the assassinations, then both of their lives depended upon this misdirection.

Isrid was receiving a similar briefing on his ship. They would soon drop out of real-space for the last leg of the journey to Karthage Point.

Nathaniel Wolf Kim wore his family name like a visible emblem to proclaim his Terran derivations, but encouraged his coworkers to call him Nathan. The man had an undercurrent of arrogance and anger that he couldn't, or wouldn't, hide. Nathan was always imposing, whether he was asking for directions on the street or interrogating subjects.

"Their intelligence adviser, personally placed by Colonel Edones. *Reserve* Major Ariane Kedros. She's had a lackluster career and little field experience. An analyst." Nathan's lip curled, but it always curled when he talked about Autonomists. They would always be the enemy.

"Edones won't be on Karthage?" Isrid was disappointed, but hid his feelings. He always practiced *somaural* control and projection. The cutthroat politics throughout the overlord's staff needed no ammunition.

"We knew we'd catch them unprepared with two concurrent inspections this early after the signing," said Maria Guillotte, seated at Isrid's right. "However, we expected Edones to delegate the preparation in Pelagos since it's not as pivotal as Karthage Point. Instead, he left the squadrons near Hellas Prime in the hands of a golem."

Isrid's interest was piqued. He looked carefully at the face of the female major, noting the gaunt cheekbones of an N-space pilot. She had a slight frame, fine features, and brown eyes. The eyes were too deep for her age, and wise, perhaps hiding pain.

"She's more than she seems," Isrid murmured.

"We broke several vault codes to get to her records," said Maria. "We were thorough."

"Edones didn't make colonel in the Directorate of Intelligence by trusting the wrong people. How heavy is Andre's workload?" Isrid used a subtle hand signal to say, *Your research wasn't good enough.*

Maria had more undercover experience than Nathan did. She could have protested that she knew how to perform surreptitious vault searches. Instead, she stiffened and made an apology with a turn of her wrist.

Nathan's dark eyes glittered. "Andre's primary mission has always been to sniff out the war criminals, although after all these years I think the trail's gone dead. Regardless, SP, I don't think we can give him extra tasking. Information has always flowed *from* him."

Isrid looked as though he was considering Nathan's words, but he was evaluating a different problem. Nathan and Maria didn't know that Andre was present on this inspection team. Isrid checked his security display on his desk. There were only the three of them in this cabin and there wasn't any monitoring equipment. He made his decision.

"Since none of us can recognize Andre on sight, I'm going to warn you that he's posing as a member of this inspection team." Isrid watched both of them. "That's confidential, but I think both of you should know."

Nathan expressed surprise. Not all Terrans could perfect *somaural* control and Nathan never had the patience to learn. However, if one wanted a career in Terra XL government, one had to be adept at reading standard *somaural* signals and understanding body language. Maria's relaxed body language should have been a clue to Nathan, but a flicker of her index finger on the side where Nathan couldn't see told Isrid explicitly that she *already knew* about Andre's new assignment.

"Why wasn't I told about this earlier?" Nathan scowled. "I'm supposed to be Andre's contact—the contact on your staff, of course, SP. Also, just because Andre's on the inspection team, it doesn't mean he's got time to support our research."

Nathan had a point, which Isrid acknowledged with a nod.

"We have a sleeper stationed at Karthage that could provide us information about this major," said Maria, ignoring Nathan's outrage. "I could activate that agent."

Isrid paused, making his final decisions. "Nathan, use your message drop to *request* that Andre dig through all the Autonomist personnel records. You may activate our sleeper, Maria, but only *after* we get through the baseline inspection. This will be the first time we've visited an AFCAW installation, so let's make the best of it."

There had been a small shift of power from Nathan to Maria, although unacknowledged.

"Certainly, SP," Nathan said crisply as he stood. He accepted his orders, but his back was tight with resentment as he left the room.

Maria stretched her legs languidly before she stood up. Her body was perfect by Terran standards: symmetrical and ideally proportioned, height between 175 and 180 centimeters, and topped by a head of smooth blond hair and flawless regular features. Isrid also knew that the rest of her skin was flawless. His gaze moved from her breasts to her small waist, then down her hips. The stretch suit hid nothing; he could see the angular lump of her hipbones and her slightly raised pubic region. He knew how soft her inner thighs were, and how she smelled and tasted.

"Do you need anything more, SP?" Maria wasn't being suggestive. Having control of practically every muscle in her body, she could radiate the fact she wasn't available.

He once thought he knew what drove Maria. Power had excited her, more specifically, his power. However, Maria had proved to be more complicated, particularly after Sabina had seduced her. Or had it been the other way around?

"No, you're dismissed," he said. Maria nodded, professionally cool and distant.

Isrid had been puzzled when, shortly before he was assigned to oversee this inspection at Karthage, Sabina triumphantly showed him a video of the two of them. Sabina purposely gave him no clue of what she expected. Was he supposed to be titillated or jealous? Moreover, jealous of whom? Sabina knew they couldn't marry Maria. Terran group marriage was merely permission to breed within specific genetic restraints, and Maria was prohibited from marrying because of genetic damage she'd received near Tantor.

He watched Maria exit, wondering whether he should ask her the questions. Did Maria know about the video? Did she mind whether he had seen it? Did she care for Sabina? He doubted it; he'd never seen Maria use sex as a way of expressing feelings.

Damn, this was—well, this situation was just plain *awkward*. Moreover, it was distracting. As a specialist in psychological torture himself, Isrid knew when people were playing head games.

Ariane glanced sideways at Lieutenant Santorini and stifled the urge to tell him to stop fidgeting. Santorini, the one and only aide thrown her way when she desperately needed more, obviously hadn't had his dress uniform recently fitted. She'd been grateful for his help, but she wished he'd stop pulling at his collar.

Leaning her way, Santorini whispered, "Everybody's here, Major, right on time. We're ready."

She glanced to her right. The senior officers arrayed outside the docking air lock looked impressive as well as apprehensive. Ariane knew that Colonel Icelos, like her, had reason to truly fear the Terran inspectors, particularly Parmet. The senior staff of Karthage Point looked as frightened as she felt. The long coats and epaulets, the gold braid, the medals and decorations, and the bright cuffs of the dress uniforms couldn't hide their tension.

In a way, their fear relaxed her and buoyed her

spirits. The Terrans, trained in their vaunted *somaural* techniques, would have problems picking out nervous guilt from this mélange of fear, hostility, and dread.

The boarding pipes sounded. The treaty didn't allow the drama of being late. Per the treaty, the Terrans had announced their inspection point two days prior to their arrival. Then they announced their arrival time twenty hours out, then twenty minutes out.

The air lock slid open and the Terrans filed out to the landing. Ariane kept her eye on the weapon detector light above the air lock. The treaty allowed AFCAW to perform active scans for weapons. None of the twelve interpreters or inspectors carried stun, compression, or explosive weapons. State Prince Parmet came through the air lock last.

The Terrans lined up on the other side of the landing. Autonomists and Terrans stared at each other. There were no Minoans here and no supervision. Fifty years of hostility wasn't easily forgotten, even if Pax Minoica had ended active warfare fifteen years ago.

The eight Autonomist officers, plus their two security guards, were a vibrant line of color compared to the twelve Terrans. Ariane's uniform was the most conservative, being a black coat edged with light blue, with blue and gold epaulets and stripes about the cuffs. The other officers wore their AFCAW red-and-gold dress coats over black trousers.

The Terrans wore grays, taupes, and other indistinct muddy colors. Their suits stretched tight over their torsos, hips, and thighs, almost looking like one-piece of clothing. They wore no obvious indication of rank, but the treaty required them to identify inspectors separately from interpreters. Perhaps the black armband identified the inspectors, Ariane thought, since the TEBI *interpreters* Kim and Guillotte wore none.

State Prince Isrid Sun Parmet, however, wore a black armband. As he moved to the end of the line farthest from Ariane, her gaze followed him. He had far more of a presence in person than on video. He was tall and broad-shouldered without having too much bulk. Most of the Terrans had similar perfection in body symmetry, probably because of their restricted birth program and eugenic controls. Parmet's smooth golden skin seemed to glow. His dark hair had a touch of gray and his green eyes glinted. He gazed at all the AFCAW officers, in turn. Ariane avoided making eye contact, looking away when his gaze rested on her.

The air lock had sealed and there was uncomfortable silence as the two parties faced each other. Ariane leaned forward and looked down the line at Colonel Icelos, who stared intently at the bulkhead wall over the air lock. He was only the facility commander. The wing commander was stationed on Hellas Daughter and she wasn't attending this first baseline inspection. The commander of the operational squadron, Lieutenant Colonel Voyage, was her representative. Jacinthe only glared back at Ariane and made no move to address the Terran inspection team.

Of course they wanted the liaison officer to handle this. Wishing fervently to be anywhere else, even the lowest level of hell, Ariane stepped forward and turned to stand between the two groups. Terran heads swiveled to look at her and she had to swallow hard to keep the knot of anger from traveling up from her stomach. These people were the enemy, and many had Autonomist blood on their hands—blood of her friends and comrades.

Everyone waited. *Welcome to Karthage Point?* Those

words would never pass her lips, not for a Terran state prince. Her jaw tightened. *I'm Ariane Kedros. I'm too young to carry this resentment. I don't have personal ties to the war.*

"Karthage Point stands ready to support the Mobile Temporal Distortion Weapon Treaty." Once her first words were out, she felt relief.

Her voice broke the tension on the Autonomist side. She saw shoulders twitch and sag, deep breaths taken, and slight stretches in several necks.

"Lieutenant Santorini will assign you quarters for the duration of the inspection. He'll also brief you regarding which corridors and parts of the station are accessible to you," she said. She felt Santorini step forward beside her, but she kept her eyes on the Terrans.

The Terran interpreters softly repeated Ariane's words in various languages. Most of the Terrans glanced about at the featureless gray walls of the station while they keyed their ear bug volume up or down. Under normal conditions, the walls displayed video from ComNet, station programs, daily orders, work queues, and schedules. Now the landing and corridor felt like a cold tomb. More important to Ariane and her overt mission, it was a tomb with no intelligence value for the Terrans.

Santorini walked to the beginning of the line of Terrans, holding his slate in front of him like a shield. At this point, Colonel Icelos dismissed the delegation formation and the Karthage Point leadership fled, quickly moving away down the corridor.

Ariane walked beside Santorini as he assigned quarters and checked in the delegation members, cross-referencing them against the roster sent by the Terran overlords. Santorini keyed Terrans to personal slates that were modified to prevent recording of information. The slates were waiting in their rooms.

Every Terran on the team was familiar to Ariane after poring over the intelligence files. Nathaniel Wolf Kim looked angrier in person. Maria Guillotte's face had beauty in static pictures but in person seemed unremarkable and without personality. Ariane looked at each Terran face as Santorini processed them, wondering if the famed "Andre Covanni" was here. That agent's penchant for causing excessive civilian casualties made him a war criminal in Autonomist eyes, but any due justice after the war had been mitigated by the Terrans' loss of Ura-Guinn. Did Andre also suffer guilt about his actions during the war?

If anyone could understand Andre, it'd be me. The voice in Ariane's head was spiteful. *I'm more of a war criminal than he ever was, if we're judging by body count.*

The jury was still out on the body count, however. In a few months, their closest telescopes would see whether Ura-Guinn's sun had survived the TD detonation. No one could know the full ramifications, however, until the generational ship arrived at Ura-Guinn.

"Major?" Santorini prompted her. They were standing in front of State Prince Parmet and his interpreter, a short man with thinning and receding hair.

Ariane looked up and, for the first time, met Parmet's gaze. The brown flecks did nothing to warm his green eyes, arrogant, unyielding, and knowing. Her rational mind told her that Parmet knew nothing of her history, yet she instinctively flinched, wanting to flee. She took a deep breath.

"Inspections will begin with storage lockers A through D, scheduled at fourteen hundred universal time." She made sure to address both interpreter and state prince as she gestured to the wall where the schedule displayed. "That gives your team a significant rest cycle. Will that be sufficient?"

Surprisingly, the interpreter gave her a warm smile and made no pretense of interpreting for State Prince Parmet, who slowly looked over the inspection schedule.

"It looks fine, Major Kedros." Parmet's voice was distant. "However, I'd like to change Ms. Guillotte's quarters. Ms. Guillotte needs better ventilation because of Tantor's Sun disease."

"Of course. Your quarters are already located near the medical facilities, but we can make room changes." Ariane nodded, hearing Santorini's quick intake of breath. "A moment please."

She took Santorini's elbow and steered him across the landing until they were well away from Terran ears and had their backs toward the Terrans.

"How does he know we have ventilation problems in A-twelve? Then he parades Guillotte's war record in front of us," Santorini said. Young as he was, he knew that only one famous battle had given spacefarers Tantor's Sun disease.

"Lieutenant, keep your voice down and relax your body," Ariane said quietly. "He's trying to put you off-balance and he'll see he was successful."

"How?" Santorini looked startled.

Ariane made a mental note to send out a briefing regarding *somaural* reading. Standard training used to include background on Terrans, but apparently not any longer. She realized that she shouldn't make such assumptions based upon her wartime memories. She described it to Santorini as the deep study of facial and body language, but avoided any mention of reading auras. Santorini would consider his aura invisible to human eyes, used solely for the transfer of personal data. Besides, she'd heard that only extremely talented *somaural* practitioners could read auras, usually under optimum conditions that involved trance or meditation. Looking over her shoulder, she saw Parmet watching them with sharp eyes.

"Relax and let go of your emotions. Can you do that, Paul?" She used his first name purposely, trying to put him at ease. Her voice was low.

Santorini nodded. "But what about his comment about the ventilation system? Do we have a leak?"

"They're only showing us that they're monitoring our unclassified maintenance chatter. We should tighten up our security, even in station maintenance, while they're here. Go ahead and make the room change Parmet requested." Ariane wished she felt as confident as she sounded. She made a note on her slate to have Karthage Security Force sweep regularly for active and inactive recording pips.

With pity, she watched young Santorini walk back to the Terrans. Feeling Parmet's gaze upon her, she left the docking air lock and landing, trying to keep her body neutral. She felt dizzy with relief when she was safely out of his sight.

CHAPTER 8

What is Truth? Truth can be written to crystal. Once written, Truth cannot be erased unless the entire vault is destroyed. But *interpretation* of Truth must be performed by intelligent beings. . . .

—Melissa Solis, Sophist at Konstantinople Prime University, 2087.005.14.37 UT, indexed by *Democritus 4* under Cause and Effect Imperatives

Change came slowly within the Athens Point Law Enforcement Force, almost as slow as decisions. After a decade of testing the use of AI interrogators, Athens Point LEF had grudgingly agreed that many suspects cracked more easily under AI because they didn't have human reactions to play against. Some suspects, however, could blatantly control their biometric responses regardless of the interrogator. Because of this, the LEF had established a tedious pendulum of question-by-AI, then question-by-human, and by Gaia, they wouldn't deviate from this procedure for anyone.

Matt woke up in a constraint chair, comfortable, but prevented from stretching. He was in a small interrogation room with featureless walls. No furniture, nothing on the walls, floor, or ceiling, existed in that room other than Matt in his constraints.

A neutral AI voice asked him for his name, physical residence, message addresses, and ComNet account names, before asking him to state why he had visited Nestor. After Matt explained his business with Nestor, the AI asked him to recount his perceptions when he entered the flat and discovered the body.

Matt answered accurately, aware that someone was reading his voiceprint for stress. They couldn't record any other biometric data without serving him a warrant. They'd already taken their physical evidence; why did they need his perceptions? They'd gotten to the flat before Matt, probably responding to an emergency call from Nestor.

But they didn't get there fast enough. The vaunted LEF, the protection that many citizens depended upon, had failed for Nestor.

Then the AI voice went away and the quiet was worse than the questioning. Hours passed, or perhaps it seemed like hours to Matt because his bladder demanded attention.

"Hey! Somebody! I need to use the urinal," he yelled.

No answer.

Time dragged by. He squirmed as much as possible in the constraint chair, but it didn't help. When he couldn't hold it anymore he urinated right there in the chair. The reclined seat and thigh supports absorbed it. In a short time, his trousers were dry and as sweet smelling as if they'd recently been cleaned.

Matt clenched his fists. They could have told him the chair was like a pilot chair, but then he wouldn't have gone through the torturous shame.

The neutral AI voice questioned him again, using most of the same questions as before but with slight variations in phrasing and order. Matt had previously believed v-plays that had the detainee losing composure at this point were unrealistic. Whenever he'd donned the virtual equipment, he'd always picked the unpopular law enforcement roles to experience. Nowadays, v-play producers spent more time enhancing "bad guy" experiences and perhaps their work was more realistic than he thought, because he was so angry that he balled up his fists tightly and his voice shook. He was a witness, not a suspect!

"What were you doing before you went to the residence of Nestor Expedition?" This was a new question.

"Putting personal items into storage," Matt said promptly, forcing his hands to open and relax. Since they could backtrack him through ComNet coverage, they would already know this.

"What type of items?"

Matt paused before answering. If they were asking him about the contents of his storage locker, then they hadn't yet gotten a warrant to open it. That meant he wasn't a suspect, regardless of how they were trying to frighten him into thinking the opposite.

"If the Athens Point LEF can convince me that my locker is relevant, then I will willingly open it for them *without a warrant*."

After Matt's answer, the AI was silent.

With nothing for his mind to do but race around, he lost all sense of time. He wondered whether he'd been drugged. In the v-plays, everyone has privacy rights so they are informed if they're being dosed. Did one have to be conscious when receiving the notification? He'd never looked into Consortium law on witness and suspect treatment. He'd never needed to. That had been Nestor's area of interest, among others.

Matt swallowed a lump in his throat. He'd known Nestor more than twelve years and just like that, Nestor was gone, cut out of his life. Unbelievable.

A door opened and a man walked in. After the door closed, the wall became featureless again, removing anything a suspect could focus on. This wasn't what happened in the v-play scenarios. First, the v-plays always had two interrogators enter, usually a man and a woman. Second, this man was thin and dapper, bearing little resemblance to the burly strong-armed v-play interrogators, except that he wore the slickly pressed uniform. No self-respecting crumb could possibly stick to this guy's coat and trousers.

"I'm honored to meet you, Mr. Journey." He extended a hand. "I'm Chief Inspector Stephanson."

Chief Inspector, huh? Matt stared at the man's hand in surprise. He tried to move his arm, and the constraint chair released his upper body. His hips and legs were still secured.

"Why am I here?" What else could he say? *Pleased to meet you*? Not under these circumstances.

"Have you checked your exposure ratings, Mr. Journey? You've gone above twelve percent."

Matt gaped. V-play celebrities would kill to get that sort of exposure. The feeds must have finally found the images from his G-145 data. That might also explain why the Athens Point LEF hadn't yet moved to examine his storage locker or the systems on the *Aether's Touch*. He'd attained celebrity status. It'd be fleeting, since net-think was so fickle.

Stephanson waited for a response, Matt said, "I didn't know that. Uh—I've been busy."

Matt saw disbelief flit through his cold eyes. Apparently, Stephanson couldn't believe that Matt didn't check his exposure numbers hourly like an obsessed net rat, as Nestor called those who spend endless hours wandering aimlessly about the indexes, thinking of themselves as informed.

"We're sorry for your loss," Stephanson said, without compassion in his eyes. "But we're holding you in protective custody. We think Nestor Expedition was murdered because of *you*."

"Why?" Matt felt a wave of nausea.

"We don't know, but someone wanted you to see his body."

Including the LEF? Were you measuring my reactions? Matt held his bitter comments inside.

"Nestor has—had other clients. He did freelance work, beyond what he did for Aether Exploration," Matt said.

"Your recent discoveries have piqued the interest of many, if you look at the rise in your exposure. Our analysts have seen a rise in rants from fringe extremist groups that believe in Terran-centrist origins of intelligence." Stephanson smiled thinly.

"If his death was related to G-145, anyone would know that Nestor wouldn't have a copy of the indexes. *I'm* the one keeping those. Besides, the data has already been released to the public domain."

Matt hedged while his mind ran wild. He needed time to sort this out. The strange remote sitting in his storage locker worried him. He could hand that remote over to Athens Point LEF, but if Minoans were involved in Nestor's murder, what would the LEF do? Would this murder be hushed up and smoothed over?

"Your friend managed an emergency command wipe, just before—or *as*—he was attacked. It scrambled his local system, but we know that a large package was sent to your ship." Stephanson paused, not so subtly expecting Matt to volunteer illumination.

Yes, what about that strange AI that Nestor hoped to transfer to the *Aether's Touch*? Matt shivered. Nestor was obviously protecting the AI, as well as the data the AI had retrieved for him. Should Matt tell Stephanson about the research he'd commissioned?

He'd asked Nestor to look into the regular payments made to the customs officials. Nestor had said it could widen—

Ariane. Did this have something to do with her?

"What?" Matt realized that Inspector Stephanson had asked him a question.

"I asked what you were doing in storage before you arrived at your friend's flat."

"Just checking on some expensive parts I had in storage." The words were out and irretrievable, before Matt made a conscious decision to hide the Minoan remote from Stephanson. Now he was committed.

"Would you be willing to hand over the package Mr. Expedition sent you?"

This question meant Athens Point LEF couldn't get warrants to search storage or the *Aether's Touch.* Not yet. Matt missed Nestor's familiarity with Consortium law. He usually didn't think of the LEF as adversaries, but he certainly didn't want them mucking about on *his* ship.

"I haven't had time to look at the package." Again, Matt lied instinctively. Why? "If it looks relevant, then of course I'll hand it over."

"Forgive us, but we'd like to be the ones determining the relevance." Stephanson's face creased again with that thin smile; perhaps he suspected Matt was lying.

Matt closed his eyes and tried to think of nice things, fond memories, and not what had just happened to Nestor.

"We can't release you on your own recognizance because of your high exposure rating. You're safer here under protective custody." Stephanson's final words grabbed Matt's wandering attention. *Protective custody.* He remembered Nestor jeering at those words as he sat splayed in his control chair, watching several feeds. *Protective custody is the new loophole for lazy law enforcement—it's an affront to CAW privacy law*, Nestor had said as he watched his favorite porn star led away by the Hellas Prime LEF, to only Gaia knew where.

"Impossible." This came out as a yelp, so Matt lowered his voice. "I have business to attend to, as you know. I demand legal representation."

"You'll get all the representation you need within our custody, and you can continue to do your business. Protective custody facilities are quite comfortable and you'll have access to your data through ComNet." Stephanson was implacable.

Matt wouldn't have access to the AI that Nestor transferred: quiescent, hidden, and waiting within the *Aether's Touch*. The LEF would probably monitor his comm and research *for his own protection*, no doubt. Once they processed and analyzed the public node data near Nestor's flat, however, their interest in Matt should ease. If so, when did his protective custody end? Matt racked his brain, wondering whether he'd ever seen that porn star in public again. Since he didn't follow that entertainment sector, he should have asked Nestor.

At the time, Nestor had been apoplectic about the new protective custody provisions, purported to be used only for witness protection. Nestor had vowed to fight them through all his free-whatever organizations, but he'd also mentioned a defense. *Too bad Sasha's such a dumb-ass*, Nestor said, *since she doesn't need a lawyer to demand—*

"I can demand transfer of custody, can't I?" asked Matt.

"As long as the receiving authority meets protection standards, and agrees to protect you by providing an acceptable security plan," Stephanson said.

"Athens Point facilities are comfortable and secure; I doubt you can find anyone else that can compare."

Stephanson's tone meant he doubted Matt could find anyone that would go to the trouble. However, Matt knew somebody who was extremely dedicated, not necessarily to him, but to Ari. The man was an asshole, to be sure, but he always seemed to know where Ari was and he was always nosing around in Ari's business. Matt's safety and freedom guaranteed Ari's job, didn't it?

"I demand transfer to AFCAW's Directorate of Intelligence. Point of contact is Colonel Owen Edones." Matt was pleased to see surprise on Stephanson's face.

The Karthage mess hall was busy when Ariane stepped from the tube, but the crowd was thinning. She'd waited until the initial rush after shift change had ended. Karthage offered two distinct buffets, as any respectable mess hall would. If Ariane went to the left, she'd go down the protected and ventilated side for crèche-get who couldn't stomach anything that was seasoned with strong spices or, Gaia forbid, had planetary flora or fauna products in it. On that buffet, there were plenty of vat-fungus-based and hydroponically grown dishes throwing off steam that quickly rose into the vents. Ariane would probably find Matt's favorite noodle dish—something he claimed had a wonderful array of flavors but which she found bland and unremarkable.

"If you please, Major." Jacinthe Voyage's voice was sharp with impatience and Ariane stepped aside to avoid blocking the line. The tall woman quickly moved toward the left ventilated side labeled 100% STATION GROWN. Ariane turned right.

Karthage shipped many of the ingredients for the

planetary dishes from Hellas Prime and its primary moon, Hellas Daughter, which supported agriculture in controlled and protected biomes. Ariane read the labels before making her choices; dishes had their contents listed to assist cultural dietary restrictions.

At the end of her buffet line came the advantage of being in the planetary food chain: beers, wines, and flora-based juices.

Ariane hesitated. She usually didn't have alcohol on assignment, saving it as a reward when her duty ended. However, the shift had been stressful and she wanted true, natural relaxation. She selected a beer with a label that promised "full-bodied flavor, with light tones of green altensporos, a grain grown in Southern Indigos, Hellas Prime."

She sat as far away from Jacinthe as possible, staying on the right side of the hall where the mélange of smells was comforting. She'd finished half her beer before she realized she hadn't yet sampled her food. She could feel her stomach warming and absorbing the liquid. No longer having any appetite, she picked at the brown meat dish with gravy and chewed resolutely. Small bubbles formed in her beer and clung to the sides of the glass; she stared into the light amber fluid and lost herself, the sounds of the other diners fading.

"Major? May we join you?"

Ariane looked up and nearly jumped out of her chair. It was the fluid voice of the state prince's interpreter, who hovered his tray over the table expectantly. Behind the interpreter stood State Prince Parmet himself, looking bored, as if he didn't care where he sat. When she looked wildly around, she saw plenty of empty tables. Why did they want to sit with *her*?

"Major Kedros?"

It was disrespectful to ask them to find another

table. She could say she was saving the five other places for comrades, an unlikely excuse because she was eating so late. Besides, she couldn't find five people on the station that wanted to eat with a black and blue, although the Terrans wouldn't know that.

"Certainly," she said. Astoundingly, the banal civility drilled into her from childhood came out of her mouth. She swallowed, feeling nauseated.

Parmet and his interpreter sat down at the table, their trays an interesting contrast. The interpreter had only meat slices, raw as well as cooked, without gravy or adornment. Parmet had only cooked and candied fruits. Neither man had chosen grain products, fibrous roots, or vegetables, but Ariane wasn't about to ask questions about their diets.

"Pardon. Didn't introduce myself," said the interpreter brightly. "Dr. Istaga. Won't confuse you with my full name. Nor bother you with its origins."

Ariane nodded. She'd read whatever Owen's staff could dig up on every member of the inspection team. Rok Shi Harridan Istaga had doctorates in anthropology and political science. He had originally been part of the inspection team quota for scientists, but CAW had questioned his background for that role. The Terran overlords had immediately sent a revised manifest, shuffling the team and introducing another person. This time they listed Dr. Istaga as an interpreter. Ariane was interested that Istaga was important enough to keep on the inspection team for a military weapons facility, even though he had no military background.

"Fascinating to have the chance to experience new cultures. Other religions." Istaga apparently thought small talk required speaking in short sentence fragments. He fulfilled all of Ariane's expectations for a mild-mannered and middle-aged academician, which made her immediately suspicious.

"I expect so, Dr. Istaga." She reached for her beer without thought, a reaction to get her through tedious conversation. She took a sip and savored it. She glanced at Parmet, and then looked away quickly. He ate his fruit and paid little attention to his interpreter's chatter; he was concentrating upon *her*.

"—in particular, the pervasiveness of Gaia-ism. Voice crying in the wilderness, giver of life, writer of DNA, et cetera. Pervasive among early colonists. Obvious backlash against patriarchal orders of Kristos and the small male-centric Mohammedan cults." Istaga rambled on, while Parmet finished his small meal and leaned back.

Ariane put down her drink and picked at her food, noting that Parmet was still watching her, his elbows resting on the chair and his hands meeting at the fingertips.

"Are you a Gaia-ist, Major?" The direct question from Dr. Istaga startled her.

"I was raised as one," she said. Her constructed identity meshed with her real religious and cultural background, so she couldn't slip up with unfamiliar beliefs. Owen had been an artist, detailed and fastidious, when building her new life.

"At this point in my life, I'm not particularly spiritual," she added honestly.

"Rather easy belief system. Sense of right and wrong, but gentle on retribution. How do you handle guilt, Major?" The mild academician's eyes became sharp.

"What?"

"If your belief system doesn't carry retribution, as Mohammedan cults do, or confession and forgiveness for bad behavior, as the Kristos orders, how do you cleanse yourself? How do you *start over*?" Istaga was unexpectedly speaking in full sentences.

"Are you speaking of me personally, or in general?" Ariane noted that Parmet's lids had lowered as if he was sleepy, but he still focused upon her.

"Much more interesting to understand the personal aspect," Istaga said.

"Well, I was taught that the sending of Kristos and Mohammed to Earth—"

"You mean Terra."

"Of course, Doctor, my apologies. I was taught that they were prophets sent by separate avatars of Gaia on Terra. When mankind dispersed into space, a planet-centric higher power didn't provide—" As she spoke, she reached for her beer with a clumsy grope and knocked the glass with her fingers. The beer in the glass sloshed and she grabbed for it, only causing it to bounce off her fingertips and tip over toward the two men. The glass went down with a solid clunk and a sheet of beer spread across the table.

Istaga slid his chair back and stood up. He clamped his hand on State Prince Parmet's shoulder. Parmet shook his head as if shaking off sleep and pushed away from the table before beer dripped over the side.

"I'm so sorry," said Ariane, waving for the mess steward. "They'll have this cleaned up quickly so you can finish your dinner. I should get some rest."

She stood up while Istaga protested that they were fine, it had been such an interesting conversation, he would like to know more about the teachings of Gaia—

"Excuse me, I have to go," she said, her cheeks flaming. Everyone in the mess hall seemed to be watching her table. She hurried toward the exit.

"Did you have enough time to read her, SP?" Dr. Istaga asked Isrid after the steward had mopped up their table.

"Not as much as I'd like. Her aura was interesting,"

Isrid said thoughtfully. It'd been a beautiful aura; he had almost lost himself in the deep blue, with an almost purplish cast, shot through with sparks of turquoise. The scent reminded him of the clean air that blew in over the seas of Quillens Colony.

"How so?"

Isrid looked at the gregarious interpreter and wondered how much he could trust him. If Dr. Istaga was exactly who his records claimed, then Isrid had little control over the man and he'd never trust him. If this man was Andre Covanni, as Isrid was beginning to suspect, then he certainly couldn't control him—but could he trust him? Isrid could message and request data from Andre, but the mysterious Andre answered only to the overlords.

"She was frank with you, but she knew what we were doing. The beer accident was contrived." Isrid glanced upward, using the universal reminder that all CAW public places, even on military installations, had a plethora of recording devices.

"Really? It looked so natural." A small smile of admiration flitted across Dr. Istaga's face. "Well done, including the flush of embarrassment."

"Probably grounded on true feelings, which helped complete the scene." The academician's admiration for Major Kedros's theatrics convinced Isrid that he was speaking with Andre.

Thus, Isrid didn't tell Dr. Istaga about the most interesting aspect of Major Ariane Kedros. Her aura had stress fractures, usually indicative of an immense emotional burden, perhaps of guilt, under her facade of crisp competence. He intended to find out why.

What a waste of a perfectly good beer.

Ariane slowed to a normal walk after leaving the mess hall. She'd felt Jacinthe's eyes on her the entire time, making her face burn. Spilling beer on visiting dignitaries (*enemies*, claimed her gut) had a good side: It might convince Jacinthe that she was the subperformer her records indicated.

She took a deep breath, rubbing the muscles in the back of her neck. Her knees were weak and rubbery with relief. Her stomach had clenched with terror as soon as she realized that Parmet was slipping into a trancelike state for *somaural* reading. CAW intelligence insisted that *somaural* reading didn't qualify as telepathy; instead, they called it "an enhanced state of empathy."

Why did it matter if Parmet sensed her turbulent emotional state? *So, I'm fucked up—does that make me any different from anyone else around here?* She was beginning to feel pleased with her acting skills.

She passed a pair of Terran inspectors coming out of uniform clothing and walking toward the mess hall. The inspectors wandered freely on the mess level, but, as Owen predicted, the Terran overlords required their inspectors to remain paired, both on and off duty.

Forever hopeful, Owen provided procedures labeled "what to do if an inspector approaches you regarding defection," as well as cautions to note any slips of intelligence or technological information. Ariane had dutifully briefed the procedures, but she doubted they'd ever be used. Owen hadn't underestimated the paranoia of the overlords, considering that even State Prince Parmet had an escort.

Dr. Istaga gave Ariane a greasy, itchy feeling, particularly on her scalp. She'd had this feeling before, when her instincts helped her come to a conclusion before logic could. There was no doubt in her mind, or in her nerves, that Dr. Istaga deserved constant monitoring.

"Hey, Major! Want to share a drink with the backbone of the officer corps?"

Lieutenant Santorini leaned against the entrance of

the Company Grade Officers Club. Inside, Ariane saw a nicely provisioned bar running the long length of the triangular room. The club was crowded with customers. Today had been stressful for the personnel assigned on Karthage. After a period of intense preparation, either they were escorting their traditional enemy about or they were confined to their quarters and the mess level.

Santorini was still in uniform. His dress coat was rumpled and hanging open at the neck. There were shadows about his eyes, but a relaxed smile on his face.

"Have a drink with us, Major Kedros," he said.

Ariane hesitated, for several reasons. The rank of major required walking a fine line. By definition, she was no longer company grade, and senior officers weren't supposed to fraternize with their subordinates. To make matters more difficult, she wore the black and blue. Intelligence officers were supposed to distance themselves from the operational rabble, while said rabble consequently disdained their company.

Should she be a prick and rebuke Santorini's less-than-regulatory attitude? Should she hold herself aloof from the lower-level officers?

But there was an easy justification, obvious when she looked over Santorini's shoulder and saw majors and senior captains mingling in the club. Generating "team spirit" and "building unit fiber" were excuses for senior officers to drink with subordinates. *Decisions about drinking aren't necessarily about control,* she thought, spitefully silencing the echoes of Matt's voice in her head.

"Why not?" She stepped through the hatch.

CHAPTER 9

We understand the basic chemistry of substance abuse
and I won't babble on here about GABA receptors and
dopaminergic pathways. We've had success using deep-
psyche neural probes, but this treatment requires *voluntary* exposure of memories so we can break the brain's
reward pathways. Another disadvantage is it only works
on addicts with "maintenance" profiles. At least sixty
percent of substance abuse occurs under the "normal"
and "binge" profiles that allow addicts to remain productive and hidden within our society. Bingeing is a special case of the reward-punishment cycle. . . .

— *We're All Addicts*, Dr. Diotrephes to Senatorial
Subcommittee on Substance Abuse, 2102.52.12.15
UT, indexed by *Democritus 15* under Metrics Imperative

Ariane woke suddenly, but not from a nightmare.
"Karthage Command: display time," she mumbled. She had to repeat herself before Karthage's systems responded. They were still learning her voice.

The time that slowly brightened on the wall was
an hour before she needed to get up for the inspection. The massive quantities of alcohol she'd con-
sumed only hours before had screwed up her sleep
cycle, one of the unfortunate side effects of too much
beer. Karthage Point had stores of many exotic beers
and she'd made a point to sample all of them. The
few lieutenants who tried to keep up with her could

still be lying under tables. Santorini slid off his chair
onto the floor before she'd left the bar.

What woke her? Looking around her small quarters, she saw that her message queue was blinking,
patiently holding waiting messages. None were high
priority; none would have sounded an alarm. Her
tongue felt as if someone had danced upon it with
dirty boots; perhaps she should get up and try to
work off the alcohol.

Sitting up, she groaned. Her altered physiology tol-
erated higher dosages of chemicals, both natural and
unnatural, but she still suffered consequences. On the
natural side, she could pump adrenaline for longer
periods, showing endurance beyond what anyone
might expect. She could also drink more alcohol, take
more drugs, and abuse her body in ways that might
harm or kill others. As for recovery, her body was a
binger's wet dream: She suffered only modestly from
overindulgence and her body shrugged it off more
rapidly than was natural, although she doubted that
most people would realize or mark that fact.

She could use some of that rapid recovery right
now. Opening her hygiene closet, she got a mouthful
of water and swished it around before swallowing.
Then she drank deeply and took care of basic functions. At least she hadn't vomited or urinated in her
sleep. She thanked Gaia that she'd never choked
while—

She paused. This was the first time she'd gone over
the edge while on active duty orders for the Directorate. It wasn't the first time she'd drunk on active
duty, because some of those hellholes she'd slunk
about in for Owen had required socializing, but it
was the first time she'd lost—*lost control, my ass. I
can call it whatever I want, but I still went on a binge.*
She couldn't blame circumstances, stress, or Lieutenant Santorini. She'd known, subconsciously, what she

was going to do last night after she heard the invitation come out of his mouth. She couldn't pretend she made a conscious decision, since her mind had already preordained and blessed the drinking. However, she'd stepped over one of her imaginary lines. *I wasn't going to lose control again, not on reservist duty.*

She looked at her reflection on the back of the hygiene closet. Her face was filling out; she'd gained back a little weight since her last N-space drop. Her dark eyes looked liquid and tortured. There was no accusation in them, only pain and knowledge.

She ran her fingers through her tousled curls and they behaved themselves, as always, but her scalp still prickled. Those little nerves of intuition had woken her. She looked at her message queue. The last message had no sender. Hesitantly she opened it, finding only text.

"Colonel Icelos is in danger."

She hadn't had time to speak with Colonel Icelos privately. No one could think they had any connection at all, yet this warning displayed on her wall, sent anonymously through a military system that *should* allow tracing. The message header indicated chaotic encryption, meaning that it originated somewhere on MilNet. She swallowed hard.

"Karthage Command: Trace origin of last incoming message," she said.

UNKNOWN displayed on the wall.

Impossible. "Command: Trace insertion point."

The Karthage systems could only cycle a moment and then blink UNKNOWN.

Ariane wasn't an expert on chaotic encryption, but she knew that message could only have been generated on military equipment. Both sending and receiving equipment had to perform the same chaotic dance, a counterintuitive concept of synchronization that Cipher had once had to explain to her.

"Command: Save current message in—*cancel*!"

It was too late. The message was autoshredding, triggered by her save command. Unless all incoming messages were copied to crystal—no, there wasn't any organization that could afford that expense. The message was gone.

She chewed her lip. Someone might be probing for information. In that case, who was the target: Colonel Icelos or her?

Someone, or some group of someones, had killed twelve people, all in the chain of descending command that had processed the Ura-Guinn execution orders. Ariane visualized the list of names exactly as she'd read them, by date of death. They'd been killed *almost* in order, in the proper sequence of descending command and control. *Almost*, because Cipher's death should have been later—she was actually at the bottom of the chain, after Brandon and Ariane. Of course, there was still the possibility that Cipher's death was an incredible coincidence.

If Ariane was right and the order of death was meaningful, then Icelos was the next target. The command post controller verified the execution order before passing it to the executing crew. Had Owen warned Icelos of the danger? She assumed so. After all, they'd hurried away to have their colonel-huddle, so Owen had plenty of opportunity.

The schedule showed that Icelos worked first shift, and this was third shift, so he could be anywhere. She put through a high-priority call to his quarters, in case he was resting, but he didn't answer. An autoanswerer told her to call again during first shift, an inappropriate response to her Intelligence Directorate authorization. With that authorization and priority, the system should have told her where he was at that moment.

"Command: Show location of Colonel Icelos," she

said. Being responsible for ensuring treaty compliance, Ariane had the authority to override privacy constraints.

She gaped at the response. Military personnel couldn't block their implanted transponders in a military facility, and Karthage showed Icelos in his quarters on level 7 *as well as* in the gym on level 8, one level outward. Showing two locations simultaneously was a system malfunction of serious proportions.

Ariane smelled a trap. She was tempted to call Command Post to report a system malfunction and have them track down Icelos, but she'd have problems convincing them it was an emergency. CP wouldn't act quickly. This was something she'd have to do herself, to get a chance to catch the assassins.

She quickly pulled on her uniform and left her quarters. It was late in third shift and there was hardly anybody in the corridors to note her hurry, or her wary checking at intersections and air locks.

As a military habitat, Karthage Point was an example of functional form that didn't waste space and money on aesthetics. To be honest, it could be called butt-ugly. Its symmetric, but inexpensive, wheel shape surrounded its artificial gravity generator. All personnel quarters were on the same level, but senior officers were located against the side shields of the station wheel so they could have views. Karthage Point wasn't intended for N-space, so windows were available and their shutters could be opened under low radiation conditions. She jogged over the curved hall, using a priority override on section air locks. Usually the wall and ceiling surfaces provided news and shift orders, interspersed with scenes of natural dawn on some planet. Today the ceiling surface glowed to provide ambient lighting and the walls were dead, all because of the weapons inspection. They offered only an institutional gray surface and she almost missed the correct hallway. She turned quickly and stumbled. This hall was dead straight, compared to the curved hall she'd left. It ended at the facility commander's quarters.

Icelos didn't answer his door.

COLONEL ERIK ICELOS IS IN THE GYM AT L8-R3. VERIFIED BY TRANSPONDER SENSORS, displayed beside the door as a result to her query.

Now the Karthage systems only showed one location for Icelos. Her priority call to the officers' gym went unanswered. Every minute, this was looking more and more like a trap.

She backtracked to the last manual tube, not wasting the time to get into an elevator and strap in for a slow trip between levels. By the time she'd climbed the ladders and gone through two air locks, however, she might have spent the same amount of time.

Level 8 was close to the outer circumference of the wheel, but was still pressurized and heated for full life support. It contained large facilities such as gyms and hydroponic farms. During third shift, level 8 was eerily quiet.

That familiar area on her scalp still prickled—she had no other word for that uncomfortable sensation. Looking carefully about as she walked, she saw nothing to alarm her. She double-checked the environmental lights above the side hallway air lock, identified with a large marquee that said AIR LOCK 8D-A. Status displayed green.

She stepped silently down the straight lateral hall toward the gym. The environmental systems showed green on both locker rooms she passed, as well as over the gym door. She hesitated.

A tiny sparkle on the edges of the door caught her attention and she reached out slowly to the door. Her fingers jumped back before touching the door and getting burned. Frost. Deep space cold.

She whirled and jogged, breathing hard, to the air lock at the end of the lateral hall. Why did the environmental status lights continue to show green? Something was seriously wrong with the sensor systems on Karthage Point. This time, she didn't use a priority override on the air-lock doors. After she cycled safely through, she instinctively raised her hand to punch the emergency alarm that would notify the Karthage Command Post and everyone else on the habitat.

She stopped, her hand in midair. She could also declare an emergency verbally, but she chewed her lip as she reconsidered the ramifications of notifying everyone, particularly Security Force, at this point.

Icelos might already be dead inside the gym, but if he wasn't, she could get to him faster than Security Force. The Karthage systems were severely impaired, possibly sabotaged, and her emergency call wouldn't change the situation. Command Post probably couldn't fix this malfunction any better than she could.

Then she had to consider the resulting investigation. The SF, following their protocols, would keep her away from the records and physical evidence. To get access, she'd have to appeal up her chain of command, and by then, all clues to the assassins would be lost.

Instead of initiating an alarm, as regulations demanded, she opened the emergency locker and pulled out a suit. This was a light-duty emergency suit, designed to adjust to many sizes and able to withstand extreme environments for no more than two hours.

"Command: Visual response only. Karthage Query: List all personnel in the officers' gym and locker rooms." Maintaining a calm smooth tone was difficult while she struggled into the suit. She felt it squirm as it shortened and tightened to fit her legs.

The gym and locker rooms should be the only areas currently at risk. She straightened, holding the suit shoulders and arms about her waist, as she looked at the two-line response displayed on the wall.

OFFICER'S GYM: COLONEL ERIK ICELOS, FACILITY COMMANDER was on the top line. The second line chilled her. MALE LOCKER ROOM: ISRID PARMET, VISITOR [UNCLEARED].

Three possibilities: Parmet had killed Icelos and was waiting for her, Parmet was in this section for some sort of skullduggery, or coincidentally, Parmet was preparing to exercise before the first baseline inspection. She discounted the last option immediately—at this point, she wouldn't accept coincidences.

Meanwhile, as she dithered, one or both men were dying.

She sealed her suit and checked the fit. She had good oxygen supply to the soft hood. She grabbed two more suits and the environmental slate from the locker, and cycled back through the air lock. Using her authorization code, she put a warning lock on the air lock doors. This warning lock would display in CP on their status boards.

The suits were uncomfortably heavy across her shoulder, but she needed her hands free to operate the slate, specialized for monitoring environmental and life support. The emergency suit was cheap and disposable, meaning it didn't have any sensors or displays of its own. She walked back down the hallway toward the gym, noting that the oxygen percentage was low. When she first entered the hallway, she hadn't been suspicious enough to worry about her shortness of breath.

CP would eventually notice the opening of the locker and the use of the slate, as well as the warning lock she'd put on air lock 8D-A. The environmental suit supported one emergency channel of communications and she tested it. No good. Were the MilNet nodes disabled?

Icelos was higher priority than Parmet. Not knowing what waited for her on the other side, she grabbed a handhold as she opened the door. There was no decompression, so she stepped to the threshold. The slate's alarm went off in her hand, vibrating as well as flashing red dots.

It felt surreal to look up at the status displayed above the door—calm green—then to look down at the slate and see blinking lights and the text WARNING! OXYGEN CONTENT INADEQUATE! TEMPERATURE DANGEROUSLY LOW! DO NOT EXPOSE SKIN! Readings from the sensors in the slate began to scroll down the right side.

At least the suits were equipped with shrink-to-fit gloves, so she hastily saved the slate's data with a single action of her thumb. Still standing at the threshold, she reached around to flip the emergency disablement switch before stepping all the way into the gym.

The door closed behind her anyway.

She whirled, her breath starting to come faster. She'd toggled the mechanical disablement switch, yet the door had closed. She was beginning to feel persecuted, and those feelings became overwhelming as the lights dimmed and a text message formed on the back of the door.

HOW CAN YOU HANDLE THE GUILT, ARI? SOON YOU'LL HAVE NO TROUBLE SLEEPING. . . .

Her eyes widened and her heart pounded. She felt the adrenaline pouring into her bloodstream as her enhanced metabolic chemistry kicked in for fight or flight—whatever it would take to save her ass.

She turned side to side, looking about the gym through her faceplate. In the dim light, she saw Icelos crumpled on the floor near one of the far weight machines. The bright text message moved around the blank walls of the gym, keeping pace with her. In the dark room the moving message cast strange shadows, making the exercise equipment look like primitive torture devices. *How can I be tracked if the MilNet nodes are down?* complained the back of her mind, and she squashed analysis for later—she couldn't afford the distraction. .

The slate was vibrating again, demanding attention. She looked down to read the message, which kept repeating.

MAJOR KEDROS, PLEASE ACKNOWLEDGE VIA HANDHELD. CP UNABLE TO ACCESS SYSTEMS FOR SECTION 8D.

No kidding. But now she knew that some part of MilNet was operating in her favor. Reassured somebody in CP had realized her situation, she pressed the ACKNOWLEDGE key. Being able to communicate gave her more confidence, although CP was helpless at this moment. She was beginning to regret her decision to not call an emergency and roust the entire station.

Icelos looked as though he'd fallen from the bench at the weight machine. His body was curled, his eyes were closed and crusted with ice, and his exposed skin looked rosy. Kneeling beside him, Ariane keyed the slate to perform an emergency query of body functions from his implants. The slate pronounced him dead. She forwarded all her data to CP but didn't know whether, or when, they'd receive it.

She stood up and reset the slate to display environmental readings. Frost sparkled on every metal surface that could cool quickly and grab moisture from the air. This end of the gym was against the outside shields. How long had Icelos been here? He wasn't wearing exercise gear.

The slate started going crazy, vibrating and blinking for attention. CP couldn't do anything for her, but they still wanted status. They'd have to wait. Unexpectedly, the darker side of the dead man's face suddenly lit up, then fell into shadow. The cycle of light and shadow occurred again.

Turning, she saw a blinking display that eerily mimicked the countdown that displayed on Naga consoles after a TD weapon was released, armed, and targeted. Ariane had seen this display countless times via simulator and once in real life. She had less than five minutes before—before what?

Carrying the two suits was wearing her down. She dropped one beside Icelos. He wasn't going to need it and she was sure this countdown was *meaningful*. Something was going to happen when the count-down hit zero.

Looking left and right through the exercise equipment, she saw no one else. She hoped the Karthage systems were working correctly when they identified the two men in this area. She decided to enter the male locker room from the corridor rather than from the gym. Would the gym door open to let her out? She held her breath. Surprisingly, it worked. *So why'd you physically disable the manual override—unless you're just fucking with me?* She wished she could get face-to-face with this assassin.

The oxygen level in the corridor had dropped lower than when she'd taken her original readings. Someone had cleverly sabotaged the air mixture, either physically or through remote system control. Ariane noticed that the irritating text message followed her along the corridor wall, while the countdown display did not.

The male locker room door opened for her and she tried the manual disablement switch again. This one worked. *Interesting. Perhaps I stumbled over the setup for Icelos's murder.* She filed that point away for later thought. The oxygen levels and temperature here had dropped lower than the corridor, but they weren't lethal yet.

It was strange how locker rooms seemed to be the same wherever she went, for whatever gender they served. Regiments of lockers lined up, split by aisles of shiny floor with benches. Parmet was sitting peacefully on the floor next to the bench in the fourth aisle. She wasn't able to access Terran implants, if he had them, but she could see that he was breathing. He wasn't dressed for physical exercise—but then, his strange jumpsuit might work well enough. She didn't see any weapons on his body; there was no place to hide them on that skintight suit. She doubted he'd murdered Colonel Icelos; after all, Parmet should be smart enough not to be caught in his own trap.

She put the suit hood on him to give him oxygen. It wasn't going to seal tightly against his civilian clothes, but it was good enough. She saw his eyes flutter as she shook his shoulder. To get him out of section 8D, he'd have to be conscious and helping.

Parmet's eyes narrowed as he tried to focus on her. He might not recognize her through the faceplate, but she hoped he realized this was an emergency. Then she saw his eyes focus above and beyond her head.

She turned around and cursed, with no one to hear her inventive blue language. The wall still displayed the text message. Above the lockers was the insidious accusation, displayed for the enemy state prince to read.

HOW CAN YOU HANDLE THE GUILT, ARI? SOON YOU'LL HAVE NO TROUBLE SLEEPING. . . .

Parmet wouldn't know about the countdown, so she tried to make a universal gesture for hurry-up-or-we'll-soon-be-dead. He looked confused and she pulled him to his feet.

With her help, Parmet was able to stagger to the open locker room door. He seemed to be doing better with every step as they got into the corridor. By the time they reached air lock 8D-A, he barely leaned on her. He watched the message wrap itself around the walls and follow them to the air lock, where it began to blink in front of them.

HOW CAN YOU HANDLE THE GUILT, ARI? SOON YOU'LL HAVE NO TROUBLE SLEEPING. . . .

Ariane took a deep breath, trying to suppress the dread that sat in the pit of her stomach. The status lights above the air lock mocked her, still showing green for atmosphere, power, etc. Air locks had redundant power feeds, with both a manual and a computerized interface to their powered operation. If the air lock had no power, it could still be operated from outside using a crude crank that was provided in panels near the doors. That is, if the crank was still there. . . .

The failure of the manual override at the gym door meant that a saboteur was *on Karthage Point*. Ariane was now in the power of the saboteur—this air lock would only work if they intended her to escape.

She pressed the plate to open the air lock. Cycle indicators began to flash and it started to open. To satisfy her curiosity, she pulled open the emergency panel. The crank was still there. So only Icelos was supposed to die today? Was Ariane being saved for some later disaster? She turned her head to see Parmet watching her.

The priority override was disabled because of the warning lock she'd issued against air lock 8D-A, so their side seemed to take forever to open. She squeezed inside the air lock as soon as she could. Parmet, now alert, sidled in behind her. She hit the panel to stop, reverse, and close the door. Both she and Parmet turned to watch the ponderous door slide toward safety. As it locked shut behind them, the emergency channel came alive inside her suit with a repeating message.

"—teams standing by. Major Kedros, please acknowledge and provide status. We have emergency teams standing—"

"Major Kedros here." She tried not to shout, but panic made her voice loud and her words clipped. "Colonel Icelos is dead. SP Parmet is injured, but ambulatory, and needs medical assistance. Send an EOD team—"

She felt the deck jerk under her feet, followed by a shudder that went through the habitat's structure in a wave. Take-hold alarms started going off, wildly shooting orange and red sparks of light about the air lock. The side to section 8D displayed warnings of rapid decompression. Her request for an Explosive Ordinance Disposal team was too late.

CHAPTER 10

[Link to ship accident] You think that Gaia, as the Higher than Higher Power, was merely invented? Let's see if *you* can avoid praying to her when *your* atmosphere is vented! Not only is she the hand that writes the DNA of all living things, she's the comforting mother that saves us from the final void of cold black space.

—*Re: Rant: Gaia-ism*, Anonymous, 2082.161 UT, indexed by *Heraclitus 8* under Conflict Imperative

"Mr. Journey, I have more important things to do than answer a custody petition from you. Perhaps your exposure ratings have gone to your head." Edones looked as slick and precise as his voice. The blue edges of his uniform contrasted sharply against the black.

He made Matt feel rumpled and unwashed, although the hygiene facilities in his protective custody "quarters" were adequate. Any place that felt temporary, however, also made him feel incomplete. That went double for any place that had to pretend it wasn't a prison. It threw off his rhythm, his schedules, and his habits. At least the LEF had returned the slate he'd been carrying when they stunned him.

"You could have denied my petition outright,"

said Matt. *But you came here in person, because you'd like to make Ari more indebted to you, wouldn't you?* He wanted to punch the perfectly groomed Edones in the middle of his mildly pleasant face, but that was a private fantasy. *Someday I'll do it, but right now I need you.*

Edones didn't answer. He turned and nodded at the man who stepped into the room behind him. This man was in a black and blue uniform also, but the regalia on his chest looked wildly different from Edones's set of ribbons. The other man had a precisely clipped mustache and was of indeterminate age. His light brown hair, cut in military fashion, ended in razor-sharp delineations against his neck. He carried a large slate, almost larger than his hand, which he held in front of him as he walked the perimeter of the room.

Matt watched silently. He'd studied AFCAW officer specialties and rank, mostly to understand Ariane's place in the military food chain, but not enlisted rank. This man had six light blue stripes on his arm and Matt didn't know whether the designation was crewman, specialist, technician, or sergeant. He'd heard all those titles, usually on v-plays.

The enlisted man handed the slate to Edones, who nodded pleasantly and dismissed him.

"We don't have to worry about being recorded," said Edones, once the two of them were alone.

"You've turned off all the ComNet nodes?" Matt doubted the military, and Edones in particular, would have that power.

"I didn't say that." Edones's voice was smooth, using that superior tone that made Matt's fists clench. "We can call it *authorized military requisition of data,* if you wish. You needn't worry about ever finding this conversation indexed in the public domain."

Edones had more authority than Matt expected. This both relieved and worried him.

"Mr. Journey, you've got five minutes of my attention." Edones sat down across from Matt and crossed his legs. "After that, I'll walk out and formally deny your petition."

"I asked Nestor to look into graft within Athens Point Customs," Matt began.

Edones gave more attention to his manicure than to Matt's words. Matt gave a bare rendition of events, minus any mention of the AI that was currently residing on the *Aether's Touch*. When Matt referred to the two packages labeled CUSTOMS and KEDROS, Edones frowned, but a hangnail on his right hand had apparently distressed him. Edones was silent after Matt finished, causing him to fidget.

"Well?" Matt asked, no longer willing to wait.

"Well what? You still haven't told me why I should care to take on your custody. What did the LEF think about the packages?"

"They haven't produced any warrants yet, so I haven't turned them over," Matt said. "Perhaps they can't convince a magistrate of their significance."

"And if a magistrate doesn't think they're significant, why should I?" Edones stopped examining his fingernails and folded his hands on his knee. He looked inquiringly at Matt, his boredom evident.

"*Because* there's graft in the Athens Point Customs offices, which might extend into the LEF. It's customary, when there's such a taint, to move the case into a different jurisdiction." Matt couldn't help being exasperated by the man's obtuseness, feigned or otherwise.

"A different jurisdiction may be called for, Mr. Journey." Edones sat up straight and his words became crisp. "But you're assuming that I *care* about the fair application of civilian justice. In this case, I don't. You've called in the Armed Forces Directorate of Intelligence, yet you haven't connected this to military concerns or uniformed personnel, and this case doesn't fall under the Consortium Uniform Code of Military Justice."

Matt scowled. Edones was trying to scare him.

"Ari might be in danger; we should send her a warning," Matt shot back.

"Impossible."

"There's no need to keep her location from *me*."

"Mr. Journey, what hubris! Major Kedros's orders are always classified. We're not trying to hide her whereabouts from *you* specifically."

"And why are her orders always classified?" Matt demanded. "Look, she might be in danger."

"Why would you think that Mr. Expedition's murder has anything to do with Major Kedros?"

Either Edones was confident that Ari's background would hold together under any scrutiny, or Nestor had been off track in suspecting Ari's records weren't authentic. Matt had belittled Nestor's "shadow" comments, but the seeds of doubt had been planted, valid or not. Matt tried to regroup his thoughts.

"If Ari's undercover, Nestor might have interested someone else in her activities," Matt said.

"She's not covert, in case you think I'm being insensitive. She's on active duty assignment to a military facility, supporting the new TD weapon treaty that we've signed with the Terrans. Why would she be at risk?"

Edones's tone and smile seemed genuine and Matt heard the ring of truth. Growing up on a generational ship didn't make him immune to politics, and Matt had still learned to read people. But something in Edones's answer was a little off; either Edones was playing loose with the truth, or he was holding something back.

"This crime probably has nothing to do with you

or Major Kedros. Your friend was dealing with a whole different class of people than you're familiar with," added Edones when Matt didn't respond. "Did you know he was dealing with illicit ruleset distributors?"

Great bullshit, Nestor! What did you foist upon my ship? To stay safely within the law, Matt should turn the AI harbored on the *Aether's Touch* over to the authorities. They'd dissect it, and after their examination, testing, and backward engineering of rulesets, there was no guarantee the AI would be the same. But if any of Nestor's odd personality still existed, it was codified within that AI, and Matt's long friendship with Nestor mandated that he protect the AI. He couldn't turn it over.

Matt changed tactics. He needed to get out of here, without calling undue attention to Nestor's activities. He'd hoped that making appeals based upon Ari would move Edones, but apparently not.

"What about the strange remote I caught? I think the Minoans are interested in G-145." Matt pointed his slate and displayed a diagram of the alien ruins on the wall. The diagram was generated by combining hyperspectral sensor data with the ground-penetrating radar surveys done with telebots. "This is what we think is under the surface of the Priamos moon."

"Yes, that diagram's on all the news feeds and explains your exposure ratings. But the Minoans won't care." Edones shook his head. "As someone who's actually *met* Minoans, I don't think they're interested in ancient ruins. And they wouldn't give a flick of their Great Bull's tail about you or your friend Nestor or Ari—or me—because they're not interested in individuals."

"I disagree. What if we find ancient technology in G-145?"

"So what if we do? Why should the Minoans care? More importantly, why should I care? You've got two minutes, Mr. Journey."

"Three reasons why: because my claim slice contains technology that could release mankind from dependence upon Minoans; because the bidder's library containing that claim data was under Nestor's control and could now be shut down; and because *I* control the leases for any research and development of that technology."

"Plenty of references to some grand sort of technology; where's your proof?" Edones raised his eyebrows with a doubtful, patronizing air.

Matt displayed shots he'd saved on his slate. On the wall, three large view ports opened and showed the artifact at different ranges. One view was at a distance that showed the complete cylindrical shape that narrowed like a cone at one end. The second was closer and from a different angle; the last was a close-up taken by the bot, showing symbols and surface characteristics.

"What is that?" Edones's eyes narrowed.

"Something that was obviously created and placed by a space-faring civilization. Something that behaves strangely like a Minoan time buoy, at least physically. Something *our* scientists and engineers could learn much from, right?"

The smile on Edones's face finally faltered. "Why isn't this all over the feeds and public forums?"

"Because I buried *this* data. Finding it requires too much analysis for the empty heads on the feeds, but plenty of others have figured it out." Matt thrust his slate toward Edones. "Take a look at the bids coming in and the backgrounds I've uncovered on some of the bidders. There are AFCAW contractors and companies fronting for *Terran* interests. Here's a former

Terran military contractor—probably still doing business with them. Oh, and look at this! Here's a company that's contracted to do black projects for your Directorate of Intelligence. Does this have enough *military relevance* for you now?"

Matt smiled as Edones took the slate and studied it, taking his time to scroll through the entries. Several minutes passed and Matt knew he'd found a soft spot. It was time for good old blackmail.

"What if, in my ignorance, I accidentally gave all the G-145 intellectual material to the *Terrans*? Strange things can happen under free enterprise," Matt said.

Edones sighed and put the slate on his knee. His blue eyes were unreadable. "What do you want from me, Mr. Journey?"

"I want out of the Athens Point jurisdiction, I want you to help me find Nestor's killer, and I want to talk to Ari."

They stared at each other in challenge for a moment. Edones was the first to break his gaze. He looked around the room and shrugged. "Depending upon what *I* get out of this, I can offer you two out of the three. But I doubt you'll find AFCAW custody as comfortable as this."

CP never answered her. Ariane tied off her suit to a grab bar, while Parmet put on the rest of his suit and did the same. They watched the decompressed side of air lock 8D-A. Ariane whispered an appeal to Gaia, praying that Karthage hadn't been built by the lowest bidder. Internal air locks rarely experienced these conditions, but so far, their pressure held as she felt the deck shudder.

They watched the habitat side of air lock 8D-A blink warnings. It was now locked and disabled as Karthage Point tried to protect its inhabitants from decompression. Karthage CP now made announcements over the emergency channel that they could hear through their suits.

"All personnel take decompression precautions. Repeat—all personnel prepare for possible decompression. Levels seven, eight, and nine, begin lockdown procedures. Repeat, levels seven, eight, and nine, begin lockdown."

If lockdowns were only directed to levels on either side of 8, perhaps the damage was confined to level 8. Glancing out the small portal to the side with habitat air, she saw the suited emergency team scampering to take hold. There was no way they'd be opening air lock 8D-A any time soon.

As the decompression warnings repeated, the shuddering continued with sharp deep protests from the station structure that she felt through her hands and feet. This probably resulted from torsional twisting around Karthage Point's central axis—not good. Only overengineering and the *careful* application of positional thrusters could hold Karthage together now.

"Levels six through ten, begin lockdown. Repeat—" CP had extended the lockdown, not an encouraging sign.

She exchanged a glance with Parmet. He took hold of the bar nearest her, and she could see his green eyes through the faceplate of the hood. They were calm, but she also saw calculated worry. Of course, he could project anything he wanted. She looked away and checked the air lock display. Their pressure was still holding.

"Gravity generator is going off-line, prepare for thruster maneuvers. Warning—gravity generator is—"

CP was plowing through their checklists as fast as possible to prevent the station from tumbling itself apart. Ships with gravity generators usually took

them off-line in this manner near gravity wells, such
as large planets and suns, for structural safety. Karthage Point wasn't designed for the forces that CP
was intending to apply, and they were doing everything they could to widen their safety margin.

Ariane closed her eyes as she felt the gravity generator go off-line. She felt nausea building from the
confusing forces upon her body. One of the Hellas
Prime–Hellas Daughter stabilization points provided
a quasi-periodic "orbit" for Karthage Point. Keeping
within this stable, bounded area required only mod-
est station keeping. However, the explosion had
pushed them off their stabilizing orbit, and parts of
Karthage were accelerating at different rates than
other parts. Any elementary school child knew what
that meant. *Tumbling.* The nightmare for all space
habitats: when the invisible forces of gravity, mass,
and momentum started tearing them apart. She felt
the mindless shrieking of the habitat through the
handhold and bulkheads as Command Post applied
stabilizing thrusters in small increments.

She jumped when Parmet heavily tapped her
shoulder. Opening her eyes, she saw him pointing to
the status above the air lock door to decompressed
section 8D. It was blinking orange and the seal was
leaking, perhaps owing to station contortions.

"CP, this is Major Kedros with SP Parmet. Air lock
eight-delta-alpha's seal is going and we're only
equipped with emergency suits."

It didn't hurt to remind CP about their situation.
She made sure to mention Parmet; it wasn't going to
look good for AFCAW to lose a dignitary, a Terran
state prince, no less, on the first baseline treaty inspection.

There wasn't an immediate response. She could
imagine the input, the messages, and the status displays the controllers inside CP were handling.

"Acknowledged, Major Kedros." Another pause. Then predictably, the same harried voice asked: "What's your estimated air supply, Major?"

She looked up at the air lock's status and decided not to include it in her estimate. She considered only the suits, which had about two UT hours of air for a midweight male.

"CP, we have approximately one and a half hours left." She gave them her shortest estimate.

"Acknowledged. You'll get top priority after stabilization. Uh—no time frame on that yet." CP went silent.

That's not good. She double-checked the status of the air lock. The leak was slow. She had a choice and she made it quickly, unsealing the hood of her suit and shutting down the air supply. The creaking of the station structure was loud and made her want to grind her teeth. She tightened her tether and made herself take slow breaths.

After significant hesitation, Parmet followed her actions.

"What if the door blows?" he asked, once his face was uncovered.

"We stay ready to seal up as fast as we can. This way, we use the air inside the air lock while we have it, since there's no guarantee they'll lift the lockdown soon." She didn't bother to tell him that if the air lock blew, the cheap emergency suits couldn't protect them from hard vacuum for long.

She studied the environmental slate, hoping to discourage his conversation. The slate tried to estimate how much oxygen they had left in the air lock, using data from the door and its own sensors. Of course, the slate didn't account for her enhanced metabolism, but she wasn't about to download her oxygen use from her implant in front of Parmet.

Under normal conditions and conservative esti-

mates, two adults could stay conscious up to four
hours inside the air lock. However, these weren't
normal conditions. Since the seal was leaking air to
the decompressed part of the station, the slate recom-
mended that they use suit resources. She jabbed at
the slate, changing the conditions and asking for
recalculation.

"We might have enough oxygen in this air lock for
an hour, provided the leak doesn't get worse." She
kept her eyes on the slate to avoid meeting Parmet's
gaze. "Go back onto suit air if you feel any problems breathing."

They drifted against the wall where they were teth-
ered, feeling the movement lightly applied by station
thrusters. Both of them watched the status displayed
over the air lock. The leak didn't get worse, but it
didn't get better either.

Ariane decided not to monitor the slate. She
thought hovering over the decreasing numbers might
only make her nervous, but she hadn't thought she'd
fall asleep. She edged into a dream, an early memory
from the war. Waiting in a dark air lock for the
enemy to attempt boarding their damaged ship,
she'd gripped her weapon so tightly that her fingers
cramped. Of course, they hadn't been as damaged as
the enemy originally thought, but her friend Erin had
still died—

She started awake when the slate began beeping.
Lights were still on. She and the slate floated on tethers; CP hadn't restored gravity. She felt short of
breath, like when she'd gone on a mountain climb
with Brandon.

"Get onto suit air and seal up," she said to Parmet.

"You're not who you should be." He didn't look
as though he was short of breath.

"Excuse me?" She looked at Parmet in confusion.
He moved closer and she backed away, pulling her-

self higher with the handhold. She glanced up at the ubiquitous MilNet cam-eye and wondered whether it worked.

"You're not who you profess to be, are you, Major? You're certainly not the sum of your records." He stopped moving and looked her over with calculation.

She'd lived enough years with Owen's handiwork to have confidence in her established identity. Parmet was only trying to frighten her, showing he'd done background investigations.

"Well, who is?" She snorted. "Right now, I'm hoping to get back to my normal life, boring as it may sound. I'm suiting up."

She panted as she turned on the air in her suit and sealed it. Parmet began doing the same, but he wasn't panting. Perhaps he'd attained some sort of control over autonomous functions such as breathing and heartbeat with his *somaural* training.

Once they were suited up, their only communication mode was the emergency channel, but they both kept silent. Ariane watched him move about, getting as comfortable as possible. When she saw his arms fold and his eyes close, she thought he was submerging into a trance. Perhaps he could slow down his oxygen consumption.

They waited.

"Do you know your name? Tell me your name, rank, and service number."

The questions pestered her. She had a whopping headache and she wanted to sleep.

"Ari," she mumbled, opening her eyes. She saw a blurred male face above her.

"That's good," he prompted. "Focus. Let's have your *full* name, rank, and service number."

No! She tried to sit up, but someone held her

down. No one could know about Captain Karen Ahrilan Argyris, who had the service number of D2-
12-2399.

Several voices were having a rapid conversation
above her.

"We have to scan for brain damage and evaluate
radiation effects."

"Motor skills look good."

"Squadron commander wants her debriefed immediately. The colonel is dead—"

"Emergency medical treatment takes precedent."

"Squadron commander thinks she's drunk. Can
you—"

"I can only read her implant for emergency data,
because she's Reserve. Unless we have her signed
release on file?"

"I have to check."

"She's not drunk."

The last voice, cool and distinct, washed over her
body and chilled her. *State Prince Parmet.*

"I'm fine." Ariane focused on the technician leaning over her. Her vision sharpened. His name tag
read STALL. On his collar, he carried the rank of senior
technician. "Ariane E. Kedros, Major." She had a common name for the Autonomist Worlds, easy to remember, but she had to struggle to remember her service
number. "Alpha-seven-one-two-six-four-seven-two."

"Good, Major. Can I access your implant for blood-
gas readings?" He held out a slate.

"Yes." She had a swarm of medical and security
personnel looming over her. A slate was shoved at
her face and she gave them her approval, using
voiceprint.

The gravity generator was back online and she no
longer wore the emergency suit. She was lying on a
gurney near the interior side of air lock 8D-A. Turning her head, she could see through the portal to

the other side, where a suited technician was using metallo-ceramic sealant foam. That meant the air lock wasn't usable, or passable, anymore. They were probably strengthening the air lock and radiation shielding from the unpressurized side as well.

Ariane looked the other way and saw SP Parmet standing to the side, now shadowed by his assistant and the funny interpreter. Nathaniel Wolf Kim and Dr. Istaga. *Not funny— dangerous.* The fog in her head was lifting. Feeling vulnerable, she sat up, this time helped by a technician.

Technician Stall was frowning at his slate. "Your blood gas readings look good, Major, but I still need to do a full-body scan."

"Can that wait?"

This question came from an impatient captain behind the medical technicians. Ariane couldn't remember his name. He wore a security emblem and was flanked by a female sergeant in full exoskeleton and armor, with assault rifle. There were six other SF behind the sergeant, also armed to the teeth.

Ariane's eyebrows rose. Were they expecting boarders? A hostage situation? Of course, she was the only one that had a good idea of what happened. The explosion might have destroyed much of the physical evidence, including Icelos's body. Her input was going to be vital to the SF.

"What if I come by for scans in an hour or two, after a debriefing?" she asked Stall. She nodded at the security officer, Captain Rayiz. She now remembered that he was the commander of the SF Squadron. He reported—had reported directly to Colonel Icelos.

Stall reluctantly agreed to later scans after Ariane demonstrated that she could stand and walk without help. A stone-faced Rayiz provided a detail to escort the Terran visitors back to their quarters, where they were to stay until told otherwise. State Prince Parmet was apparently unharmed.

Rayiz told Ariane to follow him and they marched off. She hoped that the four SFs flanking and following her were for protection. The hissing, squeaking, muscle-suited escort dwarfed both her and Rayiz. She followed Rayiz down two levels and into the Security Force Operations Center. Their escort took up positions outside the center. Inside, Lieutenant Colonel Jacinthe Voyage stood with her back to the door, looking at damage reports. She turned around and gave Ariane an edgy smile that didn't hide her satisfaction.

"What happened, Kedros? Did Colonel Icelos botch your sabotage attempt?" she asked.

CHAPTER 11

If an item listed in Section I of this Protocol is lost or destroyed as a result of an accident, the possessing Party shall notify the other Party within 48 UT hours, as required in paragraph 5(e) of Article II of the Treaty, that the item has been eliminated. In such a case, the other Party shall have the right to conduct an inspection of the specific point at which the accident occurred to provide confidence that the item has been eliminated.

—*Section V, Loss or Accidental Destruction, in Elimination Protocol attached to the Mobile Temporal Distortion (TD) Weapon Treaty, 2105.164.10.22 UT, indexed by Heraclitus 8 under Flux and Conflict Imperatives*

Isrid was silent as he was escorted back to quarters, but Nathan kept a running commentary on inept Autonomist security and inadequate habitat design, both of which had caused risk to Terran dignitaries, most particularly their state prince. His diatribe amused Isrid, even if it was only for the benefit of their escort team and the ubiquitous AFCAW MilNet nodes. Dr. Istaga was quiet.

Maria met them at the door to Isrid's suite, clearly projecting agitation.

"SP, are you all right?" Her face was pale and her voice was anxious and appropriate for any observers, but the tiny tight gesture as she palmed open the door said, *We've been compromised*. Something beyond the recent explosion had disturbed her.

"Their medical people checked me out. I was groggy, but they claimed I got off without permanent damage." Isrid turned as if to include Nathan and Istaga in the conversation, but he was checking to ensure that they hadn't reacted to Maria's message. Neither Nathan nor Istaga seemed able to project somaurally, but they would read it well enough.

Later. Isrid needed a secure room for face-to-face discussions. He could ask the Autonomists for one, but what would they infer from such a request? Major Kedros's request for an EOD team meant she suspected sabotage or planted explosives, and Isrid didn't want his inspection team put on the list of suspects by immediately calling for a private meeting. Of course, he had equipment to jam their MilNet node-to-node comm, but he didn't want to expose classified Terran capabilities. On an inspiration, he turned to the most senior person in their over-equipped, heavily armed escort.

"I'd like to have my own doctor examine me, but under a privacy shield," he said to the escort.

Luckily, the Autonomists had a great respect for personal privacy. The big brute of a man nodded, turned to the opposite hall wall, and opened a channel to Command Post. Everyone watched as a CP controller, some young female lieutenant, authorized the privacy shield for an hour and returned them a code.

Isrid had the only medical doctor on the team come to his quarters, where he invoked the privacy shield. The woman gave him a perfunctory check, then left. Isrid called in Nathan and Maria. They still had three-quarters of an hour left on the privacy shield, but he also pulled out the classified jammer and activated it, just in case.

"The Autonomists have devised a way to hide some of their warheads, under the cover of destruction," Nathan said. "They're risking the treaty, maybe Pax Minoica itself."

Nathan had gone for the most sinister, and least likely, explanation. Not that this same suspicion hadn't immediately popped into Isrid's mind, but he'd already discounted the possibility.

"I had the benefit of listening to their emergency channel during the whole episode," Isrid said. "The explosives targeted section eight-D. It's hard to damage TD warheads, and given how far their warhead storage is from section eight-D, I doubt they could make that claim stick. Besides, the treaty allows us to investigate losses."

"We've got a bigger problem than the treaty—"

"I know we've been compromised." Isrid cut off Maria's words. "I received a text message, which I supposed to be from Andre, to meet him in the men's locker room. It was an odd request, but the message was sent on the appropriate channel and decrypted correctly with our keys. I was lured there by someone using *our own intelligence keys*."

"That's not all." Maria was pale. "Our sleeper agent was given orders to physically disable items on this station, perhaps to support externally placed explosives. Our own intelligence network was used to execute this sabotage."

Isrid realized the ramifications of her words before Nathan did.

"You exposed our sleeper?" Nathan still hoped to climb over Maria in the political pecking order and he didn't see the bigger picture.

"No, Nathan. I hadn't sent the activation code yet. The sleeper contacted *me* after the explosion occurred." Maria's voice was steady and calm, but her body screamed, *You idiot!*

Nathan's eyes widened.

"How much of our intelligence network is compromised?" Isrid asked quietly.

"The whole Hellas system could be exposed. The quietest recourse we have is to distribute new keys and channel protocols in face-to-face meetings. We'd repeat agent vetting at each meeting and change out equipment."

"That would take forever," Nathan said.

Maria nodded. "I said that was the *quietest* method we had. While it might not tip AFCAW intelligence to our problem, it's not the *fastest* action we could take."

"It also means that our problem, whether it be a double agent or compromised equipment, has time to adjust and infiltrate deeper," Isrid said.

"But the Hellas system is the command center of AFCAW. We need operatives—"

A knock at the door interrupted Nathan. He and Maria looked puzzled until Isrid said, "The privacy shield. We can't get any messages through their nodes."

Nathan scowled and got up to physically open the door. Dr. Istaga stood outside.

"Sorry to disturb you, SP Parmet, but they couldn't access you through the privacy shield. There's been a stationwide announcement. A Minoan ship is inbound to Karthage Point."

Nathan went white. Isrid acknowledged the message and thanked Istaga. Maria withdrew, melting into her chair. She became so still that Isrid could barely see her breathe.

"Well, that decides it," Isrid said, once Istaga left. "I'm shutting down the whole Hellas system."

"How'd the Minoans get the news of the explosion so fast?" Nathan's lip lifted. "If AFCAW has so many leaks that—"

"It doesn't matter," Isrid said. "We can't take the

chance of being implicated in the station sabotage because the Minoans will consider that as noncompliance with the treaty. It's safest for all agents to cease operations. Our intelligence network within and around Hellas will go dead. The sleeper, if implicated, won't be able to lead the trail to us."

"But the time and effort it'll take to restart everything. The *cost*." Nathan sounded aghast, then flinched at the sharp look that Isrid gave him.

"Send out the command," Isrid said.

Nathan bowed his head and left to shut down their network.

"It's lucky you were with this team, SP," Maria said softly from her chair. "Only a state prince has the authority to shut down intelligence operations over a whole system."

Luck. Coincidence. Yes, there was a hell of a lot of *that* going around, particularly involving Major Kedros. She had operational experience beyond what her records showed, but he expected falsified records for an intelligence officer. He could see she anticipated physical sabotage at the air lock, but didn't find any. Had she already found the disablements mentioned by Maria? In that case, AFCAW intelligence already suspected a physical agent on the station. Then there was that floating message, as if this whole thing had been a test, or a punishment, for Major Kedros. This seemed *personal*, centered on her.

"If it's necessary, we'll need to divert Minoan attention." *Or divert their punishment*. He spoke quickly, having little time left under the privacy shield. "This seems to hinge on Major Kedros and we need to find out how the saboteurs know her. If we find that link, we might need to implicate her to take Minoan heat off us."

"I'll get whatever you need, SP." Maria smiled and turned back to her equipment. She loved research, digging through data and hoping for gems. And usually, she was good at it.

"What?" The thought that she might be accused of the sabotage had never occurred to Ariane.

Jacinthe smirked. "Such an *obvious* solution. You killed Icelos and planted explosives to obscure the evidence."

"That's a *ludicrous* solution." Ariane steadily met Jacinthe's gaze. "I don't have the background to get past system security and cut off station environmental control. Once you retrieve the body, you'll find Icelos was dead before I arrived at the gym. You'll also find physical evidence that this couldn't have been done without inside—"

"Sure, divert us into an audit of our own security. Or a hopeless search for a bulkhead in the wreckage." A hint of a sneer was on Jacinthe's thin lips. "Meanwhile, we're distracted from looking into you or your background."

Who's trying to divert whom, Colonel? Ariane mentally went through the chain of command that kept the cogs and gears of Karthage Point turning. Did command of the station revert to Jacinthe, as commander of the operational squadron?

Jacinthe turned to Captain Rayiz. "No word yet on who'll replace Colonel Icelos. I spoke with the wing commander. She'll wait on Hellas Daughter for the new facility commander. In the meantime, detain Major Kedros for questioning and I'll get my pilots out to oversee cleanup operations."

Captain Rayiz looked puzzled and intimidated. He opened his mouth to reply, but Ariane cut in, deciding to take the brunt of Jacinthe's ire.

"Excuse me, ma'am, but command of the facility, as well as the ensuing investigation and cleanup, has passed to Captain Rayiz," Ariane said.

Rayiz was commander of the Facility Security Squadron and Jacinthe couldn't argue with the chain of command. Ariane thought she saw a flash of fear go through Jacinthe's cold eyes, and then the woman went still. It was a deep stillness, happening within a discrete moment that might not have been noticed by anyone but Ariane. In less than a second, Jacinthe's humanity came back.

"Captain." Jacinthe inclined her head toward Rayiz, accepting his authority. "What's the status, then?"

"Right." Rayiz took a deep breath and looked relieved. "I don't have need of your pilots or vehicles, Colonel Voyage, but thanks for offering. We're collecting debris and we've already found the colonel's body. Initial indications show carbon monoxide poisoning. As Major Kedros said, the time of death recorded on his implant occurred before she went through air lock eight-D-A."

Jacinthe looked sour as Ariane tried not to show her relief. Since Karthage lost MilNet nodes in section 8D, she couldn't be sure which of her movements had been recorded. Thinking back, she realized that the floating message hadn't followed them inside the air lock, so that must have been outside the saboteur's control.

"We know the infiltration of systems was done remotely," continued Rayiz. "However, someone had to *place* the shape charge on the outside of the station and there was tight coordination between its detonation and hijacking of our systems. Command Post is going through logs to try to see when, and where, our firewalls were breached. We'll need to know what Icelos, Parmet, and you, Major, were doing in that section."

Rayiz looked at Ariane for answers.

"I received a message in my quarters—" Ariane began.

"While you were still drunk off your ass," Jacinthe said in a mocking tone. She smiled as both Ariane and Rayiz looked at her. "I have reports from the Company Grade Club bartender. I should formally rebuke you for conduct unbecoming a field grade officer, and for *that*, Major, I do have authority."

"The bartender might be mistaken about the amount I drank."

"By his observation, you drank as much as two other lieutenants who were in bad enough shape to require remedy treatments. Since they're in my squadron, I can freely obtain their implant data. The bartender will vouch that when you left, you were impaired." Jacinthe cocked her head in challenge.

Ariane's eyes narrowed. She didn't want Santorini to suffer on her behalf by having to provide blood alcohol readings or having his conduct questioned. This was all part of Jacinthe's diversion.

"Perhaps then, but not later. I'll provide blood alcohol readings for the past two shifts. For the record, I'm volunteering this data and waiving privacy rights." Ariane reached down to Rayiz's desk and tapped for a keypad display.

Jacinthe looked surprised. "That's not necessary, Major."

It was already done. Ariane had tapped in her personal codes, laid her hand flat, and let near-field data exchange occur between her implant and the Karthage node in Rayiz's desk.

"See for yourself, Captain." Ariane gestured to the display on the wall behind Rayiz.

"That's within civil sobriety limits." Rayiz pointed at an entry made at the time of the explosion, stuck in the middle of the column of time-stamped numbers.

Sure, there was a hideous spike near her last drinking round at the bar. But, as Ariane knew, her body ate up the alcohol like a machine and her readings quickly stabilized.

"That doesn't—" Jacinthe was interrupted by a station-wide announcement.

"This is Command Post, calling Condition Purple. Inbound Minoan emissaries. Repeat, Condition Purple."

Purple? Who thought that one up? Ariane raised her eyebrows and exchanged glances with a tense Jacinthe and Rayiz.

"I'm betting that's our treaty oversight. The baseline inspection has to continue," Ariane said. "Let me do my job, Colonel."

Jacinthe nodded. The antagonism washed off her face, leaving it drawn. She left, asking questions of Command Post as she took long strides down the corridor. "What's their ETA? Uh-huh. They're sending a shuttle for docking?"

Ariane watched her go. She turned to discover Rayiz watching her.

"If I were you, I'd stay under Colonel Voyage's radar from now on," he said. "I don't know what she's got against you, but then, Colonel Icelos never got along with her either."

Interesting. Ariane wondered whether Icelos had also suspected that Jacinthe Voyage had *somaural* training, but Icelos hadn't had the benefit of observing a practicing master such as Parmet.

"Colonel Voyage might not want to consider the possibility that someone on this station is involved." She worded her statement carefully. It'd be better if Rayiz independently came to her same conclusions. "I think you'll find physical disablement of the gym's door and sensors, if you can recover that bulkhead."

"You think there's an anarchist here on Karthage—

trying to stop the treaty inspection? Everyone, including some of our visitors, are military personnel."
Rayiz's forehead wrinkled.

"I'd avoid using labels that make assumptions, such as 'anarchist' or 'enemy' or 'saboteur,' and you shouldn't rule out criminal motives, such as graft, bribery, and blackmail."

"You're right." Rayiz hesitated. "This seems more up your alley, being Intelligence, I mean."

Ariane smiled at his unasked question. "I can provide help if you need it. After my statement, I'd like to observe your interview with State Prince Parmet. Remember, his diplomatic immunity can't protect him from questions routinely asked of all personnel—which means you should ask me every question that you're going to ask him."

"Right. Let's get started." Rayiz began recording.

"As long as I'm free to meet the Minoan emissaries, if and when they board."

"I don't envy your job, Major. Now, please tell me what time you left your quarters. . . ."

Contrary to Rayiz's advice, she ended up butting heads with Lieutenant Colonel Voyage only thirty minutes after she recorded her statement.

Ariane checked with the maintenance squadron to ensure that the explosion hadn't damaged any of the warhead storage bays. Karthage was required, per the treaty, to open all warhead storage bays so the inspectors could view the entire contents. That was when she found out that Jacinthe was intending to immediately move several TD warheads, mounted on Naga vehicles, to Hellas Daughter.

"You can't move those warheads to Hellas Daughter," Ariane said, as soon as she caught up with Jacinthe. This was something she had to explain face-to-face.

"They're mine to move, Major." Jacinthe was in squadron ops working with her schedulers. She was too busy to waste time on antagonism, so her words were dry and clipped.

"You'll violate the TD weapons treaty."

"I've read the treaty, Major. We're allowed transit times of five days between deployment areas." Jacinthe didn't bother to look at her.

"As of ten days after the signing of the treaty, we're no longer allowed to store warheads at *production facilities*. Hellas Daughter is defined as a production facility in the Memorandum of Understanding."

Jacinthe turned to face Ariane, crossing her arms. The schedulers, a captain and a master sergeant, stopped poking their slates and stared at Ariane.

"What would you suggest we do, Major?" Jacinthe's voice was low, deceptively calm, and dangerous. "We have a mission readiness commitment of launching ten Naga vehicles, fully crewed and with warheads, within ten minutes of launch notification. The explosion left seven of our launch ports without power, so we can't meet that commitment. Our backup has always been to move mission-ready Naga vehicles to Hellas Daughter and have them stand alert from the old test launch facilities."

"You're not allowed to move the warheads through N-space for deployment, only maintenance, and there's no other legal facilities in-system," Ariane said. She knew the list of allowed deployment sites in the Memorandum of Understanding. Whoever drafted the memorandum hadn't provided the flexibility of deploying weapons anywhere else in the Hellas system. There was only Karthage Point, and Karthage had been damaged.

"Surely there's provisions in the treaty for emergencies," Jacinthe said.

"I'm sorry, Colonel, but lowered readiness isn't

considered an emergency by the people who wrote this treaty." Ariane left the rest unsaid. *Combat readiness isn't important because your weapons system is going away. Combat readiness isn't important because your unit is being deactivated in two years—yet in the meantime, you'll still be evaluated and your future careers may depend upon your readiness numbers.*

She *was* sorry. These crew members prided themselves on doing their duty, and doing it well. The Thirty-second had the best readiness numbers, for four years running, throughout the six operational squadrons in the three Naga wings. That wasn't going to happen this year.

"You'll just have to report your reduced capability and readiness to Wing Operations." She had become what she'd always despised: an illogical administrative barrier to getting the mission done. No apologies could erase that.

Her ear bug chimed with a high-priority message from Captain Rayiz. "Major Kedros, we're ready to interview the state prince."

She quickly excused herself from the silent room.

CHAPTER 12

Alexander the Great's consolidation of cultures and his introduction of eastern mathematicians to Greek society on pre-Terran Earth is a source of inspiration within the Autonomist worlds. Autonomists still revere Alexander, and it shows when they name their children (41% of Autonomists name a child Alexander/Alexandra/Alexia, compared to 19% of Terrans). The second most popular name for females is Ariadne/Ariane, from the tales of King Minos. . . .

—*Names from Our History*, Iona Sands, 2873.042.10.05 UT, indexed by *Democritus 31* under Metrics Imperative

Edones started prying apart the bars of bureaucracy that kept Matt from the evidence of Nestor's murder. Matt had to grudgingly admire Edones's cool composure. When Matt wanted to launch at any one of the many petty officials they spoke with, and choke him or her into cooperation, Edones only smiled in his bland manner and coldly tried another tack.

Ari, however, was nonnegotiable. Messaging or speaking directly to her was forbidden. Edones insisted that news of Nestor's murder would distract Ari from her mission and he wouldn't divulge her whereabouts. Matt, however, already had a vague idea of where she was assigned; her in-system call was a clue. She was still in the Hellas system and he'd backtracked her message to the point where it transferred between MilNet and ComNet. The timing could match a common data dump point used on the route toward Hellas Daughter and Karthage Point.

"There's no need to worry her about Nestor's murder, nor your situation," said Edones.

My situation? This was the closest Edones had come to admitting that Matt might be in danger.

One sticking point was whether Matt should be allowed to leave Athens Point, considering his potential as a witness. Edones pointed out to a perpetually scowling Captain Sanna that Matt arrived at the murder scene after Athens Point Security Force personnel. What information about the murder could Matt provide that hadn't already been discovered and analyzed by Sanna's own people?

Captain Sanna was their last barrier in a long list of approval authorities. He was barrel shaped and the high collar of his uniform did nothing to alleviate the impression that he had no neck. His dark curly hair and mustache were unruly, in contrast to Chief Inspector Stephanson, who sat quietly to one side.

"We'll need background on the victim that can only be provided by Mr. Journey." Sanna's complexion darkened and the scowl lines deepened, his face seeming to cave in on itself. The next words jerked their way out of his reluctant mouth. "Besides his personal knowledge of the victim, he's executor of the victim's will."

Matt expressed his surprise to Edones through raised eyebrows. This was another reason Matt wanted to get out from under the thumb of Athens Point LEF: They were controlling his incoming messages. When would they have told him this? In their own sweet time, they might have allowed him to process Nestor's estate. He wondered why they were so paranoid, so controlling, and he tried not to think about the package titled CUSTOMS sitting on his ship. Graft in the customs departments might be indicative of more corruption within Athens Point.

"Mr. Journey can remain available for questions over MilNet. He'll also leave you signed access to view the will," Edones said.

Matt shifted uncomfortably in his seat. He wasn't thrilled about letting them see Nestor's will.

"What about Mr. Journey's ship?" asked Captain Sanna.

Perhaps they were more worried about depriving the station of income than the application of justice. Sanna didn't want to be responsible for losing the fees charged for ship resources and docking.

"I'll be—" Matt stopped when he heard the emergency alarm from Edones's ear bug. It was one of those rare alarms that was audible to everyone near the receiver. It demanded immediate attention and was designed to be rude, to stop conversations.

Edones sat upright while he pressed behind his ear to turn off the alarm. Everyone in the room looked at him as he listened to the message. A frown slowly developed on his face. Anything that could get a re-action from Edones had to be serious. Edones's uniform seemed crisper, the decorations and blue edges more distinct. His rank weighed ominously upon his shoulders.

"There's problems on Karthage Point," Edones said. "Explosions. There's been decompression."

There was a moment of silent shock in the room. Habitats were engineered to withstand storage compartments blowing out; perhaps they hadn't loaded their hazardous material correctly?

"An accident?" Captain Sanna asked.

"No accident. Sabotage," Edones said.

Matt's mouth opened in surprise. An attack on a

habitat violated the Phaistos Protocol, which had established wartime codes of conduct and had been a Minoan condition for mankind entering space. Edones seemed concerned. Matt's stomach tightened with a jerk. *Ari's aboard Karthage.*

"How'd explosives get aboard, with all our sniffers?" asked Stephanson, causing Matt to jump. He'd forgotten the quiet man seated over in the corner. The inspector had a point: No one could carry explosives near street bazaars or restaurants or other public places, much less use public transportation. The ubiquitous ComNet nodes also had sensors that were extremely effective at ferreting out explosives.

"Initial reports suggest the charges were attached to the outside of the station." Edones gave Captain Sanna a level look. "Within a few minutes, you'll be going to heightened security here on Athens Point as a precaution. Civilian habitats could be at risk until we find the perpetrators."

"But—"

"I must leave immediately for Karthage, and I'll need all my personnel," Edones continued, ruthlessly overriding Sanna. "This necessitates taking Mr. Journey with me, on an AFCAW cruiser, which certainly meets your security requirements. Mr. Journey will sign over any access you need before departing."

Both Matt and Sanna raised their voices to chorus their protest. Matt was furious; he didn't want to give Sanna unlimited or unattended access to all of Nestor's records. Sanna still wanted Matt to stay.

Edones stood up and cut them off with an abrupt motion.

"Mr. Journey, Athens Point LEF can get anything they want, given the time to request specific warrants. Captain Sanna, do you really want the expense and trouble of protecting Mr. Journey from whomever and whatever?"

Matt's objections died in his throat; he swallowed hard. Edones face was unyielding, his shoulders square and purposeful. His rank and decorations glittered. Perhaps this was what Ari referred to as "command presence." Edones looked imposing, while being *both* trustworthy and dangerous. Matt's gut clenched with resistance; he wasn't about to be suckered in by Edones's personality. *So, he's got an imposing aura that he can pull out of his ass, I'll give him that.*

"I'll leave this situation in the capable hands of Master Sergeant Alex Joyce. We'll be disconnecting from Athens Point within two hours, with or without Mr. Journey. However, I think that you'll soon be too busy to worry about him."

Edones walked out.

Alarms and messages suddenly began besieging Captain Sanna. Recalls of off-duty personnel started automatically. Stephanson left quickly and *now* Captain Sanna seemed happy to sign custody of Matt over to the man with the light blue stripes who assisted Edones.

"We need to collect the remotes you disabled earlier." Matt noticed that Joyce avoided naming the Minoans directly.

Joyce kept an iron grip on Matt's elbow. He steered Matt quickly through the hive of activity within Athens Point LEF, and out to the street. The "street" was merely a wide, busy corridor with a high ceiling, but Matt sighed in relief at the feeling of freedom.

"What should I call you? Alex? Er—Joyce?"

"You don't know much about the military, do you, son?" Joyce frowned, but dropped his hold on Matt's elbow.

Matt balked at being called "son," but thought twice before criticizing the hulking man. Initially, Joyce had looked slim, only because he was tall and well proportioned. Once Matt was walking close beside him, he proved to be massive. He looked as if he could snap Matt like a dried noodle, and his serious demeanor and quiet aura of competency were intimidating.

"No, sir, I haven't had much contact with the military."

"Don't call me sir." Joyce seemed about to add something, but paused. His face looked as though it might crack into a smile, but that was obviously too painful and his serious expression returned. "Just call me Sergeant Joyce," he finished.

"Okay, Sarge."

"*Sergeant* Joyce." The warning came out in a growl.

Matt held back the "Yes, sir" with effort.

"Is this where you have the remotes hidden?" Joyce asked, glancing left and right as they approached the storage roundabout.

"Uh . . ." Matt wondered whether the hefty sergeant was going to rudely follow him into storage.

"You don't think I'll leave you alone, after the colonel charged me with your safety?" Joyce asked.

Matt couldn't do anything but gesture resignation. As they unlocked the remotes and put them into Matt's bag, he was thinking furiously. He had to have access to his data, as well as Nestor's AI, but both were locked down tight on the *Aether's Touch*.

"I have to get to my ship," Matt said as they exited storage.

"No time. The *Bright Crescent* is starting emergency disconnection and they'll wait for no one." Joyce had a firm grip on Matt's arm again and pulled him in the wrong direction.

"Look, I'm paying for life support that I won't need. I can't afford this."

Joyce didn't look convinced by Matt's financial anguish, so Matt changed his argument.

"It'll only take a moment to put the ship into storage mode. I also have to create an access door to my data. Remember, the colonel agreed to help investigate Nestor's murder, and for my side of the bargain, I'll need that back door for assigning leases to *suitable* companies."

The ring of truth, even partial truth, is always perceptible. Joyce relented. "Do it fast, because if we miss boarding . . ." His voice deepened into that scary growl again.

"Yeah, yeah." Matt threw propriety, and safety, out the door. He turned and ran. Joyce followed, but in his gait, Matt heard the awkwardness that the planet-born couldn't hide under artificial gravity. Matt hid a smile.

Joyce stuck close to him after they boarded *Aether's Touch* and Matt wondered how he was going to enable Nestor's possibly illegal AI. He decided to use text input rather than spoken commands. Sometimes speech was too slow; perhaps Joyce wouldn't follow his commands.

Matt's fingers stopped the purchase of life support from Athens Point and started putting systems into hibernation. He set up a secure channel with identity interrogation so he could access information on *Aether's Touch*. At the tail end, his fingers flying, he activated the AI for querying.

"What'd you do?" Joyce asked suspiciously. "That's not a normal access command."

"I activated a search agent. You don't expect me to use some pathetically outmoded search engine to evaluate these proposals, do you?" Once again, Matt hoped the partial truth would work. Edones's comment regarding Nestor's activities made him more anxious about the legality of this AI.

"You'll have access to Heraclitus and Democritus. We're not primitive—hey, we've got to go." The time on the wall diverted Joyce.

"I'm done. Let me grab my things." Luckily, he kept an overnight kit packed.

Matt glanced reluctantly backward at the *Aether's Touch* after final lockdown. He was paying fees for security and insurance, but even so, he didn't like leaving her unattended. He rarely left the station where she docked. Now he didn't know when he'd be back.

He followed Joyce. They had to change levels and run through the corridors to get to the *Bright Crescent* in time. The loadmaster had closed cargo and equipment holds and was about to close the passenger air locks. He waved them through frantically.

"No problem. Like I said." Matt was panting from the run.

"You're late, Mr. Journey. Another minute and we'd have left you on Athens Point," said Edones's voice, reverberating inside the small air lock.

Joyce gave Matt a sour look.

The Minoan emissary would arrive in two hours, giving Captain Rayiz enough time to question State Prince Parmet. Rayiz allowed Ariane to watch remotely, but she couldn't have input to the session. On the other hand, she could relax in her quarters as she watched the interview in real time. She sipped hot Hellas Kaffi that she had grabbed from the mess hall, which happened to be conveniently between squadron ops and her cabin.

"At least I'm getting something good from this interview," she muttered. She tried not to yawn as she concentrated on the dreary small conference room where Rayiz was taking Parmet's statement.

Parmet, under his diplomatic status, was allowed to bring any necessary support personnel with him for his "interview." He brought Dr. Istaga, manifestly as interpreter, and Nathaniel Wolf Kim. Kim's role was supposedly as legal and diplomatic counsel.

On Rayiz's side, a major assigned to the AFCAW Judge Advocates Office ensured that he didn't over-step his bounds. Rayiz was familiar with Autonomist privacy laws, but diplomats received specialized pro-tection and Legal was there to make sure he didn't make a mistake.

Ariane noted with approval that the room didn't have any tables. The Terrans were in chairs that pro-vided Captain Rayiz with a view of their entire bod-ies, to send the message that their private *somaural* messages could eventually be translated. Rayiz was also seated, while Legal stood alertly in the corner of the room.

The Terrans seated themselves. Dr. Istaga gestured at the time, prominently displayed on the wall and showing the countdown to the arrival of the Mi-noan emissary.

"The state prince has expressed concern about meeting so close to arrival of the Minoans," Istaga said. "He's also concerned that we stay within the bounds of the treaty, per the section on treatment of inspectors."

"We have the treaty liaison officer observing, just in case," Rayiz said, waving his arm in a general acknowledgment of MilNet nodes.

Ariane saw that Legal was nodding; Rayiz was ap-parently required to notify the Terrans that she was watching.

"Ah, then I would assume that Major Kedros is unharmed," Istaga said with a smile. Parmet's face was unreadable. Kim scowled, but that seemed to be his normal expression.

"She's uninjured, but will require medical evalua-tion," Rayiz responded stiffly. "I must notify you that all standard recording is being performed, but this interview will not be publicly released until the end of the classification period."

"And when would that be?" Istaga asked politely.

"The classification period will depend upon what we discuss. If operational weapon deployment points aren't mentioned, then it'll be classified based upon our investigation of the explosion." Rayiz didn't speculate. He started the interview by stating purpose and attendees for the record.

"First, we'll ask the state prince to state his reasons for being in the male locker room in section eight-D."

Rayiz used common Greek and addressed Istaga, who turned and repeated the question in an English-like patois that sounded like what had developed on the Mars colonies.

Both State Prince Isrid and Nathaniel Wolf Kim looked earnestly at Istaga while he was translating. Parmet responded in the same language, which seemed heavily associated with hand gestures.

Ariane almost laughed at the awkward dance played out before her. Everyone in the room knew that both Isrid and Kim spoke common Greek. Everyone also knew the Mars patois allowed for *somaural* subtleties and direction, and that AFCAW would analyze the recordings for subtext later.

"SP Parmet says that he was lured there by an anonymous message, which autoshredded," Istaga said.

Ariane pressed her lips together. A third party had to be involved. If the Terrans had sent the message about Icelos to Ariane, then they already knew her background. In that case, SP Parmet had been waiting to kill *her* as well as Icelos, but that scenario no longer made sense. He had plenty of opportunity to kill her while they were in the air lock, particularly when she passed out. He could easily have made it

look accidental, given the disruption of MilNet nodes
and other distractions, such as explosive decompression of part of the habitat.

No, Parmet doesn't want to kill me. At least, not yet.
And, hopefully, that meant he didn't know her identity.

"Even if the message was specially encoded or personal, we should have a record of it being delivered."
Rayiz looked as though he was picking his words
carefully. "We don't. And our network, contrary to
Commercial Common Net, doesn't allow anonymous messages."

"Nevertheless, he says it was anonymous and that
it shredded as soon as he tried to save it." Istaga's
voice was silky.

"What were the contents? Why does he say he
was *lured*?"

Rayiz's question provoked more discussion between Parmet and Istaga.

"He prefers to not discuss the contents. They
were personal."

At that answer, Rayiz turned to look at the major
from Legal, who shook his head. Ariane sighed as she
interpreted their unspoken conversation. As long as
Parmet claimed that the contents were *personal*, he was
protected by an obscure intersection of diplomatic and
privacy protection laws. The Terrans had done their
homework when it came to CAW legal code.

Rayiz couldn't obtain anything more of interest
from SP Parmet. The SP had a good memory for
details and his story matched Ariane's from the point
when she revived him. He even recalled the floating
message perfectly, word for word.

Parmet's testimony made hers all the more believable, and vice versa. Rayiz had been skeptical about
the messages. Ariane told him the contents of the

original message *plus* the mocking messages in section 8D, even though they intimated that the saboteur's motives involved her in some way. The only point she left out was her knowledge of Icelos's background.

Over the years, she'd come to realize the power that truth held when it came to simplifying the world. So she took the chance of exposing her identity to Karthage SF in the hope they'd find the perpetrators faster—operating under the assumption that Icelos's murder and the explosion were the work of the assassins she was hunting.

The important, and unsubstantiated, part of Ariane's interview had been her insistence that the gym door was sabotaged *physically*.

"We'll see whether we find enough debris. I've talked to the structural engineers, and to check the manual disablement for that door, we'll need the entire bulkhead," Rayiz had said, probably hoping she'd been mistaken. However, he couldn't wish away the obvious: Someone had taken control of many protected environmental systems on Karthage, possibly from a remote location. That was frightening enough.

Parmet's interview ended and Ariane's view port closed. She soon had to greet the Minoan emissary and she still hadn't had time to get a report off to Owen. She checked her dress uniform, back and front, using node views. Her uniform looked trim and professional, but she doubted the Minoan emissary would care. She took a deep breath. She was bone tired and about to do what no human should have to do: interface with an alien species. For all her personal efforts to see the Minoans as Gaian-based species, she still couldn't suppress the shivers and strangeness she felt when around a Minoan.

"Major Kedros, report to docking air lock six-alpha-delta to meet inbound visitors," her ear bug announced.

She squared her shoulders and left her cabin.

CHAPTER 13

There's controversy regarding the origin of modern Minoans, but let's first dispense with net-think inferences
that they're descended from the Minoan civilization on
pre-Terran Earth. The original Minoans were a shining
beacon of civilization that dragged us out of the bronze
age, but they vanished during the Unenlightened Century
in post-Alexandrian times. Archaeologists can't explain their
disappearance, but they *can* puncture the net-think theory
of Atlantian Intervention (background laughter). Now consider the end of the twentieth century, when we make
first contact with a species that uses strikingly similar
symbology to the original Minoans. . . .

— *Marcus Alexander*, Sophist at Konstantinople Prime
   University, 2052.115.18.32 UT, indexed by *Heraclitus
   20* under Conflict Imperative

Matt followed Joyce down the narrow corridor of
the *Bright Crescent*. The uniformed personnel
that brushed past him were intent and full of purpose; everyone was a cog in the gears of their mission. Except Matt. He didn't know what sort of
mission this cruiser performed. Ariane had called this
a "lightly armed cruiser," but that didn't help him.

Matt was far out of his depth. He'd never been
aboard a military ship. He had space operational experience, of course, born and raised on the *Journey
IV*, the third largest of the sublight generational behe-

moths. Her size required class-A dock support. Athens Point, even as large as it was, couldn't service a class-A ship. The *Journey IV* required a minimum of two hundred and forty people to operate piloting, navigation, and system engineering. That number didn't include personnel for acquiring and analyzing exploration data, maintaining hydroponics and environmental, food services, medical support, component maintenance, etc. During Matt's time aboard the *Journey IV*, the soul count never dipped below eighteen hundred.

Joyce stopped at a narrow door that said LIEUTENANT OLEANDER. Before opening it, he tapped in a command and the door changed to read VISITOR.

"Your quarters," said Joyce.

Matt colored. He wanted to ask whether this lieutenant was evicted just for him, but Joyce pushed him through the door.

"You only have the small locker, since the other two are being used." Joyce answered Matt's question, pointing to one of the lockers. Poor Oleander had to get out of his quarters without moving his personal items. "Stow your stuff and get webbed in for—"

"Take hold, take hold, take hold. This is third and last warning. Prepare for undocking." A male voice sounded throughout the cruiser.

"Contrary to civilian ships, we don't check that *passengers* are webbed in before maneuvers." Joyce's glance was hard as he left, securing the door behind him. If he had substituted "useless baggage" for "passengers," his words would have matched his tone.

Matt numbly stowed his bag and quickly got into the bunk, feeling the familiar squirm as the webbing secured him. He hoped he'd done the right thing in calling Edones.

* * *

The clear tones of the boarding pipes sounded. Ariane had a moment of disorienting recognition: Hadn't she been doing this about ten hours ago? The moment felt so familiar, down to the sounds of Santorini fidgeting behind her. Yesterday she was suppressing anxiety and terror caused by the arrival of the Terran inspectors, but her mission seemed simpler yesterday, when she'd had clear lines between ally and enemy. Today she was no longer sure who might be her friend.

Parmet stood on one side of her and Jacinthe Voyage stood on the other. Flanked by indifference and hostility, Ariane felt like an empty effigy standing in the front line. Were the Minoans upset about the sabotage to the station, worried that this might affect treaty support? The answer might be to thrust the intelligence liaison officer forward as a sacrificial goat.

As usual, the most advanced sensors and algorithms that AFCAW could employ were confused by Minoan technology. The weapon detector light above the air lock flickered between blue and orange, and then decided to stay blue. There was no doubt in Ariane's mind that the light should display orange, because the Minoan emissary certainly had an armed escort.

Mankind had a century of space flight under their belts, but they'd yet to catch up with the Minoans in the area of weapons technology. They had tried to analyze the results from Minoan weapons. The wreckage of would-be pirate vessels were examined and the aftermath of genetically targeted bioweapons were still being measured, to little avail. Both AFCAW and TerranXL military intelligence had theories regarding the directed energy weapons used by the Minoans, but the theories only proved how far behind the technology curve mankind fell.

The air lock opened and a figure stepped onto the landing, carrying a baton slightly longer than its arm. This was what net-think called a "guardian," one of the mute armed escorts that protected higher-level Minoan functionaries. Clothed in flowing black to below the tops of its black boots, it had a headdress of short, sharp horns with no jewels and what looked like worked gold and platinum over the crown. The headdress still hid facial features, but as the guardian looked far right and left, it displayed a silhouette that looked like a human forehead, nose, and chin. Whether this was a generated illusion, or the actual profile, no one knew.

The guardian examined the loading platform with waiting audience and, finding no obvious threats, stepped aside for the emissary to disembark. Emissaries represented a different Minoan class or race. Their robes were always red and drifted down to the floor to obscure all their body. This emissary, given the height and graceful curvature of its headdress horns, might be an important personage. Precious metals covered the horns and each tip provided anchors for dripping ropes of jewels that cascaded down and looped back to connect to the headdress under the emissary's collar; or perhaps they connected to the emissary itself.

There was a third class of Minoans, rarely ever seen. Mundanes called them the "warrior" class and Ariane hoped never to meet one. They only showed up when nasty work had to be done with their weapons, like surgically dissecting ships used for piracy or wiping out would-be anarchist tribes.

The emissary stepped forward onto the landing.

There were fanatics who thought the Minoans were gods. If Ariane believed that she would have been facedown on the deck in supplication when finding herself this close to a Minoan. As it was, her breath stuck in her throat as she suppressed an urge to offer obeisance.

Jacinthe Voyage saluted, as one would for a visiting head of state. They hadn't saluted State Prince Parmet, but as leader of the inspection team, he wasn't acting as a head of state. Mentally, Ariane approved. This time, given the indications of this Minoan's rank, a salute might be appropriate. Ariane saluted and heard the soft whoosh of cloth whisking behind her as Lieutenant Santorini and others did the same. Out of the corner of her eyes, she saw Parmet make a shallow bow.

"Welcome, Emissary. I'm commander of the Thirty-second Naga Strike Squadron." Jacinthe cleared her throat. She was awkwardly filling the role of the facility commander, who was embarrassingly deceased.

There was silence. Ariane couldn't hear Santorini fidgeting any more. There was nothing to do but wait. Over more than a century of interacting with the Minoans, mankind had learned a few social tips. First, there was no sense in giving Minoans your name, since they seemed to only remember titles. Second, Minoans didn't use their own names when interacting with mundanes unless they were extremely high-ranking leaders. Third, one must learn to *wait* when conversing with Minoans.

The emissary's horns dipped slowly to acknowledge the greeting. It had been standing in front of Jacinthe and now took a step sideways to stand in front of Ariane and Parmet. Ariane suppressed a shiver in seeing that movement, which seemed the result of inhuman joints. The Minoans were obviously bipedal, but the red robes that moved under a nonexistent breeze gave no hints of gender or overall shape of limbs.

"This is Terran State Prince—" Jacinthe cut off the name and Parmet nodded his head. "—and our intel-

ligence liaison officer for compliance of the Mobile
Temporal Distortion Weapon Treaty." Jacinthe gestured toward Ariane.

The Minoan shifted its attention to Ariane and they
waited again. They all expected this visit had something to do with the treaty and the recent sabotage.

It took time for mankind to understand the Minoan
mind ruleset, called such because it seemed about as
inflexible as an AI ruleset. Minoans never forced their
own laws, morality, or ideology upon mankind—
they worked *strictly* within mankind's laws and they
expected the same compliance from mankind. When
they first offered the sale of referential engine plans
that could navigate nous-space (or N-space, which
was still a theoretical vista to mankind), they made
trade agreements with governments and always honored them. It all fell apart when individuals tried to
subvert their own governments, their own taxes, and
their own laws.

Minoans didn't understand idiosyncratic behavior,
defiance of authority, or individuals that bent rules
or laws, much less broke them. They could barely
comprehend individuality since the concept didn't
translate, behaviorally or emotionally. That's why piracy was lethal to practice in Minoan space, and why
Minoan weapons squashed violent anarchists until
they learned to avoid Minoan targets. Minoans understood societal rules and laws, and they expected
everyone to follow them.

They also appeared to understand aggression between governments, at least when there were rules
for warfare. In the case of the decades-long hostility
between CAW and TerraXL, everything was fine as
long as conduct fit the Phaistos Protocol. Attacks outside this protocol were labeled as war crimes. The
most notable, and most ambiguous, attack had been

the TD weapon for Ura-Guinn. Was an entire solar system a space habitat? The prohibition against destructive bombardment of habitable bodies didn't seem to apply, at least not until the effects of the weapon could be verified. TerraXL called for Minoan judgment, while CAW tried to justify a loophole in the protocol. In the end, both sides agreed to sign Pax Minoica and phase out temporal distortion weapons research, development, and deployment. The Minoans declined judgment or perhaps they only *suspended* it, waiting for the evidence to travel from Ura-Guinn.

Ariane tensed under the emissary's scrutiny. An armed Minoan vessel sat less than fifteen kilometers off Karthage. If Karthage Point was undergoing a weapons inspection under a codified treaty, then by Gaia, they'd better be following those treaty rules and protocols. This emissary would certainly be concerned about the station sabotage and Icelos's murder, if the events affected treaty compliance.

"We recognize you, Ariane-as-Kedros. I now acknowledge you under this role, Treaty Compliance Officer." The emissary's voice was pleasant, although lacking soulful quality and vibrancy. The voice sounded neither male nor female.

Shit. Even Great Bull–shit. Minoans didn't identify mundanes by name. Ariane's knees almost buckled. Parmet and Jacinthe turned and looked down at her, their eyes narrowing. Behind her, she heard Lt. Santorini and the Maintenance Squadron commander both draw in their breath.

"Thank you, Emissary." Ariane tried to respond cheerfully, as if the Minoan had merely complimented her trim uniform. "We're about to start a baseline inspection to confirm the number of warheads aboard this station. In accordance with treaty protocols, this is occurring within twenty-four hours of the arrival of the Terran inspection team. Would you like to observe?"

"I am honored to record your compliance, as well as that of Terran State Prince and Naga Squadron Commander," said the emissary gravely. "First, however, I must speak with you privately, Treaty Compliance Officer."

Jacinthe wasted no time in escorting the emissary to a conference room recently used by the Terran inspection teams. She motioned Ariane to follow. Jacinthe didn't call SF and place a security detail; Ariane shrugged and followed the emissary into the empty room. The emissary's guardian took up a post outside the door.

At this point, I'm probably safer here than anywhere else on Karthage. Besides, Minoans wouldn't do anything illegal, as defined by CAW law.

The emissary sat down with oily grace at the small conference table. Ariane went to the other side of the table facing the emissary, but remained standing. She grasped the back of a conference chair and used it for support. It gave a small peep of alarm, telling her that her grip might cause damage. She tried to relax and keep her gaze on the emissary.

The emissary's smoothly gloved hand came out from within the red robes, and dark graceful fingers reached up to a particular jewel on the chain and twirled it. Then the fingers went farther down the chain and caressed another jewel. With each touch, a faint tinkling tone rose from the chain and then faded. Ariane watched, fascinated. The movements might have looked like random fidgeting, but—

"I have disabled MilNet node recording in this room," said the emissary. As she wondered whether this Minoan had the concept of individual privacy, the emissary added, "For security of common state goals."

She waited silently. When she'd moved to her current position in Intelligence, she'd gone through additional training modules, one of which covered interacting with Minoans. She had hoped she'd never need it. Now she had to curb her apprehension as well as her expectations; the training had emphasized how different mental models led to misunderstandings. Exchange of information using common mental models worked quickly because each person anticipated where the conversation was heading.

"You have risen above your initial title and have become multiroled, Ariane-as-Kedros. You were single-roled as Destroyer of Worlds—"

The chair squeaked in protest again as Ariane's fingers dug into it. She relaxed her hands as the emissary paused. Perhaps she shouldn't be surprised the Minoans knew she was on the crew that detonated the TD weapon at Ura-Guinn. Perhaps that gave her notoriety enough, in their view, for having an individual name.

"—but I wish to address you as Explorer of Solar Systems, not as Treaty Compliance Officer or Destroyer of Worlds," continued the emissary.

"Oh." Dumbfounded, Ariane took a step backward. This was the problem with expectations. She relaxed a little; the further away from the subject of Ura-Guinn, the better.

"You are unwilling?"

"Not unwilling. Unprepared, perhaps." Ariane chose her words carefully, remembering her training. "I accept title Explorer of Solar System. Please continue addressing me in that role."

"You are partners with Aether Explorations, Limited, and you have signature authority." The Minoans had a tendency to overuse plural forms, but Ariane wasn't going to correct it. The accurate name for Matt's company wasn't important.

"Yes . . ." *Wait until the proposal is made,* her mind cautioned, and she held back the "but" qualifier that should follow.

"We have interests in leases controlled by Aether Explorations, Limited. I have requests for you."

She kept her face blank. The Minoan wanted to talk about G-145. *I'll bet you're interested.* She'd been just as excited as Matt when they'd confirmed the presence of intelligent civilization, *which might or might not be Minoan.* Then there was the problem they had with the *artifact.* She'd bet a year's salary that it hadn't been made by Minoans. Its appearance, to include the symbols on the sides, was different from all the others she'd used for N-space drops.

The emissary wasn't finished, not by a long shot. She waited.

"We can make no offers of special payments or dispensation to you, of course. We only request that you assign certain leases to the companies that we identify to you." The gloved hands emerged from the diaphanous robe, this time opening into palm-outward gestures of honesty.

Of course this was a request, because kickbacks were illegal. Ariane tried to form her answer so she didn't insinuate that the Minoans were sidestepping the laws regarding fair and open competition. From her training, she knew that was a deadly insult.

"I do have signature authority, but I rarely use it," Ariane said. "My partner, the majority owner of Aether Exploration, has more experience in these matters."

"You do not need experiences for this, since I will provide the suitable companies."

"True, but I have a private agreement regarding

division of responsibilities with my partners. Matt—
er—the majority owner of Aether Exploration usually
authorizes leases and contracts. I merely provide consultation or advice."

"Could you advise your partners toward certain
companies? As tokens of our gratitude, I could provide you with confidential information." Again, the
open, honest hand gesture caught her attention. "This
information has no monetary or intrinsic values, except perhaps to you."

The emissary sat back, unmistakably expecting her
to take some time to reflect upon its proposal.

Ariane hid a sigh. She always hated the business
side of, well, business. Even when she wasn't stepping into anything illegal, she felt dirty. Luckily,
she'd had a military salary ever since she accepted
the reserve position under Colonel Edones. It wasn't
outlandishly huge, but it was sizable enough to keep
her comfortable even if she didn't have a job. She
got monthly deposits whether she was on active duty
or not.

Ariane paused as a revelation struck her, something that should have been obvious to her; perhaps
she wasn't cynical enough after all. *I'm being paid
hush money*. It sounded so melodramatic that she almost smiled.

AFCAW certainly wouldn't want her, in either
identity, plastered across the feeds. This unwelcome
Minoan attention could be the result of discovering
the ruins in G-145. She hadn't been catching the feeds
lately because Karthage's corridor walls were disabled. *I wonder how Edones is taking all this, particularly
if I've registered a high exposure rating on net-think.*

The Minoan emissary still sat waiting for her next
words. Mundanes thought long pauses were awkward and would rush to fill the void, sometimes tak-

ing silence during conversations as offensive. Minoans considered silence respectful, considerate, and thoughtful.

"I'm sorry, but I cannot guarantee my partner's actions. Final authority rests with him." Ariane's curiosity got the better of her and she asked, "What information were you going to offer me in exchange for my *advice*?"

The emissary cocked its head sideways and Ariane wished she could see its face and get any idea of emotional content.

"We know you were dispersed with no knowledge of where all Destroyers of Worlds were sent. We thought you might value the locations of the others."

Her breath caught and her heart pounded. "You knew all of us, as individuals?"

"Always."

Ariane wondered whether Brandon had been warned specifically about the assassins. She had access to classified information because of her reserve position, but Brandon had probably returned to civilian life. If so, the Directorate might have only sent him some nebulous warnings. Brandon was probably somewhere in the countryside of Hellas Prime. He'd always valued his home planetary vistas, the natural fauna and flora of what he called "the great outdoors." Just before their last mission, he'd been contemplating separation at his next reassignment window.

She could warn Brandon, tell him everything, and risk a blatant security violation. It might be worth the destruction of her career if her warning kept him from harm. But Hellas Prime was a large and heavily populated planet. She'd have to find him first, and now she had an excellent opportunity.

"I could identify your companies to my partner and ask that they be considered, but I won't guarantee they'll get the leases they're bidding," Ariane said cautiously. Matt wouldn't want Minoan concerns getting any contracts and she agreed. This "gentlemen's agreement" could never be acknowledged by the Minoans, so what harm could come of giving Matt a list of companies? He'd get a good laugh out of it.

"That is acceptable." The emissary straightened its neck, righting its head. "The other Destroyers of Worlds are located within the Demeter Sanctuary on Hellas Prime."

Ariane nodded. That sounded like the sort of place Brandon would prefer. She pointed down at the table surface and said, "I'll need MilNet nodes to send your list of companies."

"Of course."

The emissary caressed a jewel in the string and Ariane activated a display on the table. A message arrived in her queue and she opened it: a list of companies. She didn't bother to read it.

"I can only do an anonymous drop from here to my partner in Aether Exploration, Limited. As you can see, I'm sending your list with an advisement to consider these for contract authority. Once again, I can't guarantee results." Ariane didn't add that Matt would consider this a joke, at best, when he did receive the list.

The emissary seemed satisfied and did the Minoan equivalent of closing that topic and changing the subject.

"I would now advise you, as Treaty Compliance Officer, that you have less than two hours to start your baseline inspection."

"I accept title of Treaty Compliance Officer," Ariane said.

"I also accept the honor of observing your compliance," added the emissary.

Ariane hid her sigh. Since the emissary wanted to

hang around awhile, she wasn't going to have time to get a report to Colonel Edones. All AFCAW installations would have raised their alert status because of the sabotage and passed this warning on to civilian habitats as well. The news would certainly have reached the colonel by now and he'd eventually receive the casualty list. He'd know she hadn't been able to protect Icelos.

Had Matt figured out where she was? She hoped not, because she didn't want to be the cause of any worry, not at this time. When he received this mail through anonymous drop, he'd know that she was alive and well.

Outside, Lieutenant Colonel Voyage, Captain Rayiz, and Lieutenant Santorini waited impatiently to one side. To the other side, beyond the Minoan escort, State Prince Parmet stood with Dr. Istaga. Ariane followed the emissary out of the room and shrugged in response to the questions radiating from Jacinthe, Rayiz, and Santorini. She felt shaky and the whole episode felt like a dream; she'd just *personally* negotiated with an alien.

"Let's get started on Karthage's baseline inspection," she said. "The emissary has expressed a desire to observe our compliance to the treaty."

CHAPTER 14

This year the Overlords *must* hear our petition. We desperately need funds to expand protected biomes. The protected areas we currently have are too small and they struggle to operate in this shambles of an economy. Thankfully, the war with the Autonomists is over and we're no longer seeing money sucked away to support . . .

—*Tenth Symposium on the Restoration of Terra*, Dr. Hong Cloud Chicahua, 2093.318.10.22 UT, indexed by *Democritus 29* under Metrics Imperative

Matt wasn't surprised to find himself locked in his quarters after he released his webbing. No space vessel wanted passengers rattling around, and on a military ship, this crew probably rated him lower than useless.

He pulled out his slate. His most recent message was from Sergeant Joyce. Looking stern and authoritative, the sergeant said that Matt was confined to his cabin, with the exception of mealtimes. He would be escorted to the galley for meals. Full toiletry facilities were available in his cabin. *Cheap sonic showers and sponge baths—great.* Well, Edones had warned him.

There was more. Joyce provided Matt a MilNet account that provided a conduit to ComNet, so he could access all the bids sent to his company. Matt also had access to Athens Point LEF files on Nestor's murder and Colonel Edones expected a full analysis.

Oh, he does, does he? What about the help I asked for?

At the end of the message, Joyce said, "When I've got some spare time, I'll provide my own analysis to the colonel."

Joyce finished his message tautly, without any sign-off. It was obvious the gruff sergeant didn't feel he had any time to spare on Matt's problems.

Apparently, he was facing a lonely time aboard the *Bright Crescent*. His cabin allowed only about three paces alongside the bunk. Across from the bunk were storage lockers and his "facilities," which weren't any bigger than the full-height locker beside them. Sighing, Matt threw himself on the bunk. He picked up his slate again and tested his account and conduit to ComNet.

It worked fine. He browsed over the documents sent by Athens Point, such as autopsy reports, but he avoided video taken on the scene and from Com-Net nodes in the vicinity of Nestor's apartment. He couldn't shake the memory of his friend strung up like some sort of animal carcass and he wasn't ready to see Nestor, alive or not, on video. He could do it later. The ship would be at sublight for several days before reaching Karthage Point.

Instead, Matt turned his attention to what he could now access on the *Aether's Touch*: the packages Nestor had sent before he died. There was already significant lag transferring data and attempting real-time queries to the AI back at Athens Point. He wondered what sort of acceleration this cruiser could thrust to, and not turn her crew into jelly.

"Nestor's Muse Three, retrieve and summarize the data from packages titled 'Customs' and 'Kedros.'" While it took longer for Matt to enter text questions, it made for quicker messages. Considering that

Edones was controlling and paranoid, Matt had no illusions of privacy aboard this ship. He was sure his communications going through the conduit were recorded, but at least they'd have to be decrypted. Matt pictured some disinterested lackey, probably some low-ranking military grunt, examining his messages.

A knock at the door interrupted his reflections.

"Unlock door," Matt said, wondering if it was time for his meal. *Now I know how inmates feel.*

The door was opened tentatively. Standing in the corridor was a young woman with striking eyes that reflected her green uniform, intensifying the color. Her complexion was creamy, and her face seemed to glow against chestnut hair tied back into a braid. The black name tag on her uniform read OLEANDER.

"Oh, excuse me." Matt scrambled up from his bunk. His shirt had been open; his elbows flapped awkwardly as he sealed it.

"For what?" Oleander had a dreamy confidence that wrapped peacefully around her. She made Matt feel like the proverbial awkward country cousin.

"Huh?" He ran his hands through his short hair, trying to regain his composure. "Oh. I'm sorry that I bumped you from your quarters."

"No problem. It's all part of the job. Ready for chow?"

"Certainly. Is it breakfast or lunch?" Matt hurriedly pulled on his boots.

"It's whatever you want. We're shift-based."

He followed her down the narrow halls, appreciating the deftness she used to turn the corners and maneuver past oncoming personnel. The gravity generator, in expensive ships and certainly military vessels, could be used to bleed off force into N-space and compensate for acceleration-g. Sort of like antigrav, but not really, because it didn't require the expensive power of true antigravity. Theoretically, it should feel exactly like being in "natural" free fall when orbiting a gravity well, but the human stomach seemed to know the difference. Nobody had their space stomach until they'd exercised and operated under acceleration-compensated free fall with an N-space connection. The generational ships built up to high speeds, but they did so through low acceleration. Matt's space stomach had been built up on the *Aether's Touch*, which had a surprisingly high acceleration limit.

The few crew members they met in the hall were in uniform and nodded companionably in passing. There were some sidelong glances at Matt, but no one bothered Oleander with questions.

Like they have membership in some club, and I'm frozen out. He tempered his sullen and ungracious thoughts, considering where Oleander might be bunking at this time. She'd shrugged when he apologized, since it was "all part of the job." Why did those words seem to only come from people who didn't have a "job," but were dedicated to a profession?

"Hey—Lieutenant." He caught up with Oleander. "What's your position here?"

"Weapons officer." She gave him a serene smile and motioned, indicating that he should precede her into the galley.

Matt nodded. Not only did he have nothing in common with this woman; he couldn't imagine her long, graceful fingers flying across a console and sending havoc and death via kinetic or swarm missiles. Those were conventional space warfare weapons mentioned by talking heads on the feeds. Matt shivered.

Oleander didn't carry the weight of potential death and destruction on her shoulders. She was young and fresh, unburdened by second-guessed decisions and losses like older crew. Like Ari. *Why am I comparing her to Ari?* He couldn't help himself, although the petite, gruff, dark-haired, dark-eyed Ari bore no resemblance to the ethereal and glowing Lieutenant Oleander.

"We've got the standard select-from-stores and heat-it-yourself cafeteria. We're not big enough to have cooks and stewards." Oleander gestured about the small and spotless mess that had two shiny kiosks for retrieving and heating food. In her calm voice, her words were neither an apology nor an excuse.

Matt was delighted to find several generational menu items, while Oleander went for the planetary-grown foodstuffs. The kiosks dispensed the food in low-g dishware. After they found a table, Oleander took the time to answer his questions during their companionable meal.

Matt asked polite, but general, questions about ship living conditions and military life. Eventually, this led to a deeper conversation about AFCAW officer career progression.

The important career points for an officer, explained Oleander, were getting out of the training mode of sublieutenant and then making each rank step, at the appointed time, up to the rank of major. If one could attain the rank of major, then one could work up to forty years in AFCAW service or apply for retirement after twenty-five years of service, depending upon one's assignments.

"Early retirement can be granted based upon the amount of action the officer has seen." Oleander sipped delicately at her straw.

"But we're not at war," Matt said. "What sort of action would you see?"

"Perhaps I should have worded it as *risk encountered and injuries sustained during duty*. Accidents happen in space, as you well know, and there are still

military actions against pockets of partisans and pi-
rates and anarchists. There are risky rescue missions.
People still *die* in the line of duty, Mr. Journey."

She barely raised her voice, but Matt felt abashed
nonetheless. Growing up on a generational ship, he
had a tendency to belittle the risks of living in habitats and the basic rigors of real-space travel. Once
he'd accepted a lifetime of debt for the *Aether's Touch*,
he'd found a whole new set of dangers engendered
by N-space navigation and referential engines, or
that's what the insurance companies told him.

"I'm worried about what we'll find at Karthage
Point," added Oleander. " 'Minimal loss of life' can
mean there's been life-shortening exposure to radiation. Some crew could be looking at early
retirement—are you all right?"

Matt's face reddened and his heart skipped. He'd
forgotten, at least for the past half hour, about the
explosion at Karthage. He had troubles swallowing
his mouthful of food, which abruptly took on the
texture of gravel.

"I'm fine," he said. "My pilot is a reserve officer
who might be stationed on Karthage. I'm worried
about her."

Oleander had a way of encouraging talk without
seeming to ask questions, and Matt found himself
telling her all about Ari. Coincidentally, Oleander
had also grown up on Nuovo Adriatico. Not a prime
planet by any means, Nuovo Adriatico had the bene-
fits of mild climates and genetically flexible flora, so
Oleander began dredging up memories of agricul-
tural work and bucolic vistas.

"Uh, yes, sounds beautiful." Ari made Matt uncomfortable with those same scenes of the wide open,
terrifying for all crèche-get. "You might have gone
through the military entrance academy together."

Oleander chuckled with her warm voice. "That's

unlikely. You say that she's a reserve major? Then she must be a bit older."

"Well, she does look younger than her thirty-five years, but she's hardly . . ." Matt had wandered into no-man's land. In this day of near-relativistic speeds, extended lifetimes, and reconstructive surgery, it was rude to speculate about anyone's age and he was about to tread on this sanctified ground for two women at once.

He retreated promptly. "I think she just made major, before she started working for me. She works for Edones in the Directorate of Intelligence."

Oleander looked politely interested. "Ah, the Directorate. I didn't know they had slots for reservists."

"Ari said it's a specialized slot, the only one. She regularly gets hazard pay, I guess."

"Must be a thrill junkie." Then, when Matt frowned, she demurely finished her drink pack through her straw and added, "Well, I really don't know what intelligence officers do for a living."

"But this ship carries the Directorate's seal, and you work for Colonel Edones." Shouldn't Oleander, with obvious military clearances, know what went on in the Directorate of Intelligence?

"Here's where I shrug and say, 'I only work here,' and that's the truth. I'm a weapons officer who can be assigned to any Fury Class Cruiser, regardless of mission. So I get only what I need to know for the particular operation—in this case, all I know is we're transporting personnel to Karthage at maximum sub-light-speed."

Matt then learned how the *Bright Crescent* operated. Colonel Edones was the "mission commander," while Lieutenant Colonel Lydia was the "ship commander." Oleander acted as though there was distinct delineation between their authority, but Matt was left with a muddled idea that Lydia might be allowed to override

Edones under certain tactical situations even though
Edones outranked Lydia and provided the missions for
the ship. Matt was pleased that Edones wasn't in
charge of everything aboard the ship, but that also
meant that most of the ship crew members wearing
green uniforms didn't know diddly about what Edones
and Joyce and their cohorts did.

Same as me—I have no idea what Ari is doing. Matt
rubbed his neck as he remembered Nestor's comment, as outrageous as it seemed then, about Ari
being a shadow. The bustle of the galley faded from
his senses as he stared at his empty food containers.
The comment Oleander made about Ari being a thrill
junkie made him think about the injuries Ari always
tried to hide whenever she came off assignment. She
clearly felt an obligation toward Edones and a com-
pulsion to "do her duty," even if it might mean enormous risk.

*What a bastard. Edones manipulates Ari for all he can
get, putting her into only Gaia knows what kind of danger.*

Overall, Matt had a pleasant meal with Lieutenant
Oleander, but he was in a gloomy mood when it
ended. After Oleander escorted him back to the
cramped quarters, *her quarters,* Matt still didn't feel
inclined to dig into the reports or gory video provided by the LEF. His blinking message queue gave
him an excuse to procrastinate.

He had a message from Ari! Looking at the UT
stamp, he sighed in relief. She'd made this anonymous drop after the explosion occurred at Karthage,
so he could assume she was safe.

The contents were surprising, though. Ari talking
about business? She hadn't shown much interest in
the business side of his company. Up to this point
she'd avoided using her signature authority, even if
it involved—Minoans? The video showed Ari and a
Minoan, where Ari was saying something like "I'm

sending your list with an advisement to consider these for contract authority. Once again, I can't guarantee results."

Matt smiled as the list of company names scrolled onto his small wall. First, Ari was safe and well. Second, she'd had the Minoans identify their own shell companies for him, saving him time and giving him leverage over Edones.

He watched the video again. Ari looked competent, as always, but not fresh. After working with her for several years, he could see the telltale signs of fatigue and strain. Regardless, Matt was impressed. How many AFCAW officers could coolly negotiate, one-on-one, with a Minoan? Edones might have, and he had more experience than Ari, given their respective military records. However, Ari had a hardened edge and sad pragmatism that presumed she'd do what was necessary for the mission. She'd already been there, already made those difficult decisions. Matt was still certain: *She's seen combat, even if her records say she hasn't.*

That edge hadn't formed yet in Lieutenant Oleander. Edones had experience and command presence, but he hadn't seen combat either, because he'd been in Intelligence as the war was ending. *But Joyce saw combat.* Sergeant Joyce had the same grizzled edge of acceptance and pain that Matt felt in Ari. Matt bet they'd both seen and done things that couldn't, and shouldn't, be described.

Thoughtfully, Matt turned his attention to the packages titled "Kedros," now available locally. What had Nestor discovered, and what did it have to do with Ari?

The baseline inspection was grueling, being eight hours of mind-numbing activity. Isrid was tired of meticulously comparing serial numbers of warheads with the AFCAW inventory. He found no discrepancies and there'd been no chance to collect any interesting intelligence, not with the damned Minoan emissary looking over his shoulder. Isrid and Dr. Istaga had been paired with Major Ariane Kedros and her assistant. For some reason, the emissary decided to tag along with their group.

Isrid gratefully watched the emissary attach itself to Ariane Kedros as she combined all inspection results, while he and Dr. Istaga bid farewell. He was escorted to his quarters, where he found Maria. He'd seen her signals earlier. She had intelligence to discuss, something she thought was valuable.

Dully, he wondered what could possibly compensate for his decision to shut down all intelligence operatives in this system, one of the primary solar systems controlled by CAW. Overlord Three wasn't going to be happy with him. At best, his career might continue in a desultory, unspectacular manner, but at worst, he might be charged with anything ranging from incompetence to treason.

"You have to see this for yourself, SP." Maria's golden brown eyes glittered strangely and she moved with suppressed energy. *Revenge can be ours,* shouted her flicking fingers.

"Do we need another privacy shield?" Isrid asked. He rubbed his eyes, tired.

"Already requested one." She motioned to a side table, where their jammer was operating. After seeing his resigned expression, she added, "AFCAW can't know how I got this."

"How *did* you get it?"

"I left recording pips in the conference room we used, on the off chance I might get something interesting. They were scheduled to deactivate in a couple hours so the SF wouldn't find them during their daily sweep—which is pathetic, by the way, since they only scan for active devices."

Now he was interested. "They went active when the Minoan emissary went in?"

"They certainly did." Maria was triumphant. "For privacy, the Minoan used the same sort of shield that we do, meaning there's no force field or other comic-book tool. They merely issue node override commands, just as we do. But being so structured and proper, the Minoan didn't suspect secondary sensors on an AFCAW station, playing over undocumented frequencies."

Maria waved her arm and the video started on the wall. Isrid stood behind her and watched. It was passive; it didn't have active focusing and depth of field changes that everyone expected from network nodes. This meant Major Kedros moved in and out of both focus and frame as she leaned on the table or moved closer to the emissary, but the audio was surprisingly clear.

"Stop! Replay," Isrid said after the emissary addressed Kedros as "Destroyer of Worlds."

"She knows that name," Maria said. "She could be one of the original crew members."

The Minoans had only used the title "Destroyer of Worlds" at one event that was unclassified and accessible by any Terran or Autonomist citizen. At the opening negotiations brought about by Pax Minoica, the Minoans had addressed the vice president of the Consortium of Autonomist Worlds as *Destroyer of Worlds*. This was because the vice president had been responsible for the weapon *execution*, even though the president and senate had authorized it.

"She seems a bit young to be one of the original crew." Isrid tried to cautiously suppress his excitement. Was it possible that he'd found one of the original executioners, a war criminal, and right here at Karthage Point?

"Age is relative nowadays," Maria said.

Isrid watched the rest of the meeting on video, savoring his surge of anger, fanning the embers after he'd suppressed them for so long. Now he could avenge what happened to his brother. He tried to shut down the little internal voice that suggested the celestial objects in the Ura-Guinn system might have survived.

By the time the video showed Major Kedros sending off her message, Isrid was a surprising turmoil of conflicting emotions. Kedros had saved his life. He didn't know how crèche-get or autonomists viewed this, but in Terran terms, he owed her gratitude and more. This was a troubling and mitigating factor, and possibly the reason for Maria's sidelong glances.

Then there were the Minoans, and their interest in Kedros's civilian life. If they wanted their appendages on these leases, then the Terran overlords would expect him to investigate, perhaps get a Terran share of the work.

If this was the test that Overlord Three had anticipated, then it was agonizing to set aside his own need for vengeance.

"How much time do we have?" Isrid asked.

"We have forty-three more minutes under the privacy shield, one hour and twelve minutes until boarding call, and one hour after that, we disconnect from Karthage." Maria was complete and precise, as always.

"I need to know what Kedros's partner, and this Aether Exploration, have been doing—"

"I've got that," Maria said. "You asked me to look into Kedros's background, just in case, and this is what I got from public sources on ComNet." Maria brought up another display. "The initial data from

Aether Exploration indicates ruins of a *space-faring* civilization, which may not be Minoan. The time-space slice that was part of the Aether Exploration claim is now open for working bids, whether it be for mining, surface exploration, archeology, whatever—but Aether Exploration has control over leasing the claim work to whatever contractors they want."

Isrid raised his eyebrows. They'd all been distracted in the past day or two and now he wished that everyone, including him, had paid better attention to Major Kedros's civilian history.

"SP?" Maria had turned around and moved closer, her face looking up to his. "Are you going to make her pay for what she did?"

"Certainly. Not, perhaps, in the way I expected. Or wanted."

Maria's pupils had expanded, as they always did when she was excited and stimulated. He felt her fingertips trace down his hips on either side and he caught both her hands in his.

"We don't have much time," he said. "Bring me Major Kedros. If you're detected, I must be blameless."

Maria smiled.

CHAPTER 15

Radiation is the biggest threat in space. Thank Gaia we developed aerogel, directional polymers, and metallo-ceramics, combining them into effective metamaterial shielding before we left Helios (Sol). Today we use implants that monitor dose rates as well as cumulative exposure in real time, but that doesn't mean you can forget about radiation poisoning or damaging doses. Remember to have a medical professional review your implant's history at least four times a year, even if you haven't received any alarms. If you lose shielding or have unplanned or nonroutine EVA, get to a medic *immediately* and have your radiation exposure evaluated.

— *Spacecrew Bulletin*, 2102.021.18.01 UT, indexed by *Democritus 12* under Cause and Effect Imperative

"It's about time, Major."

Senior Technician Stall used that calm tone that all medics learned, managing to sound gently chiding, motherly, and authoritative all at once. He was the only tech in the dimly lit sick bay during this shift, and he had no one to treat.

"What do I do?" Ariane sagged as exhaustion crashed down on her. There should be no more decisions to make, at least for a while. She'd do as told, then go to bed and sleep through a whole shift. Maybe a couple of shifts.

"Since you're a reservist, I'll need thumbprint plus

voiceprint release of your records. I'll have to update your profile and put in warning limits for future exposure." Stall shook his head. "You and that Terran prince, or whatever he is, sure got off lucky. With the shielding blown off, you might have received whopper radiation doses and been grounded for the rest of your life. As it was, the orientation of the moon and the station, plus the debris cloud, reduced your exposure considerably. Of course, our crews managed to get temporary shielding into place quickly, but even so . . ."

She nodded wearily, no longer listening, and blindly thumbed the slate he extended. Stall continued to chat while he set up his equipment.

When he pointed to the whole-body scanner, she numbly bent down and unsealed her boots. She climbed onto the gurney and he adjusted its height, still talking.

"Sorry to take so much of your time, Major, but considering what you've gone through and the date of your last scan, it makes sense to do it now. Don't worry, this type of scan won't add to your rad dosage. . . ."

He slid her into the cylindrical scanner. His words faded a bit, but after he positioned her, she could still hear him talking.

". . . take an hour or two. I'll be puttering about here and there, so . . ."

Deep, dark sleep took her.

Furtive movement woke her. Someone was pulling her gurney slowly, carefully out of the scanner and the silence was damning. She would have expected Stall to be chattering on about the results.

Nathaniel Wolf Kim made several mistakes. The first was pulling her out feet first. The second was vastly underestimating her. The third was being the only one near the side of her gurney. Before Ariane saw who was holding the hypo, she'd twisted her hips, brought up her leg, and aimed a quick kick where a face should be.

Without her boots, she didn't have the effect she'd hoped for when her foot connected. But she did connect, and as she rolled off the other side of the gurney, she saw Kim's nose was bleeding.

Kim might have assumed she'd *let* him drug her, but he wasn't stupid enough to come by himself. Maria Guillotte was at the foot of the gurney, pulling it. Another "inspector," whose name currently escaped her, stood to one side.

"Emergency code! Nine-one-one!" Ariane yelled. They were brave enough to attack her right here on Karthage—were the MilNet nodes disabled *again*? Perhaps she shouldn't waste her breath.

She dodged Maria's blow. Maria had hand-to-hand training but she used subduing moves, so Ariane had the advantage. She didn't have a problem going all out and killing the Terran bitch, but Guillotte and Kim and whoever-he-was obviously wanted Ariane alive.

"Get behind her."

They showed no fear of being recorded.

"I'm trying—" Grunt.

Kick. Twist. Door to sick bay was closed, no way out. Any weapons? Nothing to grab.

"Hold her—"

Break grappling attempt. Aim blow to ribs and push away.

Thanks to the rejuv and the enhanced metabolism, Ariane had strength beyond what she should for her body weight and size, but she wasn't superhuman. Moreover, she was exhausted and outnumbered.

"Take her down—"

They finally got smart. The third TEBI agent took a sacrificial blow to the ribs as he sagged onto her back. She staggered under his limp weight and they had her. Embarrassingly, this only took a moment or two. She continued to struggle as they shot the drugs into her.

"Give her more! More, Nathan!"

"Good God, what does it take?"

The security was piss-poor on Karthage Point. *Really gotta get on Rayiz . . .*

Matt hesitated before opening the package titled "Kedros." This *was* what he wanted, right? This probably violated Ari's privacy, but curiosity finally drove him to open it.

The initial cross-referenced data, supposedly supplied by Nestor's Muse 3, confirmed what Matt already knew about Ari. She was thirty-five years old, born in 2070, and had lived her formative years on Nuovo Adriatico. With her test scores, she attained early entry to AFCAW at twenty years of age. She transferred to the Reserve after her two obligatory assignments, first as weapons officer, then Naga maintenance. She spent the next seven years working assignments for the Directorate of Intelligence, in between her N-space piloting jobs. Nestor had linked information regarding the Reserve point system, and had asked the AI to hypothesize as to her missions.

That was where the data became too erratic for analysis. Ari popped up in the strangest places, but of course, recognition algorithms for processed video were notoriously unreliable. There were links between Ari and Edones. Matt took a little time to drill down on that data. Edones had his fingers in many different technologies and industries. For Gaia's sake, he operated on the board of directors for three civilian companies! Matt wondered whether this was personal business or duty for the AFCAW Directorate of Intelligence.

However, Ari's life looked ordinary as long as he ignored the interpolations and postulations made within the mission timelines. Near the end he ran into a protected note made by Nestor, which read "Correlation, LOC?" Accessing it required authentication. Matt hesitantly provided his own, and was allowed access.

The note merely highlighted certain correlation and level of confidence figures, hence Nestor's "LOC" notation. The numbers were supposed to quantify the validity of the information by showing how each entry was indexed by differing AIs, differing models, and the level of confidence one could apply against that entry. The AFCAW mission entries had such a low level of confidence that one could dismiss them as nonsense—for instance, it didn't seem possible that Ari had been sighted in an establishment later shut down by AFCAW as an illegal arms dealership.

The specific numbers that were highlighted were high, meaning that Nestor's AI had found explicit index corroborations. Did Nestor think they were too high? Matt scanned along the timeline of Ari's life. Before 2090, the LOC values were pegged at ninety-nine percent. At the year 2090, the levels of confidence began to hover in the low nineties. Just to compare, Matt looked at the entries on Edones. Even the highly correlated facts for Edones pinged randomly between eighty-nine and ninety-eight percent. Normal fluctuations could be expected in the course of collecting data from billions of nodes.

Matt leaned back. *This is absurd—now I'm going to be suspicious because the data are* too *perfect?* Apparently, Nestor had distrusted these results and marked them for Matt.

The boundary was significant. The year 2090 was auspicious because—Matt sat up. In 2090, he was seventeen years old, still getting acclimated to "normal society" in the generational orphanage. The war had been going on for so long that sometimes the battles didn't register exposure ratings on ComNet. Civilians seemed safe because of the Phaistos Protocol, but military deployments and the weapons development contest between CAW and TerraXL was grinding down economies on both sides. Then CAW finally used a temporal distortion warhead. . . .

And everything changed. In many ways, life changed for the better, but not immediately. Matt remembered the panic and localized rioting, fed by the fear that the Minoans would retaliate for the damage to the time buoy network. Ships and crews were lost if they were transitioning exactly when the Ura-Guinn sun and time buoys "glitched." Data packets evaporated and businesses, economies, and governments faltered. Tedious manual inventories and censuses had to be performed. A whole solar system disappeared from N-space (no inventory needed for *that*). Net-think went insane, postulating the use of Minoan genetic weapons on CAW populations or supposing that TerraXL would retaliate by using *their* TD weapons. Prices of food and manufactured goods rose at phenomenal rates, kicking economies into uncontrolled inflation. Hoarding ensued. Transportation and shipping were disrupted as people tried to move their families to places they thought were safe.

"Mr. Journey, are you ready?"

Sergeant Joyce's voice jerked Matt out of his reverie. Joyce's face was in large display, split over the cupboard doors.

"Ready?" Matt responded coldly.

"The colonel would like a report from you, regarding the results of your analysis." The display closed.

Matt hadn't gotten anywhere on Nestor's murder, but he was beginning to think that Nestor had uncovered more than he should regarding Ari and Edones. By the time Joyce arrived to let him out, Matt had convinced himself these military bastards were covering something up—if they were obscuring Ari's background, they might be hiding information about Nestor. Edones seemed to know more about Nestor's activities than he did, so his questions built inside him and stoked his anger as he followed Joyce. Perhaps Nestor poked his nose into classified information when he looked into Ari's past.

When Matt entered the colonel's opulent cabin, a bit of self-preservation kicked in and he didn't say any of the confrontational phrases circling in his head. He reminded himself he was on a military ship, controlled by Edones.

"Was military intelligence watching Nestor?" Matt's fingers curled, but he relaxed them before his hands formed into fists. He stood in front of Edones's desk.

Edones's eyebrows rose and he did something entirely unexpected: He began to laugh. His laughter was so surprisingly honest that Matt was derailed. When he turned to look behind him, he saw the corners of Joyce's mouth were twitching. He felt a surge of embarrassment.

"What's so funny?"

"Why would we spend our precious resources on watching your friend? Do you think we care one iota about a young information broker who spent most of his credit on porn and illicit AI?"

"*Somebody* was watching him and they didn't like what he uncovered." Matt narrowed his eyes and pressed his lips together sullenly.

Edones grinned and shook his head. "We're all recorded, Mr. Journey. Through ComNet, every node in a public habitat provides video and audio, to be fixed forever in crystal. Nobody would have any problem *watching* Mr. Expedition."

Until now, Matt never thought of the ComNet nodes as intrusive. If anything, he'd considered them as safety monitors. Many people installed nodes throughout their flats and paid for AI safety overwatch on their children and elderly relatives. Besides, one could always pay for a privacy shield, right?

"What we're trying to figure out is whether anybody *cared* about your friend's activities, in a way that led to his murder," Edones said. "By the way, you were right in suspecting Minoan technology in that remote, but we have no idea who was running it."

But I might, given the list of companies that Ari sent. There seemed to be no point in chasing after the owner of the remote, unless it proved important to solving Nestor's murder. Matt walked silently over to the chair that Edones pointed at and sat down.

"We also haven't found any connection between the remotes and your friend's murder. We were interested in hearing what your analysis has uncovered, Mr. Journey."

Matt ground his teeth every time Edones used the condescending phrase "Mr. Journey," but it was better than some other addresses he could think of. He didn't want to admit that he hadn't started going through the LEF data.

"I was looking through Nestor's last set of research, trying to find any motives for his murder," Matt said.

"And did you?"

"Not really," Matt muttered.

"While you've been napping, Sergeant Joyce was doing real detective work. He's finished the tedious job of identifying everyone, through ComNet, who

was near the flat entrance shortly before Mr. Expedition's murder. The entrance is recessed, as you know,
and there isn't accurate node coverage, probably by
design. Despite that, we've got a section of ten meters
on either side that we can use. With a narrow window of time, we've got over a hundred names and
none of these names can be connected to your list
of bidders."

Joyce had been doing what Matt had avoided, for
personal reasons. He nodded toward Joyce, hoping
that it'd be taken as thanks. Edones displayed a list
of names.

"Just because there's no match to a bidder doesn't
mean that you won't recognize someone from this
node coverage. Do you know any of these names,
Mr. Journey?"

Matt watched the names scroll down the wall.
"No."

"We sliced the list based on background. We're
going to go through every slice, with the best facial
view caught on ComNet. Here's the slice for visitors
and nonresidents of Athens Point. See if you recognize anyone."

Matt watched about fifteen faces, names, and occu-
pations flash by. He shook his head.

"People employed by independent services or the
entertainment industry."

About twenty faces this time and Matt still shook
his head. "Nope, don't recognize anybody."

"All people associated with Athens Point operations."

Matt shook his head. They went through two more
slices and Matt didn't recognize anyone.

"Last slice. Government contractors and em-
ployees."

More faces.

"Wait! Go back!" Matt's eyes widened.

There, about one block from Nestor's flat, was temperamental Mr. Customs. His real name was Hektor Valdes.

"You initially mentioned corruption inside Athens Point Customs," Edones said. "Do you have proof of illicit dealings? How do you know this man?"

"Valdes was the customs inspector when we last docked," Matt said. "He and I had an—er—an altercation."

Edones's eyebrows went up and Matt had to explain the entire conversation. The argument ended up sounding childish and irrelevant, even to Matt.

"I guess he had some past problem with second-wave prospectors," Matt finished lamely.

"And his bad humor was an indication that he was on the take?" Edones asked.

"No, Nestor told me about it. He said many of the officials received payments for something. The payments were small, so he thought it was for information. I asked him to look into it for me."

This might be the reason Nestor was killed. Matt thought about the package titled "Customs." He didn't want to hand it over to Edones until he'd gone over it himself. If there was something that didn't reflect well upon Nestor, he wanted a chance to filter it.

"This is enough to get the LEF going again. They're stymied by dead ends." Edones cleared the display and turned around, leaning back and crossing his arms. "I've done my part of our agreement; it's time to sign over your leases."

"*I'd* rather wait for some results. This inspector may not be guilty of anything, other than being obnoxious," Matt said. "I also need time to plow through Nestor's will and records."

"I've done my side of this bargain, Mr. Journey."

"Doesn't this all seem a little too neat and clean?

We haven't got any motive. Then there's the question whether Athens Point LEF has the backbone to investigate the Customs Department."

"I can't influence the Athens Point LEF."

"Besides, there're too many other things that don't make sense." Matt leaned forward. "In particular, Ari's strange background."

Edones shrugged, his face blank.

Matt pressed on. "Look, I don't know how it was done, but I can tell that her history, perhaps her identity, has been altered."

"Crystal doesn't lie. And the government can't keep secrets—it's too big and inept."

"It doesn't have to. A small task force, working secretly, some time around the year 2090, could keep a lot of secrets. Particularly while everyone's attention was riveted on peace negotiations." Matt kept his voice casual, his fingers kneading the arm of the chair.

"You're speculating. What's in crystal is accepted as truth and I'll defend the data to my dying day." Edones sighed. "However, such defense may soon be moot. We've received the casualty report from Karthage."

Matt had already received a message from Ari, so he knew she'd survived without injuries. She probably wasn't supposed to be dropping him messages, anonymous or not, so he tried to look concerned. His acting abilities weren't the best, but then, Edones hadn't confirmed that Ari was even on Karthage.

"Is Ari all right?" When Edones lifted an eyebrow at his question, Matt added, "Look, I already know she's on Karthage Point."

"Don't worry, Mr. Journey. She's probably fine, although I haven't received a report from her recently." Edones's smile was coldly impersonal and not reassuring. "However, the explosion got another one of my protected flock."

Matt realized the implications of Edones's words. "She's in danger." None of this sounded, or felt, real.

"I've known Major Kedros a lot longer than you, Mr. Journey. I expect she's well aware of any danger."

"Did you expect this?" Matt clenched his jaw. He felt adrift; this conversation had depths beyond his knowledge.

"She knew the risks when she accepted the orders. Yes?"

Edones looked over Matt's shoulder. Matt turned to see Sergeant Joyce turning up his ear bug while making a vague motion. He was receiving a private message.

"New message from Karthage CP, sir. The baseline inspection was completed successfully, with an *onsite Minoan observer*. The Terran inspectors left three hours ago. And, specifically addressed to the supervisor of Major Kedros"—Joyce frowned—"the Orderly Room has declared Major Kedros AWOL. Missing and assumed to have left the station without leave."

Matt quickly faced Edones.

"That can't be true." Matt's words came out in a rush. "She'd never abandon her post. Ari's a stickler for performing her duty."

"Well, that's one thing we agree upon." Edones began to drum the top of his shiny desk with his perfectly manicured fingertips.

"You remember Ura-Guinn?" Brandon's eyes were darker than she remembered. Angry. He had been angry. After the mission.

Where have you been? she wanted to ask, but her mouth was numb, her tongue inert.

"Was it just our crew? Blowing away a system without authorization—who else was in on it?"

"No." She tried to shake her head. Couldn't.

That's not how it happened. The memory filled her mind; she saw Brandon striding through the hallways of Thera Point, home to two Naga Strike Squadrons under the Fourteenth Strategic Systems Wing.

Brandon's temper was infamous. Ari tried to keep abreast of her furious crew commander, dancing sideways as well as she could under station-g. Behind them, Cipher shuffled along solidly but she looked dazed.

"Be careful, Brandon," said Ari. "Don't do anything stupid. They didn't trust us with the truth, but at least we got back all right."

Brandon stopped abruptly and turned to her. He reached toward her temple and when he pulled back his hand, he held a chunk of her loose curls.

"*This* is all right?" He thrust the hair toward Ari and she recoiled, her hand flying to her scalp. "They *should* have told us the payload was real and they were blowing the weapons' facility, so we could do our mission the way we trained. They *should* have warned us to dose ourselves and drop out of normal space sooner, but they didn't! We were disposable. *Expendable.*"

"We're crew. We followed orders." Ari flinched as he scowled and resumed his march toward the Operations Center. She touched her temple gently and dislodged more hair. She'd pushed through nightmarish N-space without drugs, an experience that could cause disassociative insanity. She'd be under medical supervision and intravenous nutrition for days.

Ari stopped walking. She looked despairingly at Cipher. "He'll ruin his career."

"We just destroyed an entire solar system, Ari. I don't think he's worried about his career." Cipher's eyes were dull.

"No, he's thinking about his *crew*, even if he's being unprofessional about it. Cipher, get a grip on yourself." Ari grabbed Cipher's arm.

"What about the civilians on that colony? Doesn't this violate the Phaistos Protocols?" Cipher's dark eyes blazed and she pulled away.

"I don't know. All I know is that we did what we were ordered to do, and by Gaia, I got us back alive." Ari was exhausted, her knees and legs beginning to quiver as if they'd give out at any moment.

Shouting and thumping spouted out of the Ops Center. Ari and Cipher rushed into Ops to find Brandon trying to throttle the director of operations—he leapt the chain of command, ignoring the squadron commander and attacking the Wing DO. The squadron commander stood watching with a bloodless face, not moving. Everyone looked shocked and frozen, so Ari and Cipher worked alone to pull their crew commander off the DO.

"I didn't sign up for suicide missions—neither did my crew." Brandon's voice sputtered. He lost his breath and let them push him against the wall, where he slumped.

"Captain, *no one* in squadron ops was told this was anything other than a fancy recon mission. We didn't have advance warning." The squadron commander's face was still drawn. "We thought you were lost with the other ships that were transitioning. You've got your pilot to thank for that." He nodded at Ari. "Good work, Lieutenant."

Ari put it down to dumb luck. She'd dropped them out of real-space before the TD wave destroyed the Ura-Guinn buoy. They had fully transitioned to N-space before the destruction of the time buoy caused a "glitch" to shudder through the buoy network, losing anyone in direct transition.

"A ship from the Directorate of Intelligence is docking. Apparently they intend to debrief us." The DO gave Brandon a dark look. "We'll talk about insubordination charges later, Captain."

Suddenly she and Brandon were alone. He looked older. Different place, different time?

"We violated the Phaistos Protocols, didn't we?"

Her mouth worked, twisting and fighting her. "No."

Brandon's eyes darkened. His face became sharper.

"Valid orders." She couldn't make her mouth work right, not without his command.

His lips curled back from his teeth. Brandon melted into Nathaniel Wolf Kim. His eye was blackened, and one side of his face bruised and swollen. She remembered doing that with a well-aimed kick. Her head restrained, she slid her gaze from side to side to see gray walls and the familiar shape of a hatch on a ship. Kim stood in front of her and he jerked his head sideways to talk to someone.

"You've got to keep her under," Kim said.

"I can't give her any more. The problem is her ultrarapid metabolism. We'll have to recalculate the safety margin."

"No, the problem is that I haven't any neural probes. Guess I'll have to get physical." Nathaniel Wolf Kim smiled. "I'm going to enjoy this."

CHAPTER 16

Since its inception, the Phaistos Protocol has governed wartime prisoner interrogation. It only protects lawful combatants and civilians [see Minoans Define Anarchists as Subhuman], and obedience to the Protocol rests upon faith in reciprocity from one's enemy, as well as fear of Minoan retribution. Nevertheless, Terran Intelligence tortured AFCAW prisoners during the war in ways that went unnoticed by Minoan observers. Consider the challenges: No physical marks could be left on victims, modern use of bright made sleep deprivation techniques obvious and time-consuming, while claustrophobic environments are ineffective against anyone trained to pilot N-space. . . .

— *Modern-Day Torture*, Zacharias Milano, 2097.363.11.00 UT, indexed by *Heraclitus 23* under Conflict Imperative

Darkness. Pain. Needles dragged along her skin and peeled her raw. She writhed as the pain forced its way under her fingernails, tearing them away. *It's not real. Only pain-enhancing drugs.* She panted as the pain faded, but she knew that it would come again at some random moment. *Uncertainty is the interrogator's friend.* She shrieked at the sensations when they battered her again.

Then her hood was ripped off and she was blinded

by light. Nathaniel Wolf Kim's face hovered, barely discerned through her streaming eyes.

"There's no one here but you and me," he said. "No one is going to rescue you."

"Ariane Kedros," she whispered. This time they weren't trying to control her will and she could talk. "Major in the Armed Forces for—"

"Major Kedros is listed as AWOL. No one will come for her. Besides, you're not Major Kedros. *You* don't exist. What's your real name?"

She felt the effects of another drug being pumped into her bloodstream. Kim's face distorted and her heart pounded. Shadows crawled and twisted around him. Shades of N-space terrors that she couldn't quite remember.

"Four billion people gone," he said. "That's genocide. Slaughter. Butchery." Rage poured from his mouth and his eyes.

"I followed orders," she said.

"There were no orders." He slapped her face hard. Again and again. She tasted, swallowed blood. She was strapped into a slanted table and couldn't move her head. Every time his arm drew back, she twitched in agony, trying to dodge.

"You had no orders. Admit it, you're a war criminal." His voice sounded on the edge of insanity.

"Authorized."

"Your military crew went rogue."

"No. Did my duty." She coughed. Maybe she'd drown in the blood running down her throat.

He hit her again.

It had been six hours since Maria and Nathan had sabotaged the MilNet nodes and kidnapped Major Kedros. Maria had devised a clever method for getting Kedros off Karthage, although she had to give up the ventilator that allowed her to sleep. During that time, Isrid was involved with the signing of treaty paperwork, the departure, and getting the ship under way in such a public fashion that he could deny ever knowing what, or who, had been stowed in one of the lowest-level storage holds.

Now he was free to view Nathan's handiwork.

"I didn't authorize physical torture," said Isrid, tearing his gaze away. He saw Maria watching the video with an absorption combined of revulsion and fascination.

"The subject is extraordinarily resistant to will-power inhibitors, perception distorters, drug-induced pain, *and* she's an N-space pilot who's had a recent drop. I had to step things up." Nathan shrugged and looked perplexed. "I assumed that we needed a breakdown, as soon as possible, for a public state-ment of guilt."

Isrid understood Nathan's confusion. Since when did his staff need authorization for physical torture? During the war, Isrid condoned whatever it took to break the subject and achieve the goal or intelligence. *But the war's been over for fifteen years*, nagged an inner voice.

Maria looked puzzled also. A hand splint, neces-sary to support small bone growth stimulation, ham-pered her *somaural* communication.

Isrid felt out of step with Nathan. He still burned for revenge but his feelings felt shallow beside Na-than's. In addition to plain old anger, Nathan could draw from a sadistic streak that had strengthened over time. Fifteen years, however, had left its mark on Isrid and he couldn't watch this interrogation with cold objectivity. For the first time, he felt a certain . . . *distaste*.

Nathaniel Wolf Kim moved out of Ariane's sight, which gave her a small respite. When he returned, he held a baton or club, thin enough to wrap his hand around. He held it up in front of her eyes.

"You can save yourself if you'll give us a public statement. It can be short; all you need to do is admit that you violated the Phaistos Protocol."

"No."

He tapped her solar plexus sharply and knocked the breath out of her.

The constraints didn't allow her to shake her head. He drew his baton back again and she panicked, trying to speak, trying to wheeze the words out. "No. Had—valid release orders. You want—kill me. Jus— justify it."

Kim cocked his head, his eyes narrowing. "Four billion people gone. Don't you deserve to die?"

She didn't answer. He drew his arm back slowly and she waited for an agonizing moment. Pain exploded below her knees and her sight faded into whiteness.

Isrid closed his eyes. Even though he told himself that the subject was the enemy, his emotional self reacted to a large man whacking a young woman across the shins with a bat. Why was this bothering him? He'd seen much worse, done much worse, during the war. Perhaps he'd become weak; perhaps he'd changed because of marriage and children. He now had two adolescent daughters by Garnet, who didn't look much younger than Major Kedros—the enemy, the subject.

"I cracked one of her bones but I thought I'd show you the progress, SP."

The satisfaction in Nathan's voice made Isrid's stomach clench, but he wasn't a *somaural* master for nothing. He hid his reaction.

"Did you get the doc in?" Isrid asked flatly.

"Yes. She'll be ready for more soon."

"I want the doc to mend the bone and keep her unconscious. We don't need breakdown."

"What?" Nathan looked incredulous, belatedly adding, "SP?"

"We need Major Kedros to sign leases *voluntarily* or her signature can be legally contested. Isn't that right, Maria?"

"Uh, yes, SP." Maria was quicker, and more flexible than Nathan. She also had the benefit of having researched Aether Exploration's leases and knowing what Kedros could sign. "But if you need the leases for G-145 to stand up in CAW courts, the best defense is to keep the signer alive."

Nathan struggled to compose himself. "This is about paperwork? Money?"

"If her business partners contest her signature, she needs to be able to testify that she did indeed sign the leases willingly. I'm not sure you're going to get that after . . ." Maria glanced at Nathan and her voice trailed away.

Nathan looked lost and blind, with no target upon which to spend his rage. Sitting down, he curled his trembling fingers into fists, his eyes staring uncomprehendingly down at them. Isrid saw the years of impotent rage settle into Nathan's face, lining it and making him look older than his years.

"I've got the leverage to get Major Kedros's signature, as well as her support," Isrid said. "I'll deal with her personally."

"And then what, SP?" Nathan's voice was harsh and grating. "Are you telling me that she'll live, that she'll go free? After what she did to Ura-Guinn?"

"I don't know yet." Isrid was tired. What did the overlord want? He didn't have the answer yet. He used *somaural* signals: *Patience, Nathan. Times are changing.*

Isrid realized that he couldn't have *spoken* truer

words. *Somaural* communication could have that electric illuminating effect, when the body felt truth that the conscious mind refused to acknowledge. Civilization was changing for the three war veterans in this room; they had to shed their battle-weary grudges and adjust, when required by external forces, to more productive pursuits. Otherwise, Isrid and his staff were doomed to obscurity.

"I've tried to serve the League conscientiously, SP, but I can't support this approach." Nathan glowed with his anger, his hands still balled into fists. "I'm going to file a complaint with the overlord."

"That's political suicide." Isrid allowed his real concern to show in his voice, betraying ambiguous feelings. Nathan and his rages had become a comfortable, well-worn blanket, protection against change. On the other hand, perhaps it was time to get younger blood on his staff.

"Perhaps, then, it's time for me to resign." Nathan stood up stiffly, pride screaming from every tense line in his body.

"At least wait until we return from this inspection," Parmet said. "Continue your duties, and when we're back on Mars, I can see about transferring you to another SP's staff."

Nathan nodded. His face was closed, but his emotions were clear to anyone who had known him as long as Parmet. Besides bewilderment, there was disappointment and sorrow. And of course, anger, which never left Nathan alone for long.

"Don't do anything you'll regret, Nathan." Maria's voice was soft.

Nathan didn't acknowledge her words as he left the office. Maria lingered. Isrid gave her an opening, cocking an eyebrow at her.

"Are you sure you're not being influenced by your personal feelings, SP?" Her voice was hesitant, but then, she'd never trod this territory before. Isrid suspected she had an aversion to emotions, both talking about them and feeling them.

"How so?"

"This woman saved your life. Perhaps your false sense of mercy is based in gratitude."

"We need to meet our overlord's objectives before satisfying our personal needs. I'm trying to keep us employed, and Nathan would do well to remember that." *As would you*, he added with a flick of his fingers and wrist.

Maria nodded and left Isrid alone with his thoughts.

Did he have personal feelings in this case? Hell, yes. His urge to avenge his brother was strong, yet in direct conflict with some strange desire to protect Major Kedros. It wasn't because she was helpless, or seemed helpless. After subverting the security systems it had taken three of his people to subdue and kidnap her. Major Kedros had the constitution of a bull.

It was her sense of duty, her insistence that she'd followed orders at Ura-Guinn and would have done so again, if ordered, that spoke to him. Her *loyalty*. He admired its strength and purity. Her loyalty would be his weapon, his leverage.

He didn't address the nagging thought that still slithered about in his brain: Why didn't he answer Maria's question?

At first, Colonel Edones and Sergeant Joyce didn't want Matt to accompany them onto Karthage Point.

"You don't want my leases to be worked by Terran defense contractors, do you?" he'd asked.

As it was, Edones seemed distracted and he relented. Matt was issued green crew coveralls with no military insignia. Walking behind Edones and Joyce,

Matt realized that their black uniforms with the blue trim stuck out far more on Karthage than his operational coveralls. Matt turned down the visitor safety briefing being transmitted to his ear bug, in favor of trying to hear the whispered comments between people who passed Edones and Joyce. He saw sidelong glances but couldn't quite catch any muttered comments.

They stopped at Command Post first. Edones said they'd have to handle the inspection mission first, and Ariane's "situation" second. The CP personnel were duds on both accounts. They didn't know anything other than the times they transmitted their status reports. Order of reports: the explosion, the damage assessment, the arrival of the Minoan emissary, the inspection results, the departure of VIPs, and finally, the Kedros AWOL notification.

"I should have been notified immediately that a Minoan emissary arrived to observe a weapons inspection." Edones's voice could have frozen the room, but the young lieutenant commanding the CP shift held her ground.

"Sir, we put together the distribution list according to the regs." She tapped her slate and a copy of the message, with headers, appeared on the wall. "See, there's the Directorate of Intelligence XO, XI, and XT offices. They must not have redistributed the message."

The message recipient list looked like a snarled network of unreadable acronyms to Matt, but all the military types inside the CP nodded as if they understood. Matt looked around, bored. The Karthage command post could have been on any station, until he noticed the obvious blank spaces on the wall. MilNet monitoring nodes probably told the CP shift that he wasn't "cleared" for classified—*like being unclean.*

"I'll need to talk to the Naga squadron commander and the facilities commander." Edones was finished with CP.

"Sir, the facilities commander—"

"Of course, I would mean the *acting* facilities commander."

"Yes, sir."

Next, they moved to a depressing conference room, where only two news feeds and the CP announcement channel displayed on the walls. Edones made a call, requesting somebody to meet with him. After a few minutes, a tall, slim woman officer with obvious generational background entered the room.

After observing Lieutenant Colonel Jacinthe Voyage for a few moments, Matt ranged through several opinions about the woman. Initially he thought it refreshing to find a generational orphan so highly placed on Karthage. Then he decided that Jacinthe epitomized everything that v-plays taught him to expect from the military: the arrogance, the rigid adherence to irrelevant regulations, and the lack of empathy. Her military training must have beaten out her generational upbringing.

She and Edones talked about inspection results that Matt didn't bother to follow, then moved on to the subject of Ari.

"Face it, Colonel. You put your faith in an unreliable and unremarkable reservist. Now she's skipped out on you." Jacinthe smirked.

"Perhaps." Edones seemed preoccupied, interested in the inspection reports that were scrolling in front of him.

Matt gripped the arms of his chair tightly and it peeped a small alarm of warning. He froze as he saw Joyce glaring at him and he bit back his words. He'd sworn to Joyce and Edones, in the names of Gaia and St. Darius, that he'd remain quiet on Karthage. His movement caught Jacinthe's attention and she looked at him, her gaze cold and unreadable. Then her eyes flickered away. She hadn't asked who Matt was or why he was in the room. Perhaps she knew; she could have queried Karthage systems before briefing Colonel Edones.

Matt looked at Edones. Why didn't the bastard stick up for Ari? After all, he'd selected her for this mission.

"You realize that Major Kedros's missions are special access only," Edones said casually. "So you shouldn't take her records quite so *literally*."

Jacinthe's face went wooden and Matt got the feeling that she was reassessing.

"I didn't think the Directorate of Intelligence would use reservists for sensitive missions," she said.

"It's obvious you didn't think, Colonel Voyage." Edones's voice was sharp. "Since Major Kedros's *unofficial* performance is exemplary, I can only believe there's a driving reason she left Karthage. Have you investigated?"

Jacinthe stiffened. "Since she was attached to my squadron, I directed the SF commander to do the normal investigation. He did so, to my satisfaction."

"Then I'd like to speak, face-to-face, with him." Edones nodded in dismissal.

After Lieutenant Colonel Jacinthe Voyage left, Matt's emotions burst out.

"She obviously doesn't like Ari—how do you know she doesn't have something to do with Ari's disappearance? Why didn't you ask her more questions?"

"Because, Mr. Journey, this is the military." The corner of Edones's mouth twitched. "You don't have to *like* your coworkers, your subordinates, or your superiors, to do your duty. Nobody has to like you either, so personal opinions regarding someone's personality aren't supposed to be relevant to an investigation. We're not into fuzzy feelings like the generational ship crews."

Joyce cleared his throat. "Colonel Voyage might not be likeable, but she's respected. We've looked at squadron performance and they've done well on evaluations under her leadership. One thing to consider, since Major Kedros came in as intelligence liaison officer, is that it'd be natural for squadron members to distrust her."

"Why?" Matt was amused to see Edones and Joyce shift uncomfortably at his question. These military types were shy about examining psychological motives—not that Matt liked the way generational ship lines managed their people. The adage "the ship is your parent and the crew is your family" could be literal depending upon how long the mission took in relative time. Any general unhappiness, malaise, or malcontent was nipped in the bud, or bludgeoned to death, by counseling. Anyone who opted off, like Jacinthe or Matt or Nestor, had to go through torturous touchy-feely seminars to prove that they believed the generational ship life wasn't for them.

"Major Kedros was an outsider to the squadron, so many of the squadron members would keep their distance," Edones said.

"Because she wore the black and blue," Joyce added.

"Yes. The Directorate of Intelligence falls under the Inspector General, and they have a naturally antagonistic relationship with operations," Edones said. "Ops has to be evaluated and the evaluators aren't ever going to be loved or appreciated, nor should they be."

"So Ari's true mission required that she be an outsider?" Matt asked.

"Nice try." Edones's face was bland.

"It's as obvious as the Great Bull's balls that Ari was here for more than the treaty." Matt shrugged. "Maybe Colonel Voyage sensed that."

"All gargantuan genitalia aside, Mr. Journey, you're the last person I'd give clearance to see Major Kedros's orders."

Matt's attempt to get Edones to admit that Ari had a secondary mission was interrupted by the arrival of the SF commander, Captain Rayiz. Rayiz glanced toward Matt and raised his eyebrows in question to Edones.

"He's not cleared for classified, but I doubt your findings on Major Kedros will be a problem," Edones said.

"They're official use only."

Edones nodded. "My authorization for release to Mr. Journey is already on file."

Rayiz summarized the results of his investigation. The last time Ari was recorded by the Karthage systems had been when she checked in with Senior Technician Stall at sick bay. The tech was called away to a minor medical emergency.

"Where?" asked Edones.

"The Thirty-second's training bay, cab number three. Colonel Voyage had punctured her hand on some equipment and the wound needed to be sterilized and closed."

The tech came back to an empty sick bay, but since the scan he'd started had finished correctly, he thought Major Kedros had left for her quarters. He updated her records per her new radiation exposures and went about his work. No one knew she was missing until she didn't show for the inspection completion briefing at the Ops Squadron.

"Any sign of a struggle?" asked Edones.

"In sick bay?" Rayiz's eyebrows rose. "I didn't ask the tech. If there was, I'm sure he would have volunteered that information, even called the SF when he came back to check on the scan."

"What did MilNet show?"

"Uh—we don't have recordings from sick bay for that time."

Matt noticed that Edones had gone still. A moment before, Edones's fingers had been drumming the edge of the desk in front of him and now they lay quiet.

"What happened to your MilNet coverage?" Edones asked.

Rayiz's face blanched. "We had a regularly scheduled test of the MilNet nodes in sections six-Delta through six-Gamma. They somehow got stuck in test loops for half an hour."

Edones tapped his slate and a slice of Karthage Point displayed upon the wall. Below the diagram Matt saw the word UNCLASSIFIED printed in bold black letters. He could see those sections included medical facilities and guest quarters. Edones tapped again, and the names GUILLOTTE, KIM, and TRAVIS appeared, displayed in red on three separate guest quarters. Another tap. The word KEDROS floated in blue above one of the medical examination rooms.

"So we can't track the actions of these four people, which include three TEBI agents and my operative." Edones's voice was so soft that Matt had to strain to hear him. "Let me guess: You went back to your published node test schedule *before* the inspectors left?"

Matt hadn't thought Rayiz's face could get any more ashen, but it did.

"We thought we could stop randomizing unclassified tests. After all, the inspection was over."

Edones poked a little on his slate. Matt suspected that Edones had authorization to Karthage Point's security records, so he wasn't surprised to see

Edones point the slate at another wall and bring up video displaying a line of people going through an air lock. Their clothing was alien. These were the Terran inspectors and they wore tight, clinging jumpsuits that were devoid of interesting decoration and color. Unlike Autonomists, they stuck to the range of natural skin and hair colors. Perhaps because of this limitation, there was a *sameness* about their features, height, hairstyles, and clothing. Several of the Terrans were women.

Edones froze the video on a woman wheeling a crate-size piece of luggage. She had straight and smooth medium blond hair, cut bluntly at chin level. Matt thought she was attractive enough, but her generic and regular features seemed to rule out any chance of being beautiful. She'd never stand out in a crowd.

"Maria Guillotte has Tantor's Sun disease and required special medical equipment. We examined everything when she boarded." Rayiz swallowed hard.

"And now you're realizing Guillotte's equipment could easily be dismantled and stuffed into vents—where we'll probably find it. Do you realize you've allowed them to kidnap a CAW intelligence agent? From what we know of TEBI, she's now being interrogated, perhaps tortured, all because of your sloppy security."

Matt's stomach lurched at Edones's biting words. *Interrogation. Torture.* Having been on a generational ship during wartime and always protected by the Phaistos Protocol, he tried to fit those words into his reality. The thought of Ari undergoing torture sickened Matt, and by the stricken look on Rayiz's face, it affected him. Edones and Joyce remained emotionless.

"Sir, we didn't know Major Kedros was at risk

from the Terrans. After the explosion, we were distracted. I should have been warned—"

"I noted that Major Kedros's request for more frequent deep scans was ignored by your office, Captain. We'll be performing our own scans to ensure that the Terrans didn't walk away with other sensitive material," said Edones.

So Ari's only sensitive material to you? Matt thought Rayiz's protests carried merit. Edones's proclivity for secrecy was the root of this problem and Matt still preferred to blame him for putting Ari into danger in the first place.

"We ran periodic scans according to regulations covering visiting heads of state," Rayiz said.

"My equipment is different, Captain." Joyce stood up. "Let me have a look at every part of the station that Major Kedros went through."

Rayiz's eyes widened. "That's a lot of real estate."

"Then we need to start now, Captain." Joyce motioned Rayiz to exit.

As he left, Rayiz glanced sideways at Edones, whose face might have been set in stone. After the hatch closed behind them, Edones turned away and Matt thought he saw the facade slip out of place. For a moment, anger slid over the cold politic features before Matt saw the back of Edones's head.

"What happens now?" Matt directed the question tentatively toward Edones's back.

"We wait." Edones turned around, again his pleasantly bland self.

Did Edones have *feelings* for Ari? Somehow that thought made Matt uncomfortable.

After he got the medical reports, as well as confirmation that Major Kedros's bone was healing, Isrid headed to the hold where she was kept. When he

climbed down to the lower level, he found Dr. Istaga
waiting for him.

"This level has limited access. It's only open to me
and my staff," Isrid said coldly.

"Certainly, SP." Istaga smiled ingratiatingly.

This was a Terran ship and they no longer had to
worry about spying ComNet nodes, but Dr. Istaga
kept his hand and wrist close to his body when he
signaled: *SP Hauser told you who I am, and to whom I
must answer.*

Isrid had thought Istaga couldn't project, but he
was wrong. Most *somaural* masters moved with a pre-
cision that implied their specialty. Istaga slouched
and his body and physical movements didn't look as
though he did any daily exercise, yet he was able to
project complex sentences. He hid his abilities well.

"I understand," replied Isrid aloud. "But unless
you want to produce identification and clearances,
you still must leave this section."

"I wanted to warn you. I know who, or rather
what, you're holding." Dr. Istaga gave a nod of disdain toward the hold where Major Kedros was kept.

Istaga's subtext was clear, stating that Overlord
Three would receive his independent report. If Overlord Three passed this on, the entire top echelon of
the League could know that Isrid captured one of
the crew members that detonated the *only* TD warhead, the warhead used against the League. When
they dealt with the Consortium, the overlords preferred to have a united front—and that usually didn't
include forgiveness.

"What does Overlord Three want from me?" Isrid
was tired of guessing.

"I don't envy you your choices. Most overlords
like initiative in their state princes, but not too much.
You've got a fine line to walk, keeping the welfare

of the League in mind. Remember that Overlord Three must pass a vote of confidence within a year."

"What would you do?" asked Isrid.

"Me? Personally? I'd take out all sweet acts of revenge possible upon her body and put her out an air lock. But *I'm* carrying around mental baggage from the war and *I* don't carry the responsibilities of a state prince." Dr. Istaga wagged a finger.

Isrid glared at him. Dr. Rok Shi Harridan Istaga, also known as Andre Covanni, wasn't leaving him with any advice of value.

"You're a state prince," Istaga said softly. "Even though she saved your life, she offers the League a boost of morale with a statement of guilt. Humiliation at a Terran trial for her war crimes might be even better. Consider what would be best for the League when you make your final decision."

CHAPTER 17

Am I the only one disturbed by the latinization of Common Greek? Latin phrases have always played a part in our insanely complicated legal code, but now it's insidiously creeping into our everyday language! [Link to examples]

—Rant: *Purity of Our Language*, Stan Gregorios, 2104.345.12.15 UT, indexed by *Heraclitus 21* under Conflict Imperative

When Isrid entered the hold, he turned off all cam-eyes and monitoring equipment. He knew, just like Nathan, that all interrogations should be documented, but he couldn't afford records of *this* decision, *this* interview. It would be controversial because no solution would please everyone. It'd also give his political rivals too much material.

The ship's scrubbers worked vigorously, but they couldn't clear the smells of blood and sweat. He walked over to the table and looked down at Major Kedros. She was conscious.

After seeing the results of Nathan's handiwork numerous times, Isrid expected that she'd look worse. The swelling around her eyes had gone down enough to let her see. The bruises on her face were already turning green. Under stimulation her bone was mending quicker than the norm, according to

the ship's doctor, who told Isrid privately that
Kedros might be the result of minor, but successful,
rejuv.

Isrid heard that AFCAW had dabbled in rejuv, although it was dangerous and unreliable. Instead of
attempting full-body rejuv procedures, TerraXL med-
icine focused in the area of genetic design and eugen-
ics, but Isrid had ordered the doctor to take as many
samples from Major Kedros as possible while she
was unconscious. He didn't want to pass up the possibility of snagging medical advances for the League.
It was a violation of CAW privacy law, but honoring
that was laughable, considering what they'd already
done to Kedros.

"Major Kedros."

Her eyes focused on him, but they were devoid of
fear or hope. She was naked and vulnerable, yet she
had no fear of dying. Not now. He knew he'd made
the right decision.

"I know you want to die," he continued softly.
"That'd be the easy way out for both you and me.
Instead, I'm guaranteeing that you'll get off this
ship alive."

As he expected, alarm and pain flashed through
her eyes. Her mouth tried to form a one-word question. *Why?*

"I won't insult Nathan by saying that you're tor-
menting yourself more than we could, but I'm happy
to see that you're shouldering the guilt for what
you've done. I'm stopping your interrogation, so you
can consider *what you owe us for Ura-Guinn.*"

He paused. As always, naming the system where
his brother had probably died caused a surge of pain
and anger. He savored it while he traced along her
neck and her jawbone with his fingers. She flinched
at his touch and he smiled.

"Truthfully, Major, part of me would be disappointed to see you break, and the other part would revel in your pain. But you saved my life, so I have a debt to pay—rather small when compared to yours, wouldn't you say?"

She closed her eyes.

"You must bargain for the same clemency for *others*. That will be your punishment, and after I pay this debt, if we see each other again, don't expect the same mercy." Isrid released her restraints and left the hold immediately.

She estimated several hours had passed since Parmet had removed her restraints. She dozed, trying to regain her strength. Then she limped about the small climate-controlled hold, designed to store sensitive goods or be converted to temporary quarters. She wanted to assess her prison, but also to find her uniform. Where were her damned clothes?

Currently, the hold was decorated in late-twenty-first-century torture-chamber style. In the center of the floor was a convertible stretcher with a skeleton restraint, where the occupant could be horizontal or slanted to almost vertical. This was where she had been when she woke.

The hold lacked a full hygiene closet, but there were rudimentary waste and water facilities in a closet set flush in the wall. She relieved herself, ignoring decorum. Let the watchers make the assumption that she thought she was unobserved. The baton that Nathan had used on her was neatly stored in one of the lockers, with a few other basic torture implements.

There was no mirror, but she probed about her face, neck, collarbone, breastbone, and shoulders. She pulled off flakes of dried blood and she winced from the bruising, but she didn't think that any bones had been broken. Her legs were a different story. Her shins throbbed and displayed massive purple and green bruising. Stippled pricks, perfectly parallel, stood in rows drawn across her right shin. It looked like the effects from a bone growth stimulator. She was familiar with what the stimulator did, temporarily, to the skin.

They'd treated her and allowed her to heal, after they'd beaten her. Did they fix her, only to torture her again? She vaguely remembered Parmet leaning over her and saying there'd be no more torture. More specifically, he said there'd be no more *interrogation* and insinuated that she should be grateful. In exchange for—for what? Parmet obviously wanted cooperation and information.

She clenched her teeth, feeling hungry, sore, tired, and *most* uncooperative at this moment. Besides, what could she give them? She doubted they'd be interested in most of Owen's dirty little missions. The fact that she'd broken an arms smuggling ring or rooted out a double agent hardly seemed worthy of Parmet's attention. He certainly wouldn't risk the Mobile TD Weapon Treaty or angering the Minoans, just for that.

He also appeared unconcerned about pursuit or justice; he probably banked on AFCAW ignoring this little kidnapping, to keep the treaty together. She could understand that. She doubted that Owen would risk Pax Minoica for an expensive embarrassment like her. Nathaniel Wolf Kim was right; she was alone.

Brandon. Did they want him also? She started pacing again, clenching her jaw. They wouldn't get Brandon's location from her, not voluntarily. Her memory was hazy about what happened while Kim interrogated her, but she was sure she'd never give up Brandon.

"Step toward the closet wall and turn your back

to the door. Keep your hands away from your body."
Maria Guillotte's voice sounded in the room.

Amused, Ariane did exactly as ordered. This
wasn't a v-play. Did they think she could overpower
all her guards, race naked through a fully manned
ship, and overpower the pilot and controllers in a
ridiculously lengthy combat sequence? Ariane had run
a good amount of v-plays during the long stretches
of second-wave prospecting, but she could tell the
difference between drama and real life.

The door opened and closed behind her. She
smelled food. Her stomach rumbled and kicked.

"Turn around. Keep your hands in view and your
back against the wall," Maria said.

Where did Maria think she was going to hide her
hands? Ariane slowly turned around. She heard hollow noises in a sequence that indicated she was behind a dual-hatch air lock for separately pressurizing
this hold.

Parmet and Maria stood in front of the closed
hatch. Parmet held a food tray and Maria held a stunner, aimed at Ariane. Strangely, this was the first
time she felt self-conscious about her dress, or lack
thereof, but she held her head high. While her situation was similar to many plucky heroines in v-plays
and she had the advantage of *knowing* how to pilot
the commercial TM-8440 used by the Terrans, she
saw no hope of escape. The stunner Maria carried
was standard TEBI issue; it was accurate and aimed
with professional and unwavering ease. Ariane
wouldn't get through the first hatch, much less to
ship controls or an escape pod. Besides, an escape
pod only meant a lingering and painful death.

"She looks well enough, SP. Be cautious." Maria
made a motion with the hand that didn't hold the
stunner. That hand was splinted.

"I hope I did that." Ariane nodded at Maria's hand and smiled.

Maria's eyes narrowed.

Ariane didn't say anything more. It wasn't wise to provoke an armed TEBI agent and it might not take too much to irritate Maria, particularly if she knew Ariane's history. Searching her memory, Ariane couldn't remember from the background briefs whether Maria had relatives on Ura-Guinn.

Parmet stepped forward and put the tray of food on his side of the constraint stretch, now set horizontal, then stepped back. Maria and Parmet were acting as if she were a dangerous caged animal, poking her with sticks while they stayed safely behind Maria's stunner. The food smelled wonderful. They hadn't given Ariane leave to step forward, so she stayed where she was, her back against the bulkhead. Her impatience with the silence goaded her into speaking first.

"Well, if you're not going to kill me, then you're risking the entire weapons treaty."

She said this in a deadpan voice. She was *tired* of hiding. She couldn't escape her wretched life through alcohol or drugs or N-space. Not that she wanted to kill herself—but if she could stop the expansion of the galaxies, stop the motions of the planets, and step away from her life as if it never happened, she would.

"No, you're staying alive." Parmet's green eyes were wide and honest, his face open. His voice was gently chiding and familiar, as if at any moment he was going to say, "Ari, please just call me Isrid."

She knew he was playacting with the subtle use of *somaural* projection, but she couldn't help relaxing her stance. It was an involuntary reaction to his non-threatening body language and she tried to compensate by stiffening. Maria had a knowing smirk on her face, probably quite aware of the tricks that Parmet was using.

"Why?" Ariane asked.

"You have to be able to attest to the real story," Parmet said.

"Which is?"

"You went AWOL, overwhelmed by the terrorist bombs, weapons inspection duties, whatever, by stowing away on our ship. Of course, you'll probably be stripped of your commission."

Parmet smiled warmly, but Ariane snorted.

"For payment of transporting you to Hellas Prime, you're going to sign over the leases managed by Aether Exploration," continued Parmet. "Don't bother to argue about their significance. We already know what your civilian company discovered and we know you've got signature authority. You'll sign them voluntarily, and your voice stress must pass any duress limits. After that, you'll be on Hellas Prime, alive and able to testify that you did this all willingly."

Her mouth dropped open; then she collected herself. "Why, in Gaia's name, would I *ever* agree to such a fairy tale?"

"Because I know where your fellow crew members are hidden." Parmet's voice was silky. "I can publish their location on ComNet for everyone to see."

An involuntary shiver went up her spine. *How can he know where Brandon is?* She started to cross her arms over her chest—an involuntary reaction of protection—and stopped when she saw Maria twitch her weapon.

"Come, Major Kedros. We both know there's an assassin out there, waiting to finish all of you." Parmet's voice became gently chiding again.

"How do I know that you're not the killer?" Ariane clenched her jaw. She was lying, trying to get time to think. She knew Parmet wasn't responsible for the explosion on Karthage and therefore wasn't the assassin.

"All you have to know is what *I* know, and what I'm bargaining with." Parmet raised and twitched his hand in a liquid motion. A familiar voice, the voice of the Minoan emissary, filled the room: "The other Destroyers of Worlds are located within the Demeter Sanctuary on Hellas Prime."

That's how they knew. Ariane didn't bother to argue about what "Destroyer of Worlds" meant, or find out whether they recorded the entire conversation, or how they'd obtained the recording.

"There are thousands of people on that sanctuary. You wouldn't know who to target," Ariane said.

"That'd be up to the *someone* who's pursuing your crew. I'm only publishing the information." Parmet shrugged. "All the more reason to cooperate with us and not put innocent people in danger."

"How do I know I can trust you? You might release the information anyway after I leave." She might be able to get to Hellas Prime and find Brandon, warn him—

"She's thinking that she can find her crew before we can, SP." Maria's voice was level.

"That's impossible, Maria. And we'd release the information before she hit the surface of Hellas Prime." Parmet smiled, his eyes focused on Ariane. "This will be a long-term relationship, where each side has leverage."

"Blackmail, you mean," Ariane said.

"Whatever you want to call it. We can find your remaining crew members—we *will* track them down—and you can always try to claim coercion to rescind these contracts. The advantage for *you* is that having you alive, supporting your signatures, is better for us than killing you. The automatic investigation and suspension of your signatures issued within six months of your death would not be in our best interest. Until the six months pass, of course."

"CAW has such incredible legal snarls; the Consortium must have been established by lawyers," Maria said in an offhand tone, as if commenting upon the service at a restaurant.

Ariane slumped against the wall. It all boiled down to Matt's business and her military career versus Brandon's safety. What was a bit of money and her career, compared to the life of someone she'd respected, perhaps even loved?

But she had to consider other losses. Matt, as well as Owen, would never trust her again. *I can live with that, if it keeps Brandon alive*. It would also keep her alive, for six months at the least, but she didn't look forward to that. *Matt shouldn't have trusted me in the first place*.

Maybe she should try delaying tactics—but somehow she knew that this was the only chance Parmet was going to give her. It'd take him hardly any time, and cost him nothing, to publish Brandon's location. There were plenty of crazies out there and at least one real assassin. . . . She squared her shoulders and took a deep breath. "What do you want me to sign?"

Parmet pointed to the wall on his right, where a display appeared. Ariane saw approximately fifteen leases on the right side of the view port, with eight companies on the left side.

"*All* these leases are offered by Aether Exploration?" she asked, a bit perplexed.

"These are the ones for which you have signature authority. They cover the research, development or exploitation, from mining to archaeology, of the small moon that Aether Exploration charted."

She didn't need to be told *which* moon. For a moment, she wondered why Matt had split everything up into small leases and contracts. Did any of these leases explicitly cover the artifact? Regardless, this many leases would require significantly more coordination between contractors, Aether Exploration, and the CAW SEEECB. She shrugged. It didn't matter; she'd never be dealing with Aether Exploration again.

Parmet decided which company was applying for, and receiving, which lease. Maria handed Ariane a slate and she signed, using her public password for voiceprint and her thumbprint. There'd be no question that she signed these contracts. Parmet also required that she provide a standard free-will statement, which she recorded in a steady voice. There was no way Matt could rescind her signatures, because she *wanted* these contracts to stand. They were Brandon's safety net.

"Is that enough?" Ariane handed the slate back to Parmet by leaning over the stretcher. "I don't know how believable it'll be. I don't usually authorize the contracts."

"Oh, we'll make it believable," said Maria.

Ariane heard the snap and sizzle of the stunner. As she spasmed into unconsciousness, she hoped she'd broken Maria's hand, and she hoped it'd hurt.

Isrid watched Maria check Kedros's still body.

"She's out. For how long, though, I don't know." Maria prodded and kicked Kedros in the ribs. When there was no reaction, her lips widened in a satisfied smile. She glanced toward Isrid and he saw her pupils were widening and her respiration rate had increased. Maria was intoxicated with rendering Kedros helpless.

"If this works, then we're going to rise in the overlord's eyes like a shooting star. We, meaning myself and my staff." His hand, brushing by his hip and flickering, said, *Anyone who doesn't support me will be left behind.*

She knew he meant Nathan and he saw her nipples harden through her suit. The rivalry between them would never die. Still standing over Kedros, she holstered the stunner. "And if this doesn't work?"

"I think it will." He told Maria what he wanted her to do. After all, he promised Kedros she'd leave his ship alive, but he didn't say in what condition.

Maria was amused, but a bit puzzled. "Don't we need to protect her from the assassin you mentioned?"

"No." Isrid shrugged. "I'd like her to last at least six months, but if we're clearly blameless, her signatures would probably stand through the investigation. We do need to get as far from her as possible, and quickly."

"Your plan works best if she lives. Nathan will be displeased, but your debt to her is paid."

"I arranged this primarily to hold on to those leases," he said sharply.

"Certainly, SP." Maria leaned over and straightened out Kedros's body. She traced down Kedros's breastbone with her finger. "But there's now a connection between you two."

She was referring to the belief that significant emotional exchanges and debts—blackmail probably qualified as well as saving a life—could connect two auras. The connection showed as visible blotches and stains. Isrid hoped that Kedros's blue and turquoise wouldn't be tinged with his orange red. It'd be a shame, even though the colors were complementary.

"As between you and Sabina?" Isrid asked.

"I was told that you saw the video." Maria had worked her way down to Kedros's hips and legs. If Isrid didn't know better, he'd assume she was ensuring that Kedros didn't wake up damaged or in pain. Maria's fingers became distracting, at least to him.

"You can search our auras, SP, but I doubt you'll find any debts. You know I'm not looking for a *connection* in the bedchamber." Maria's lips parted and her tongue caressed her upper lip. She was looking down at Kedros. "Can I dress her when the time comes?"

"If you want." His tone was careless. He had to find out, however, whether she understood that Sabina's attention didn't change anything. "I understand Sabina's urges, but what *are* you looking for in the bedchamber? To use your euphemism."

Maria stood up and walked toward him. Her gaze slid sideways to the table and the skeleton restraint. She smiled, every part of her body expressing, suggesting.

"Experimentation." She stepped close and he felt her fingers release the seal at his crotch.

A good thing too, since his erection was demanding attention. Isrid rewarded himself with one of those perks that comes the way of state princes.

Edones, Joyce, and Matt had squeezed every drop of relevant information they could from Karthage and had regrouped in Edones's office on his cruiser. Now Matt was so angry that he thought his head would blow apart.

"What do you mean, you can't do anything?" he shouted at Edones, all decorum dissolved. "You know she's on the Terran ship and you're not going to have it boarded?"

"I told you: With the state prince aboard, they have diplomatic immunity."

"That's Great Bull–shit. I've read enough interstellar legal code to know that diplomatic immunity doesn't cover criminal actions, such as *kidnapping*."

Matt wasn't boasting; he'd studied the ISS code pretty thoroughly before launching his business.

"Maybe so, but accusing a Terran state prince of a crime under ISS is way beyond my authority."

"They subverted AFCAW security—hell, they probably tried to blow up Karthage Point! One call to Alexandria Port Security or Hellas Prime Customs and you'll have stopped them." This seemed so simple to Matt. They just needed to catch up, since the *Bright Crescent* was following the same flight plan as the Terran state prince's ship.

"Captain Rayiz cleared their departure. There's nothing to connect them to the explosion and everyone has alibis," Edones said. "The explosives were set on the outside of the station, and Rayiz is already tracking down a possible lead with a contractor's maintenance drone."

"But Ari said there had to be someone on-station to help—and you don't have an alibi for anyone in section eight-D before the explosion. That includes the Terran state prince." Matt had viewed all the unclassified interviews.

"It also includes Major Kedros." Edones used a calm, reasoning tone. "Karthage security has degraded atrociously, considering their MilNet outages. The new facilities commander is having them wipe all their systems, rebuild them, and reinitialize them with chaotic key particles. All expensive procedures, opening a window of vulnerability—"

"I was asking about Ari," Matt said, his anger now smoldering in the pit of his stomach. "What are you going to do about *her*?"

Yes, that was what it all came down to: *Ari*. Matt watched Edones and Joyce exchange a glance. Edones looked a little uncomfortable. *Maybe now I'll get the truth.*

"Major Kedros will realize that the weapons treaty

is our highest concern," Edones said. "We can't afford risking this treaty with a—a political incident between us and the Terrans."

"Like rescuing her? For Gaia's sake, you said they're torturing her!"

Matt stood up with clenched fists. Joyce went into a stance that meant Matt would suffer a lot of pain if he launched himself across the shiny desk and throttled Edones. There was a tense moment before Matt sat back down and forced his hands to relax.

"We can get the AWOL charges smoothed over and we might be able to save her career. However, Major Kedros knows she can't put us in a position of choosing her safety over the stability of the weapons treaty."

"I don't give a floating fuck about her *career*, or your treaty."

"It's not *my* treaty. Everyone's duty in AFCAW is to keep the peace. Pax Minoica is now embedded in our culture, our lives," Edones said.

A chime from Matt's ear bug stopped his reply. Matt had an incoming message, marked private, from his ship. His ship? The *Aether's Touch* had no active . . . uh-oh, Nestor's Muse 3 was apparently taking its own initiative.

"Uh, I have a private incoming message. Can I borrow a slate?" Matt flipped his tone one hundred and eighty degrees, becoming unexpectedly polite. He reddened when he saw Joyce's eyebrows go up.

Edones nodded, and Joyce reached in the side pocket of his crew coverall leg and handed Matt a slate. Matt ignored their watching eyes as he dumped the message to slate. He read through the results and couldn't help widening his eyes.

"News?" Edones asked in a light tone.

Matt looked up and glared at him. The MilNet systems had probably siphoned off a copy for these jerks to look at later, but he might as well show Edones the contents since they concerned Ari.

"Some of my leases were signed by Ari a few minutes ago. I think you'll recognize the companies that are now holding the leases." Matt handed the slate back to Joyce.

"All Terran-funded shell corporations." Joyce's voice was grim.

"Just what we didn't want—what are you grinning about, Mr. Journey?" Edones's voice became sharp.

"They're not going to kill her, don't you see?" Then, as Joyce's and Edones's puzzled looks remained, Matt added, "You guys need to read up on CAW contract law. As part of probate, all signatures the deceased makes within six months of death are suspended, pending investigation. They can be reinstated, but if it looks like death didn't occur naturally or the deceased was coerced—"

"Or murdered?" Edones nodded. "But what happens when you contest her signatures?"

"They're valid, and Ari had the authority to sign those leases. Now *I'm* being coerced." Matt's voice was flat. "They're waiting to see what I do. If I contest her signatures, the resulting investigation might suspend the leases for as long as a year. Not only that, I'd expose them as kidnappers and they might as well kill her. They know I know that."

The office was silent for a moment.

"This is a quandary." Edones's voice was as flat as Matt's. "We can't have the enemy controlling the leases and subsequent contracts in Pilgrimage-G-145."

Anger surged through Matt's blood again. Edones's suggestion *was* the equivalent of refusing to pay a kidnapper's ransom. Did this bastard think he'd risk Ari's life?

"First, there is no '*we*.' This is purely my decision

and I'll let her signatures stand." Matt's voice was low and vicious. "Second, there is no *enemy*. Not for me. The war ended fifteen years ago. Third, don't be thinking I've got nothing to hold over you, Edones. Ari had signatory authority to less than half the contracts. I reserved some for my signature only."

Edones grimaced, which Matt interpreted as relief.

"You surprise me. I didn't expect you to hold healthy amounts of distrust toward your business partners."

"I trust her." Matt glared back. "I was trying to get Ari interested in the business without overwhelming her."

"Major Kedros may not be the reliable business partner you're hoping for, Mr. Journey."

"Why?" Matt asked bluntly. "Does it have to do with all the years of altered records? Is she connected to Ura-Guinn?" Matt tossed out the questions quickly, hoping to provoke a reaction.

But there were no twitches in Edones's too-perfect facade. Matt watched Edones with narrowed eyes. There was also a little nagging voice in the back of his mind; perhaps he had distrusted Ari, deep down.

"It was the Consortium that originally funded the G-145 mission. We should benefit from the proceeds, not the Terrans."

Edones was taking another tack—didn't the man ever give up? This objection, however, Matt was prepared for, after working J-132. Governments were usually the biggest financers of generational ship missions, where the designations G-145 and J-132 were *mission numbers* and not astronomical designations. The generational ship lines always had to consider the unpredictable political environments; circumstances might not be the same after they took fifteen, twenty, or, in the case of G-145, approximately twenty-six years to drag a Minoan time buoy out to a system and open it to N-space traffic. This was why generational ship lines had offices near both the Consortium and League nerve centers.

"J-132 was financed during the war also, but by the League. My company's already been through one interstellar and multigovernmental opening." Matt smirked. "Our SEEECB has a counterpart under TerraXL. They exchange information, approve the contractors, and give me a *qualified* list of contractors. Some of them are Terran and they're bidding for my leases. Don't worry, the Consortium can get its cut from any new system."

"There's still plenty of room for AFCAW contractors?" Edones asked.

"Certainly. That's why I'm not going to be contesting Ari's signature."

Matt had layered and interwoven the lease coverage, providing what he thought were checks and balances. It was lucky he'd done that, because now he had to play the Minoans against CAW against TerraXL, and he couldn't let Edones know that. He was unsure of what it would mean to give the Minoans a seat at the table; they were an unknown in this game of dividing the resource pie. Moreover, Matt had no doubts that this was a dangerous game, particularly when dividing G-145. Nestor might have been murdered for it. Just because the SEEECB had approved a contractor didn't mean they were automatically clean, with no connections to organized crime.

"We have an hour before we reach Alexandria Port and I believe Athens Point LEF has questions for you. Shouldn't you be helping them?" Edones asked, effectively changing the subject.

CHAPTER 18

Ha. You Autonomists think you've shed all the outmoded Sol technology. You're the new colonies, innovative and brilliant. You think Hellas is the center of art, society, and science. Gibber on, you morons. Universal time is still run by Terra's orbit and your measurement units were developed, for the most part, on pre-Terran Earth. So don't go . . .

—*Rant: Because I Can*, Lauren Swan Kincaid,
2105.045.02.55 UT, indexed by *Heraclitus 12*
under Conflict Imperative and *Democritus 17*
under Metrics Imperative

The economies of the Prime planets were booming and Hellas Prime was no exception. Alexandria was the largest city in the southern hemisphere of Hellas Prime, sprawling over seventeen thousand square kilometers. It wasn't the most densely populated, with about eleven million people and an urban plan that incorporated strips of greenbelt to allow natural flora and fauna to migrate through the city. Alexandria was reputed to be the most beautiful city on the most prominent Autonomist planet in the Consortium. Consequently, it also boasted the highest property taxes.

Even the crown jewel of Hellas Prime, however, had its seedy neighborhoods. One of these was the

Karaborsi Canal, where liquor, drugs, and prostitution flowed, if not freely, then economically. The Alexandria Addict Commons purposely abutted the Karaborsi Canal, since "retirement" to the Commons didn't require any actual dropping of habits. The only requirement for keeping supplies moving across the fence into the Commons was a friendly relative willing to send stipends, whether credit or goods for barter.

Hellas Daughter was in decline and the moonlight was faint. The weather stayed in that uncertain evening drizzle, as if committing to steady rain was too strong a statement. Tonight in particular, Thales wished he'd taken his mother's advice as he stomped back to his position at the front admittance counter of the Commons.

Get a doctorate and go into genomics, she'd said. *That's what's hot.*

Thales had disagreed. He didn't want to go through that much schooling and take on that many debt-years. He didn't think genomics would be a viable long-term career. Now what was he doing? *I'm an orderly—just strong-armed security.*

Earlier in the evening, Thales had quelled a small tempest with the residents before it developed into a riot. He was going to have to talk with Dr. Phan, one of the staff rehabilitation therapists, about his choices for interactive v-plays. To get their v-play, residents had to agree that they were rehab possibilities. They also had to agree to subject themselves to rehab messages presented in the v-plays.

Dr. Phan had made a bad choice. He'd picked a drama where a character was degraded by his alcohol use, and drowned because of the degradation. Most of the residents that went interactive chose to be the main character and vicariously experience the alcohol, as Dr. Phan had predicted they would. The v-play caused strong reactions when the main character cleaned his feces-smeared trousers in a swift deep stream that would ultimately lead to his drowning. These reactions weren't quite the ones Dr. Phan had hoped for, because the designer of the v-play apparently didn't have a good grip on alcohol abuse.

"Where's the drugs?" screamed a resident, Carolyn. But then, she was never satisfied with the v-play experience. Thales had to eject her from the connection.

"Wouldn't happen. Nobody shits their pants—nobody eats if they're a drunk. You *piss* your pants, you don't *shit* your pants." Another resident, Tank, was methodically trying to stop the v-play interaction by pulling out the sensory feeds in the connection panel. His nickname was unfortunately descriptive, and Thales had to call for extra muscle to get Tank back to his billet.

After this crisis, Thales had settled back in at the front desk and opened view ports to his favorite feeds beside the displays within the Commons. Through the glass doors, he saw a long, dark car pull up outside. It was too nice for this neighborhood, probably a rental. He saw two figures get out and struggle with a third limp, insensate form.

A check-in. Sighing, Thales changed all the public view ports to generic landscapes. The view ports behind the admittance counter still displayed, but couldn't be seen from the other side. The Commons management didn't like visitors seeing the living conditions of the residents.

Hearing the doors whoosh open, he arranged his smile, raised his head, and froze in surprise. He'd thought he'd seen everything—but perhaps not.

The future resident was a young woman with a lolling head of dark hair. Thales could smell the reek of alcohol three paces away. Her eyes fluttered a bit,

indicating she'd probably taken smooth with her alcohol. She wore an AFCAW uniform. None of this
was unusual. Crewmen and -women were often
brought in to sober up, and an AFCAW superior usually showed up to chew them up and check them
out, not necessarily in that order. AFCAW took care
of their own.

The two escorts, however, captured his attention.
They looked similar in body size and weight, but
their clothes were all *wrong*. They were tight and
stretchy and the color of mud, with no lights or displays or decorations. Thales knew they were Terrans
since he was devoted to his feeds. He had watched
a hurried interview with the Terran state prince,
who'd hit Alexandria Port only a couple of hours
ago. The state prince said he was here for a short
bout of "sightseeing," as he'd called it. When he later
wandered the port's shops with his security, crowds
of remotes followed him and loaded their video
onto ComNet.

Thales had never expected to see Terrans standing
at his front desk. "May I help you?"

"We'd like to commit this woman," said the male
Terran, frowning. He looked grouchy, perhaps because of his blackened right eye and the bruises on
the right side of his face.

"You want to *admit* her?" Thales said.

"Of course." The female companion smiled
warmly at Thales. Her hand was splinted, but she
looked concerned for the young woman they held up
between them.

"Do you have custody or power of attorney for
this person? Do you have authority to waive her privacy?" Thales brought up his admittance checklist on
the countertop.

"We found this woman. We were told we could

drop her off without signing anything. . . ." The woman's voice dropped off into a slightly questioning tone.

"You don't have to provide your names, ma'am," Thales said, marking the drop-off check boxes titled "Good Samaritan" and "Anonymous," which were misleading. He wasn't going to point out that since the Commons was partially government funded, the lobby was a public place. Because of that, the admittance area was noded and this event would probably be indexed in the public domain.

"Will you be making a donation?" Thales asked hopefully. Then, when the Terrans looked at him quizzically, he added, "It might make her stay more comfortable." *And boost my quarterly bonus.* His mother had warned him away from civil service and now he knew why. The salary was pathetic.

"I don't think we'll pay anything for this woman's *comfort*," the male said stiffly. The female nodded in agreement.

Thales shrugged, but he pressed his lips together in irritation as he marked "Unfunded."

He displayed a map on the wall and pointed to it. "We'll need you to identify where you found this woman, while I call medical support."

The Terrans pointed out a well-known alley near Karaborsi Canal, and Thales was surprised that they'd only seen *one* insensate drunk sleeping it off beside a popular bar and brothel. Once the on-call medic arrived with a stretcher trailing behind him, the Terrans displayed their misapprehensions about CAW privacy law.

"What do you mean, you can't analyze for alcohol and drugs?" The Terran male sputtered with outrage and looked as though he was personally affronted. The female made a fluid gesture with her hand and

he immediately quieted after giving her a vicious
look. Thales figured the woman was in charge and
the man resented her.

"She's in good shape. If her vitals indicated some
sort of distress, then we'd be authorized to take measurements for medical purposes," Thales said. "Otherwise, we'll log her name and rank, since it's public
information. We'll get more data after she sobers up."

If she sobers up. Thales watched the Terrans lean
the slight woman—he never remembered the
names—against the stretcher. The constraint netting
squirmed and tightened as the medic rotated the
stretcher to horizontal and onto its expensive antigrav. Thales usually didn't bother to look at the future residents, but this time the woman's face caught
his eye. It had been bruised from a beating, possibly
a couple of days ago. *Just what I need: another trouble-
maker.*

"Hey, she's a reservist," said the medic, pointing
his slate at the wall. "Are we still required to send
a message to AFCAW?"

Thales turned to look at the display, and the Terran
female rotated smoothly and immediately, but her
curiousity seemed feigned. The Terran male looked
at the wall almost as an afterthought. *They know this
woman.*

Thales read the unusual information on the wall.
The woman's public record listed her as an AFCAW
Reserve officer, but also as a civilian N-space pilot.
She actually had to take drugs to make her living. In
Thales's experience, he'd expect this woman to ex-
hibit what they called "supercontroller behavior."
She had to regulate her doses of strange substances
so tightly that she'd probably only let loose in safe
environments, in places she knew, not in Karaborsi
Canal bars.

Everything was suspicious about this admittance,

but Thales had no guidance on what to do, and he was tired. He noted the woman was currently on active duty, but she seemed to have two supervisors. In that section of the AFF-5290, it read: "Lieutenant Colonel Jacinthe Voyage (Liaison Assignment); Colonel Owen Edones (Directorate of Intelligence)." What did that mean?

"I'll have to check the regulations to see if we're supposed to notify her supervisors." Thales sighed. It was his bad luck to get a problem child tonight.

"In the meantime, where does she go?" asked the medic.

"Induction Three."

When the medic's eyebrows rose, Thales jerked his head resentfully to emphasize his decision. This woman would cost Thales extra research and time, so why not throw her into the harshest tank with the hard-core addicts? It'd teach her a lesson.

"Anything more you need from us?" The Terran woman was already drifting back toward the doors.

"No, ma'am," Thales said.

As she turned and walked through the doors, her companion walked casually close to the admittance counter. He glared at her back, and then at Thales, who resisted backing up a step or two. The Terran then touched a switch under his skin near his wrist and laid his hand on the counter. At this universal gesture for transferring data from an implant, Thales looked down on the counter.

Not surprisingly, it was a bribe. He was offering Thales a credit of five hundred thousand Hellas drachmas, or five hundred HKD. This amount wasn't going to change Thales's life, but it could pay his subsidized rent for two months. It was a provisional transfer, and to qualify, all he had to do was notify the provided contact of Major Kedros's admittance within the next ten minutes.

Thales recognized the number. It was for a black market provider of transplant organs, still hot business because less than thirty percent of the population had the cellular biology capable of accepting their own vat-grown organs. Thales looked up and saw the female Terran getting into the car, apparently unconcerned with her companion's tardiness.

Looking into the male Terran's eyes, Thales nearly flinched at the anger he saw in the gray-green depths. Without dropping his gaze, Thales tapped his fingers and moved the provisional deposit into his account.

Ariane tried to move away from the hard hands pushing, pulling, but she couldn't. *Leave me alone.*

Hands went through her pockets, pulled at her uniform. Ripping off parts of her jacket.

"Any jewelry?" A male voice.

"Just on the uniform. Don't know if there's a market for it, though." A younger male voice.

She tried to open her eyelids, but they were just too heavy. She couldn't raise her head, feeling weightless, yet helpless. Did she feel good? Did she feel?

More hands, roughly pushing her hair around, examining her ears and her neck. She couldn't protest. Someone was taking off her boots.

"Too small for me." A female voice.

"Sell 'em over the wall." The same male voice.

Questing fingers opened her collar and moved downward, exploring her undergear and her breasts.

"She's not stacked, but she's firm." The younger male voice.

"No," Ariane said. That one word exhausted her.

"Wait till we find what credit she has, Smith." Authoritative woman's voice. Same as before? How many people were crowded around her? If she could only open her eyes—

"Yeah, you horny bastard."

"You want some smooth, don't you?"

"This might be better."

Fingers fumbling at her belt. She kicked out wildly, but someone lay across her legs and held her down. She felt dizzy, as if she were circling a great whirlpool.

Did she pass out? Voices above her rose in argument. The weight was gone, and then somebody kicked her in the ribs. She curled in pain and got another kick in her kidney area.

"Ain't worth nothing."

"Wait till her relatives or CO arrives, and squeeze them."

Then they were gone. She was alone, as she wanted.

This time the probing was different, like the military medical exam she had every year. Her eyelids almost worked, opening a slit, but the dim light was painful. There were two people looming over her and they had slates. Neither of them had white coats and her vision was too blurry to see any military rank.

Leave me alone.

"Excellent kidneys and liver—almost like she never abused. Lots of alcohol and smooth in her bloodstream. It'll take a while to flush the organs." The voice was puzzled. "Still waiting for full typing."

"What's at the top of the list? Might as well fill the most expensive requests."

These people were different. Where was the first rabble?

Someone was pulling down her pants, but this time she didn't think sex was the objective. A fog smeared her eyesight and she could barely make out the figures, one starting to undress her and the other near her hips and holding a slate. Now she could aim.

"Hey!"

She had connected her right foot with the figure trying to pull down her pants, and then twisted to hit the wrist or forearm of the other with her left foot. She heard a slate skitter across the floor.

"Help." The word came out of her dry mouth as an unintelligible croak. She tried to get up, but only managed to roll and fall on the floor. She must have been on a bed or stretcher.

"Strap her down."

A weight pressed her down as she tried to sit up. Suddenly there was tape over her mouth and around her wrists. She tried to keep kicking.

"Give her something! She's coming up."

"On top of what's already in her bloodstream? It'll ruin the liver for sure. Don't know how she's even moving—"

Pain exploded on the side of her head. She heard other voices. Arguing with raised voices.

"Stop that."

"Who the hell are you? You're not the LEF."

"Leave her alone."

"We got here first."

"Yeah, unless you want to pay—"

Sizzle-whack! Shock baton or stunner set on high power. She knew that noise. Screams. Shouting. *Sizzle-whack.*

Quiet. She felt as if she were floating to the top of a pool. Somebody was putting her on a stretcher, but it felt as if it were happening to someone else. A cool hand touched her forehead.

"Don't worry, Ari. You can sleep now."

Did she know that voice? It was tantalizingly familiar, but more than anything she wanted to go back to the darkness. *Please leave me alone.*

CHAPTER 19

Before the Assumption of Holy Avatars back to Gaia's Heart, a young man named Darius entered the Kristos Order of the Three Crosses. Brother Darius was given the mission to serve the Order on the new colony on Titan. In this harsh environment, Darius learned he had a gift for ministering to those who must trade their life-times for passage to the stars. Darius chose to leave Titan, beginning his faith-challenging travels on the . . .

— *The Chronicles of Saint Darius*, approximately
2052 UT, reindexed in 2066 by *Heraclitus 5*
under Flux Imperative

"You shouldn't accompany us, Mr. Journey."

"I got the necessary shots," Matt said. "And if you want AFCAW's fingers in G-145, then you'd better let me go along."

"Your threats are wearing thin," Edones said.

As if my threats worked on you anyway, you manipulative bastard. When they docked at Alexandria Port, Matt wanted Edones to march over to the Terran ship and confront them about kidnapping Ari. Of course, that didn't happen. Edones was convinced his blessed treaty was at stake and no amount of pressure from Matt could sway him.

Then two messages arrived, almost simultaneously, announcing Ari's admission into the Alexandria Addict Commons: An official notification came to Edones and Nestor's Muse 3 sent Matt a similar report. That AI of Nestor's was becoming damned useful, and Matt hoped he'd be able to keep it. Edones hadn't voiced much interest in the package Nestor had sent Matt, at least not the kind of interest the LEF had shown.

Captain Sanna and the Athens Point LEF were making pests of themselves. As soon as the *Bright Crescent* had arrived at Alexandria Port with Matt, they'd wanted to have a long discussion with him regarding Nestor. He'd begged off with an excuse that he had an emergency, which was true. Then he'd caught up with Edones and the faithful Joyce as they were leaving the ship, intending to depart the orbital port for Hellas Prime. They were impatient to go, but Matt demanded that he accompany them. Edones and Joyce, of course, resisted.

"You haven't had enough time to build up resistance to the allergens." Joyce was referring to the planet-specific shots that Matt recently received.

"I'll tough it out," Matt said.

"When did you last go planet-side?" Joyce asked.

"Doesn't matter."

Joyce looked doubtful. "There's going to be a lot of open sky."

"I can handle it," Matt said firmly. He hadn't been on a sucking gravity lump for—well, for more than a decade. He'd have problems, but he'd adapt. Eventually.

"We're riding down on a rock. Have you been medically cleared?"

"Of course." Matt's heart sank, but how else did he figure they'd get to Alexandria proper with minimal delay?

Edones and Joyce exchanged a glance. Edones

shrugged and said, "Fine. You get to take care of him."

The words were directed to Joyce, not Matt. Joyce gave Matt a hard look, causing the man's face to flame up again. *Now I'm a babysitting job*?

Matt had previously ridden a reusable reentry vehicle, fondly called a "rock," but it wasn't his favorite way to get planet-side. He stoically followed Edones and Joyce through preflight briefings and signed all his waivers. Afterward, he paid careful attention to the fit of the equipment he was renting: helmet, mouth-guard, pads, g-suit, ear protection, and gloves.

He didn't panic until the three of them started climbing into the cramped vehicle.

"Where's the pilot?" He looked wildly around. At some point, a rock became aerodynamic and entered planetary air traffic; hence, the nondestructive landing that made them reusable.

Edones turned to look at him. Joyce rolled his eyes.

"I'll be piloting," Edones said. "Any problem with that?"

Yeah, lots of problems. Matt wanted to demand to see Edones's license, last qualification date, aero and glider scores, but instead he quietly said, "No." Subdued, he climbed in behind them and webbed into the seat. The egg-shaped interior of the rock held four people; couldn't they have hired a commercial aeropilot?

Matt tried to quell his quivering stomach. Almost anyone could get an aeropilot license, he reminded himself. But his crèche-begotten instincts said that moving through space was safer than moving through atmosphere. Air tore a vehicle up and there were so many things to slam into, namely the *surface*. There were also all sorts of orbital objects about Hellas Prime and *tons* of air traffic—

He was building his worry into panic. He'd soon be hyperventilating if he didn't stop this. He opened his eyes to see Joyce watching him with a stern expression, which sobered him.

"Besides, these things practically fly themselves," Edones said cheerfully, looking over the instrumentation. "Let's see. Where's that autopilot switch?"

Matt gulped, but when Joyce gave a gruff bark of laughter, he stiffened. They were having fun at his expense. Matt felt his face flush with anger, but that was better than fear. He was going to deal with his contrary instincts as rationally as he could.

When the time came to disconnect from Alexandria Port, Edones became all cold efficiency, much to Matt's relief. The professional discourse that helped the rock fire its small thrusters and head it into safe ballistic reentry was almost soothing. It didn't seem as though there'd be any problems until it came time to deploy glide surfaces and dodge the ground, which he'd white-knuckle his way through, like before.

He checked his webbing, put in his mouth-guard, let his gloves and boots strap in, and closed his eyes, if only to avoid looking out the front windows. Why did aerodynamic vehicles have to have windows? They were distractions and radiation hazards. N-space-capable ships couldn't have them and they got along fine with instrumentation. However, when the shaking and g-forces intensified, he snapped his eyes open.

"Alexandria Control, this is RRV-9236. First attempt to deploy G-S." Edones's voice strained against the forces.

"Acknowledged, RRV-9236."

The voices were tiny and metallic because the speakers in the helmet were cheap and they couldn't connect to his implanted ear bug. Matt's fingers clutched his handholds. Deploying the glide surfaces was the riskiest point in this flight. A small double-finned tail had to pop up and fins would have to extend from the sides, without getting ripped off or damaged. This was where one had to have faith in the engineers and maintainers, but just to be safe, Matt prayed to St. Darius. *There are twenty to thirty successful rockfalls a month to Alexandria—please, please let us be one of them.*

Every year or so there was also a failure, and that's why their ballistic trajectory had them going straight into the New Agean. It was also why he had to sign waivers: *Yes, I know I'm stupid to strap into a rock and aim myself at a planet surface, but I accept the risks because of the need for expediency and I agree to release . . . blah, blah, and more legal blah.* If the glide surfaces couldn't deploy, then they'd have to hope that the rock didn't explode and the emergency chute deployed correctly. If so, they might survive smacking into the ocean.

Net-think said it was safer to fall by rock than fly on an airliner, but that was based upon twisted statistics. Since far fewer people were carried in rocks, Matt knew that rocks weren't safer on a per-person basis. But then he didn't like to travel by airliner either.

The RRV jerked and Matt's helmet slammed into the sloping side. The surface, as seen through the front windows, twirled as Edones played with the instrumentation.

"Alexandria Control, this is RRV-9236. G-S deployed. We have aero."

"Acknowledged, RRV-9236."

They'd passed the most difficult hurdle of their flight as Edones changed them slowly into a glider and headed toward the special runway for rocks in the southern hemisphere, right on the edge of Alexandria proper. Matt had to admit, *privately*, that Edones seemed to be a competent and mature aeropilot. The man followed his checklist steps precisely and exhibited a calm familiarity with the instruments.

Matt stretched surreptitiously and discovered sore muscles from fighting the turbulent ride. His fingers were tight and he tried to stretch them out. Glancing at Joyce, he realized the sergeant had fallen asleep. He'd *slept* through that?

Joyce woke up, however, as they came closer to landing. He and Edones looked out the windows and pointed out landmarks to each other while Matt closed his eyes and tried to relax. Then he had to keep his eyes open for the actual touchdown, as if being prepared would help him. Gripping his handholds, Matt was silent through the smooth landing and subsequent taxi and cable hookup. He tried to steel himself, because the worst was yet to come.

Luckily, they didn't have to jump out of the RRV directly into the wide, wide open. Instead, they were towed into a hangar with low cover. After pulling themselves out of the rock, all three of them did the "spaceman shuffle" as ground crews that never worried about shifting gravity or free fall cavorted about the RRV and checked it for damage. Edones headed for a door in the hangar, followed by Joyce and Matt. As last in line, Matt saw that both Edones and Joyce loosened up quickly as their planet-side upbringing started to take over. Their legs began to push away from the deck easier, their bodies began to sway and bounce.

Then Edones opened the door. Through it, Matt saw the wide open waiting for them. The sky was deep blue, almost aqua, but a few clouds scudding across it and the wind ruffling Edones's hair ruined any deception of it being a habitat dome.

Matt clenched his jaw as he stepped through the door. *Think of it as a ceiling. You're not going to spin off.* The ceilings of Athens Point corridors were high and could display as sky, when there weren't commercials moving across—*but it's not the same. Don't look up; don't look at the horizon!*

"We have a rental car waiting," Edones said as Matt crumpled. "Oh, for Gaia's sake! Get him up, Joyce."

Nothing Matt's conscious brain said could keep his body from flinching and going down onto the safety of hands and knees. Growing up on a generational ship and spending so many years under cover overwhelmed his cognizance. Without a deck above his head, his instincts wanted EVA apparatus, tethers, and the familiar sound of air supply to keep him from flying off into—whatever.

The deck was rough and black, absorbing the sun's heat so well that Matt's hands were almost burning. He saw Edones's feet continue toward a car, while Joyce squatted next to him.

"Amazing what some men will do for love," Joyce said dryly into Matt's right ear.

What the hell?

"What?" Edones's voice was sharp.

Matt raised his head, with difficulty, to see Edones standing a few meters away with his hand on the door of the car. Edones frowned, his eyes narrow as he watched Matt and Joyce.

"I'm helping my *employee*. She's gotten me through a lot of dicey situations and she deserves the same support from me." Matt said this through gritted teeth, keeping his voice low.

"Just giving him some words of encouragement, sir," was Joyce's answer to Edones.

"Encourage him into this car, will you?"

"I need a moment. Give me time to adjust," Matt

muttered, but Joyce grabbed the neck of his coveralls and hauled him to his feet despite his protests.

"You need to get over this for the sake of your *employee*. Keep looking at the ground and stay steady." Joyce kept his hard arm around Matt's torso, guiding him to the car.

With each step, Matt felt better and by the time he reached the car, he was on his own feet. It wouldn't have been so bad if they hadn't landed in the middle of a deserted prairie, for Gaia's sake. He felt comfortable inside the car, even though Edones and Joyce wanted to open their windows in the front seats. Matt couldn't find any position in the back that avoided the breeze coming from their windows.

The rental car was legally constrained to only operate on autonav. Edones told the car their destination and it smoothly turned and took them around the hangar. It edged into traffic along a wide boulevard that went westward into the city. The landing port was on the outside edge of Alexandria, which explained why they'd landed in the wild.

"Look at that."

"Beautiful."

Edones and Joyce were pointing out a raucous display of orange, yellow, brown, and green to one side of the road. They were flowering plants about three feet high, with bright petals and dark brown centers. They looked tangled and chaotic to Matt, wildly encroaching onto the boulevard. They needed tending and he thought they looked garish in the bright sunshine. Purple sprigs appeared here and there, peeking out from the warmer colors.

Matt started sneezing and his eyes watered. His sinuses clogged quickly and he used one of the extra ampoules he'd been given for planet-side irritants. He wished he had more of them. Of course, if Edones and Joyce closed their windows, he could breathe the air from the car's particulate filters. They probably thought they were toughening him up by exposing him to hot, dry wind full of pollen, dust, bugs, and only Gaia knew what else.

Matt sat back and crossed his arms, refusing to complain. *Next they'll be shoving food grown in dirt at me*—but there was only so much he'd suffer for Ari. Joyce's sly comment irritated him, but perhaps that's what Joyce intended. Matt knew he'd gone beyond feeling "professional" about her, but this wasn't about love. Soon after he'd hired her, Matt concluded that he and Ari wouldn't be compatible—hmm, in that way. Both he and Ari tended to date attractive (pretty) and nontechnical (dumb) sorts. Sometimes Ari even went for the nonprofessional (couldn't hold a job) types. He was realizing that both their tastes ensured that neither he nor Ari formed permanent relationships, which was a revelation of sorts, but not close to Joyce's insinuation.

Matt shifted his attention to the traffic on and beside the roads. They'd periodically passed through greenbelt and lightly populated suburban areas, but now had reached business and manufacturing districts. The day was apparently a nice one for those planet-born; he could see that Edones and Joyce were trying to suck up every photon possible of the late afternoon sunshine.

Matt, on the other hand, was trying to prevent sensory overload from the breeze, the warm dry air, the pollen, and the dust. Another bout of sneezing overcame him.

When he finished and could breathe again, he watched pedestrians wandering on the sidewalks, doing window-shopping or whatever sort of business people do under the open sky. Remotes weren't a plague on planetary surfaces; they became too expensive if they had to deal with wind, rain, dust, stronger gravity, and sporadic node coverage. Besides, most government and industrial facilities didn't permit their use and many businesses, such as restaurants, salons, resorts, and merchants with real inventories, paid for facility shields. Remotes only abounded on space habitats, unfortunately, where kits and parts were readily available, and ComNet coverage permeated every cubic foot of public space.

His body gradually relaxed; he was getting used to the wide open. The sun was setting. Tall buildings threw most of the boulevard into shadow and they dashed through blinding rays of sunlight only at the intersections. They'd been on this same road for the entire trip, and Matt started to get bored and impatient.

"When are we going to get there?" He couldn't suppress the tired whine in his voice. "Shouldn't we be at the Commons by now?"

Joyce turned around to face him, looking as if he was desperately trying not to laugh.

"What's so funny?" Matt crossed his arms.

"Sorry. I just had a flashback of a trip I took with my sons." Joyce snorted.

Matt raised his eyebrows. He'd never imagined that Joyce had a family. Where did they live? When did he see them? Did they go on assignment with him? Matt sidelined his questions and pointed at his watch.

"It *has* been over two hours," Matt said. Just to be sure, he double-checked that his watch was synchronized with a UT source.

"Alexandria's a big city; we're having to cover most of its width." Joyce sounded as if he were placating a child, which didn't sooth Matt's nerves.

"Can you check the car's nav?"

Joyce leaned forward and tapped on the nav

screen. "We've got another forty minutes," he said shortly.

"The summer rains have started," Edones said, unexpectedly turning around. "Did you bring outerwear, Mr. Journey?"

Matt shook his head. Yet another thing that the planet-raised always thought about; didn't they realize that year after year of opening a door and stepping out into the wide open made them different? They tried to acclimate the generational orphans from the ship lines, but it wasn't the same. Matt didn't know anybody from his orphanage who had settled planet-side. Everyone went back to space, one way or another.

"We can stop and get you something." Edones waved vaguely at the merchandise outlets they were passing.

"I'll be fine. Don't delay on my account." Matt's voice was tight. He leaned back in the seat and looked away.

That was how his own stubbornness led to him shivering uncontrollably in the lobby of the Addict Commons. He was drenched with warm rain when he ran from the car through the automatic glass doors into cool air. Shaking his dripping arms, he waited as Edones came in and threw back his hood. Both Edones and Joyce had ultrathin coats folded in the cargo pockets on their uniforms.

The lobby was white and institutional, devoid of seating. The heavy attendant behind the desk appeared to be younger than Matt and was wearing the standard healer-green tunic, but it was dirty. Was that blood smeared across his lower torso? The attendant's dark eyes flickered over Matt and dismissed him, focusing instead upon Edones's uniform.

"If you're here for that Major Kedros, you're too

late," said the attendant. "She was picked up last night."

Her hangover felt familiar. Waking to disorientation and the aftereffects of overindulgence had become customary. She was starving; her body was processing smooth and alcohol, but when? Where?

Ariane quietly groaned as she raised her head. She squinted against the bright light. After her eyes adjusted, she realized that curtains were drawn but the rough weave glowed with direct morning or afternoon sunshine. That, combined with the secure feeling she couldn't fall out of bed, meant she might be on Hellas Prime. The gravity was too strong for Hellas Daughter.

Ariane rolled to move herself to a sitting position and *did* fall out of bed. Whether her body hadn't adjusted to the gravity or whether it was the hangover, she didn't know. Luckily, the bed was on a low platform and she caught herself before her face hit the slate floor. The rough, natural surface felt cool to her hands.

She pushed herself up and sat on her knees. She was wearing some sort of hospital gown that tangled and twisted around her thighs. Her fingers caressed the slate tiles, the rough grout, and the dark wood of the bed platform. Her glance traveled about the room, noting the dark heavy beams on the ceiling, the adobe walls, and furniture made from dark wood and leather in clean straight lines. The curtains were natural, made of rough-woven cloth in a light color that complemented the olive and cream bedding, the multicolored slate, and the tan walls.

The temperature was mild, reminding her of summer on Nuovo Adriatico. She smelled the sharp spice of late summer flowers. A breeze ruffled the curtains and moved through the high-ceilinged room to an open doorway that was twice her height. There was an open beam across the top of the opening and she could see more slate continuing into a foyer.

Her nerves basked in the restful natural materials. They were also pricey. The decorating, the materials, the open windows, and the modern structure all said that they were expensive, under their Zen-spa-retreat style.

Ariane leaned back onto her heels, and her shin complained by sending a shooting pain up and down her leg. She remembered Nathaniel Wolf Kim, holding a club. Flashes of images: Kim, Parmet, Guillotte, an unshaved face leaning close to hers—the Addict Commons. Was that before or after she signed over Matt's future to Parmet? She was going to be sick.

She staggered into the unobtrusive bathroom. She barely saw the high windows and slanted sunshine traveling up the walls before she made for the ubiquitous toilet. Down on her knees. Arms braced on the bowl like an old friend. Dry heaves. *This is familiar*.

She had no food in her stomach. When had she last eaten? How much alcohol and smooth had the Terrans pumped into her? She was sure they used legal substances, but Gaia only knew how much. Her implant would show blood sugar and alcohol levels over time, as well as the current UT. She pressed the access contact embedded under her skin and pointed toward the most likely wall, commanding a display.

Nothing happened. She tried all the walls, just in case. The rough adobe was an unlikely displayable surface, but she'd seen amazing things done with thin organodisplay materials. She tried voice-only ComNet access and decided that there were no active nodes available. Somebody had taken naturalness to the extreme. The slate continued into the bath, where there was both a shower and large soaking tub. Somebody also had a lot of money and wasn't shy about spending it on luxurious amenities.

Ariane craved a hot shower. She stepped toward the shower, dropping her gown, and shied away from movement she saw in the corner of her eye. It was a full-length mirror so, unfortunately, she glimpsed her entire body in its current glory. She usually prided herself on keeping her frame trim and muscular. Now the green and yellow bruising that marched up her legs, reappeared on her shoulders and arms, and covered her face overwhelmed any possibility of looking healthy or sexy. That was old bruising, but there were new bruises on the insides of her thighs. She remembered the face of a young man, unshaven, leering over her—had she been raped?

Her heart pounded, yet she was numb. She started the hot water and stepped into the shower, hoping to shed the feeling of slime and filth. She leaned against the wall and let the water pour down her back. Fragments of memory floated about in her head, with enough glimpses of close sneering faces to disturb her; she tried to piece the wreckage together and figure out what had happened in the Commons. Nothing made sense.

She felt carefully around her vaginal area, prodding for sensitivity. She didn't have any pain or bruising. Should she get a medical exam? An exam could identify all abuses to her body, including rape. She didn't have to worry about pregnancy, thanks to her implant, but did she want to *know* what happened in the Commons? She couldn't tell anybody about the actual kidnapping if she was going to protect Brandon. Besides, going to a medic and saying that she didn't *know* what had happened to her was a humiliation she'd never expected.

Maybe later. When she had her cover story pieced together. When her flashes of memory made sense.

Ariane shivered and pushed up the temperature of the water. Only by the grace of Gaia had she avoided this fate in the past. She'd experienced blackouts before, but she'd always had confidence in her surroundings to keep her safe. She'd been careful to do her drinking and drugging with people she trusted and she stuck with people who took care of her. She always had people she could call.

Like Matt—and look how I screwed him. As far as he's concerned, I went on another binge and signed over his contracts in a fog of alcohol and smooth. He warned me, and now he'll never forgive me. Worse, she knew that faced with the same circumstances, she'd sign over the contracts again.

Placing her forehead against the slate, she cried silently. Painful, wracking gasps—if that was crying. *I'm so tired of this existence. Owen gave me a spanking-new life and I ran it into the ground too.*

She didn't know how long she stood in the shower or how much water she wasted; she didn't care. Eventually she steadied. There wasn't any point in regrets. Even if she could live everything over again, she couldn't see herself doing anything different. She'd make the same decisions. *I'm born to be a fuckup in whatever life I'm given.*

Ariane turned off the shower, stepped out, and toweled off. Looking down at her discarded gown with distaste, she searched about and found a folded white robe in a cabinet. She wrapped herself in the thick, thirsty, clean fabric.

She circled several times around the bath and bedroom in her bare feet, searching for her uniform. She'd have settled for *any* clothing, but it looked as though she was stuck with the robe.

The rooms were so large that she now called it a

suite, since it had a foyer. Peeking her head out of
the foyer double doors, Ariane discovered a large
central hall that was open on both ends. She saw the
flash of pink and white as someone entered doors at
the far end, toward the center of the complex. Was
this some sort of hospital? Her suite was on the outer
part of the hallway. Beyond her suite, a fountain
splashed in the open air of a patio. Drawn to the
delightful sound, she walked onto the patio and
found a man was sitting on a low platform, facing
outward to the setting sun.

In her bare feet, she was so quiet the man didn't
notice her. He wore only loose trousers. He wasn't
healthy; crisscrosses of scars, unmistakably from surgery, sprawled across his back and torso. He was
flexible enough to sit in a lotus position, but he had
tubes in his neck, shoulders, and down his arms. Implants for analysis and dispensing drugs appeared as
raised lumps on his upper arms and thighs.

Her feet felt the transition from smooth, cool slate
to warm sandstone. She padded around to the side
of the platform to study his face, seeing rivers of pain
etched on the unfamiliar features of indeterminate
age, anywhere from forty to eighty years. His eyes
were closed, the eyelids lightly covered with fine
wrinkles, the lashes dark but thin.

She turned to the view he faced and drew in her
breath. They were near the edge of an escarpment.
Below her stretched a wide valley that was the prod-
uct of erosion. It was wild, perhaps greenbelt. On the
other side of the valley, grasslands rose into foothills;
then foothills merged into rough mountains, kilometers away. The sun setting behind the mountains
made them more ominous, turning them dark with
bright edges. Rays of light shot out across the hazy
sky, deepening it to aqua with firebrands for clouds.

"Now you see why I bought this land." The man's

voice made her jump. She turned to see a stranger's face looking up at her. His unfamiliar smile pulled crookedly to one side, probably because of nerve degradation or internal scarring.

"Welcome to the Demeter Sanctuary, Ari. Your registration at the Addict Commons was a matter of public record and I arbitrarily decided to check you out, so to speak, overriding the objections of a black market organ broker. I hope you'll like these accommodations better."

His voice had roughened and changed with age and pain, but in his eyes, she saw that familiar flecking of green within brown.

"Brandon?"

CHAPTER 20

Here's an update on Ura-Guinn for all you net-rats. You say you've had enough of that and you're tired of glitch data conspiracies? Well, my little netlings, they say they'll know for *sure* what happened—in about four months, when the light-speed data reaches us. Yawn. *Riiiiight.* On to more interesting things, such as my analysis of the Marino versus Simons blockbuster match . . .

—Dr. Net-head Stavros, 2105.298.21.01 UT, indexed by
Democritus 29 under Hypothetical Effect Imperative

"*S*he's gone?"

Thales stepped back from the counter, in case the agitated man reached across. One of the uniformed men, the tallest one with the mustache, reached out and placed a warning arm across his chest.

He'd seen this before. That was a mistake, to *care* too much about an addict. Nothing good could come from an addict. Addicts pulled anybody who cared about them through the muck and mire; they bankrupted their caregivers of wealth, energy, and spirit, like vampires. Thales had seen caregivers break down in relief when addicts checked into the Commons. Regardless of whether the caregivers were parents, siblings, children, or lovers, they'd had their trust betrayed countless times for any small chance of a high. He knew why these caregivers gratefully sent stipends to those inside the Commons: It was much cheaper and easier than having the addict live with them.

Not that life got better for anybody when alcohol and drugs were removed, a sour revelation to Thales that rendered his workdays both endless and useless. Sometimes addicts could be cured. It often took voluntary neural probing, plus reprogramming, plus therapy, plus group support for such a success, but in the end, everybody who cared about the addict would be gone. Why? *Because human nature is perverse.* After all their nagging, whining, and martyrdom, caregivers found they didn't *like* the new drug-free addict. Or they'd been controllers and they could no longer dominate the drug-free addict. Or they discovered they carried too much resentment toward the addict. Pick any reason.

Addicts couldn't win, because their relationships went up in flames whether they used or not. The corollary for everyone else was *never care about an addict.*

Thales felt no compassion for the agitated man, who apparently hadn't yet learned that rule. He was lean and tall, looking out of his element, like any other crèche-get on Hellas Prime. Raking his hand through his short blond hair, the crèche-get stepped back to stand behind the two military men and shiver in the conditioned air of the lobby.

The military man with all the silver on his collar had Thales's attention. His uniform displayed the familiar AFCAW emblem on the right breast pocket, but had some emblem involving a candle on the left. More importantly, the black uniform with the light blue edges matched the uniform that Major Kedros had worn, as it'd looked when the Terrans brought her in. Now the uniform was dispersed among the residents of Induction Three.

"I'm Colonel Edones." The man's bland plastic face formed into a cold impersonal smile.

"Yes, sir." Thales kept his tone respectful. He had the feeling he shouldn't screw with this man. Colonel Edones might not *care*, but he wouldn't accept incompetence and he probably saw through lies with the easy facility of someone who kept secrets himself.

"I have authority to access Major Kedros's private data." The colonel set his hand on the counter to perform near-field exchange with his implanted identification, and gave his public password.

Thales looked down to check authentication. Colonel Edones was exactly who he claimed to be. Military supervisors never responded this quickly, and they usually sent a noncom to collect their wayward charges. Dread tightened Thales's stomach into a knot.

"Now tell me what happened to Major Kedros," the Colonel said.

Tell this cold reptile of a man that his charge had vanished, leaving behind a dead black-market organ broker? Thales's instincts told him that he should divert this pesky colonel away from the Commons. He quickly put a spin on the story, grabbing the safest conclusion for his purposes.

"She's gone, leaving us a murdered man. We finished cleaning up her mess when I came on shift. EMT was called in about three a.m., they called *both* LEF and the coroner. I'm betting that, by now, Major Kedros has been charged with murder." Thales's voice was tight as he looked down at his tunic. Damn, he'd gotten blood on it when he helped the coroner load the body onto the stretcher, but that gave his story veracity.

The crèche-get's mouth dropped open and he glanced at the two military men, who didn't react to Thales's words.

"What did ComNet get?" Edones asked.

"Thanks to privacy law, we don't have ComNet nodes inside Induction," Thales said. "It's not legal confinement."

"Who signed for her?"

"There's no requirement to check *out* of Addict Commons, as opposed to checking *in*—"

"There's our tax drachmas at work," the crèche-get said in a nasty tone.

Thales ignored him and instead sent the menu to the opposite wall. "Here's what's available, given the nodes on the lobby, the exits, as well as the public reports filed by the LEF. Excuse me, but I have to change."

The lobby was silent as the three men turned to the displays he'd provided. He saw them all whip out slates before he turned away. It took him about half an hour to replace the tunic and tidy himself. He dawdled, hoping that Edones and his entourage would leave by the time he got back to the admittance counter.

No such luck.

Colonel Edones and his sergeant were conferring in low tones over a slate while the crèche-get stood to one side with a pale face, his arms crossed. As Thales slid onto his stool behind the counter, Colonel Edones looked up and watched him with bland lifeless eyes, making him shiver.

"We've gone through your reports, as well as the Hellas LEF analysis," Colonel Edones said. "From interviews, they've been able to piece together what happened."

Thales's gut tensed. He was surprised that Edones had access to Hellas LEF data. What was more worrisome: Had the LEF issued warrants against ComNet packet routing? They'd never done that before.

"She's safe. Get in the car," Edones said to the crèche-get.

"But—"

"We know who picked her up, from the LEF paperwork. She's safe." Edones nodded at the sergeant, who hustled the crèche-get outside, where they both got into the car.

Colonel Edones watched them go. He walked to the counter so he could stare at Thales eye to eye.

Thales flinched. He'd been mistaken; the Colonel *cared* about the missing woman, although not in a lost and victimized way.

"The Hellas LEF identified the dead man fairly easily. Do you know him?" Edones tone was frigid.

"No, I'd never seen him before." Thales was telling the truth, but he began to sweat.

"They connected him to illegal and *involuntary* organ brokering."

"Well, then, his death is no great loss. But murder's murder, isn't it? Are they charging Major Kedros?" Thales kept his voice steady.

"No, it's valid self defense. Besides, final cause of death was high-voltage stunner," Edones said, leaning closer. "Major Kedros didn't have any weapons, and interviews of your inmates indicated that a third party used weapons to rescue Major Kedros from becoming an involuntary organ donor."

"They're residents." Thales's voice was soft and hoarse. His mouth was dry.

"What's that?" Edones leaned closer.

"They're called residents, not inmates."

"I suspect they're also called organ fodder, when they're in good enough health. The LEF has already issued a warrant to examine all calls made to and from the dead man for the last two days."

Edones's voice was quiet, but Thales could hear him quite clearly since he was leaning over him across the counter.

"Are you insinuating that someone called this broker when Major Kedros checked in? Are you accusing *me*?" Despite his best efforts, his voice squeaked.

Edones stared at him coldly.

Thales licked his dry lips. The ComNet nodes could pick up their conversation, even if it was quiet. Perhaps he could provoke Edones into threatening or libeling him. He sensed the man was tense, like a tightly wound spring.

"She was just an addict. The scum that Gaia cleans off her planets every day," Thales whispered.

Instead of losing control, Edones smiled. "She was the wrong target to choose. She was under my protection."

The words puzzled Thales, but before he could respond, Edones straightened and stepped back.

"The Hellas LEF needed a bit of prodding to look into this matter fully. Apparently, they've let similar incidents slip by them in the past, but I've remedied that." Colonel Edones brushed some imaginary lint from his uniform. "I can't imagine a worse torture for anyone than watching the excruciatingly slow jaws of the LEF close around them."

The colonel turned smartly and went out to get in his car, leaving Thales sweating and shivering in the lobby's conditioned air.

Ariane dropped to her knees on the patio stones, which still radiated heat from the afternoon sun. She extended her arms toward the sick man, and then dropped them after he made no movement. "Brandon, is that you?"

"Yes, unfortunately, this is me." Again the crooked smile.

"How did you find me?" Then, as his previous words registered, she asked blankly, "Black market organ broker?"

"I've had my staff following you. Of course, we were notified by our automated agents when you were checked into the Addict Commons."

She looked at him dubiously as she tried to remember. "Did you come for me personally? I remember that somebody had a stunner."

"That was my security. They're probably still filling out forms for the Hellas LEF. They'll come through fine since it was self-defense, or at least to prevent you from being portioned out to the highest bidder."

"Thank you." Her tone was fervent; being kept alive in a vat, unconscious, until her body lost too many parts to continue, wasn't her idea of a decent end.

"You don't have to worry here, Ari. This sanctuary is secure and I have top-notch protection."

She searched his face and eyes, now level with hers. She had never found out whether Brandon had been charged for his attack upon the DO. After Ura-Guinn, she had been hustled off to sick bay, while everyone else was sequestered by the black and blue. When she was healthy enough to keep her food down and her hair was growing out again, the only person she could question was Lieutenant Owen Edones and *he* hadn't been bubbling with answers.

As Ariane looked into Brandon's eyes, she sadly recalled the squadron commander's face, the stark reality of what had happened etched into the man's features. *He's dead now. They're all dead, except for Brandon and me.* Brandon looked as if he'd been through the grinder already, and she'd trashed whatever was worthwhile in her own life.

"Why all the surgery?" Ariane asked, avoiding all the other questions she wanted answered. *Where did you go? What have you been doing with your life, and with whom?*

"This is what can happen when rejuv fails. Of course, AFCAW has paid for this, many times over. They helped build my empire from defense contracts." The resignation in his voice had an undertone of bitterness. He looked down and his hands traced some of the scars on his bare chest. "I burn up my own organs, but luckily, I'm one of those people that can grow my own and accept them gracefully."

"You sound different." Ariane felt awkward. The patio stones were beginning to press painfully on her knees and she sat back on her heels. This wasn't the same Brandon, who lost control of his emotions freely and frequently.

"From what I can see under all those bruises, you didn't have facial reconstruction. But something's different about your face." He grinned.

"I had the nose straightened and refined. You know, I'd bashed it up, way back when . . ." Another altercation in a bar that she didn't want to rehash, particularly with Brandon. She'd been protecting her nose jealously ever since; she hoped Kim hadn't broken it again.

His expression sobered. "You know, Ari, the Addict Commons are dangerous. Especially the ones in Alexandria."

She winced, suppressing glimpses of the nightmare. She wanted to protest that she wasn't responsible for ending up in the Commons and she didn't want him disappointed in her, but she paused. Did that matter anymore? His respect was less important than warning him about the Terrans and the assassin that was still roaming around. He said he had a good security staff; how much would he have told them?

"Brandon, you're—*we're* in danger," she said.

"No doubt." He chuckled. "We've always been in danger, top of the hit list for any crazies out there. I have my people keep an eye on the fringes, just in case."

You have no idea how much *danger, particularly if they can get onto a military installation.* Before she could reply, one of the monitors on his chest began to blink and beep. It was about as thick as Ariane's finger and semi-buried into his skin.

Movement at the periphery of her vision caught her attention; a medic was walking toward them. She was probably answering Brandon's monitor. Her vivid hair, flamboyantly copper with green highlights, stood out starkly from her medically white tunic and pink trousers. She hadn't reached the patio when Ariane's scalp began to tingle. It hadn't been Brandon's voice that had haunted her, that had pushed familiarly through the fog of alcohol and smooth.

"Brandon? Who came to the Commons to get me?"

Brandon closed his eyes, smiling faintly in the fading sunlight. The early gloom of evening was starting. Ariane watched the attendant approach. She ignored Ariane and knelt beside Brandon, professionally turning off the blinking monitor and checking measurements. A delicate barrette shaped like an insect with long filigree wings held back her thick shoulder-length hair over her right ear.

"You know your liver function's degrading, Mr. Leukos. You shouldn't be out here in the evening temperatures," she said in that tantalizingly familiar voice. She picked up the light jacket that had been beside Brandon and draped it around his shoulders.

Brandon sat tranquilly, his eyes closed, his peaceful expression unchanged, and his legs arranged in the lotus position. The attendant looked up, her dark eyes meeting Ariane's without surprise.

"Hello, Cipher," said Ariane.

*   *   *

"So you think Ari's safe with this Leukos fellow?" Matt sat alone in the backseat, looking at his slate after getting results from Heraclitus and Democritus models. "From what I can find, it sounds like this guy might be a customer of organ brokers, legal or illegal."

"Mr. Leukos is ill, true, but he has the means and the ability to accept his own vat-grown organs." Edones replied in a disinterested tone, watching the city lights go by.

"Hmm. Well, I suppose if you're rich enough to have whole hospitals named after you, there's no need to scrounge in the black market gutters."

Neither man in the front seat responded to his low mutter.

They were heading north by way of the central expressway of Alexandria. The light rain that regularly swept into the western parts of the city had faded away as the rental car smoothly rolled through villages and districts. The car was displaying exit names on its windows. In Matt's peripheral vision, they blurred together, one after another, into the inky night. The constant hushed hiss of the wheels was hypnotic.

Matt shook his head. Even when distracted, Edones avoided giving him a direct answer. How did Edones know so much about Leukos, and how did Ari fit in? Matt had been trying to find the connections, but so far, he'd been stymied. He set his slate on the seat beside him.

There was no connection between Reserve Major Ariane Kedros and Mr. Bartholomew Leukos; even the AI models, with their formal answers, seemed taken aback by the absurdity of such a query—or that might be his imagination. Mr. Leukos was extraordinarily rich and shrouded in the privacy that only the rich could afford. He was twelve years older than Ari and had no military background, other than being rejected for duty by reason of his medical condition, the nature of which was heavily protected by privacy law. Leukos had initially started his business empire with a small defense contract and then bought another contractor, and then another. Today, Leukos's corporations dominated much of Hellas Prime's manufacturing and transportation industries for the defense sectors.

According to the analysis Matt could perform quickly against the AI indexed information, Ari and Leukos shouldn't know each other. However, Edones had immediately relaxed when he thought that Leukos had snatched Ari out of the Commons, because "she was with friends." While not claiming friendship, Edones said he had "had dealings with Leukos in the past."

They were on their way to the Demeter Sanctuary where there was a good chance of finding Leukos, but Edones was taking his own sweet time. He seemed reluctant to call upon Leukos, and Matt suspected something more between these two men than only "differences of opinions," as Edones had said. Part of Edones's delaying tactics involved driving through the central Alexandria nighttime light displays and going to dinner. Matt seethed and fidgeted, although he admitted he was hungry.

He wished he had time to have Nestor's Muse 3 do a full-fledged analysis on Bartholomew Leukos. Would there again be an interesting division between almost-perfect and less-than-perfect documentation? If so, would the transition point again sit at 2090, when Ura-Guinn was blown out of N-space by a TD warhead?

He wouldn't know until he was willing to invest a good amount of accelerated AI time, as Nestor had done for his investigations of Customs. Thinking of Nestor, he guiltily picked up his slate again. He'd put off the LEF's questions long enough. This emergency with Ari had taken all his attention. Now he had the time to grind through Nestor's "Customs" package and the LEF data, which he'd loaded onto his slate, just in case. He pulled out his stylus.

CHAPTER 21

Unresolved guilt can fester, immobilize, and cripple. It can hinder health, productive action, and positive relationships. If directed inward, it becomes shame, which destroys self-esteem and individuality, often leading to substance abuse or emotional numbing. The least likely outcome, unless another psychiatric disorder is involved, is transference or sociopathic behavior. . . .

—*Guilt, the Real Thing*, Brett Inez,
2102.292.19.04 UT, indexed by *Democritus 21*
under Hypothetical Effect Imperative

Ariane smoothly pushed to a standing position and saw Cipher's hand jerk into the deep pocket of her white tunic. She was carrying a weapon.

Conclusions crashed about in Ariane's mind, rearranging details and reversing assumptions with amazing speed. The mind can swiftly rearrange the chain of causality, once a premise is changed. Ariane almost staggered from the weight of her conclusions. She'd read and reread the reports on the plane accident, but that had only reinforced her belief that Cipher was dead.

But Cipher was very much alive. Owen had told Ariane to find a traitor, someone who knew the classified release process and the operational chain of command as it existed in the past. Someone clever, like Cipher, who'd been known to scavenge parts and cobble them together into inventive equipment. She'd even refurbished crypto equipment—before the inaccurate report of her untimely death, that is. Her genius with software systems and encryption explained the subtle equipment sabotage behind the murders. Ariane still balked at the biggest question: Why? Until she could answer that, she wasn't sure she could accept her own wild conclusions.

"What's the matter, Ari?" Cipher's eyes darted from Ariane to Brandon, keeping her hand in her pocket. She smirked. "Did you expect a lovers' reunion?"

Her question wrenched Ariane back in time, filling her with the same stomach-clenching guilt. How long would she have to pay for that? Getting physically involved with Brandon probably qualified as the worst decision of her lifetime. It had almost torn their crew apart. *It's been over for fifteen years, so let's move on.*

Ariane shook her head, trying to ground herself in the present. There were more important things to consider now, such as *murder*.

"You can only lose your past by accepting it. Introspection, meditation, and acceptance," murmured Brandon.

Cipher rolled her eyes. "Spare us your pearls of wisdom."

Ariane watched Brandon smile wryly. What the hell was wrong with him? Didn't he know that people had been dying? Didn't he care?

"What have you been doing lately, Cara?" she asked softly.

"There's no Cara Paulos anymore." Cipher's voice was rough. "There's no Karen Kambas anymore either—not after she revealed her true past to her husband. He couldn't take it, so she lost her husband

and children, and then her life. Now there's only a faceless employee living off the fringe largess of Leukos Industries."

Cipher had children? Ariane's eyebrows rose. "I'm sorry, Cipher."

"Don't be. He saw me for what I was." Her broad face twisted.

"Maybe you shouldn't have told him who you were." Ariane tried to be delicate. How *stupid*; what was Cipher thinking?

"You can't share your life, you can't wholly love each other, until you're honest with each other." Anguish crossed Cipher's face.

"You didn't need to expose yourself to have a meaningful relationship."

"Says the woman who's never had anything but one-night stands," Cipher jeered. "You won't share someone's bed regularly, let alone start a relationship. Too much honesty for you, Ari?"

Ariane paused. Cipher's words stung because they were true, but she was more interested in their other insinuation—exactly how long had Cipher been tracking her? *She might have been doing this for Brandon*, said her positive side, the side that didn't want to face the truth.

"I admit to being cautious with my new identity," Ariane said. "As for your husband—"

"He was right to take our children and get restraining orders against me. That way they couldn't be tainted."

"As we are?" Ariane asked, taking a step sideways. She stopped when Cipher jiggled her hand meaningfully.

Meanwhile, Brandon slowly and carefully extended his legs. He continued his exercise by gracefully stretching his back and hamstrings. Ariane saw his loose trousers tighten on more clumps of monitors built into his thighs. He might be systemically sick, but at least his muscles were flexible.

The landscape lights brightened and shone about the edge of the patio. Behind her was the low wall indicating the edge of the escarpment. She faced Cipher, Brandon, and the long wing off a central core pavilion. No lights shone from the rooms.

No one to hear cries for help. No ComNet nodes to detect an emergency call. *I'd be an idiot to let Cipher know what I suspect.* And yet she ached to know *why. Why did you kill all those people, Cipher? Why did you try to kill me?*

"All of us are tainted," Cipher said. "That's why you're here, Ari. But you know that, don't you?"

The LEF had physical evidence tying Mr. Customs, as Matt still privately called Hektor Valdes, to Nestor's apartment. ComNet placed Mr. Customs at Nestor's apartment at the right time. The problem was that the LEF couldn't find a murder weapon and they couldn't establish a motive. Mr. Customs maintained his innocence and he had talented legal representation.

Mr. Customs had a mild-mannered exterior that could probably fool a judge or jury into thinking he couldn't commit murder, but he had a stout, strong body—Nestor would have been no match for him. Mr. Customs also hid a violent temper; he'd been previously charged with assault, but never convicted. The LEF staff psychiatrist decided that Mr. Customs was highly motivated by money, as are many, but Mr. Customs and his financial records didn't fit the muscle-for-money profile. He had received, however, a recent payment that was suspicious because of the size and timing. The LEF had run into a dead end trying to trace it. That was all of their evidence regarding payment, unfortunately.

Matt opened the "Customs" package. Nestor had established a pattern of message-payment pairings that went back approximately seven years. Payments were made to everyone, at some point, inside the Athens Point Customs department. Matt's Mr. Customs, currently charged with Nestor's murder, appeared at the end because he'd been recently assigned to Athens Point.

Nestor hadn't completed the analysis. He'd back-traced the messages sent by the inspectors, and while determining they all had the same destination, he hadn't identified the location or recipient. What were the messages, and why the payments? The disappointment was that Nestor had only started to correlate the message-payment pairings to external events; his last hypothesis had been that they were related to the arrival and departure of ships. Sure, the last couple of years had the *Aether's Touch* listed, but other ships were identified also. They had vaguely familiar names to Matt, but he didn't immediately see the relationship.

Back-tracing messages and identifying termination points, however, was Matt's specialty. He had a wonderful little algorithm sitting on *Aether's Touch*—Matt felt the car slowing. Knowing that he was asking a lot from the burgeoning AI, he sent a command to Nestor's Muse 3 to find the common connection between the docking of the ships and to use his algorithm to back-trace the messages. If the AI was capable of performing those commands and correlating the data, he'd have to wait for results.

"Time for dinner," Joyce said. The car parked.

Edones seemed intent upon torturing Matt. They entered a gourmet restaurant that specialized in "organic Hellas Prime foods." Their menu proudly trumpeted that all their vegetables were grown planet-side (in dirt) and that their meats, fish, and poultry were raised under "free range" conditions (meaning the animals ate whatever they could scrounge). Imagine that being a selling point! Matt nearly gagged at the thought of the foreign microbes that crawled over all the food, not to mention the inherent allergens, albeit in "immeasurable amounts guaranteed to have only subclinical effects."

After long consultation with the wait staff, while Joyce and Edones rolled their eyes, Matt was able to order a side dish of hydroponic noodles. However, that was the only concession this restaurant made for those with "delicate sensibilities." For his entree they suggested the bluefish, which they compared to space carp grown on generational ships. The dark blue flesh lightened to a faint bluish white when heated, but Matt had to send it back for additional cooking. It was still stronger tasting than the fish to which he was accustomed.

Matt's ear bug chimed during dinner, announcing results from Nestor's Muse 3.

"Excuse me for a moment," he said to Edones and Joyce. Relieved that he could stop picking at his food, if one could call it that, he pulled out his slate to take the analysis privately.

He kept his eyes on the data that scrolled over his slate, avoiding the sight of Edones and Joyce eating dripping red-brown slabs of meat and violent green, orange, and red plants. They said they'd ordered different dishes, but their plates had looked equally nauseating to Matt.

Soon the results from Nestor's Muse 3 grabbed his attention. This AI was a fortuitous gem gleaming through the soot and glut of information. The initiating event, according to Muse 3, for every message-payment pair, was the docking or disconnecting of a ship. The connection between all the ships was *Ari*. The inspectors were paid to report the comings and

goings of ships that listed Ariane Kedros as crew.
Muse 3 then thanked Matt (*huh?*) for the useful algorithm that had helped narrow down the destination
of the inspectors' reports and how they were paid.
Then Muse 3 had taken upon itself to make one more
connection. Gaia, he loved this AI!

Matt slammed the slate down on the table to get
the attention of Edones and Joyce.

"Leukos Industries can be connected to *both* the
Karthage explosion and Nestor's murder," Matt said
when the others looked at him.

Joyce looked skeptical and went back to eating his
dinner, cutting another piece of meat enthusiastically.
Edones raised his eyebrows and waited.

"Leukos Industries holds maintenance contracts for
Karthage. Under that contract, they lease telebots that
perform external maintenance on the habitat. Captain
Rayiz said the explosives were planted externally—"

"More than thirty contractors have telebots floating
about Karthage. You need something more incriminating than maintenance work." Edones speared a
chunk of orange flesh, twirled it, and popped it into
his mouth. He chewed slowly and obviously, savoring the taste and texture.

"I agree that the Karthage link is tenuous." Matt
looked away from the food. "But the most incriminating point is the connection between Leukos Industries and Nestor's murderer."

"Athens Point LEF already has that fellow in
custody—what's his name, Joyce?"

"Hektor Valdes, sir. They've got physical evidence
against him and his alibi was busted by ComNet,
but he hasn't fingered anyone and they can't trace
the money."

"*I* can trace the money," Matt said. "My search
agent just sent me results."

Edones's eyes narrowed, but he waited. Joyce began eating faster.

"Mr. Valdes was paid, as were all the other inspectors, to report on Ari. I can prove this later with a statistical report. All these payments were small, but they're much easier to trace than the large one that they suspect was payment for Nestor's death. The small payments came through Aegis Airlines, a large corporation where it's hard to pin down where every drachma goes. These payments used a previously unknown and, according to the Aegis accountants, unassigned account number. However, these transactions trace back to a line item in Syracuse Financial, another huge corporation, that proxies for Leukos Industries on the board of Aegis Airlines. The line item breaks up and one link leads to a private Leukos account used for maintenance and payroll on the Demeter Santuary."

"That's a pretty fantastic chain, where every link has to be proven," Edones said.

"Hell, that's a pretty fantastic *agent*," said Joyce, after he swallowed. "How much privacy law did you break?"

Matt ignored Joyce and pushed his slate in front of Edones. "Read it for yourself."

"You haven't traced the important payment, the one that might have paid for Mr. Expedition's murder," Edones said after a few moments of review. Then, as Matt's fists were starting to ball up in frustration, Edones added, "But I'll agree this warrants investigation."

As before, when Edones made his decision, he moved quickly. He paid the bill displayed on the tabletop and stood up. "Sergeant, start looking over the other cases for connections to Leukos Industries while I get us an aircraft. In particular, I want the

crypto equipment from operative one-three-three put
through an entire overhaul and inspection."

What other cases? What crypto equipment?

Edones made a call through his implant as he
wound his way between tables of diners. Matt heard
something like "stealth hovercraft" and "top of the
Pagkrati building" and "AFCAW authority," followed by some numbers. Matt looked to Joyce for
answers, but the burly sergeant stuffed as much dinner as possible into two more bites, pushed his chair
back, stood, and whipped out a slate.

"Better start moving, Mr. Journey," Joyce said.
"We're still on the hook for your safety and I don't
see the colonel taking the time to get you an escort."

Matt blanched. The second thing worse to getting
into a rock, by his definition, was getting into a planet-
side aircraft. At least, this time, Edones wouldn't be
piloting.

After Cipher's comment about taint, Ariane
watched Brandon for reaction, but saw none. He
carefully arranged his legs back into a lotus position
and closed his eyes.

"I've tried to teach you how to empty yourself,
how to be at peace." His words were clearly for Cipher, although he didn't turn toward her.

Cipher shrugged. "So I can get to the point where
I don't care about *anything*? That's not my definition
of peace."

Brandon only inclined his head a fraction, keeping
his eyes closed. It seemed a well-worn discussion between them.

"How have you been watching me, Cipher?" Ariane asked.

"Leukos Industries has many resources." She
smirked.

"I asked her to look for you, Ari. Particularly

after—after the military said we were in even more danger," Brandon said quickly. If he'd talked to Owen, then he wasn't going to admit it. *And I'm still in the dark regarding Brandon's involvement.* There was nothing to do but force the issue. Ariane squared her shoulders and stepped forward.

"Don't move, Ari." Cipher's right hand came out of the pocket and she aimed what looked like a miniature stunner at Ariane. The ministunner probably couldn't be lethal, but at this point, there wasn't any reason to pretend. Ariane's shoulders sagged.

"Why'd you try to kill me, Cipher?" She watched both their faces for reactions.

"I didn't." Cipher smiled thinly. "It wasn't your time. Only the command post controller had to die. I expected you'd figure out where Brandon was and come here eventually, but I didn't know it'd be by such a circuitous route."

Brandon's face had crumpled in disappointment as soon as the ministunner appeared. Hadn't he had any suspicions? There was shock in his eyes, but very little surprise at Cipher's words. Deep down in his heart, Brandon might have suspected, but couldn't face the truth.

"I still don't know *why*." Ariane's voice broke. "All those innocent people? Why, Cipher?"

"They weren't innocent! They had to pay for billions of lives lost." Cipher's voice became shrill.

"What about the passengers in the airliner crash you arranged? They were innocent," Ariane said.

Brandon stared dully at the ground in front of his low platform. Why didn't he say something?

"That wasn't me." Cipher's eyes darted to look down at Brandon. Maybe she still cared about his opinion, maybe she still valued his respect. "That crash was a piece of good fortune that jumpstarted my plan. With a little altering of the manifest before it went into crystal, I was able to get Edones off my back.''

"And our prior commanders?'' Ariane opened her hands outward in question. This gesture also allowed her to edge closer to Cipher, who was standing behind and to the side of Brandon. There was no flicker in her eyes, no tremble of the hand holding the stunner: Either Cipher hadn't noticed her movement or she wasn't intending to use the stunner.

"They deserved to die—for the 4,000,650,271 souls in Ura-Guinn.'' Cipher's voice started climbing again and the hand holding the stunner trembled. Her eyes looked wild.

Even Nathaniel Wolf Kim had generalized the casualties. *Four billion people gone.* Cipher had learned the numbers, obsessed over them. Was that a sign she was going deeper into the bottomless gulf of Kaos?

Brandon raised his head and his gaze met Ariane's. There was no hope in his eyes, only a dull sort of acceptance. *Cipher will kill us all, and Brandon won't make a move to stop her.*

"Why?'' Ariane asked, looking at Brandon. "They were only following their orders. Just like we did our duty—what we'd been trained to do.''

"Good old Ari, falling back on military indoctrination. Why'd you stay in? Do you like being Edones's gofer and his pet prodigy?'' Cipher laughed, her voice breaking as if she were on the edge of tears. "Don't look to Brandon for help, Ari. He's retired from life, letting others like me run his businesses and handle his money. That's his answer, but not mine. Don't we deserve to die for what we did?''

"But I'm asking: Why now? When there's *hope.*'' Ariane continued to hold Brandon's gaze. "The treaties signed under Pax Minoica are working. We're drawing down and destroying the TD weapons.''

"Peace treaties are meaningless when vengeance is demanded. Getting rid of the weapons will be pointless, unless we punish those who'd dare to use them," Cipher said.

"The Minoans don't think the treaties are pointless." Ariane answered Cipher, but her attention was on Brandon. "The light-speed data will be here soon and then we'll know the extent of damage to Ura-Guinn. We can prepare to *help* the survivors. Only four months left, Cipher. Plenty of people have *hope* that the sun's still there and operating."

Brandon's gaze sharpened and he gave Ariane a barely perceptible nod, answering her unspoken question.

"Don't tell me you believe the analysis of the glitch data?" Cipher's lips twisted in disdain. "That's a government conspiracy."

"Scientific communities on both sides have analyzed it," Ariane said.

"Then it's a scientific conspiracy."

"But in four months—"

"And what happens in four months?" Cipher was gesturing with the stunner, her eyes glinting from the landscape lights. "Punishment of the guilty should have been swift—instead we waited and *we forgot*. I can't let people forget."

"Punishment has to wait for justice, and justice must wait for proof." Ariane's voice was steady. "In this case, the evidence only travels as fast as the speed of light. You're counting your casualties before the fact, Cipher."

"Perhaps we should punish the *intent* to destroy Ura-Guinn's sun, not the fact. You're always falling back on cold logic—don't you feel any remorse, Ari? Any feelings? Or is that what you're always looking for at the bottom of a bottle?" Cipher gestured widely, and unwisely, with her weapon.

Ariane was taken aback, first by Cipher's illogic, then by the sudden personal attack and her movements. It seemed as though Cipher *wanted* her to jump and struggle for the weapon—or was subliminally urging her to do so. That was puzzling, and her emotions cooled.

"Are you angry because I stayed with AFCAW?" Ariane changed the subject. "Because I took assignments with the Directorate of Intelligence?"

"You thought you were protected by Owen's magic." Again, the wide gestures that said, *Attack me. Go ahead, try it.* "His secrecy corrupts, doesn't it? Little by little, from the inside out. By now you're rotten inside, and *that's* why you secretly want to die."

"Ah—just to quibble, but I'm remarkably attached to my life right now." Ariane intended to bait Cipher with her remark, but she felt a quiver of surprise; she *meant* it. Cipher clearly wanted to take out all three of them together in some macabre murder-suicide plan, but she, *Ariane Kedros*, wanted to live.

"We deserve to die," Cipher shouted, extending her arms. As she yelled, Brandon rolled backward and to the side, hitting Cipher in the knees. Cipher went down with a grunt, landing on her left side and temporarily immobilizing her arm. Her left hand was still stuck in her pocket and she used her right hand to cushion her fall awkwardly. She dropped the miniature stunner.

Ariane leapt, landing on Cipher and trying to keep her pinned to the ground. That didn't work, since Cipher weighed more. Cipher's body had undergone fifteen years more aging than hers had, but it hadn't gone through significant abuse in the past two days. Ariane tried to go limp to prevent Cipher from pushing her off. Catching movement in the corner of her eye, she saw Brandon trying to pick up the stunner.

"Don't stun her," shouted Ariane.

A dark shape silently blotted out the stars above. Ariane instinctively ducked and stiffened, which allowed Cipher to push her off. Cipher was on her hands and knees, pushing toward the short wall between the patio and the steep edge of the escarpment. Ariane grabbed on to Cipher's leg as she felt the distinctive teeth-grinding vibration of a large antigrav generator. It felt like metal scraping against metal silently inside her head.

Cipher kicked, almost upright, trying to free her other leg. Ariane felt pain explode along her shoulder. Her arm loosened about Cipher's leg, but she pushed herself off the patio stones and launched herself at Cipher again. They went down together, rolling. Cipher pulled away using the waist-high wall for support as she stood. Ariane, still on her knees, clutched at Cipher's tunic. For a moment they looked into each other's eyes.

"Now you can sleep, Ari." Cipher smiled and sharply pushed her away.

Ariane tried to hold on, but the pain in her shoulder weakened her grip. She heard the sound she feared, the sound of the stunner. One of her hands still held Cipher's tunic and she reacted instinctively to the sting of a close stun—her hand jerked away, letting go. Cipher's smile stretched into agony as she slumped backward.

"No!" Ariane screamed as she irrationally grabbed for Cipher's twitching legs. She couldn't hold on as Cipher went over the wall. She turned to see Owen and Joyce crouching at the open side doors of a hovercraft currently on antigrav. Owen held a stunner—did he understand what he just did?

"Dead-man-switch! Explosives!" Ariane shouted into the eerie silence.

The more precise definition was *conscious*-man-switch, but Owen figured things out. It didn't matter whether Cipher was still alive. She heard him shout. The pilot switched on the conventional VTOL engines and they whined into action. They'd need altitude fast.

She ran across the patio to where Brandon crouched. He had apparently realized what had happened and was talking into his implanted mike as he pressed the switch in his jawbone.

". . . evacuate everybody in the west wing. Good." Brandon raised his voice to be heard over the engines. He released his mike switch and said to Ariane, "Cipher moved all visitors, except for you, out of the west wing this afternoon."

"We have to go." Ariane pointed toward the hovercraft.

Brandon nodded. He was able to walk, but couldn't climb or jump. The pilot lowered the hovercraft and Ariane helped boost Brandon, while Owen and Joyce hauled him into the hold like a sack of grain. They were losing precious time. All Cipher's automated agent needed was confirmation of unconsciousness. How often would it poll her implants?

"Go, go, go!" shouted Ariane as soon as she had a secure grip on the handhold with her good arm.

She felt the ground fall away. Her clenched hand ached as she tried to swing and extend the other toward Owen. She saw Joyce holding on to Owen and a familiar face behind them both. *Matt?* Someone grabbed her free hand and the pain along her shoulder caused her to yelp. Her vision grayed at the edges.

She felt a force hit her back, like a wall moving through space. The hovercraft jerked and lunged. Hot burning arrows of pain pierced her lower legs and it felt as if her skin were ripping off her back. She screamed. She heard grunts of pain above her.

Gaia, please save me.

CHAPTER 22

Now for news from the Terran scene. An astounding
shake-up on Overlord Three's staff has State Prince
Isrid Parmet moving up to fill the position of assistant
for the Exterior. There's been rearrangement internal to
Parmet's staff also; our feed received an exclusive report
that Nathaniel Wolf Kim has resigned, although the Terrans are mum regarding the reason.

— *Interstellarsystem Events Feed*, 2105.300.19.05 UT,
indexed by *Heraclitus 17* under Flux Imperative

An angel? No. A man in white. He lectured her
in a stern voice.

". . . multiple lacerations—internal bleeding and
significant loss of blood—torn ligaments and cartilage
in—cracked collarbone, dislocated right shoulder, broken left thumb, three cracked ribs, cracked . . ."

She tried to focus on him as words rushed out of
his mouth, stomping over each other and intermin-
gling. He had AFCAW medical technician insignia
on his collar.

". . . welds started in your lower leg—problematic
when considering your classified condition—can't
perform bone growth stimulation again until . . ."

Classified condition? *It's not my fault*, she wanted
to say. She closed her eyes.

* * *

She remembered Owen had blood running down his face and neck. The right side of his face had looked like chewed-up meat. Now it was covered with plastiskin and was healing.

She tried to ask him about Brandon, but only a sigh came out of her mouth.

"Don't talk, Ariane," Owen said. "You've lost almost twenty percent of your body weight. They're pumping calories into your body and they've got you drugged, but they also have to suppress your metabolism."

"Brand?" she croaked.

"He's fine. He's having a liver transplant, a little earlier than usual, but they knew it was coming and they'd already grown him one. Now go to sleep."

Contrarily, she struggled to get out another question. "Others?"

Owen gave her a strange look and then said, "Everybody else in the hovercraft was protected because of its pitch. Only you and I caught the shrapnel, but you took the brunt of it."

Her mind had been cycling through Cipher's remarks, in particular the ones made about Owen. She worked her tongue and managed to get some more saliva into her mouth for her next question. "Cipher crypto? You?"

Owen sighed. Apparently, he knew exactly what she was asking.

"Yes, knowing her talents, I tried to recruit her. She did one job for me, but we both realized she wasn't suited for intelligence. Soon after that, she ostensibly died in the airliner accident. When we collected her equipment, I made the mistake of not having it broken down immediately and checking the internal seals. The outside seals looked good and unwittingly, I gave her what she needed to generate, encrypt, and decrypt military keys."

Stupid, but we were all played by Cipher.

"I'm sorry, Ariane."

A sincere apology from Owen? She hoped she remembered this. She closed her eyes and slipped back into sleep.

This time it was Joyce she saw when she woke. Her mind didn't feel so fuzzy; perhaps they were taking her off the drugs. She noted the new stripe on his arm.

"Congratulations on making master sergeant."

"Thank you, ma'am. Had to see for myself that you were recovering."

"Perhaps to remind me that you had to save my ass this time?"

"It was an honor, ma'am." He snapped to attention.

"Cut the bullshit, Joyce. I suppose this makes us even."

"Yes, ma'am, I s'pect so." He grinned. "Until next time."

"If there is a next time," she muttered, feeling fatigue attack her again.

"You always say that."

"This time . . ." She closed her eyes.

This time was different. The *threat* of discovery, capture, and torture had been stimulating and motivating until actually experiencing it. Now she knew how she measured up: After having the shit knocked out of her, she'd broken and given the Terrans exactly what they wanted by turning on her business partner and employer. Then she was dumped in the Addict Commons, and the inmates . . . She shuddered. *What, but for the grace of Gaia, makes me any different from them?* The distinguishing mark of addicts was their *untrustworthiness*, whether they lived on the dole or made their own way in the world.

She thought a lot of time passed, and when she opened her eyes, she was surprised to see Joyce still standing there, looking as though he was internally debating about what he would say next.

"Your employer, Mr. Journey," he said hesitantly. "He went through a lot and he did help us, regardless of what the colonel says."

" 'S that so?" Her tongue was getting thick and her eyelids heavy. A pang of sadness ran through her. She doubted she'd ever see Matt again.

"Never seen the colonel so angry, once he figured things out."

She wanted to follow up on that, but her eyelids slammed down.

Ariane didn't remember hospital soft foods tasting so good. What were the shreds of meat in this soup? Perhaps she shouldn't ask.

"Cipher installed that meditation platform for me over three months ago," Brandon said softly. "She said she finally understood the power of meditation, but that was a lie. Owen's analysts say she planted the explosives when it was constructed. She planned all this."

Ariane finished gulping her soup. *Gaia, I'm still so hungry.* At least this meant she was healing. She wiped her mouth and pushed the tray away. Looking around the small private room, she itched to be up and walking, but she'd been told to stay in bed for twelve more hours. She'd been awake for two.

Brandon sat beside her bed in a mobile chair, as it'd be another couple of days before he'd be allowed to stand and walk on his own. Although the explosion hadn't harmed him, he looked worse than she did, with tubes plugged into all his implants and bags hanging from his chair.

"Any chance she survived the fall?" Ariane asked.

Brandon shook his head. "Nobody thinks so, considering that the explosives were set deep enough to cause ground rippling. Tons of debris and dirt have cascaded down the side of the gulley. They're digging through it, expecting to find her body—mostly because Owen thinks she didn't want to come through this alive."

"Well, Cipher was always thorough. She wanted to make sure we all died together, so much so that I wouldn't be surprised if she left explosive packages littered all over your property."

Brandon snorted. "That's what Owen said, right before he slapped a specialized AFCAW search warrant on me and had teams crawling all over the Reserve—before my legal staff could respond and block him."

"Wouldn't it be best to let them search?"

"You've worked for Owen so long that you're beginning to think like him, aren't you?" Brandon's voice was cold.

It felt as if she'd been slapped in the face, and she flushed with anger. "Look, I got firsthand experience with Cipher's work when she blew a hole in Karthage Point. With all your disdain for the military, consider that they're at least constrained from doing *that* by the Phaistos Protocols. Besides, Cipher wouldn't have had the resources to assassinate, poison, and explode people and places if it weren't for your Gaia-be-damned business empire!"

They stared at each other in silence. She heard the hurried footsteps of staff in the corridor intermingled with the shuffling steps of patients. The AFCAW physical rehabilitation wards on Hellas Daughter were busy.

"You're right." Brandon broke first, looking away. "I shouldn't have withdrawn from active management, because that allowed Cipher to move in and

take over operations. When she contacted me for a
job a year ago, requesting secrecy, anonymity, and
reclusion, I should have been suspicious. She said
she had run her second life into the ground, which
was certainly believable. I only cared that she was
able to give me news of you."

"Really?"

"Of course, I was angry that you were still in
AFCAW."

When she opened her mouth to correct him, Brandon added, "Or at least, in the Reserve and being a
toady for the Directorate of Intelligence. But I got
over all that, like I had to get over all my anger about
the failed rejuv."

"Got over all what?" Had she just missed something here? It was amazing how failed hopes could
be so quickly rekindled, and with the hope came
painful memories.

"You can get over the past, Ari, like I did." He
leaned forward eagerly. "You could find peace on
the Demeter Sanctuary. Get rid of the nightmares. I
know you have them."

"Provided that our EOD teams can safely disarm
the two explosive devices they found. One in the
Demeter operations center and one in your study."
Owen sauntered into the room, followed by Joyce.

Brandon's face tightened as he turned his chair to
face Owen.

"I'm sure you've got some sleeper agents in your
systems, given the particular talents of Cara Paulos,"
continued Owen. "If your lawyers allow us, we can
do a system audit for you. It'd save you a bit of
money."

"Thanks, Owen, but no. I'll take my chances with
a civilian audit. Get your people off my property."
Brandon turned his chair and headed for the door.

"Certainly, Mr. Leukos." Owen's voice was bland.

Brandon stopped in the doorway, twisting to look back at Ariane.

"I mean it, Ari. The Sanctuary's doors are always open for you. Think about it." He gave Owen a dark look and then he was gone.

Joyce scanned and secured the room. Ariane sighed. It was debriefing time.

The grilling went on and on, exactly as she expected. Since she'd conversed with a Terran state prince longer than anyone else in AFCAW, bargained with a Minoan emissary, and survived torture from TEBI agents, Owen wanted every detail he could get from her. For the times when she hadn't been under the influence of drugs or alcohol, her memory was too good. She hoped many of the scenes that seemed etched on the inside of her eyelids would eventually fade away.

One benefit of this debriefing was that information had to flow both ways.

"Did Parmet or his TEBI agents give you any indication that they'd be shutting down their intelligence network?" asked Owen.

"No. When did that happen?" she asked.

"We're pretty sure a Hellas-wide shutdown went into effect. What was the time, Joyce?"

"Approximately an hour before the Minoan emissary docked at Karthage, sir."

"By the way, we think that can only be done by authority of a state prince. It must have come from Parmet himself," said Owen.

"Ah—the last piece of the puzzle clicks into place." She smiled. "I knew that someone helped Cipher from the inside, because Cipher had doors physically disabled. Now I know that person was a Terran agent, because SP Parmet shut down his network so the Minoans wouldn't connect the sabotage to his own agent."

"Captain Rayiz mentioned that you had suspicions about a physical saboteur, but not about a *Terran* agent," Owen said.

"I think Cipher infiltrated and used the Terran intelligence network. She used Parmet's own agent to get her work done on the inside of Karthage. Damn, she was clever." Ariane shook her head.

There was silence as Owen and Joyce stared at her. After a long pause, Owen delicately cleared his throat.

"Are you going to tell us *who* the Terran agent is, Major?" he asked.

"Maybe, if we can come to an agreement."

"I don't bargain."

"Wrong, Owen. Every conversation I have with you is a *negotiation*, one way or the other."

Owen sighed dramatically. "You sound like Mr. Leukos now. What do you want?"

"I'd like to control a little more of my own soul," she said.

Joyce quickly looked down at his slate, hiding a smile.

Owen's eyes narrowed. "What's that supposed to mean?"

"I'd like—I need—" She swallowed, not realizing how hard this was going to be. While she trusted both these men with her life, this was different. This was worse than learning to strip down in front of crew, because that was only physical. This might mean losing their respect.

They waited.

"I need addiction treatment," she said, trying to keep her voice steady.

Joyce didn't seem to react at all.

After a moment, Owen frowned. "I already said that was risky, and neural probes are out of the question for you."

"There must be treatments that don't involve reprogramming." She waved her arm, indicating her surroundings. "Look at the facilities that AFCAW has. Surely there's group therapy and individual therapy, with cleared therapists . . ."

"We'll see what we can find," Owen said, after her voice trailed away. Joyce wrote something on his slate.

That was it? She was expecting her career to blow up in her face. In the military, you didn't admit to having problems. You could fall down slobbering drunk and throw up on the wing commander's shoes at a party, but you didn't walk into his or her office and declare you had a problem. You could swiftly find yourself in charge of only a small desk and under constant supervision and observation.

However, she filled a special reservist slot, so perhaps this hadn't been an earth-shattering request after all. Maybe all she had to do was push Owen a little bit. She took a deep breath and squared her shoulders, feeling lighter by taking this first step.

"Lieutenant Colonel Jacinthe Voyage is the Terran agent," she said.

Owen raised his eyebrows. "I'll agree that she seems unpleasant to work with, but—"

"You can't know anything about her personality because she's trained in *somaural* techniques. I'm sure, having seen enough of their performances by now," Ariane said firmly. "She pretended extreme hostility toward me to undermine my job. She also tried to derail Captain Rayiz's investigation and might have managed it, if we hadn't been diverted by the arrival of the Minoan emissary."

"We could look into her background quietly, but I'll need more than your opinion on her *somaural* training and hostility. Remember, you wore the black and blue, so you made an excellent target." Owen's mouth twitched in a brief smile.

"Jacinthe knew what physical evidence I was searching for, before I mentioned what had happened, or where it happened. She slipped up and said Karthage couldn't start a *hopeless search for a bulkhead in the wreckage*, before I ever explained the problem of the gym door to Captain Rayiz. That's what his people have to find to prove sabotage of the manual override for the gym door—so Cipher could prevent Colonel Icelos from leaving the gym, if he realized what was happening. This was the one part of Cipher's trap that she couldn't do remotely."

Owen still didn't look convinced.

"In addition, she tried to usurp Rayiz's authority and have her own squadron comb the wreckage. She obviously hoped to find the incriminating bulkhead before Rayiz—has he found it yet?"

"I don't know. They're still trying to establish who, or what, set the explosives," said Owen. "If it turns out to be a bot, they'll have problems determining if the owner lost control if they can't find its memory module intact."

Ariane nodded, having a quick visual flash of Matt and the bot they'd left in G-145. She also felt a small pang of loneliness; she wouldn't be part of the planning, or the operations, to recover it.

"Lieutenant Colonel Voyage was also the one that called Technician Stall away from medical when Major Kedros was kidnapped." Joyce brought the conversation back to Jacinthe.

She hadn't known that; now she wished she could go back to Karthage and have a one-on-one with Jacinthe Voyage. Her fingers tightened into a fist.

"But that was after they shut down their Hellas intelligence network." Owen was quiet for a moment, thinking. "Okay, besides another look at her background, we'll keep an eye on her. We can leave her in place, hoping she'll be picked up as an operative when they rebuild their network."

After he asked everything he could about Karthage, Owen told Ariane about Nestor's murder. She was saddened. Nestor always tried to act like a tough little pervert, making adolescent advances toward her, yet there was something endearing about him. Apparently, the latest theory was that Nestor had dug too deep into Ariane's background and attracted Cipher's attention. The theory didn't explain how she picked Hektor Valdes for her dirty work, since she already had plenty of customs inspectors in her back pocket. However, the LEF was slowly digging up evidence to prove that Mr. Valdes was paid, or blackmailed, to ensure Nestor's silence. Whether they'd put together a case that could stand up in court was questionable.

"Mr. Leukos's legal staff is zealously protecting his empire, but they're also protecting Cara Paulos and her crimes. The Athens Point LEF is attempting to push through their second warrant."

Cipher might have arranged Nestor's murder, but Ariane was ultimately the fault. If she hadn't been working for Matt, Nestor would still be alive. *Yet another reason for Matt to hate me.*

Surprisingly, Owen seemed to want to avoid the subject of Matt as much as she did. After Owen and Joyce left, she fell into a deep sleep of emotional and physical exhaustion.

Several days passed before she checked her message queue. It was stacked. Both the Athens Point LEF and Karthage SF wanted to talk with her. They were only two of many agencies that wanted a "word" with her. There was also the DiastimBot Instrumentation Company, the Hellas LEF, the Administration of the Alexandria Addict Commons, Interpol's

Office of Black Market Organ Brokering, Solicitors for
the Demeter Reserve, the accounting offices of Aegis
Airlines, the internal audit department of Syracuse
Financial, several insurance companies . . . who were
all these people? She scrolled down the list and
raised her eyebrows when she reached the bottom.

Less than an hour ago, a message had arrived from
Matt. It was text, not the most common format for a
personal message, but still used for expediency, privacy, or brevity. Signed with Matt's official Aether
Exploration, Ltd., signature, the message read: "Your
job is still open, awaiting your return. We miss you."

We miss you?

Matt rubbed his temples. Exactly as Nestor had
warned, splitting and layering these leases was an
administrative nightmare, not only for him but also
for the CAW Space Exploration, Exploitation, and
Economics Control Board. The SEEECB flunkies, as
they were not so affectionately called, had to track
leases and contracts, as well as manage permits between contractors. The companies doing actual work
on the site, whether mining or exploring, were often
subcontracted to a contractor of the lessee. When considering the numbers of subcontractors, contractors,
and lessees, across several functional areas that had
to communicate with each other—well, out of sheer
frustration, the SEEECB demanded that *Matt* put together a reporting and organization matrix.

Not that he regretted doing this. It was worth it just
to see the unflappable Colonel Owen Edones go pink
with frustration. Edones had been concerned with Ari
signing away leases to the Terrans, but at the time,
Matt *implied* he'd give Edones control over how other
leases were awarded. Edones lost his cool restraint
when he found Matt had already dispersed the remaining leases between AFCAW contractors and com-

mercial companies that had Minoan funding, causing a three-way snarl with the Terran-based companies.

"Everything will require integration between contractors, even the smallest archaeological or scientific analysis," Edones said. "How is anything going to get done?"

"That's the point," Matt said, which didn't endear him to the colonel.

That might have been the reason he was marched out of the "situation" at the Demeter Sanctuary. Edones assured him that Ari was going to be all right, but she was being treated in a special AFCAW hospital and couldn't have visitors.

Edones's last words were spiteful and Matt remembered them word for word. They had the unmistakable ring of truth. "I doubt Major Kedros will be interested in continuing to work for you, Mr. Journey, considering what she *suffered* for your leases."

Joyce escorted Matt to transportation off Hellas Prime. This time, thank Gaia, he traveled by sedate space elevator. Joyce gave him a final warning.

"You squeezed the colonel, so I'd lie low for a while." Joyce grinned. "After all, you don't want him poking around that 'agent' of yours. Or looking into what Mr. Expedition did in his spare time."

Then Joyce winked and said good-bye, but stayed around to make sure that Matt got on the elevator. Matt still remembered him waving as the elevator started up the cable. *Those bastards know all about Nestor's Muse 3, maybe more than I do.*

Leaning back, he ran his fingers through his short hair, massaging his head and trying to ease the tension. The object of his discontent noticed this.

"Matt, do you feel all right? I have read that erratic eating habits can lead to headaches."

Great, now it's getting motherly. I should have expected Nestor to program emotional mimicry.

"Muse Three, you shouldn't believe everything you read," Matt said aloud.

He wished he could shut down the AI's interface for a while, but net-think cautioned that burgeoning AIs needed interaction. Since he'd been back, Muse 3 had pestered him with questions about his business, even requesting repetitive "verbal renditions" of G-145 missions. The account of the wayward bot that required his rescue by Ari had started feeling like a bedtime story. All this interaction was tiring him.

"Matt, I detect Ariane Kedros walking up our ramp. She'll be at the air lock in—"

"Ari!" Matt bolted out of his chair and was up the ladder to the main deck in record time. He barely paid attention to the AI's words.

"—sorry that you do not have adequate preparation time, perhaps for a shave and sonic shower," finished Muse 3 as he ran down the corridor to the personnel docking air lock.

Shave and shower? What was the AI babbling about? Matt rubbed his jaw, realizing that he did indeed look a little grubby. What did it matter? Ari had seen him in much worse shape.

He pushed open the air lock door when she was only a pace away, her arm extended to tap for a call. She jumped backward and he saw that she was still limping from her injuries.

"Matt," she said, hesitantly.

"You look good, Ari." She looked thin and underweight, as if she'd done several drops in a row. There was plastiskin on one side of her face.

"*Good?*" She laughed, and the haunted look in her deep brown eyes changed to sparkling humor. "Have you had your eyesight checked?"

"Well, you look like you're healing," he said hastily.

"I hear my job's still open," she said.

"Sure is."

He'd stubbornly hoped for her to call and then decided only a couple of days ago to hire another N-space pilot. But he never got around to searching the job boards because there was always something better to do, some message or report or question from Muse 3. He hadn't even gotten around to cleaning out Ari's cabin, once he had decided she wasn't coming back.

"I thought you'd be filling a cushy position on the Demeter Sanctuary." He gestured for her to come aboard *Aether's Touch.*

"I decided I couldn't retire to a life of quiet meditation yet." She walked ahead of him, purposefully, to the control deck. He watched her touch her consoles almost lovingly, the way he often did, as she checked status displays. He smiled.

She turned and smiled back at him, but again, he sensed hesitancy.

"Matt, there's things about me—"

Impulsively, he cut her off. "I don't care."

"You might not like what I've done in the past or what I'm doing in the present. About those leases—"

"It's not going to be a problem," Matt said. "Besides, I know what I need to know. There's no one else I want backing me up in new space. We work well together; we're *crew.* That's enough for me."

"By the way, the message . . . ?"

"Message?"

"Why *we*?"

"*We* what?" He looked at her blankly.

Her smile faltered. "You sent a message, didn't you?"

Matt paused. No, he hadn't. He'd been too stubborn to beg her to come back, even though his company teetered on the brink of ruin without an

N-space pilot or an intellectual property broker and administrator.

"Welcome home, Ari." Muse 3 broke the silence.

She started. "That's *Nestor's* voice. What's going on?"

"It's a long story, and it can wait. Welcome back." He threw an arm around her shoulders and hugged her to his side, making sure to keep it brotherly and gentle, given her injuries.

"Hope you're ready to go back to G-145," Matt added. "We've got a lot of work to do."

"And we missed you," said Muse 3.

"Shut up, Muse Three."

DISCOVER THE "THRILLING"* STARDOC NOVELS

Smart and savvy surgeon Cherijo Torin—
a genetically-enhanced human engineered to be a
model of perfection—has ventured across the
universe in and out of danger and love. Torin is
driven by two great forces—her sworn duty to heal
the sick, and her constant fear of the demented
man who created her...

Stardoc
Beyond Varallan
Endurance
Shockball
Eternity Row
Rebel Ice
Plague of Memory
Omega Games

*Booklist

Available wherever books are sold or at
penguin.com

THE ULTIMATE IN
SCIENCE FICTION AND FANTASY!

From magical tales of distant worlds to stories of
technological advances beyond the grasp of man, Penguin has
everything you need to stretch your imagination to its limits.

penguin.com

ACE
Get the latest information on favorites like
William Gibson, T.A. Barron, Brian Jacques,
Ursula K. Le Guin, Sharon Shinn, Charlaine Harris,
Patricia Briggs, and Marjorie M. Liu,
as well as updates on the best new authors.

ROC
Escape with Jim Butcher, Harry Turtledove, Anne Bishop,
S.M. Stirling, Simon R. Green, E.E. Knight,
and many others—plus news on the
latest and hottest in science fiction and fantasy.

DAW
Patrick Rothfuss, Mercedes Lackey, Kristen Britain,
Tanya Huff, Tad Williams, C.J. Cherryh, and many more—
DAW has something to satisfy the cravings of any
science fiction and fantasy lover.
Also visit dawbooks.com.

*Get the best of science fiction and fantasy
at your fingertips!*